WITHIN THE WIND

Seeking Spiritual Deliverance

A Novel

by

David W. Stewart

ISBN: 0976302918
EIN-13: 9780976302919

Coreopsis Publications, LLC is an independent limited liability company chartered by the state of Florida. Coreopsis Publications, LLC was created to publish and promote the books and writings of David W Stewart.
Phone: 321-223-0830
Website: www.coreopsis.gs
Contact the author by e-mail at david@coreopsis.gs

COREOPSIS
PUBLICATIONS, LLC

This book is dedicated to the men and women of emergency services in all capacities

Epigraph

*"We are not human beings
on a spiritual journey. We
are spiritual beings on a
human journey."*

Pierre Teilhard de Chardin

Acknowledgements

I want to thank Lou Belcher of Footsteps, Inc. for editing and for her suggestions on voice and theme. I am grateful to my best friend, Marsha Becker, for reading every section as it came off the computer and providing excellent suggestions on character traits and continuity. I appreciate the support of my critique group: Holly Girard, Jerry Johnson, and Bob Wise. I want to recognize the encouragement of the Colossus Roundtable: Lou Belcher, Kee Briggs, Sally Fairchild and Toni Sweeney. I would also like to thank the University of Florida Press for the wonderful publications they produce on Florida's original inhabitants, Florida's Lost Tribes.

PROLOGUE

"Do not go where the path may lead, go instead where there is no path and leave a trail."

Ralph Waldo Emerson

It had been more than two years since Bonnie had first stood on the path leading into the Ais Sanctuary and seen the spiritual world unfold before her eyes. It had been almost three years since she experienced the seizure that had signaled her spiritual possession by the ghost of Julie Gustafson, the sixteen-year old who had lost her baby to kidnappers on the day it was born; the baby that had turned out to be Bonnie herself.

During the time that Julie's spirit possessed her, Bonnie found out many things about herself. She found out that her real father was Cody Wilkins, leader of a gang called the Swamp Rattlers. She found out that she had been sold to the couple she knew as her parents on the black market and they had raised her as their own without ever telling her she was adopted. She discovered that there are intermediate realities between the final spiritual realm and the temporal realm in which we live.

Three years ago, Bonnie had asked the spirit of fire to show her the truth and – through Julie's spirit – it had shown her a part of the truth. When Julie's spirit departed for the final kingdom, it left something behind in Bonnie's soul, a spiritual presence, which allowed her to continue to see into the spiritual realm. Since that time, Bonnie visited the Ais Sanctuary often to walk with the spirits of the former inhabitants and enjoy the tranquility of the ancient forest. The place attracted her as if she had once lived among these primitive people, natives of the old Florida.

During these three years, Bonnie had continued her work as a paramedic at Coreopsis Hospital. Her relationship with her best friend, Justin Parker, had grown during that time and she had moved in with him a year ago. Just recently, she had found out she was pregnant. None of this made her forget the husband and son she had lost several years ago in an automobile accident, but it gave her hope for a new beginning – dreams of a new life with Justin and their baby.

Bonnie thought of these things as she followed the path leading into the Ais Sanctuary, ambling beneath the ancient oaks and the magnolias with their red cones declaring Christmas in August.

CHAPTER 1

"Fate rules the affairs of mankind with no recognizable order."

Seneca

Bonnie meandered along the shady path on the grounds of the Ais Sanctuary, a nature preserve dedicated to the memory of the original inhabitants of this region of Florida. She approached a large lake, slipped off her shoes and socks, rolled her jeans up to her knees, and stuck her toes in the water to test the temperature. It was warm and soothing to her tired feet. She waded slowly in the shallows at the shore of the lake. It was a good way to relax after working a shift as an emergency medical technician.

Ever since Julie's spirit departed, Bonnie had the ability to perceive the spiritual world. She knew that one of the resident spirits of the Ais Sanctuary was moving with her – a silent, hazy companion. Normally, Bonnie's discernment of otherworldly manifestations was subliminal; however, within the refuge, she could see images of the ghostly inhabitants and their ethereal surroundings. During the last three years, she often came to the Ais Sanctuary to enjoy the tranquility. Her spiritual

1

companion this afternoon was a young native man, slender and nimble.

The surrounding woods were silent, except for several birds discussing whatever might concern them on a warm Florida afternoon. There were no raucous sounds, only the twittering of neighbors. The swishing of Bonnie's legs through the water was the only other noise disturbing the silence of the area. It was too isolated for traffic or town noises to intrude. She sleepwalked around the perimeter of the lake with her eyes half closed.

As she walked with her back to the sun, Bonnie felt a change. The air, which had been warm and pure, became heavy and sticky. The sounds of the birds stopped. The wind picked up and began to swirl around her. She stopped and turned toward her spiritual companion. The young man was gone. Instead, a great blue heron stood facing her. It came up to Bonnie's shoulder. Its armored beak bobbed as it thrust its head back and forth, and its black-browed yellow eyes glowered at Bonnie. She reacted with a startled sound.

The large bird made no noise. Behind the heron, Bonnie saw a monstrous wave of water coming toward them – taller than a medium-sized palm tree. She felt the sand pulling away beneath her feet and the wind began to howl, pushing her forward toward the giant bird and the oncoming wave. The wind pressed Bonnie into the water and every cell of her body tensed as the stress penetrated her bones and tissue. The storm tossed her about like popcorn in a kettle, and she gagged on the water forced into her mouth and involuntarily sucked it into her lungs.

Whenever she came to the surface, she could see a shoreline in the distance. She saw buildings tumbling beneath gigantic waves, trees, pulled up by their roots in the wind, lifting the earth into the air, and vaulting along the land. Debris flew in every direction.

As quickly as the storm started, it subsided. The darkness lifted, the wind diminished to a gentle breeze, and Bonnie was sitting in one foot of water – soaking wet, but unharmed. The big bird was still there. Inside her head, it uttered one message... "Behold the wind"...then, it flew away.

At first, Bonnie did not know what to make of the experience. Her jeans and blouse were heavy on her, so she walked from the lake, removed her outer clothing, wrung the water out, and put it back on. Then, she walked around the shore to retrieve her shoes. She had left her cell phone with her shoes, so she picked it up as well and retreated to a bench along one of the paths.

She had to call Justin. She and Justin had lived together for the last two years. They had discussed marriage but had not gotten around to it. This week, however, Bonnie had found out she was pregnant, so she expected Justin to come forward with a ring any day. Bonnie had promised to meet Justin for dinner at Suzie's Shrimp Shack. He had acted suspiciously as if this might be the night.

Bonnie told Justin what had happened at the Ais Sanctuary. Justin was a third generation Floridian and a sailor, so Bonnie knew he kept track of tropical storms

"I don't know of any big storms out there, do you?" Bonnie asked.

Justin answered without pausing. "There's a new tropical depression near the Cape Verde Islands."

"What's it called?"

"TD-7. Tropical Depression 7. If they name it, it will be Tropical Storm Dirk."

"That could turn into a hurricane."

"I suppose. That doesn't mean it would come anywhere close to here."

Bonnie did not want to seem silly, but she was uneasy about her vision. "I don't feel good about this. The heron definitely gave me a warning."

"I know," said Justin. "I take your premonitions seriously, but we'll just have to see what happens. So, are you coming by the house before dinner?"

"I'll have to, I'm soaking wet."

"Okay. We'll drive to Suzie's together."

"Right. I'll see you in about thirty minutes.

Bonnie went back to the edge of the lake and looked out over the surface. Now, it barely rippled in the late afternoon breeze. A few small cumulus clouds floated slowly from north to south. Even though she and Justin had been together for more than a year, she was a little nervous about getting married again. Her previous marriage had ended disastrously when an automobile accident killed her husband and four-year-old son.

Bonnie drove through her neighborhood and looked at the trees and houses. She wondered what a truly big hurricane would do to them. She stopped in the driveway and looked at the yard and house she had come to call home. A big storm could destroy it all. She parked her car and went into Justin's study to let him know she was home. He turned to look at her and she plopped herself down in his lap and put her arms around him. He pulled her face down to his and gave her a long kiss. It still gave her a thrill and she felt her body quiver slightly.

"You're soaked," said Justin.

"Now, so are you. You'll have to change."

"I'll wait for you. I want to finish these figures and then I'll be right back."

Bonnie went to their bedroom, undressed, took a quick shower, and pulled on slacks and a colorful blouse. She went to her computer and googled the National Hurricane Center. Just as Justin had said, there it was:

SEVENTH TROPICAL DEPRESSION OF THE SEASON FORMS...

Bonnie read the advisory carefully. It didn't seem like much. Then, she remembered the scene from the lake, and shuddered. This storm had a lot of time to strengthen. She turned off her computer and went into the living room to wait for Justin.

***

Earlier that same day – in Belize, Central America – Ladamien Upton stood at a dock in Corozal Bay and held a Colt Model .635 submachine-gun where everyone could see that he had it. He was not concerned with the immigrants coming off the ship, the Salazar; they did not pose a threat to him. Most of them were happy to be disembarking and heading to new homes. The rifle, however, would dissuade inadvertent passers-by from saying anything to local authorities.

Ladamien was a former linebacker for the notorious Glades Central High School Raiders in Belle Glade, Florida. At six feet four and 235 pounds, he towered over most people. By menacing with his bright white teeth, which he knew stood out against the stark black background of his face; he could back most people down without speaking. With the weapon, he intended to leave no doubt that he was not someone to mess with. Any local residents that observed their human trafficking operation would keep silent.

The Salazar had sailed to Belize from Djibouti, but the refugees on board came from all parts of the world. Ladamien's gang, the Swamp Rattlers, expected him to transfer the cargo of human beings from the ship to buses, and then to transport them from the landing to an encampment two kilometers outside of Subteniente Lopez, a stone's throw from the Mexican border. The captain had anchored the ship in Corozal Bay, well away from any coral reefs, and a motorized raft was carrying the migrants from the ship to the shore

Belize, which adjoins Guatemala to the east, was perfect for human trafficking. It had open access to the Caribbean Sea with many isolated harbors where passengers could land. It afforded easy entry into Mexico or Guatemala, either of which could be a gateway to the United States and Canada. Ladamien had already paid the ship's captain and the customs agent. As the refugees, mostly girls and young women came ashore, Ladamien's partner, Alberto, selected the appropriate passport, and passed it to the agent, who stamped it. After the agent had authenticated a passport, Alberto dropped it into a black satchel at his side.

There were sixty-two immigrants in all, so it took almost two hours to get them off the ship and into the buses. The raft only carried six at a time and the ship had anchored several hundred yards from the shoreline. The women, accepting whatever fate lay in store for them, chatted with one another, while the men smoked and spoke occasionally. Ladamien identified at least seven languages with which he was familiar. His assignments took him all over the world and he was becoming an expert at recognizing foreign tongues.

The Swamp Rattlers were not a low-class operation. Ladamien knew the history. They might have been a petty gang at one time, but not anymore. They started back in the chain gang era in the south, sometime in the late forties. Guys who escaped banded together and learned how to live in the Okefenokee Swamp and the Everglades. They poached and robbed around the swamps. Some of the original gang members considered themselves modern day Robin Hoods. As they grew in numbers and power, they eventually interested some of the more established gangs in the Chicago area who set up a headquarters in Atlanta.

The big boss, Alberon Randazzo, lived in Atlanta, and manipulated several gangs, including the Swamp Rattlers. Leroy Greene, the boss of the Swamp Rattlers came from Chicago and lived in Miami. The larger gang base had allowed the Swamp Rattlers to expand its activities to include trafficking in weapons, drugs, currency, and people. As far as Ladamien was concerned, the Swamp Rattlers were a business and he had a job.

"Hey, Ladamien, dig that chick." Alberto pointed to an especially attractive Cambodian girl. "How'd you like to get a piece of that?"

Ladamien had made up his mind a long time ago that these refugees were cargo, and nothing else. "I'm married, man," Ladamien, answered. "I don't need no woman besides Aggie."

"How'd you ever get tied up with a blond, white woman, anyhow?"

"I ran into her at the state football championship. She was a cheerleader for the other team." Ladamien thought back to the incident. "I tried to intercept a pass, went off the sidelines, right into her − bowled her over. She wasn't mad or nuthin'. That's how I knew she was a good sport."

Color hadn't mattered to either of them. He and Aggie had just clicked. Ladamien continued, "She was the smartest, prettiest, most fun girl I had ever met."

"You ran into her." Alberto chuckled. "Literally."

"Yeah, and then she kept running into me until I agreed to marry her. I didn't mind."

Ladamien continued to watch the immigrants file onto the buses. In his mind, they were probably one hundred percent better off where they were going as compared to where they came from. Oppression remained rampant in countries like Zimbabwe, Burma, Cuba, Iran, and Laos. Ladamien figured that passage through Mexico or Guatemala into the United States or Canada offered these people a chance to find a meaningful life and security.

The facts were that more than 20 percent of the

women were already HIV positive and most would end up as prostitutes. Probably, all of the men would end up in labor camps. Ladamien was aware of these facts but had decided that the risk for these escapees was worth the prize – possible freedom. He knew the value of freedom. His soul was committed to the gang. He was as much a slave to the Swamp Rattlers as these refugees were to their buyers.

"This is the last one," said Alberto. "It's time to drive to the camp." Alberto took out his Uzi submachine-gun and zipped the satchel closed. Once they entered the encampment, they might need to keep the local broker and his associates in line. They were probably thugs, and not trustworthy. Alberto boarded one of the buses and Ladamien stepped aboard the other.

Ladamien stood in the front of the bus. The bag over his shoulder held his own commission plus the money to pay the camp guards, the bus drivers, and Alberto. The camp director would be happy to see him. After that, Ladamien would go to Belize City and fly back home to Merritt Island, Florida, where he lived with Aggie and their nine-year-old son, Simon.

The neighbors would believe he had returned from another trip designing airports for his company, Airport Design Partners, LLC. The company was legitimate and Ladamien was the chairman of the board; however, the Swamp Rattlers funded the company and used it to launder money from its human trafficking endeavors.

So far, Ladamien had kept his record clean, and Interpol had not connected Airport Design Partners with human trafficking. Ladamien knew it could be a matter of time before they found out about him. He would have to leave the United States to go into hiding. Aggie and he had talked about it many times. There was also a possibility that authorities in another country might capture him or someone might kill him. It was dangerous work, but the Swamp Rattlers paid him well. The gang had been a reality in his life since early childhood, so he did not question the morality of his work.

Money was not the only pheromone that kept Ladamien loyal to the Swamp Rattlers. The Rattlers gave him status in both the gang and public communities. Within the inner circle of the Swamp Rattlers, he was a heavy hitter – a close friend of the gang's boss, Leroy Greene, and influential in conducting the gang's business. In the business world, he was owner and board chairman for a multi-national, billion-dollar corporation. Even though he was only a front man for the gang, it made him a legitimate authority in his neighborhood. Most of all, however, he knew he would be able to provide opportunities for his son, Simon, that his own family had never been able to offer him. It was worth the risks. Besides, Ladamien was addicted to the adrenaline rush.

Before he had come up to Belize, he and Aggie, had taken a short vacation in Jamaica without Simon. Aggie had suggested it might be a good place to live if they had to move. She worried more about the police catching him than he did. Ladamien left her in Jamaica when he came to Belize. He suggested she explore the island before she returned to pick up Simon from the neighbors. He was not sure if

Jamaica would be a good place to hide but it would not do any harm to have Aggie look.

The drive from Corozal to the camp was less than ten kilometers over good road, so it only took a few minutes for the buses to make the trip. Estuardo Martinez, the camp director, was standing alongside the road to meet them after they went through the gate. Ladamien watched as Alberto exited the first bus and handed Estuardo the satchel containing the passports. Estuardo then walked back to Ladamien's bus. The driver opened the door and Ladamien came down the steps.

"How are you, amigo?" Estuardo asked.

"I'm fine," said Ladamien. "Let's go inside to split up the money. I'll let you pay the drivers." Ladamien did not trust the people at this end of the transaction. He had previous bad experiences with brokers in places like Oman and the Dominican Republic. "I'll follow you."

Estuardo led the way up a path to a small cabin in the corner of the impoundment. Alberto followed them. He had left the refugees to the camp staff. His job now was to stand guard outside the cabin while Ladamien completed the deal with Estuardo.

Ladamien entered the hut behind Estuardo. Inside, a small table sat in the middle of the room. Four chairs posed randomly around the room. Ladamien motioned Estuardo to sit, and then he sat across from him, put his bag on the table, and took out three envelopes.

"That's yours," said Ladamien, pushing a sachet in front of Estuardo. "You can count it."

Estuardo took the money out and rippled

through it. "It looks okay," he said, and put the cash back into the envelope.

Ladamien pushed the other two packets toward Estuardo and pointed at each one. "That's for the drivers," he said, "and, that's for the camp guards."

"Good," said Estuardo. "We'll get more when the buyers come to collect. It's a good day's work. Where do you go now?"

"Home," replied Ladamien. "Home, sweet home. Do you have a car out there for Alberto and me? We need to get to Belize City."

"It's out there, fueled and ready. Here's the key." Estuardo opened the center drawer of the table, took out a car key, and handed it to Ladamien.

Ladamien picked up the key and left the cabin. He handed Alberto one of the two remaining envelopes from the bag. "That's for you, my friend," he said. "Thanks for covering my back."

Ladamien and Alberto walked to the car, got in and drove south toward Bueno Vista and Belize City.

"I'm gonna sleep for a week," said Ladamien

***

In Merritt Island, Florida, Ladamien's nine-year-old son, Simon, was playing with his friend Buster. Simon saw his mother peek out the back door of the Thurston's house and he waved to her. He knew she was there to pick him up.

"It's my mom," he told Buster. "I'm gonna have to go home."

"Where's she been?" asked Buster.

"Jamaica. She and my Dad are thinking about

moving there."

"Where's Jamaica? Is it near New York?"

"Nah. It's way out in the Caribbean, south of Miami."

"Why would you move there?"

"My Dad's job. He builds airports. He's gone all the time. He'd be closer to his job."

Buster pushed a toy bulldozer through the sand, leveling it. "Does your dad drive a bulldozer or anything?" Buster asked.

"Nah. He's an engineer. He designs airports and bosses around the guys that build them."

"My dad's an engineer too, but he designs rockets."

Simon heard his mother call. "Come on Simon, we've got to go home now."

Simon got to his feet and brushed the sand off his knees. "Maybe I can come back tomorrow," Simon told Buster. "Ask your mom if we can go fishing."

"I don't know if she'll let me," said Buster.

Buster was such a baby. Simon gave him a look of disgust. "Ask her."

"I will."

"Good." Simon ran toward the house to find his mother.

Simon found Aggie in the kitchen talking to Buster's mother. "Buster and me are going fishing tomorrow. Okay."

"Has Buster asked his mother?"

"No. But he's gonna."

"Where do they go?" Buster's mom asked Aggie. "Is it safe?"

"Oh yes," replied Aggie. "They just go down to the river. At the end of that dirt road off Tropical Trail."

"I guess it would be alright then. Will Buster need a pole or a line?"

"I'll bring him one," said Simon. "I'll bring him a good one."

"We'd better go home, young man," said Aggie. "I haven't seen you for a week." Aggie turned to Buster's mother as she prepared to leave. "Thanks for keeping him, Janice, and thank Steve also."

"He's no trouble. When is Ladamien coming home?"

"He hasn't called me yet, so I'm not sure."

"Come over for lunch tomorrow. You and Simon can eat with Buster and me. Give us a chance to talk."

"Alright. Can I bring something?"

"Make some of that potato salad. That would be nice."

"You got it." Aggie started to leave. "C'mon Simon. We need to get you cleaned up. Then, I'll show you some photos from Jamaica."

Simon didn't know if he wanted to look at pictures, but he was glad to have his mom back home. "I'm coming," he said as he ran ahead of his mother. "I'll see you at the house." Simon ran along the path between Buster's house and his. He went into the garage and started looking at fishing poles. He loved to fish and looked forward to showing

Buster how much he knew about it. He had already picked out two poles when his mother found him.

"You can leave those on the porch until tomorrow," Aggie said. "Now, go in and take your bath while I set up the TV to look at the camcorder."

Simon's mother had put his change of clothes on the back of the toilet. Simon had a ritual with his bath. He had a whole set of warships and he staged mock battles between his navy and an enemy navy commanded by the mysterious pirate, Captain Red Blood. Captain Red Blood was the scourge of the seas. He robbed unsuspecting sail boaters, killing all on board and sinking the vessels. He was a bad dude but he had a lot of money. Simon's navy always won, but Captain Red Blood always escaped.

"Pow! Pow! Boom!" Simon fired his cannons.

Aggie stuck her head in the door to the bathroom. "Wrap up the battle. I've got the video set up."

"Okay, Mom. I'll be right there." Simon dried off and then wiped off his ships and put them back on the shelf where he kept them. He put them away carefully. One time, when he didn't, his father had thrown them away, telling Simon that if he didn't put his toys away, the same thing would happen every time.

Simon slipped on the clean clothes and went into the living room to join his mother.

"Where is Jamaica?" Simon asked. "Is it close to Miami?"

"Not really," answered Aggie. "It's a big island, south of Cuba – in the Caribbean Sea."

"Do they have pirates? Did you see any of them?"

"There are pirates all over the Caribbean, even in Florida. Most of the pirates are farther south, closer to South America. Your Dad introduced me to one or two of them, but I didn't want to get to know them. They mostly stay out of sight"

"I bet Dad knows lots of them."

"I imagine he does. You can ask him."

"When is he coming home?"

"I don't know, dear. I expect him to call. Now, let's watch the videos." Aggie started the camcorder.

Simon watched the playback. There were many pictures of beaches and he saw his father wave from the water. The last part of the video showed mountains, jungle, and wild desert.

"What were you doing there?" Simon asked.

"At first, I was just looking at property. Later, I went into the interior to look for a rare bird, the Blue Mountain vireo."

"Did you find it?"

"Yes. I photographed one. It's on my other camera."

"Are we going to move there?"

"I don't think so. We don't have any reason to move right now."

"Good. I like playing with Buster and being able to walk to the river. I don't wanna leave Merritt Island."

"Jamaica's nice too. You could fish there, and go snorkeling. You might like it."

Simon thought about it. It would be more exciting if they had pirates there. "I guess. Especially if I saw more of Dad. That would be nice."

"Yes," Aggie agreed, "that would be nice. Do you have homework tonight?"

"I had some, but I finished it before I left school."

"All right. If you want to watch TV, I'll fix our supper."

Simon was pleased to have his mother back home. He wondered when his Dad would call

***

Chief Maureen Louise "Rusty" Douglas walked around Coreopsis Fire and Emergency Station Number 2 and marveled at the newness of the facility and equipment. The freshly painted walls had no marks or blemishes. The stainless steel pipes and fixtures still sparkled as they did when first removed from the box. The floor was pristine, with no grease stains or tire marks. Even the smell was unsullied, without the aroma of gasoline or sweaty rain gear. It was a sharp contrast to Station Number 1, which had endured forty years of wear and abuse.

Just like a new car, thought Rusty, *undriven, untarnished, and uncorrupted.* It reminded Rusty of the bicycle her parents bought her on her tenth birthday. Her family had not been poor, but a new bicycle was a big deal. Rusty felt the same responsibility to keep Station Number 2 immaculate that she had felt to keep her new bicycle unscratched and well maintained. As the newly appointed station chief, she was accountable for the entire operation.

She felt the same way about her crew as she did about the new station. She wanted them to function perfectly. Gus Frantze, the senior chief and department head, had given her free reign in selecting her team. Recently, she had found out that one of her most experienced paramedics, Bonnie McConnell, was pregnant and would be unavailable after the following month. Rusty was happy for Bonnie, but disappointed that she would be losing a key member of her squad at a crucial time.

Rusty walked around to her office and sat behind her clean desk with its empty top. *Not bad for a country girl*, she thought. *Not bad at all. I guess I had better get an in basket.*

***

Bonnie sat in the passenger seat as Justin pulled his Prius into the parking lot at Suzie's Shrimp Shack. A short afternoon rain had come through, so the parking lot was wet. The storm had darkened the sky, and the streetlights had come on automatically. Bonnie followed Justin into the restaurant. The owner, Suzie Bastogne met them at the reception desk.

Suzie was an institution in Coreopsis. Her seafood restaurant attracted visitors from all over the county. Suzie was a large woman with a boisterous voice. She wore her hair in a half ponytail, which she called a donkey-tail because the hair poked out in all directions.

"I made reservations," Justin said to Suzie.

"Of course you did, sugah," Suzie responded. "I have a special table set up for you and Bonnie."

Bonnie was suspicious now. Suzie Bastogne did not usually come out and seat customers herself. Bonnie looked at Justin and raised her eyebrows. "What's going on?" she asked.

Justin did not say anything. He put his hand on the small of Bonnie's back and urged her forward to follow Suzie. Suzie led them into a dimly lit side room. The table in that room was set with a flourish of orchids and two glowing candles in the center. An unopened bottle of champagne chilled in an ice bucket at the side.

"The champagne's on the house," said Suzie. "Pearson will take your orders." Suzie motioned to the young waiter who had followed them into the room, and then she turned and started to leave.

Bonnie spoke before Suzie was out of the room. "What are we celebrating?"

"Any time there's a new life coming into the world – it's a cause to celebrate," Suzie said. She turned and came back to the table.

"I can't drink the champagne," said Bonnie. "It wouldn't be good for the baby"

"What would you like, sugah?" asked Suzie.

"Mineral water would be fine," said Bonnie, "maybe Pellegrino."

"Get two more glasses, and bring the Pellegrino," Suzie said to Pearson. While Pearson went to get the glasses, Suzie expertly opened the champagne and handed the bottle to Pearson when he returned.

Pearson filled three of the glasses with champagne and the other with mineral water. Suzie raised hers. "A toast," she said, "to good parents, healthy children and a better world."

"Amen," Bonnie said automatically, even though she knew a toast was not a prayer. She savored the sparkling water as it tickled her tongue and bubbled down her throat.

Suzie left and Pearson asked, "Can I bring you something?"

"Leave the Pellegrino," said Bonnie.

"A menu." Justin added.

When Bonnie and Justin were alone, he reached inside to his jacket pocket and produced a small velvet box. Bonnie knew immediately what it was. Justin opened the box and pushed it across the table so she could look inside.

"Do you want to ask me something?"

Justin looked puzzled for a moment and then straightened up. "Of course. Will you marry me? Be my wife?"

"Because you love me or because we're having a baby?"

"Can't it be both?"

Bonnie smiled. "Is it?"

"Yes."

"Then it's yes for me too," she said. "Would you refill my water?"

Justin hastily refilled their glasses. Bonnie noticed that his hands were shaking almost imperceptibly. When he had finished pouring, she asked, "Do you want to put the ring on my finger?"

"I'm sorry," he said, "I'm not thinking very clearly. Naturally, I want to put the ring on your hand. I'm just a little flustered, that's all."

"That's okay," said Bonnie. "We're both supposed to be excited. I know I've looked forward to this day for quite a while."

Justin put the ring on Bonnie's finger, kissed her hand, and then kissed her on the lips. When she opened her eyes, Bonnie saw Pearson waiting at the doorway. When they had finished kissing, she motioned the waiter to come to their table.

After they had ordered, Justin cleared his throat. "Superior Sports and Entertainment has offered me a position and a large contract."

"An architectural project?"

"Yes."

"That's great."

"Yeah, but I'll have to spend a great deal of time in Atlanta for the next one or two years. They want me to head up a design team for their new headquarters in the United States."

Bonnie thought about it. Between her job and his, they did not see each other enough already. She wanted Justin to move ahead in his career.

"It sounds like a great opportunity. Probably I should plan on quitting my job and be available to travel with you and prepare for motherhood. Anyhow, the hospital won't let me continue to go out on emergency calls after I reach my fourth month. Tell me more about this new job."

"Andre' D'aubigne called me yesterday. He complimented me on the work I did with the sports complex. Superior Sports and Entertainment is going to pursue more markets in America. He wants to locate a headquarters in the U.S."

"He wants you to design it?"

"He wants me as a member of the team that's designing it."

The waiter brought their salads and Justin waited for him to leave.

"I told Andre' I would have to talk to you first," said Justin. "I wanted to know what you would think."

"Take the job. I'll come up and see you occasionally to start and then I'll move to Atlanta permanently. I want to be with you when the baby comes."

***

That afternoon, Ladamien had dropped Alberto off at the Philip Goldson International Airport in Ladyville, Belize. It was a half-hour drive from Ladyville into Belize City where Ladamien made his initial stop at the First Caribbean International Bank. He wired most of the money from the Corozal job into his business account. Ladamien knew that the money would end up credited to profits from an airport project in Zaire Africa.

To most of the world, Ladamien designed airports. In fact, his company did provide engineering services for airports, including construction and modifications. Ladamien, while not a graduate engineer, had a practical understanding of production and finance. This practical knowledge helped him manage the company – or, at least, pretend to manage the company.

Ladamien checked into the Bachelor Inn and

paid the desk clerk to retrieve his suitcase from the storage room behind the check-in station. He entered his room on the first floor and hung the do-not-disturb sign on the door before he locked it and secured the chain. He threw the suitcase on the bed, opened it, and retrieved a cell phone from one of the side pockets. There was only one contact on the cell phone list – Aggie Upton. Ladamien pressed the dial button. Aggie answered after four rings.

"Hey babe." said Ladamien, "Are you at home?"

"Yeah," answered Aggie. "I got back from Jamaica earlier this afternoon."

"Did ya see anything you liked?"

"I went back into the mountains and took some nice bird photos."

"I gather you wouldn't want to live in Jamaica."

"Not really. It's like most of those Caribbean Islands. Nice to visit, but no place you'd want to live."

"But you had a good time?"

"It was better when you were there with me. Yeah, I enjoyed myself, but I'm glad to be home."

"You picked up Simon?"

"Yes. He's fine. He has to go back to school on Monday. Janice told me he did well while I was gone."

"He's a much better student than I ever was," said Ladamien.

"When are you coming home?" asked Aggie.

"I fly back tomorrow. Pick me up in Orlando…around five o'clock?"

"Great. God, I've missed you, and I know Simon has too."

"See you tomorrow. I love you."

"Love you. Bye."

Ladamien hung up the phone. He put it back in the suitcase and lifted the lid covering part of a false bottom in the suitcase. He removed a 9mm automatic hidden in the suitcase and placed it under a pillow on the bed. He also took out a pair of pajamas and placed them at the foot of the bed.

After a quick shower, Ladamien slipped on the pajamas and laid out his clothes for morning. He had plenty of time before he had to catch his plane, but he was always prepared to get going quickly. He fell into a light sleep watching sports news on the TV.

Ladamien had been asleep for about four hours when a knock on his door awakened him. He sat up in bed, and then heard the knock again. It wasn't just any knock, it was the special Swamp Rattlers knock — one long, three short, two long, a pause, and then one heavy rap. Ladamien knew it was probably a fellow gang member, but he took the pistol out from under the pillow and held it in front of him while he crept to the side of the door, undid the lock, and opened it to the end of the door chain.

"Who's there?" he asked softly.

"It's a brother," answered a husky voice. "It's Jamal. Let me in. We gotta talk."

Ladamien pushed the door to, undid the chain lock, and opened the door slowly.

Jamal slipped through the door and closed it behind him.

"What are you doing in Belize?" asked Ladamien.

"I'm down here to pick up some goods," answered Jamal. "Leroy asked me to come warn you about something."

"What's Leroy's problem?" If the leader of the Swamp Rattlers was concerned, Ladamien was concerned as well.

Jamal continued. "That Chicano you were with, Alberto."

"Yeah," said Ladamien.

"The local police picked him up at the airport. Right after you dropped him off."

"What rap? Anything to do with our business?"

"The police had a warrant, some civil case. Nothing to do with you. Leroy's concerned he might give you up."

"Alberto's a banger," said Ladamien. "He won't rat out."

"We can't take a chance. You're our connection. We need to keep you clean. How you fixed to get out?"

"I got a return ticket on Taca International into Orlando. Aggie's gonna pick me up."

"Leroy wants to see you in Miami before you go home. I've got your ticket."

"Man, he complicates my life. I'd better call Aggie."

"I'll wait. Give me your Taca ticket and I'll get it turned in."

Ladamien opened the suitcase and took out the cell phone. After he dialed Aggie, he handed the airline folder to Jamal. Aggie answered the phone and Ladamien could tell she had been sleeping.

"You're going to hate this," said Ladamien over the phone.

Aggie yawned at the other end. "You're going to Miami before you come home."

"How'd you know?"

"I know Leroy. I'd be surprised if you came straight home. Are you still going to want me to pick you up?"

"No. I'll rent a car. I'll probably have to head right back out."

"Who's there with you?"

"Jamal. Did you ever meet him?"

"He played football with you at Glades, didn't he? Yeah, I met him. Kick him for me, will you."

Ladamien looked over at Jamal. "Aggie says hi."

Jamal waved his hand to indicate he returned the greeting. "Hi back," said Jamal. "You ready to go? This ticket's for six a.m."

"I gotta hang up honey. I'll call from Miami."

"You better leave the niner with me," said Jamal, reaching for the pistol. "That'll get you in trouble at the airport."

Ladamien handed Jamal the gun. "Don't lose it. I'll want it back."

Jamal stuffed the pistol under his belt. "Did you stash the money?"

"First thing, I put it in my business. Made it legit."

"You got a for-real business?"

Ladamien was proud of his enterprise. "Airport Design Partners, LLC. Would you believe I have a contract with the very airport I'm flying out of?"

"You actually do any work for them?"

"There are engineers out there working for me. I'm an executive."

"And that's how you dry clean your money?"

Ladamien nodded. "I'm all packed. Should I leave the car here? The submachine-gun is in the trunk."

"That's fine," said Jamal. "I'll make sure everything's returned."

Ladamien handed the car keys to Jamal and left the room key on the dresser. He picked up his suitcase and followed Jamal.

CHAPTER 2

"Every new adjustment is a crisis in self-esteem."

Eric Hoffer 1902-1983

Every day was a long day for medical emergency services. Bonnie arrived at work Saturday at 6 a.m., just in time to join the crew in answering a call that would stay with her for the rest of the day. When they arrived on the scene, the county fire team had already arrived. Bonnie grabbed her medical kit and went inside the house. She found Brad Quince, a fire emergency specialist in the bedroom. The fire crew had a gurney already in place and they were lifting an elderly woman onto it.

"Got your vitals monitor ready?" asked Brad. "She's barely alive."

"Let me take a look," said Bonnie. "Tell my guys to bring in the portable monitor." Bonnie started applying some sensors to the woman while she checked for broken bones or bleeding. "Is there someone around to give us some idea of what happened?"

"Valerie's in with her husband," said Brad. "What do you need to know?"

"She looks like a cancer patient. If so, we need to

get hold of her oncologist."

Bonnie's team hooked up the vitals monitor and started to take readings.

"BP 93 over 64," said Dante, one of the crewmembers. "Pulse 96. It could be worse. I'm putting her on an IV and oxygen. She's probably dehydrated."

Valerie came in with the woman's husband. He was also elderly and clearly distressed.

"This is Mr. Ward," said Valerie. "He says his wife tried to get out of bed and fell. He couldn't get her back up, so he called 911. She's a cancer patient. Dr. Gonzalez is her oncologist."

"She's strapped," said Vince, one of Bonnie's crew. "We're going to the ambulance with her. We have the ER doctor in the loop. They're expecting her."

"What's your first name, Mr. Ward?" asked Bonnie

"Zack." He sounded uncertain, as if he had to look it up in some remote portion of his mind.

"Okay Zack," said Bonnie, "come with me. You can ride in the jump seat next to me and fill me in a little more."

Bonnie mulled over her conversation with Mr. Ward all day long. He had opened up, and his statement, while rambling, had been clear enough to Bonnie. His wife, Hannah, didn't want to die in the hospital; she wanted to be home, in the house that she and her husband had shared for seventeen of the fifty-three years that she and Zack had been married.

"Did Dr. Gonzales ever recommend hospice?"

Bonnie had asked.

Zack confirmed that the doctors had recommended hospice but he thought he could handle everything. He didn't want strangers in their home. "Hannah didn't like anybody messing with her but me," he had said.

Bonnie had looked at the old man. His wife couldn't last much longer. There was a good chance she would never leave the hospital. When they arrived at the emergency room, the staff took over and moved Hannah to intensive care. Bonnie found Zack sitting in the waiting room – alone.

"Do you have any family?" she asked. "Locally, I mean."

"We have a son. He lives in California. Haven't talked to him for a long time."

"How about good friends?"

"Not really. We kind of stick to ourselves."

"Go to church?"

"Not for a long time. We don't belong anymore."

"Did you resign?"

"No. We just quit going. I'm sure they took our names off their list."

"You might get back in touch with them. They might be pleased to hear from you."

Mr. Ward just nodded.

Bonnie felt sorry for him. She understood that he had no one other than Hannah. Hannah, who would soon be gone.

"Hospice isn't just for the sick," said Bonnie. "It's for the caregivers as well. People like you who need help and may need to talk to others later on. "

"You think hospice would help me."

"Talk to Dr. Gonzales again. Think about it. It's not up to me to tell you what's best." Bonnie hesitated, and then followed up on her next thought. "My friend Lucy has a prayer group that meets every Wednesday evening. I'll ask her to add Hannah to their list. If you'd like to join them, I imagine she'd give you a ride."

"It's probably all women. I'd be the only man."

"I happen to know that they have two men in the group."

"Do you think Hannah's gonna make it?"

How could she answer a question like that? Bonnie knew she had dug herself a hole.

"We got your wife here in time," Bonnie answered evasively. "She's a very sick woman, but only the doctor can answer your question honestly. Ask him."

Bonnie got up to return to work. "I've got to go, but I'll talk to Lucy. I'm sure she'll be in touch."

Bonnie could only imagine how difficult it must be for Zack. If Hannah returned home, and he agreed to have hospice care, the emergency medical team would no longer respond to a 911 call. It was a decision to let Hannah die. The memory of going through the deaths of her husband and son gave Bonnie a special empathy for Zack's loneliness.

The team had had four more calls that day and Bonnie was eager for some solitude when her shift was over. She went home, cleaned up, changed, and had a snack before she drove to the Ais Sanctuary.

She called Justin on the way and told him where she was going.

"Don't be too long," Justin cautioned. "We're supposed to go over to Dan and Sheila's for dinner."

"I remember," said Bonnie. "I'll be home by six thirty."

When Bonnie arrived at the Ais Sanctuary, she decided to take a path to the south that she had not traveled before. This path led through lowlands bordered by cattails and mallows. In addition to the constant buzzing of insects, there was an occasional croaking of frogs. The path seemed to go beyond the limits of the Ais Sanctuary and Bonnie suspected she was in that other world – the mystical world she had experienced during her possession by Julie's spirit.

Bonnie reflected on her previous psychic possession by the errant spirit of a sixteen-year-old girl who had her baby taken away at birth – the baby that turned out to be Bonnie. Julie's spirit – her mother's spirit – was gone, but it had left something inside of Bonnie's soul. That something stirred inside of her today.

As she walked, she left the marsh and came into a pine wood. At the end of the path, she saw a train depot with two Pullman cars standing on the track. She walked through the deserted terminal and entered the car on her right. People from her past, some living, and some dead, filled the car. Her parents were there; her departed husband and son; her friends from school; and, others, including Hannah, the old woman from that morning.

"Bonnie," said a large woman near the door. It was Roberta, one of her friends from EMT training.

"We've been expecting you."

"Where am I?"

"You're in that place of eternal existence, where all of the events of your life are preserved."

Bonnie nodded.

"Go on in." Roberta pointed to the passage into the next car.

Bonnie walked through the door and across the grating into the next car. The car was empty, but Hannah followed her and sat down behind a small dining table facing Bonnie. Hannah's face was serene.

"Are you alive or is this an apparition?" Bonnie asked.

"My body died this afternoon," Hannah said. "My spirit has passed on. You are only seeing a vision."

"How did Zack take your passing? I gather you were married a long time."

"Fifty-three years. Our whole lives," said Hannah's image. "He is sad but accepting."

"What was it like being married that long?"

"It was everything. Zack was all there was in my life. I was everything in his. Nothing else counted."

Bonnie sat down at the table across from Hannah and placed her hands on the table. "You were very fortunate."

"I see that Justin finally proposed," said Hannah. "May you have a long and happy time together."

"Thank you," said Bonnie. "I'm very happy."

"I have come to warn you that there is something evil that wants your daughter's soul. Beware of the daughter of the wind."

The old woman's statement shocked Bonnie. She found herself back on the path walking through the pinewood, heading toward the Ais Sanctuary exit. She hadn't known her child would be a girl. Sha had not suspected a malicious presence. She pondered Hannah's warning. It troubled her.

We'll name our daughter Crystal, Bonnie thought. The name just popped into her head.

***

Early Saturday afternoon, Ladamien checked through customs at Miami International Airport, proceeded to the interline lobby, and spotted his contact immediately. Sapphire, another gang member, was standing at the exit to short-term parking. She was a tall woman and her tight purple slacks and shirt combination studded with gold sequins stood out like a neon sign on a dark street.

"Is that your only bag?" Sapphire asked. She started walking toward the exit, and Ladamien followed her.

"This is it," answered Ladamien. "I was only in Belize for two days."

"I thought you were in Jamaica too."

"Aggie was with me. She took most of our stuff home with her."

"How's she doin'? Leroy talks about her like she's some kind of angel or somethin'."

"She is an angel," said Ladamien. "She's just fine. She went birding in Jamaica after I left."

"I love the tropics. I suppose she feels the same

way." Sapphire pointed to a BMW 535xi sports wagon. "That's my carriage." Sapphire opened the back. "Throw your things in there."

Ladamien put his suitcase in the back and Sapphire closed the lid. They both got into the car. Sapphire exited through the Sun Pass lane and drove toward the Dolphin Expressway. Leroy's estate was located on Star Island, an exclusive residential community accessible from the MacArthur Causeway. Leroy had invited Ladamien and Aggie down twice, so Ladamien knew the layout.

Leroy's estate was similar to the Governor's Mansion. The main residence dominated several adjoining buildings used to house staff and visitors. Leroy had a reputation for conducting business at all hours. The Swamp Rattlers' global activities occupied his attention twenty-four hours a day. The inner sanctum within Leroy's residence was a high-technology war room that tracked gang activities.

As they approached the gate to Leroy's estate, Sapphire slowed down. The entry opened and Sapphire waved to the guard as they drove through. Ladamien knew that no one would get past that guard unless he or she was expected or was one of an elite group in Leroy's inner circle. Sapphire drove around the complex and parked in a stall with her name above it.

"I'll take you into Leroy," said Sapphire. "He wanted to talk to you as soon as you got here. Leave your bag at the corner. Someone will take it to your room."

Ladamien followed Sapphire along a path that went under an arbor covered with bougainvillea and around a pool deck where a man and a woman sunned themselves. They entered a sun porch overlooking the pool. Leroy sat at a glass top table with a drink in front of him.

Leroy was a big man, as tall as Ladamien and twenty pounds heavier. He undoubtedly had a Heinz 57 heritage. His skin color was Polynesian and his facial features were a rough combination of Negroid, Mongolian, and Caucasian. He waved to Ladamien and motioned for him to sit down at the table.

"How was your trip?" Leroy's voice had a cultivated Louis Armstrong character to it – hoarse, but melodic. "How's that beautiful wife of yours?"

"Aggie's fine, still beautiful. The trip was uneventful, except for the news about Alberto. What's the scoop on him?"

"He had a gambling debt, to a policeman. He paid the man about twice what he owed him and they let him go."

"So, he's okay."

"Back in the Caymans where he lives." Leroy took a sip of his drink. "I want to talk about your business, Airport Design Partners, LLC."

"It's legitimate," said Ladamien. "It's an actual business, with customers and employees."

"I know," said Leroy, "I know. It's the perfect cover. How would you like to grow your enterprise?"

On the inside, Ladamien was skeptical, but he knew Leroy wasn't asking a rhetorical question. He was making a polite demand. "What do you have in mind?" Ladamien tried to sound genuinely enthusiastic.

"I have a policy," said Leroy, "I picked it up when I was a kid in Chicago. I only do business with people that have money."

Ladamien didn't consider this an epiphany. He nodded in agreement.

"Ever since the war started in Iraq and our country began hunting terrorists, some of my best customers have had a difficult time with liquidity, cash on hand."

"The Feds are watching the banks more closely?"

"Yes. Some of my methods don't work as well as they once did."

"However, I assume..." Ladamien didn't want to upstage his boss "... our friends all have airports that could use redesign?"

"Exactly. Airports, seaports, railways. Many engineering projects."

"It would take a genius to manage all of that," Ladamien said. "I'm just an old cane breaker. I ain't no genius."

"I can buy genius," said Leroy. "What I can't buy is loyalty. You would still be the owner and chairman. We'll just launder our money through your business. You can take ten percent off the top."

"The Feds might put some boundaries on where we could sell our services."

"In most instances, the US Agency for International Development will applaud your good work. After all, a company like yours has many ways to cut costs and employ locals. You'll be a hero to them."

"Even to this new administration. What if they

find out I'm a Rattler?"

"How're they going to find out? I'm not going to tell them."

"I'm still accountable to the Internal Revenue Service. It's easier to hide small amounts than it is large sums."

"It's also true that the easiest place to hide some things is in plain sight. We'll just hire some clever lawyers to make sure you stay legitimate."

"What if I get caught transporting cargo?"

"That's behind you. Where do you want to live?"

"You serious? Aggie will be delighted. I'd be home more, wouldn't I?"

"That's the idea."

"I'll have to talk to Aggie. She'll want a good school for Simon."

"So, you're okay with expanding your company?"

"Sure. I mean it's perfect. Thank you."

Leroy pushed his chair back and started toward a sliding glass door that led to the interior of the house. He stopped at the door.

"Go home," said Leroy. "You can get a flight into Orlando and be home for dinner. Sapphire will drive you to the airport."

***

Although it was Saturday, Rusty looked for Bonnie at the Coreopsis Health and Fitness. She expected the day crew to work out in the evening, every day. She took the latest bulletin from the National Hurricane Center with her to give to Bonnie. Bonnie had called her about the vision of a storm and it had sparked Rusty's interest. Rusty had been at Tulane University when Hurricane Katrina struck New Orleans, so she had a special interest in tropical storms. She wanted to keep Bonnie apprised on the progress of tropical depression 7. She spotted Bonnie at the free weights and waited for her to take a break. Bonnie approached Rusty with a bottle of water in her hand.

"Well," said Rusty, "your storm is still a tropical depression, but it is strengthening." She handed the sheet of paper to Bonnie.

Bonnie read aloud, "...tropical depression a little better organized...no immediate threat to land..."

"That's encouraging," said Bonnie. "Maybe it's not my storm."

"It's too early to tell," said Rusty. "Read on."

Bonnie continued, "...at 11 a.m. EDT the center of tropical depression 7 was located about 1,615 miles east of the Lesser Antilles. The depression is moving toward the west near 17 mph."

"That's still a long way from us," Bonnie remarked.

"Yeah," agreed Rusty, "but it's moving in the right direction.

"...maximum sustained winds are near 35 mph."

"Isn't that average?" Bonnie asked.

"It sounds a little better organized than the average depression," answered Rusty. "If it weren't for your vision, I wouldn't be too concerned yet. Because of your vision, I'm gonna watch it closely." Rusty decided to change the conversation. "How's your workout going?"

"I'm about done," answered Bonnie. "I'm going to take a few laps in the pool, and then go home."

"Just before I came over, that old woman you brought in earlier – Hannah Ward – she died."

"I know," said Bonnie. "I had a vision."

"When? I just left the hospital," said Rusty. "She only passed away a few hours earlier."

Bonnie tipped her head and smiled. "I had an episode in the Ais Sanctuary. Besides, it wasn't hard to see that she probably wouldn't make it."

Rusty shook her head. "You and your revelations. Is there anything you don't see?"

Bonnie just smiled.

Rusty thought about Hannah Ward and the effort they had made to save her life. Failure to accept hospice by obviously incurable patients was a sore subject with Rusty. "I wish terminal cases would get on hospice," said Rusty. "It just wastes our time and their money to bring them in."

"I suppose it's hard to give up hope on someone you've loved for more than fifty years."

"Hope is one thing, denial is another." Rusty felt that it was important to deal with life realistically. Wishful thinking was wasteful thinking her mother had taught her. "They're gonna have to deal with it sooner or later."

"I suppose," Bonnie said. "When's the new equipment coming in?"

"The ARGO is coming in next Wednesday. I want you and Vince to get trained on it."

"What is it?"

"It's an amphibious rescue vehicle," Rusty answered. "You know those flooded places like we had during Tropical Storm Faye?"

Bonnie nodded. "Yeah."

"The city of Melbourne actually used one during Faye to rescue seniors and help with cleanup. This baby will go through the water. Get you in anywhere. Their designers streamlined it too. You can go between the trees."

"And it can go directly into the water?"

"Yep. Totally amphibious."

"Sounds interesting. Anything else?"

"Some panels for the backup generator. The electrical department will put them in. We'll be without emergency power until we validate the system." Rusty realized that she was probably ignoring the subjects most important in Bonnie's life. "How's the baby, and when is the wedding?"

Bonnie's face went soft, adopting a gentle smile. "The baby is fine. We haven't scheduled a wedding date yet. Justin's been awfully busy."

"Let me know," said Rusty. "I want a special invite."

"Will do." Bonnie pulled her towel around her waist and headed toward the locker room. "I'm going to hit the pool," Bonnie said over her back. "See you tomorrow."

Rusty headed into the mat room to stretch, but as she wandered through the health center, she checked to see whom from her various crews was there. She insisted that each of them follow a rigorous workout routine. She saw all of the crewmembers she expected, except for Dante, one of the EMT's. She would ask him about it tomorrow. There was no schedule, or even a hard requirement. She just wanted to make sure her crews stayed in shape.

After Rusty finished her stretches, she moved to the treadmill. She saw Gus Frantze, the senior chief and took the machine next to his. Gus, in his middle fifties, plodded along at a steady pace. Rusty quickly began to jog, and then to sprint. She kept this up for about ten minutes, and then backed off to an easy lope.

"How's it coming at the new station?" Gus asked.

The hospital had promoted Rusty to chief three months earlier, at which time it gave her command of the new station.

"God, it is so neat. When I get the ARGO this week, we'll have our full complement of vehicles." Rusty slowed her pace. "We'll validate the emergency power system next week. We're already doing a booming business."

"How about your crews?"

"That fire supervisor I hired from New Jersey – he's been a big help."

"Doug? I knew you'd like him."

"The crew members like him, too. He has so much experience." Rusty got off the treadmill and wiped it down. "Well, on to the weights. Did I tell you about Bonnie's vision?"

Gus stopped walking and bent forward to listen. "No. I thought she was done with her episodes."

"She thinks we're about to have a whopping storm."

Gus shook his head. "I hope she's wrong."

***

It was Saturday evening, and Simon and his mother were eating dinner when his father arrived home. They were sharing the pound-and-a-half trout that Simon had caught that morning.

"Can I have a taste of the fish?" asked Simon's father.

Simon was proud that he had caught a tasty fish big enough to eat.

"I caught it this morning," said Simon. "Me and Buster went fishing."

"I know," said Ladamien. "Your mother told me over the phone."

"Buster's not too good yet, but I'm learning him."

"If you're a good teacher, he'll be an expert in no time."

"He keeps getting his line tangled."

"Me too," said Ladamien. "Maybe you can teach me."

Ladamien sat down at the table and turned to speak to Aggie, who was putting a T-bone steak in the oven for Ladamien. "Did you tell Simon about how my job has changed?"

"I thought we'd all discuss it together," said Aggie. She looked at Simon and held a finger to her lips. "It's kind of a surprise."

His father and mother proceeded to tell Simon how his father's business was doing so well that he would not have to travel so much. They could move to a bigger house in a nicer neighborhood with better schools. Simon did not understand all of it, but his parents seemed pleased. He went to bed thinking they might have a boat and a dock. That would be fine.

***

When Simon awoke and came into the kitchen on Sunday morning, his father was drinking a cup of coffee and eating a doughnut, which he occasionally dunked in the coffee. The morning paper lay open on the table.

"Have you ever seen a pirate?" Simon asked.

His father looked up from the paper. "Yep. Quite a few."

"Did ya ever talk to one?"

"Sure. In my line of work, I talk to pirates pretty often."

"Are they cruel?"

Ladamien put his hand to his mouth and seemed to ponder the question. "I'd say they are ruthless. I mean, that's their business."

"But they're filthy rich, right?"

"Sometimes. Not always. They get in a lot of trouble."

"If we move, can we have a big boat, and a dock?"

"Sure. We can all go fishing together."

"Yeah. Mom likes to fish too."

"I know she does. Your mom's a good sport."

"I love her."

"Me too. What would you like to do today?"

Simon thought about it. They could go up in an airplane or out in the ocean; go see a ball game, or a movie; many things.

"Let's go play miniature golf," said Simon. "Afterwards, we can get some ice cream." He liked these things because they could do them as a family. He liked having his mother and father together.

"Sounds reasonable," said Ladamien. "Go ask your mother."

Simon found his mother in the laundry room washing clothes. "Dad says we can go play miniature golf and have ice cream. He says you have to okay it."

"Sure. We need to go in the morning before the afternoon rains start. Tell him I'll be ready to go as soon as I get these clothes in the dryer."

Simon ran in to tell his father. "Mom says okay, as soon as she's ready." After telling his father, he went to his room to put on shorts, a shirt, his Reeboks, and a lucky visor his father had brought him from Curaçao. Without the lucky visor, he could not make a putt; with it, he could not miss. The writing on the blue visor advised, Solid Gold, Mon, a phrase Simon's father had told him was more Jamaican than Curaçaon. When he returned to the living room, his parents were ready to leave.

The miniature golf course was actually in Cape Canaveral, so as Simon's father drove across the causeway to the beach, Simon could see the big cruise ships moored at Port Canaveral. They looked to him like floating cities. He also saw dozens of sailboats and motorboats, some large and some small.

The place where the government launched rockets was farther up the coast, out of sight from the road. Simon had seen quite a few launches, including the Space Shuttle. Simon's third grade class had taken a tour of the Cape Canaveral Air Station and the Kennedy Space Center. The missiles had fascinated him, and he had learned the names of many of them.

As they turned onto State Road A1A, Simon heard his parents talking about their neighbors, Buster's parents.

"I think the Shockleys are going to have to move," said Aggie. "Janice says that Steve got his layoff notice last week,"

"Did she say when?"

"They aren't sure. Steve's looking for a job."

"Tell her to have him send me a resume. Maybe I could use him."

Simon tried to digest all of the changes going on in his life. He would be moving, Buster would be leaving, and third grade would begin at a new school.

Simon's father parked outside the miniature golf course and Simon ran to pick out his club. His parents ambled along behind him. When they walked to the first hole, Aggie shot first. She holed out in three putts. Simon's father also took three shots to sink his ball. Simon lined up his putt carefully and touched the brim of his lucky visor.

His ball rolled up the ramp, over the hump and dropped in – a hole in one. It was a good day.

* * *

It was early Sunday morning. The NHC had

upgraded Tropical Depression 7 to Tropical Storm Dirk, but it was still 2,600 miles from the US mainland. Bonnie was in the jump seat of the rescue vehicle on its way to another mishap. Vince was driving the ambulance, which followed the fire truck through traffic. Both had their lights flashing and sirens blaring. Doug Forsythe, who was piloting the fire truck, maneuvered skillfully toward the expressway.

Ever since State Road 409 opened up connecting Coreopsis to Interstate 95, the Station 2 emergency team had to answer at least one call a day for an accident on I-95. Because of the high interstate speeds, these accidents were usually serious, involving a significant injury or fatality.

As they came upon the accident, Bonnie could see that the Florida Highway Patrol was already there, routing traffic away from the scene of the wreck. It was a single vehicle mishap and the car, a late model gray Nissan Altima, was hanging in a tree less than one hundred feet off the east side of the northbound lane. It had apparently flown through the air and come to rest about ten feet above the ground. The rear of the vehicle pointed north and the roof faced toward the road.

Bonnie looked about the scene, as they came to a stop, to see if anyone had been thrown clear of the car. She did not see any bodies. A tree limb had impaled the Altima through the rear window and held the car tight against the tree.

The fire crew sprinted out of the truck and sprayed the accident scene with foam, in case there was any leaking gasoline. One of the crewmembers was pushing an access platform in place as Bonnie exited the rescue vehicle and came toward the automobile.

"I saw two people inside," said Doug, the fire chief. "It appears their seat belts held them. I'm not sure if the airbags went off or not."

"Did you get the windows open?" Bonnie asked.

"We're going to pry the windshield off to give access. Once we get a support under the side, you or Dante can climb up and get inside. We do not want the car tumbling out of the tree. Wear gloves. There's bound to be jagged metal in there."

"Can you open the door from the bottom?"

"We'll get the Jaws of Life in there as soon as you tell us the people are secured. We don't want them falling out either."

Bonnie waited while the firefighters popped the front windshield to open up the vehicle. She climbed onto the platform, and then up a ladder braced over the hood. After that, Bonnie was able to work her way into the car and perch astride the driver's seat. The driver, a man, was up under the steering wheel. The passenger, a woman, curled up against the passenger side door. Her hands covered her head.

Bonnie heard a noise she recognized immediately. She reached down and was able to open the driver's side door and push it up. It was heavy, but it stayed out once she had it all the way open. She poked her head over the top of the car.

Bonnie spoke loudly so Doug could hear her. "There's a baby in this car. I heard it. Tell Dante to come up above the open door. I'll find the baby and hand it out to him."

"What about the others – the driver and the passenger?" Bonnie heard Vince's voice from beneath her. "Are they alive?"

Bonnie positioned herself between the driver and the passenger so that she could check the vital signs of each. She saw Dante outside the windshield opening. He was throwing a mat over the hood of the car so he would have something to hold on to and avoid slipping.

"The woman has a strong pulse," Bonnie told Dante, "The man's pulse is elevated but weak. I do not see any signs of profuse hemorrhage. They're okay for the moment."

"I'm not okay," a woman's voice said. "I can't feel my legs."

Bonnie bent over the woman curled up against the right hand door. "Stay still, we'll have you out shortly. The loss of feeling is probably temporary." Bonnie tried to use a calm voice, hoping to reassure the woman. "Did you have a baby with you?" she asked the woman.

"Oh my God," said the woman. "Martin. My baby boy. He was in his carrier, in the back seat. It was strapped down."

Bonnie looked over the seat into the back. A tree limb had come through the back window and forced the rear cushions forward. The branch had pushed the car seat to the right and Martin was half-hidden by the cushions and the back of the car seat. The belt still secured the boy, and now he was screaming. *Probably frightened*, Bonnie thought.

Bonnie tried to move the seat cushions but they would not budge. She was finally able to undo the straps holding Martin in his car seat and she removed him from it. She worked her way back to the front and handed Martin to Dante.

"That's one," Bonnie said. "We're going to have to be careful with his mother. She says she can't feel her legs. Tell the fire crew they can go ahead and pry that right door open. Her seat belt is holding her and she's out of the way."

"What about the driver?"

"I'm checking him now," said Bonnie as she worked her way through the open door so she could position herself above the driver.

"What's your husband's name?" Bonnie called over to the injured woman.

"Jerry," the woman answered in a weak voice.

Bonnie knelt down close to the man. His face was gray, as if drained of blood.

"Jerry." Bonnie spoke in a soft voice. "Jerry. Can you hear me?" Bonnie checked his pulse rate. It was slightly elevated.

The man muttered something that Bonnie interpreted as recognition.

"Jerry," Bonnie asked. "Do you know where you are?"

Bonnie heard the noise from the Jaws of Life and saw a crack of light through the passenger side door. There was a loud splintering noise.

"Wha...?" said Jerry. "What was that?"

Bonnie saw one of the firefighters pulling the

door open. She saw Vince's face as he started to prepare the woman for extraction.

Bonnie heard Vince talking to the woman. "We're going to take special care with your back."

Bonnie turned her attention back to Jerry. "Where do you hurt?"

"My chest. How is Susan? Is Martin okay?"

"You've been in an accident," said Bonnie. "We're taking you, Susan and Martin to the hospital. You're all going to be all right."

"I feel sick."

"That's not unusual," said Bonnie. "Do you need to throw up?"

"I don't think so," replied Jerry.

Bonnie watched as Vince put a neck brace on Susan. He and Doug then strapped Susan to a backboard and lifted her down. Bonnie lost sight of her. Dante poked his head through the passenger side door.

"What's the deal with him?" asked Dante.

"I think he has a spleen injury," answered Bonnie. "He's going to be heavy. Let's get Vince up here to help us."

"Ron's here with me," said Dante. "We've got a stretcher ready."

Bonnie knew that Ron was one of the firefighters – almost as muscular as Vince was.

"Take him out from the bottom," suggested Bonnie. "It would be much harder to lift him from up here."

"Let me get in from over here," said Ron. "I'll lift

and you can guide."

Jerry moaned and fussed as Bonnie worked him out from under the steering wheel. Ron lifted him over the seat and out through the passenger side door. Dante came up to help Ron, and took Jerry's shoulders from Bonnie. He and Ron positioned Jerry on the stretcher and strapped him down. They then handed him down to Vince and Doug at the gurney. Vince started an IV at once.

Vince and Dante loaded Jerry and Susan in the back of the ambulance. Bonnie improvised a baby carrier for Martin and positioned him next to her on the jump seat. She reached over and caressed his cheek. He reminded her of the son she had lost, Timmy. Martin was quiet now, but his eyes continued to follow every motion that Bonnie made. Bonnie felt tears squeezing out between her eyelids.

"You're going to be okay, little fellow," she said. "I'll take good care of you." Bonnie knew she probably would not see the child again, but it made her feel better to comfort him.

Vince turned on the siren and flashing lights. He pulled the emergency vehicle out onto the interstate behind a Coreopsis police vehicle that escorted them to the emergency room.

CHAPTER 3

"We sail within a vast sphere, ever drifting in uncertainty, driven from end to end."

Blaise Pascal (1623 - 1662)

Ladamien awoke early Monday morning, while it was still dark. He could see the clock on the dresser. It read 3:18, too early to get up, but if he stayed in bed, he was concerned his sleeplessness might disturb Aggie. He slipped out from under the sheet, which was all the cover they needed, and tiptoed to the door. He would fix a glass of warm milk and come back to bed more relaxed.

Ladamien stopped at the door leading into the hallway and looked back at Aggie. He could barely see her in the illumination of the nightlight. Her face was soft and loving – *like visions of the Madonna*, thought Ladamien. Her medium-length hair, which she referred to as dishwater-blond, framed her face like a radiant halo. She was lying on her back, and one smooth calf, ending in a well-formed foot, stuck out from under the sheet. She was so beautiful to

Ladamien that he had trouble taking his eyes from her and leaving the bedroom.

Ladamien snuck out of the bedroom and pulled the door closed without a sound. He went into the kitchen, took the milk from the refrigerator, and poured two cups of it into a small saucepan. He went into the pantry and found a box containing packages of instant hot chocolate. *Just what the doctor ordered*, thought Ladamien. While he waited for the milk to heat, he sat at the dining room table and sipped from a glass of water.

Leroy's proposal had hit Ladamien cold. He had not had time to think through all of the ramifications. Even though he had explained it confidently to Aggie and Simon, he was not sure it was entirely a good thing.

Should they stay in the United States or perhaps move to another country? Would Leroy truly be satisfied to let him run a business, or would he have him running around the world on other matters? Ladamien wanted more security, more family life – more Aggie and more Simon. Leroy did not care about any of that and Ladamien did not trust Leroy.

Ladamien finished mixing his hot chocolate and went out onto the back screened porch. There was a light rain, a typical Florida summer rain with large drops and a steady patter. In a heavier rain, the street in front of their house would flood. They could certainly afford a better place even if they stayed in Florida. Ladamien listened to the chorus of frogs – soprano, tenor, alto, and bass – and occasionally a contrabass.

He had no choice in the decision about his

company. He had no choice in how Leroy wanted to use him. He was a Rattler, pure and simple. Ladamien needed to be more open with Aggie. She was smarter than he was and had a woman's intuition as well. She might even have more influence with Leroy than he did. Ladamien finished his cocoa and sat watching the rain. He heard the sliding glass door open and close behind him, Aggie sat down next to him.

"What's wrong, honey?" she asked.

"Couldn't sleep. Jes' thinkin' about Leroy and the company. If it's the right thing."

"Sometimes, it's hard to know about the right thing. Most people would say what you do is wrong. A lot of people would say our marriage is wrong."

Ladamien chuckled softly. "I'm sure our marriage is right."

"Me too, hon," said Aggie. She sat, pensive for a few moments. "We went through this stuff about the gang before we married. You told me how you hated the drugs and such, especially what it does to kids, but didn't mind rescuing people from bad countries and being a front for the airport company."

"That's all true," said Ladamien, "but if I start laundering money for Leroy, I'll be supporting many a' those things I don't agree with. Drugs, illegal weapons, robbery, and extortion – and that's just a few."

"Don't be naive. You're already doing that." Aggie went into the kitchen and came back with a cup of coffee. "I watch TV, I read, and I listen to you. You're not just rescuing those men and women from bad places – you're selling them to corrupt people. What if one of those women was me? What if one of those boys was Simon?"

Aggie had never criticized him for what he did. Ladamien assumed she accepted the circumstances, the same as he did.

"I thought you understood." Ladamien felt like a little boy emptying his pockets before a grade school teacher. He did not want to admit how much his conscience bothered him.

"What if you just told Leroy you won't do it?" suggested Aggie. "Tell him your conscience won't let you."

Ladamien could not believe his wife had said that. Maybe she did not realize the gang's code of ethics. Maybe she did not know Leroy as well as he thought she did.

"I don't know what Leroy would do. He might have me killed, maybe you, and Simon."

"You don't know that. Leroy's not going to have you killed. He needs you as much as you need him. Besides, I don't think your conscience bothers you all that much."

"You're right. I don't know what he might do. I do know that Leroy's offer means more money. It'll be less time in the field and more chances to be with you and Simon." Ladamien stood up and thrust his right fist into his left palm. "I'm gonna take Leroy's offer. What're you gonna do?"

Ladamien saw the expression on Aggie's face soften. "I'm with you," she said. "I knew what marrying a gang member would be like when I said yes the first time. So, if we move, where are we going? I don't want to live where it's cold and I don't want to go where it's crowded."

Ladamien was relieved. As long as Aggie was not going to leave him or be a bitch about it, he could deal with Leroy and the crime. His conscience might nag him occasionally, but he could dismiss it, he always had.

"You want to move, leave Merritt Island?"

"Yeah. Move someplace fancier, bigger, with more to do."

"Like where?"

"Nothing exotic, like India or Brazil. A foreign country might be okay – maybe Australia or New Zealand – but I'd rather stay in the U.S., preferably a college town. Some place with culture and educational opportunities."

"Maybe like New Mexico or Arizona?"

"I don't like the desert and Simon wants a boat."

"It sounds like you want to stay in Florida."

"Hey. There's a thought."

Ladamien put his hand to his chin. "Sounds like Boca Raton, St. Augustine, Ft Myers, or maybe Apalachicola."

"Yeah. Just think. We can afford to live in Boca."

"Yes. I like the location. Good access to the business community. Florida Atlantic University. We'll look very respectable – a corporate executive, livin' in an upscale neighborhood with a fancy house and all."

Ladamien saw Aggie smile and took her hand. "You ready to go back to bed?"

Aggie got up and took Ladamien's arm. He felt

the soft cushions of her breast against his body. "I thought you'd never ask," she said.

Ladamien could live with their decision. Aggie seemed content and he did not have to confront Leroy. He could live with the gang's activities. Besides, if he didn't do this work for the gang, someone else would. Where else could he make the kind of salary they offered?

***

It was 5:00 Monday morning, and Bonnie's shift did not start until 8:00 a.m. Justin poured a cup of coffee and sat down across from her. She looked in the newspaper to see if there was an update on Tropical Depression 7. She found a small article in the weather section and read it aloud to Justin.

"The National Weather Service has upgraded Tropical Depression 7 to Tropical Storm Dirk. Dirk is located about 1,195 miles east of the Lesser Antilles, moving toward the west-northwest at nearly 16 miles per hour. Maximum sustained winds have increased to nearly 65 miles per hour with higher gusts extending outward up to 80 miles. The National Weather Service expects Dirk to become a hurricane within the next 24 hours and it could threaten the British Virgin Islands within the next 92 hours."

"That's still a long way from Florida," said Justin.

"It's coming here." Bonnie marked the location on a large hurricane-tracking map that she had taped to the kitchen wall. There was no doubt in her mind. She could see the image of the blue heron as if it were standing in the room with her. She knew the county would not begin to respond until the National Hurricane Center issued an official hurricane watch.

Bonnie finished her coffee and ate a quick breakfast of cereal and juice. She took a shower and went into the bedroom to put on her uniform. She saw the ring box from the night before sitting on the dresser. She placed the box in the center dresser drawer, out of sight and looked at the ring on her finger. Still half-dressed, she went back into the kitchen to talk with Justin.

"You know, sweetie, there are still some things to be done before we are actually married."

"I know," said Justin. "We can file a pre-application tonight online, and then we can go by the courthouse whenever you aren't working."

"Okay, but what about the ceremony? I'll at least want to have my parents come down."

"How much of a ceremony do you want?"

"Nothing fancy. Just a simple church wedding."

"I'll talk to Reverend Scanlon. See what he suggests."

"I'll take off work tomorrow. We can see him together and file the application as well."

Bonnie went back to the bedroom to finish dressing. The image of the baby, Martin, had been in her head ever since they took him to the hospital. She wanted to go to the hospital and check on him before she reported to the station.

Bonnie drove to Coreopsis Hospital and took the elevator to the pediatric ward. She went to the nurse's station and looked up the head nurse, Phyllis Denver.

"Phyllis," Bonnie said. "Do you remember the baby that came in yesterday? Martin. I don't know the last name."

"Tibbett," said Phyllis. "Their last name is Tibbett. What about him?"

"Is he alright? May I see him?"

"He's doing fine. We're keeping him under observation because we don't know how much of a jolt he may have received in the accident. I'll take you to him."

Bonnie followed Phyllis back to a crib where Martin was sleeping. "He reminds me so much of Timmy," said Bonnie.

"Does it make you think about having another baby, trying to get back in the family way again? Justin would love that."

"I don't have to think about it. I'm pregnant." Bonnie watched Phyllis' eyes widen.

"Are you sure? When did you know for sure?"

"I'm in my third month. Dr. Hester confirmed it two days ago."

"Have you told Justin?"

"Of course. We're getting married" Bonnie flashed her engagement ring where Phyllis could see it.

"That's wonderful. When is the wedding?"

"We haven't set a date yet."

"Do you need any help with the arrangements? Invitations or anything."

Bonnie smiled at Phyllis. "We need to discuss it. I only have a few minutes. My shift starts at eight. I'll call you. All right?"

"Can I tell the rest of the staff?"

"Sure. It's official"

As Bonnie left the hospital and headed toward her car, she felt lightheaded. My God, She told herself, you are thirty-two-years old and you have been married before. You are going to have a child, a daughter. Get a grip.

"But I'm so happy," she said aloud.

Bonnie arrived at work on time and went directly to the locker room. A crew from the graveyard shift was still out on a call. She could see their personal belongings still scattered about. She saw Vince coming from Rusty's office.

"Where's the third shift ambulance crew?" Bonnie asked Vince as he came into the locker room.

"There was a shooting. Out at that bar, Wiley's Junction. Some gal's husband and a boyfriend got into it. The police had to secure the scene before Bill and Tracey could go in. They're on their way to the hospital now."

"That's the second time this year there's been trouble at that bar."

"I know. There's been some talk about closing it down."

"Could the city do that?"

"They could, but they won't. The owner, Fred Hansel, he's an icon. His family has been here for a hundred years. His father opened that bar in the forties."

As Vince finished his sentence, Tracey Dickinson, a third shift paramedic trudged in and gathered up her belongings. She looked at Bonnie and Vince – dejectedly. Her short black hair was tousled and wet.

"God, what a scene." Tracey slumped down on the bench. Tired tears drenched her eyes. "Drunks and guns." She stood up, straightened herself, slammed her locker shut, and stomped out.

***

Simon was dreaming when his mother's voice woke him. He was fantasizing about the boat his father had promised to buy. It was a large inboard motor boat with outriggers and swiveling fishing chairs. In Simon's dream, he had hooked a big cobia and played it almost to the boat. His father had the fishing gaff in his hand. He was leaning over the gunwales, preparing to bring the fish aboard. His mother was capturing the event on the camcorder.

"It's a school day," he heard his mother say. "Simon, time to get up."

"I'm up, mom." Of course, he was not up, but he was awake. Simon threw the covers off and stretched. Then, he squirmed out of his pajamas and sat up. He retrieved some underwear from his dresser and pulled on a pair of jockey-style underpants, a short-sleeved t-shirt, and crew socks. Over these, he added a pair of jeans, a yellow and green polo, and jogging shoes.

Simon heard his mother call in from the other room. "Your breakfast is on the table. Wash your hands before you eat."

Simon went into the bathroom, washed his hands, and dried them on his shirt. "Where's Dad?" he asked as he came into the dining room.

"We stayed up late last night deciding where we want to move. He's been working hard, so he's still asleep."

"Where we gonna move? Will I have to go to a new school?"

"We're thinking about moving to Boca Raton. It's a nice community north of Miami. They should have good schools. It's a high-tech place."

"Can we have a boat there?"

"Oh yeah. It's right on the water."

"Does Dad think it's a good place?"

"As far as I could tell. It's closer to the people he works with." Aggie signed a paper and put it in an envelope with a ten-dollar bill. She licked the flap and sealed the envelope. She wrote something on the outside and handed it to Simon. "Here, give this to Ms. Hodges. It's your permission slip to go on the field trip to the zoo, and ten dollars to pay for your ticket and lunch."

"How come I have to pay and some of the other kids don't?"

"Your Dad makes good money. Some of the youngsters, their parents don't have a job, or they aren't paid very well. The economy isn't good right now."

"But, we're not rich."

"Compared to most of the people around here, we're pretty well off. Some of them would probably consider us rich."

"Can I have some money to spend at the zoo?"

"No. It's a school function. You won't need anything."

Simon saw his mother look up as his father came

in from their bedroom.

"Why don't you give him a five?" said Ladamien. "He might want to feed the animals or something."

Aggie went to her purse and came back with two dollars that she gave to Simon. "Here's two," she said, "that's enough."

"Thank you," said Simon.

"I didn't expect to see you until later," Aggie said to Ladamien. "You want some breakfast?"

"Just coffee," said Ladamien. "Maybe some toast and jelly." Ladamien placed his hand on Simon's head. "You ready for school, son?"

"I like my teacher, Ms. Hodges," said Simon. "She doesn't ignore me when I raise my hand."

"That's good. What time do you have to be there?"

"After 7:45 and before 8:00," said Aggie. "The school sent out a message on their web page not to drop the kids off before 7:45."

"Why's that?" asked Ladamien.

"They have a special program for children whose parents have to leave them before 7:45. If you want to bring them early, you have to sign up for the program."

"Dad," asked Simon, "how long are you going to be home this time?"

"Two more days," answered Ladamien. "Then, I have to fly down to Puerto Rico to meet with my banker and Leroy's lawyer. We're going to discuss the changes to my company."

Simon was surprised that his father had to leave

so soon. "So, I'll only see you in the evenings," said Simon. "Unless," and Simon looked up at his mother, "you'd let me skip school one day."

"Not a chance," said Aggie. "If you want to go to a good college and become a lawyer, you need every day of school you can get." She looked at her watch. "Speaking of which, we'd better get going."

Simon watched his mother put a cup of coffee and a plate of toast on the table in front of his father and give him a healthy kiss on the lips. "I'll be back shortly," she said.

Simon shuffled out to the car. He was disappointed that he would see so little of his father. His mom was okay as mothers go, but she'd never talked to a real pirate. The whole lawyer idea was hers as well. Simon wanted to own a fishing boat and take people out to catch tarpon and sailfish.

"What's Puerto Rico like?" he asked his mother as she drove him to school.

"Pretty," answered Aggie. "Kind of crowded. Sort of foreign."

They pulled up in front of Lewis Carroll Elementary School; Simon got out of the car and looked around to see which of his classmates were already there. He spotted Scotty McLausen under the overhang. Scotty was always bragging about something.

"Hey, Scotty," Simon said boldly, "My dad just came back from the Caribbean and he talked to real pirates."

"There ain't no real pirates no more," said Scotty. "The British killed'em all."

"It ain't so. My dad talked to some of them just last week. He says they're ruthless."

"Your dad's prob'ly a liar."

Simon had just decided there was no sense arguing with Scotty when Jennifer Purdy, the class know-it-all came over.

"There are still pirates," said Jennifer. "I saw a PBS special just the other day. The pirates have real fast boats. They hijack sailboats, steal them, and sometimes even kill the people that own them."

Simon gave a so-there look to Scotty and walked toward the classroom.

***

Chief Maureen L. "Rusty" Douglas was learning what managers in any enterprise understand. In spite of computers and instant communications, the average executive still faces numerous meetings and mountains of paperwork. Telecommunications has not replaced face-to-face discourse. Whatever goes through the central processing unit still starts and ends with hardcopies.

Rusty was accustomed to physical duty, so the switch to the desk was difficult for her at first. The senior station chief, Gus Frantze, coached her and gave her greater insight into why she needed to exert so much administrative effort.

"It's a team effort," Gus had told her. "It starts with you and me and goes all the way to the top."

Rusty was sitting in the weekly status meeting for the city. The Coreopsis vice-mayor, Gwendolyn Tress, ran the meeting with all of the mid-level supervisors in attendance. Normally, Gus did the emergency services report and Rusty just listened. This morning, however, the vice-mayor had scheduled Rusty to make a report.

Rusty listened as the various departments reported – finance, legal, utilities, roads, planning, police, and so on. Finally, it was her turn. She had a power point presentation to back her up.

"Station 2 has finished all mandatory certifications and passed a state inspection with very few dings. At this time, the city can consider the station operational. We still have some minor verification to complete, but the station is ready."

"Could you respond to a major catastrophe?" asked the vice-mayor.

"Anything except a snowstorm," answered Rusty. "We don't expect one of those."

"It's hurricane season. Do you expect one of those?"

Rusty hesitated; could she tell the vice-mayor that she had an employee who talked to spooks – spirits that told her the storm of the century headed toward Coreopsis?

"We are especially well prepared to deal with a hurricane."

Rusty was going to let it go at that, but she saw the chance to make a point. She continued. "The first hurricane of the season is out there right now, Hurricane Dirk. The National Hurricane Center upgraded it less than four hours ago. We do not know if we are in the target area yet, but we should know by next weekend. We are watching it closely."

Vice-mayor Tress nodded and looked around the

room. "Are there any questions for Chief Douglas?"

The police chief raised his hand. "You have a lot of overlap with unincorporated areas of the county. Are you satisfied that you have an adequate agreement with county emergency services?"

"We have a response map that we agreed to with the county, and we both review it regularly. As far as I'm concerned, no victim will ever go untreated because of a territorial misunderstanding."

"Does legal agree with you?"

The city attorney answered. "As you all know, we are in the process of transferring emergency services from Coreopsis Hospital and the city to the county system. As soon as we iron out the details, the county will manage all emergency medical services. In the meantime, we are working according to the emergency response scheme to which Rusty referred. We would rather handle a territorial disagreement than a wrongful death suit. I think that explains Rusty's position."

The Coreopsis Hospital administrator said, "We have a similar agreement with the other hospitals in the county. No one should go without emergency help regardless of where it occurs."

As the discussion continued, Mayor Tom Moline entered the room with a woman everyone in the room knew, the city receptionist and scheduler, Beatrice Blocker. They sat down behind the vice-mayor. Before the meeting ended, the vice-mayor asked the mayor to take the floor.

"As you all know," Moline began, "the city of Coreopsis is new, even by Florida standards. It has only been fifty-eight years since the state incorporated us. We are fortunate that during much of that time we have had a receptionist and chief scheduler who has made those jobs much more significant than just occupying a desk."

The mayor turned to Blocker. "Come up here, Bea," he said. "Tell everyone how long you have been on the city payroll."

"Forty years," said Bea as she joined the mayor at the head of the table.

"What was your most memorable moment?"

"Besides the birth of my grandson? Probably the completion of SR-409 and opening Coreopsis to I-95. That's the most coordination I ever had to do."

"I can vouch for that," the mayor said. "Without Bea's persistence, it might never have happened."

The mayor picked up a trophy the vice-mayor had placed on the table. "This is only a symbol of the appreciation and respect that Coreopsis has for your diligence and devotion. To make it more meaningful, there's a bonus check for one thousand dollars that goes with it."

Bea looked suitably impressed and everyone in the room applauded.

"Thank you," said Bea.

The vice-mayor closed the meeting and many of the attendees stayed to exchange information. It was an opportunity to air out questions in an informal setting. The mayor pulled Rusty aside.

"I thought you might have some personal news to report today."

Rusty was puzzled. "Like what?"

"My sources tell me that one of your most

notable crew members might be getting married."

"You mean Bonnie?"

"Yes. Has she talked to you?"

"Absolutely. She's going to have a baby and she and Justin are getting married as soon as they can arrange the wedding."

"Well, I guess that confirms that. Is she going to keep on working?"

"She hasn't turned in her notice yet, but I expect her to quit and move to Atlanta with Justin."

"Why Atlanta?" the mayor asked.

"Justin's work," answered Rusty. "I don't believe it will be permanent. Perhaps a year or two."

"Will she return to work when they come back?"

"I wouldn't be surprised, but we haven't discussed it."

Rusty stopped to congratulate Bea and then left. She drove back to the station, parked and saw Doug, the lead firefighter, as she went inside. "Have you seen Bonnie?" she asked.

"She and her crew went out on a routine transport call about half-an-hour ago," Doug answered, and then he pointed toward the street. "There, they are coming back now."

Rusty met the crew as they vacated the ambulance. She took Bonnie's arm to get her attention. "Would you come to my office as soon as you're ready?"

Bonnie nodded. "Sure. Is anything wrong?"

"I don't know," Rusty said. "We'll talk."

Rusty scurried to her office and shuffled papers

while she waited for Bonnie. She left her office door open so Bonnie could come in without knocking. She saw Bonnie come through the door. "Close the door behind you," said Rusty, and then she motioned for Bonnie to have a seat across the desk from her.

"How's your day?" Rusty asked.

"So far, so good," said Bonnie.

"The mayor was asking about you." Rusty saw Bonnie frown. "Oh, nothing serious. I just confirmed that you are pregnant and getting married."

"Is that it?"

"I thought we ought to make a plan," Rusty said. "The rules won't let you stay on an emergency crew after you reach your fourth month."

"I know. I think I'm going to resign."

"Let me know when you know for sure. I'll start greasing the slides."

Bonnie got up to leave and paused at the door out. "Thanks," she said. "I'll let you know."

"Oh," Rusty interjected before Bonnie closed the door. "I understand your storm is now a hurricane."

"I know," said Bonnie. "And, it's still coming here." She turned and left, closing the door behind her.

Rusty picked up the phone to call Gus. She could not wait for Bonnie's decision to start reinforcing her crew.

CHAPTER 4

"What we anticipate seldom occurs: but what we least expect generally happens."

Benjamin Disraeli

Tuesday at 10:00 a.m., Bonnie entered Rusty's office. She had already been out on two calls that morning, so she felt she was well into her workday. Rusty was pulling a folder out of her file cabinet.

"You wanted to see me?" asked Bonnie.

Rusty returned to her seat.

"You know I have to relocate you before the end of October. There's too much risk after that."

Bonnie knew the policy and she knew that Rusty couldn't ignore it.

"Any ideas?" Bonnie asked. "Remember, I told you I would probably resign."

"Until I receive your notice, I have to assume you are still working for the hospital," said Rusty. "However, I have to move on finding a replacement. I talked to Gus this morning. He could transfer Kathie Turbinov over here right now to take your

72

spot. I wouldn't have to hire anyone."

It hurt Bonnie to think they could replace her so easily; however, she knew that Kathie was a good EMT. Gus had tried to hold on to her for some time. He probably saw this as an opportunity to solidify his staff.

"I guess there isn't any reason to delay the inevitable," said Bonnie. "Do you want me to finish out the month?"

"Yes," answered Rusty. "Finish the month here, and I'll make any arrangements you desire with Gus."

Bonnie started to get up to leave. Rusty motioned to her to stay seated.

"I know this is hard for you," said Rusty. "It's not easy for me either. You're a good paramedic. I'll be pleased when you come back."

"Six months is a long time. It could be two years."

"Marriage and motherhood," said Rusty, "I've never experienced either. I have been an EMT for a long time. It's awfully hard to erase that from your blood. Once an EMT, always an EMT."

Bonnie didn't say anything. She knew the decisions she was making, including those being made for her, were the right ones. She also knew that Rusty had a point. There was something special in being a first responder.

"Oh," said Rusty, "have you checked on your storm recently?"

"How did it get to be my storm?"

"Okay, Dirk. It's a category 2 hurricane, wind speed about 105 miles-per-hour."

"Where is it?"

"It's still in the ocean. They have warnings up as far north as the Turks and Caicos Islands. That's about six hundred miles from Miami."

"Still coming our way," Bonnie remarked. "How long before we know if it's headed here?"

"Five, maybe six days. It should start veering north."

Bonnie shrugged and got up to leave. "It'll be a category four or five by then." She stopped at the door and looked back at Rusty. "It's not going to veer."

***

Bonnie left Rusty's office and found Dante in the break room. "This is my last month in emergency," she said.

"It's probably best," said Dante. "You don't want to put your baby at risk."

"Of course I don't. It's just that I still feel so good."

"That's great. You ought to hope it stays that way."

"I'll miss you guys."

"What about Justin? You gonna marry him?"

"Yes. I accepted his proposal."

"Well," said Dante. "You might just decide to be a stay-at-home mom."

The alarm in the station went off. Vince was already heading toward the driver's seat of the ambulance. Bonnie opened the center door and strapped herself into the jump seat. Dante positioned himself in the back.

Vince turned on the intercom and updated the crew on the call.

"We're headed to 715 Pompano. Subject described as older male – confused, dizzy, with rapid heartbeat, fast breathing, fever, and chills. Subject has fainted. Caller is wife, elderly, unable to move victim."

"Sounds like sepsis," said Bonnie.

"Maybe," agreed Dante, "but from what? Hey Vince, do they have any medical info on this man?"

"ER says he's a known diabetic," said Vince.

"That could go with sepsis," said Bonnie. "We should put him on oxygen, and probably a saline IV. Make sure ER agrees."

"Depending on what you find at the scene," said Vince, "that's a go."

The ambulance pulled up in front of a single family home. Bonnie jumped out, went to the front door, and knocked loudly. "Emergency, we're coming in."

An elderly woman in a housedress opened the door. "It's Charles. He's in the hallway."

Bonnie hustled into the hallway and found an older man wearing boxer shorts and a t-shirt on the floor. He was breathing rapidly but appeared alert.

"Where does it hurt?" asked Bonnie.

"My stomach," said Charles. "It's never hurt so badly. Down low, here." The man pointed to an area above his groin.

Vince and Dante came in with the stretcher.

"Put him on the gurney and start the oxygen," said Bonnie. She turned to the woman. "What's your name, ma'am?"

"Lynne. Lynne Yeomans."

"Okay, Lynne. Do you have all of Charlie's medications? It will help if we take them with us."

"Where should I put them?"

"A plastic bag will work fine."

Vince and Dante were rolling Charles out the door when Bonnie took the bag of medicine from Lynne and started to head for the ambulance.

She spoke to Lynne. "We can't take you with us. Get a ride to the hospital and I imagine Charles will be in the emergency room."

As Bonnie entered the ambulance, all thoughts of her own future had left her mind. She was back in the flow.

* * *

Bonnie decided to take her lunch break at the hospital. She let Vince and Dante take the ambulance back to Station 2. She arranged to ride with the courier when she was ready to return. She planned to check on little Martin after she ate. She went through the cafeteria line, purchased a fish sandwich, cole slaw, and sweet tea, and then sat where she could catch the news on TV.

The TV announcer pointed to a map that showed a well-formed tropical cyclone in the east Atlantic Ocean. It appeared to be about 2,000 miles southeast of Miami. "The National Hurricane Center places the center of Hurricane Dirk about 695 miles east of the Leeward Islands," said the announcer. "Dirk is a category 2 hurricane having maximum sustained winds of 110 miles-per-hour with higher gusts. Hurricane force winds extend up to 35 miles from the center, and tropical storm winds reach outward more than150 miles."

Bonnie listened carefully. She tried to estimate how much longer before the storm reached Coreopsis. *Seven days*, she thought to herself, *give, or take two days.* She looked away from the TV and saw the pediatric nurse, Phyllis, coming toward her. Phyllis sat down across from her.

"I was getting ready to head to your floor," said Bonnie. "How's Martin?"

"His aunt picked him up this morning. The doctors plan to release his parents this afternoon."

"I guess I won't see him then."

"I'm surprised you had the time to come over here."

"I've already been out on three calls. I needed the break."

"What kind of shift do you work?"

"Right now," said Bonnie, "we have three eight-hour shifts at each of the two stations. I think Gus is about to change to four twelve-hour shifts split between the two stations."

"That's the way many emergency services are structured," said Phyllis. "Coreopsis is probably just catching up."

"I'm leaving emergency services, so I won't be affected."

"The pregnancy? The four month rule?"

"That's it. Um, must go. I have to catch the

courier."

Phyllis waved Bonnie away. "Good luck."

***

Bonnie walked out of the hospital cafeteria and crossed the street to a bench in a small park where the courier would pick her up. A small pond sparkled in the center of the park. Bonnie saw a great blue heron stalking minnows among the cattails and reeds at the edge of the pond.

The heron left the pond and lumbered up to her. It stood on one leg, tucking the other leg up under its abdomen, and stared into the distance – toward the east.

Bonnie heard the voice distinctly in her mind. "Behold the wind."

The heron lowered its leg and walked stilt-legged back to the pond. Soon, the courier van pulled up in the circular drive and Bonnie slid into the front seat. The courier was a shriveled black man named Israel, who Bonnie knew was a Florida native.

"Do you know if the local Native Americans had any myths about the blue heron?"

"The blue heron was one of their four original chiefs," answered Israel. "A symbol of wisdom and a great fisherman."

"Who were the other chiefs?"

"The hurricane, the alligator, and the manatee."

"How do you know? Are you making it up?"

"I saw the heron looking at you. Was it talking to you?"

Bonnie shook her head. She could hardly believe

she was having this conversation. "It said...'Behold the wind'...that's all."

"Seriously," said Israel, "it told you that."

Bonnie nodded.

Israel wheeled the van into the health and fitness center. "I've got to drop a package here. I'll be right out."

When Israel returned, Bonnie decided to question him further. "Have you been through many hurricanes?"

"I grew up farther south, on the west coast of Florida. I have been through a bunch of them. They don't come here so often. Lately, though, they seem to be getting worse – like Andrew and Katrina."

"What if a storm like Andrew came through here?"

Israel whistled through his teeth. "Is that what you think the heron's telling you?"

"I had a vision, out at the Ais Sanctuary. I saw buildings coming down, trees flying through the air."

"That's what it would be like alright. Just the thought scares me. Have you told anyone else?"

"Yes, but they won't do anything until the National Hurricane Center tells them to."

"I'm sure they don't want to generate any false alarms."

"I know. I just hope we're prepared."

"We're here," Israel said, as he pulled up in front of Station 2. He held up his hand to get Bonnie's attention. "If the heron's talking to you, the warning is meant for you personally. Be careful for yourself."

Bonnie got out and ambled back to work. Maybe it was a personal warning. If so, what did the heron expect her to do? She couldn't change the wind.

***

That afternoon, Simon came home from school and talked his father into taking him out to the jetties at Port Canaveral. It wasn't the best time for fishing out there, but Simon wanted more time with his father.

Ladamien called in to Aggie. "Hey babe, Simon wants me to take him fishing, at the jetties. Wanna go?"

Aggie came into the living room pressing her hand to her forehead. "I've got a little headache. You two go," she said. "I know Simon's been aching to get some time with you alone."

"Are you okay?" Ladamien asked Aggie.

"I'll be all right," said Aggie. "It's just a summer cold."

Simon did want to spend some time on his own with his father.

"You wanna pal up with your old man?" asked Ladamien.

"Well, yeah," answered Simon, "but I'll miss mom?" Simon looked at his mother. "Are you sure it's okay?"

"Your mom isn't feeling well," said Ladamien, "We'll spend some time together and talk man stuff. You can tell me about school and I can tell you more about pirates."

"Cool." Simon was eager to hear more about

pirates and he knew his mother wasn't keen on the subject. "Can we get some ice cream before we come home?"

"If you do," Aggie remarked, "You'd better bring me some as well. Rocky Road. I'll even clean the fish."

"We'd better get going," said Ladamien. "We don't want to be out after dark."

It took less than twenty minutes for Simon and Ladamien to load up the pickup and head out for the jetties. The Ford 150 had a sticker on it that allowed them to enter Jetty Park. Ladamien drove them south on State Road 3 and turned east on State Road 528. They entered Port Canaveral and followed the road along the south docks. The road through Jetty Park twisted around and they parked within sight of the jetties. They had brought frozen bait with them, so it didn't take long before they were walking along the pier that extended over the jetties.

Simon looked out at the water. To the south, he could see that two- to three-feet waves were coming onto the beach. Inside the port, the water was comparatively smooth and the tide was in. He selected a rig with a medium weight sinker and attached it to his line with considerable skill for a nine-year-old. He baited his hook and cast his line into the channel. The sun was at ten o'clock in the west, so he figured they had about an hour to fish. He sat down on the folding stool they had brought with them and watched his father cast his line and sit down next to him.

"Where did you meet pirates?" Simon asked his father.

"Miami, Cuba, Indonesia, Guyana, Nigeria, Somalia. There are pirates in lots of countries."

"Do they carry swords and swear a lot?"

"They talk pretty rough alright, but they carry automatic rifles. I haven't seen any of them carrying swords, except in movies."

"How did you meet them?"

"They helped me in my business, transporting people."

"People to build airports?"

"Something like that, yeah."

"Wow! And, they had big ships."

"Mostly, they have real fast boats. Sometimes, they steal or borrow a ship. I don't think they own them." Ladamien pointed at Simon's line. "Check your line. I think I saw it tighten and then slack off."

Simon started to reel in his line, and then it tightened up. He began to reel harder. After a short battle, he hoisted a black drum up to the deck. "Mom knows how to fix drum real good," said Simon.

"We'll keep it," said his father, apparently agreeing.

As Simon baited his hook, one of the large cruise ships sailed past, heading out to the Atlantic Ocean. Simon noticed that there were no passengers on its deck or balconies.

"Look Dad, there's nobody on that ship. Aren't there usually people out on deck waving and everything?"

"That is unusual," said Ladamien. "It looks like they're going out empty,"

"Why would they do that Dad?"

"They may be changing ports, or going to dry dock for maintenance. Of course, it could mean there's a bad storm coming and they don't want to get caught in port."

"Why would they do that?"

"They can ride out a storm better at sea than in port. I heard there was a hurricane brewing. Their captains would know better than anyone."

"How would they know?"

"The cruise ship industry is enormous. They have a lot of money at stake. Their captains are the best. They look at atmospheric conditions and know where a storm is headed many days ahead of time."

"That would be a really good job. It would be like living on the ocean."

"It takes a lot of training. Speaking of which, tell me about your school."

"Aw, it's just school."

"What classes are you taking?"

"I have reading, writing, social studies, and math. Oh yeah, and Spanish, but I don't speak it much yet." Simon looked at his father to see if that was enough. His dad just continued waiting. "Sometimes, we have music. I play the recorder."

"That sounds like a good schedule."

"It's okay. There's a boy in my class named Scotty. He thinks he knows everything. He said there wasn't no such thing as pirates."

"Did you tell him he was wrong?"

"No. This girl, Jennifer – she told him. She's

pretty smart."

Ladamien started reeling in his line. "If we're gonna pick up ice cream, we'd better leave."

"Okay," said Simon. "I caught my fish."

***

It was Wednesday, and Bonnie arrived at work before 7:00 a.m. Vince, the ambulance driver, met her outside the locker room.

"Rusty wants to see us in her office," Vince said. "She wants us to meet the ARGO representative."

Bonnie opened her locker and put her lunch bag inside. "Do I need to take anything with me?"

"Not that I know of. She just said for me to tell you to come to her office."

"Let's go." Bonnie closed her locker and walked out of the locker room. Vince walked beside her.

"It seems like we're spending a lot of time in training," Vince remarked.

"The new station's only been open for six months," said Bonnie. "Rusty tried to get all of the latest equipment. Some of it is new to us."

"That part is kind of exciting." Vince stopped outside of Rusty's office. "I'd just rather be going out on calls instead of going to class."

"Now that State Road 409 connects Coreopsis to I-95, we'll have all of the calls we can handle within a year. I know of four new subdivisions being built around the station."

Bonnie opened Rusty's door a crack. "Are you ready for us?"

Rusty was sitting at her conference table with a

sandy-haired man in a camouflage jump suit. Rusty motioned them into her office. "This is Mark Baldwin, the ARGO dealer from Eau Gallie."

Mark pushed his chair back and remained standing until Bonnie had taken her seat. He gave brochures and business cards to Bonnie and Vince, and then he seated himself. "We'll take the ARGO for a trial run, but I wanted to fill you in on some facts first. The vehicle you're getting is the 8X8 Avenger."

"Sounds like a fighter plane," said Vince.

Mark smiled. "There was a World War II torpedo bomber, an Army air defense system, and a Dodge automobile – all named Avenger. This Avenger is an amphibious motor vehicle."

"Totally amphibious?" asked Bonnie.

"Twenty miles per hour on land," Mark answered, "two and a half in the water. It holds enough fuel to last eight hours."

"How do we get it to where we're gonna use it?"

Rusty answered. "We bought an all terrain carrier that can transport the ARGO, a medical unit, or a fire command module. You will be testing that as well."

"Where are we going to test it?" asked Vince.

"Take it out to the Puzzle Lake area off of State Road 46," replied Rusty. "There's a variety of terrains out there. Take it over to the St. John's River and check it out on the water."

"Sometimes the current in the St. John's is more than two miles per hour," remarked Bonnie. She asked Rusty the question that was bothering her. "Do you really want me to undergo this training? I'll be leaving."

Rusty answered quickly. "I know that, and if Kathy were already here, I would probably send her. I want your evaluation, the benefit of your experience. Tell me if this vehicle will do the job."

"Alright," said Bonnie, "I can do that."

Mark rose and started toward the door. "I'll show you how to deal with the current in the river." He opened the door and turned to Rusty. "Thanks, Chief. I'll take good care of them."

Mark led Bonnie and Vince through the station and out the back door. "The chief decided to keep this combo in the back garage. It isn't rapid response equipment and it's best to keep it all together."

Bonnie saw a flat bed truck parked at the side of the back garage – the hangar – as the maintenance crew called it.

"What's on the truck?" asked Bonnie.

Mark waved his hand toward the truck. "The medical module and command station are on the truck. Facilities still has to finish getting the bays ready. Our vehicles, the ARGO and the transporter, are in the hangar." He turned to Vince. "You want to bring them to us?"

"Sure," said Vince. "Give me the keys and I'll drive them out."

"The keys are in the transporter. We'll wait for you."

Bonnie watched Vince open the hangar door and go inside. Soon, the transporter pulled out of the garage and stopped on the apron across the lot from where Bonnie and Mark were standing. She saw the Avenger mounted on the back. It was smaller than she had expected it to be.

"How long is the Avenger?" Bonnie asked.

"Ten feet long and five feet wide," answered Mark.

"How many people does it hold?"

"Six on land, four in the water."

"Who all has used it and what for?"

"A resort in Virginia uses one as a rescue vehicle, boat hauler, and observation platform. A town in British Columbia uses it for mountain rescue in the snow. Costa Rica used it to get supplies to remote areas and perform rescues after a major storm." Mark paused. "Should I go on?"

"No," said Bonnie. "It sounds versatile."

"It is," agreed Mark. "As a matter of fact, your neighbor, Melbourne, used it during Tropical Storm Faye."

"How did Melbourne use it?"

"To evacuate seniors during the storm and to clean up debris afterwards."

Vince stuck his head out of the transporter cab and yelled. "You guys gonna jaw all day, or you wanna go check this mother out?"

"That's Vince," said Bonnie. "He's always impatient." She cupped her hands to her mouth and shouted. "We're coming, already."

Mark and Bonnie walked across the lot and got on board the transporter, Mark in the front with Vince and Bonnie in the back. Vince pulled out onto the highway.

"Bonnie's a psycho," said Vince. "She told the chief we're gonna get a real bad storm this year."

Bonnie saw the look of surprise on Mark's face when he looked at Vince. "That's psychic, pea-brain," she said, "and, I'm not. Besides, I only told Rusty that I had a vision. It might not mean anything."

Vince did not want to drop it. "She talks to spirits out in the woods, and…"

Bonnie interrupted. "Be quiet. We don't want to be talking about that. Mr. Baldwin isn't interested."

Vince stopped talking and Mark Baldwin sat facing straight ahead.

"If we do have a major hurricane," Mark said, "you'll be glad you have the Avenger."

Bonnie believed in fate. She was sure they would use the Avenger this year. "I'm sure we will," she said.

***

After Bonnie and Vince returned from testing the Avenger, Rusty called them into her office. Bonnie entered Rusty's office and saw that Vince was already there, sitting at Rusty's conference table. Bonnie sat down next to him.

"What did you think of the ARGO?" asked Rusty.

"The carrier handled real good," said Vince, "and, the Avenger went on and off the carrier real easy."

"The Avenger is great for what it does," said

Bonnie, "but it has limitations. Twenty miles per hour limits its range for emergencies. Two and one-half miles per hour in water is a little anemic. It means I had to turn into the current and kind of crab walk across the river. I had to enter the water upstream of the current. It took me a while to get the hang of it."

"Is it totally amphibious," asked Rusty, "as advertised?"

"As advertised," answered Bonnie. "It's buoyant and maneuverable. If you have to get into flooded areas, it will get you there."

"You may get a chance to find out," said Rusty. "Let me finish with Vince and I'll tell you more."

Bonnie knew better than to ask Rusty what she meant. Rusty would tell her when she was ready.

Rusty turned to Vince. "The hangar crew has the command station and the mobile medical units mounted in their bays. I would like for you and Doug to go check out those units with the hangar crew. Figure out how long it takes to mount them on the carrier and get underway."

"Are you going to leave the fire command module on the carrier?" asked Vince.

"I think that makes sense, don't you?"

"Maybe during the dry time of year, but I would leave the Avenger on there during the storm season."

"Well, you and Doug figure it out and make a recommendation. Now, go. I want to talk with Bonnie."

Vince left the room and closed the door behind him. Rusty turned to Bonnie and opened a folder for

Bonnie to look at.

Rusty opened the conversation. "Gus and I are more aware than most people of your psychic powers. We both remember when the spirit of that girl possessed you and how you were able to help that government agent capture a gang leader. We believe you have special extrasensory powers. We decided to press the National Hurricane Center about Hurricane Dirk and asked them what their models are predicting."

"What did they say?"

"As you know, they're very conservative. They cautioned us that Hurricane Dirk is still almost 1300 miles from the Florida mainland and couldn't possibly make landfall here for at least five days. However, they added that all of the models show Dirk continuing on a westerly course. They admitted they would probably be issuing an alert for the Bahamas and the US coastline sometime in the future."

"Sounds like the beginning of something. Did their models make any prediction as to where the storm would come ashore?"

"They all indicated somewhere between Miami, Florida and Brunswick Georgia."

"That's a long way apart."

"Not for five days out. Actually it's a significant level of agreement, especially, according to the National Hurricane Center, for the level of activity in the upper atmosphere at this time."

"So why don't they issue a hurricane watch now?"

"That's not the way it works. Everything they were telling us was unofficial. Without Gus' influence, I doubt they would have talked to us at all. They won't issue a hurricane watch until they are sure the hurricane is 48 hours away. A lot can change in three days."

"So, what did you decide to do?"

"We can't do much about the county until the National Hurricane Center issues an alert. We have more leeway within the city and with city resources. That's where you and the Avenger come into play."

"How's that?"

"Gus met with Mayor Moline and filled him in on his conversation with the National Hurricane Center. Moline suggested they discuss the situation with the center director at the Kennedy Space Center (KSC). The center director checked his own sources at NOAA, the National Oceanic and Atmospheric Administration and told Mayor Moline that he was concerned about the possibility the storm could affect KSC operations."

"Wow! Y'all acted pretty fast."

"Dirk is already a category 2 hurricane. If it comes here, it could easily be a category 4 or 5. We have to take your premonition seriously. Even if it's a false alarm, it's potentially too devastating to ignore."

"I know what I saw. It's not a false alarm."

"Have you had any more visions?"

"When I came back from the hospital, the blue heron came up to me and repeated its message... 'Behold the wind'."

"Behold." Rusty looked pensive. "That's a

strange word. Why not beware?"

"Oh," Bonnie remembered her vision of the Pullman train and Hannah Ward. "I did have a vision where someone used the word 'beware.' However, it was in reference to my unborn daughter."

"So, you've had several visions about this storm."

"Yes," said Bonnie. "The courier told me something interesting. He said the blue heron was one of the original chiefs for the local Native Americans."

"What do you think that means?

"Maybe behold is more of a request for reverence, rather than fear."

Rusty just shrugged her shoulders and shook her head. "Whatever," said Rusty. "Let me tell you what we decided to do."

"Yes, I'm eager to hear." Bonnie could tell from the change in Rusty's voice that Rusty thought their decision was significant.

"Mayor Moline believes that if a major storm comes through Port Canaveral all of the causeways across the Indian River Lagoon will be closed for several days. Coreopsis is the only city with a major hospital that would have access to north Merritt Island and the Kennedy Space Center."

"By using State Road 3?" asked Bonnie.

"Exactly," Rusty confirmed. "Furthermore, if we set up an emergency medical station at the space center, we could provide first response and transport to the civilian population. NASA designed the Vehicle Assembly Building to withstand a major hurricane. The Kennedy Space Center director has agreed that they could provide us space in the Vehicle Assembly Building and access to the center."

"Wouldn't the county evacuate Merritt Island anyway?"

"Evacuations are never 100 percent. We would have to prepare to perform search and rescue operations as the storm allowed." Rusty paused. "There are many unanswered questions. No matter how we prepare, there will always be unforeseen complications. That's why we want to do this, even if it only turns out to be an exercise."

"That makes sense. Kind of like a drill."

"Precisely," said Rusty. "We want you to coordinate it for the city."

"Whoa. I'm no leader, and Justin and I filed for our marriage license. I have a wedding to plan."

"Nobody's asking you to lead. NASA will provide the leader. They look at it as an opportunity to test their own preparedness. I'll make sure you have time to plan for your wedding, but with this storm, you may have to schedule around it anyway."

"True. What will I do with NASA exactly?"

"You'll report to Vice-Mayor Tress and evaluate the need for our resources. As our interface to the team leader, you would oversee the preparation of procedures, including integration with NASA and the county."

"I assume there is a county representative on the team."

"There is, but more as an observer than an active participant, at least for the moment." Rusty leaned forward and looked intently at Bonnie. "Gus and I believe your premonition. We want to be ready for the worst-case scenario, Dirk as a category 5 hurricane headed directly for Coreopsis. We're using this exercise as a means to get ready as early as possible without risking our credibility. It's your job to make sure we are prepared for the nastiest storm imaginable."

"I'll do my best," said Bonnie, "but a medical and transport presence at Kennedy Space Center is only a small part of the total effort needed to get ready."

"Gus and I will coordinate the additional effort with the mayor. Remember, I grew up in Slidell, Mississippi. I was going to Tulane when Katrina struck. I know the stakes in underestimating this storm. I'm determined to make sure we're ready."

Bonnie nodded her head in agreement. "We can only hope."

***

After Bonnie left her office, Rusty picked up the phone and called Gus. "I talked to Bonnie. She's on board."

"Good," said Gus. "We've stirred up a hornet's nest at the county. They want to know what information we're acting on that they don't have."

"What did you tell them?"

"I'm telling everyone that we assessed our procedures and decided we were lacking in our support planning, that we are concerned what happens if we become a shelter center for north Brevard."

"Did they buy it?"

"The county people believe it, especially since

they will have an observer involved in our mock drill. Some of the other folks were skeptical."

"Did you talk to the Port Authority?"

"Yes. They say they have too many unique requirements to be interested in our exercise. Interestingly enough, the big ships are already leaving port. I guess they're expecting Dirk to come here also."

"They're probably looking at the same data as the National Hurricane Center."

"They have to be very conservative. Those ships probably cost $100 million each."

"What about Patrick Air Force Base, did they call?"

"No. They will stay with standard procedures. They can clear the air base quickly and they know their vulnerabilities."

"So, is that about it?"

"Rusty, there's one thing you should know. The mayor is strongly behind this exercise. As a matter of fact, he doesn't look at it as an exercise."

"I'm a little surprised. Is there a reason?"

"I told him we were acting on Bonnie's premonition. He reminded me that people had been down on Bonnie before when she looked goofy but turned out to be the real deal. He told me that he believes not only does history judge leaders, but the Almighty also judges them. If this turns out to be a false alarm, we need to make sure we learn from it. We can explain it." Gus paused. "However, if it is a true warning, and we chose to ignore it; we could never live with the aftermath. He doubts that history would ever forgive us."

"That's a big view for a small town mayor."

"That's Moline," said Gus. "He asked me to share his feelings with you and Bonnie. Tell her the mayor is behind her and she should make sure she doesn't screw this up."

"Understood," said Rusty, "I'll talk to her."

Rusty hung up the phone, went to her computer, and checked the latest advisory from the National Hurricane Center. Dirk was still a category 2 hurricane far out in the Atlantic.

***

Bonnie left Rusty's office still unsure of what Rusty expected of her. She had been prepared to resign and now Rusty had assigned her to a team expected to prepare for the very storm she had predicted. What was she expected to do? She did not have to wait long to find out.

Vince waved to her. "Hey Bonnie, there's someone on the phone from NASA that wants to talk to you."

"Already?" said Bonnie. She went to the wall phone in the ready room. "Hello, this is Bonnie McConnell."

"Bonnie," said the voice at the other end, "This is Eduardo Martinez. The center director has appointed me to head up an emergency readiness team. I understand you're my contact for Coreopsis."

"Yes. I just left a meeting with my chief. Do you have a plan?"

"Not yet. I think that's our first task. Can you

come to a meeting later this afternoon, say at 3:00 p.m.?"

"Sure. Should I bring anything?"

"If your city already has an emergency plan you might bring that, also an inventory of your resources."

"I'll see what I can do. I won't have much time."

"Is three too early?"

"No. I'll be there."

Bonnie hung up the phone and went to Rusty's office.

"I need a copy of our emergency plan and an inventory of our resources," she told Rusty. "The NASA team leader wants to meet this afternoon, at three."

Rusty went to her bookcase and took out a one-inch report. "Here's the plan. It contains a list of resources but it needs updating. What's the team leader's name?"

"Eduardo Martinez."

"Tell Eduardo we'll get him an updated inventory tomorrow. You'd better go. You have to get a badge. You know how to do that?"

"Yes. I've gotten a badge before." Bonnie left the chief's office and drove her car across the NASA causeway to the badging station. After she entered the building, a medium-sized man with graying hair came to meet her.

"Bonnie?" the man asked, extending his hand.

"Yes," Bonnie answered. "Are you Eduardo?"

"I am. They have your information. All they have

to do is take your photo and they will issue you a badge. It will be valid through September 30. That should be long enough, don't you think."

Bonnie nodded and approached the counter where she saw the camera.

"Give me a picture I.D.," said the young woman at the counter.

Bonnie pulled her wallet from her purse, removed her driver's license, and handed it to the woman.

The woman checked the information on Bonnie's driver license against some papers she had in front of her and then pushed the papers toward Bonnie. "Sign these," said the woman, "while I make a copy of your license."

Bonnie read the papers that described the rules and regulations regarding access to the center and signed them. The woman at the counter motioned to Bonnie to stand in a spot allocated for taking photos. Bonnie smiled dutifully and the woman took her picture. Soon, she returned with a badge with Bonnie's picture on it and some numbers.

"What do the numbers mean?" Bonnie asked.

"Those are the areas you are allowed to go into. The Vehicle Assembly Building, and the Industrial Area, including the Headquarters Building."

Eduardo came up to Bonnie and led her to a chair. "We have to wait for the county representative," said Eduardo. "We'll all go in my car after he gets his badge."

"Who is it?" asked Bonnie "Do you know?"

"Keith O'Reilly. He's an aide to one of the

commissioners."

"I know him," said Bonnie. "He's sort of political."

"What did you expect," said Eduardo, "a technical expert?"

Bonnie shook her head and shrugged her shoulders. Everything with the commission was politics. She saw Keith coming through the door. "There he is now," she said. Keith looked toward her and Eduardo. Bonnie waved at him.

Keith waved back and came toward them. Eduardo rose and went toward him. Bonnie remained sitting against the wall.

"We'll wait while you get your badge," Eduardo told Keith. "You can leave your car here. We'll all go in my van together."

"Where are we going?" Bonnie asked.

"We'll meet in the headquarters first," answered Eduardo. "Take a look at the maps and discuss our boundaries. Then, we'll head out to the Vehicle Assembly Building and I'll show you where we're going to set up a staging area."

"I have our inventory and equipment specs with me so we can figure out the space requirements," said Bonnie.

Eduardo nodded. "Good. We may have to take what the operations guys are willing to give us. We're not their first priority – yet."

"It sounds like you believe this storm may come here."

"I'm paid to plan for the worst. Terrorist attacks, storms, catastrophes on the launch pad – I have to consider any and all of those."

"That's quite a job. Doesn't it give you nightmares?"

Eduardo cocked his head and looked at Bonnie as if the question had never occurred to him. "I deal with reality," he said. "I dream about the beach." Eduardo started to walk toward the door. "Keith is ready," he said. "Let's go."

Eduardo led them out of the badging station into the parking lot and pointed out a government van parked in a reserved slot. "We'll take my van into the center."

"Will our badges allow us to drive through the guard gates?" asked Bonnie.

"Oh yes," answered Eduardo. "I just want us to stay together for this first meeting."

Bonnie noticed that Keith commandeered the front seat next to Eduardo without offering it to her. She wondered what he would contribute to their effort. She listened to his conversation with Eduardo.

"How many more shuttles launches does NASA have planned?" asked Keith.

"None," answered Eduardo. "We are keeping one assembled and ready to launch. It's only a matter of time before we are told to stand down completely."

"The lay-offs are continuing?"

"Yes. We are trying to find jobs for everyone. There are some retraining programs and financial assistance for new businesses. "

"What do you think about this storm?"

"I think we'd better be prepared."

"Aren't we always?" said Keith. "I don't know why this would be any different."

Bonnie detected cockiness in Keith's voice that made her uneasy. Protecting Coreopsis was one thing; the rest of the county had many areas that were more vulnerable. She assumed that Keith was aware of that. When they arrived at the headquarters building, Eduardo came around and opened the door for her. Keith left the van and waited for them at the front entrance.

"Thank you," Bonnie said as Eduardo escorted her to the sidewalk. They met Keith at the door and went inside.

"We're going to the third floor," said Eduardo, as he led them to the elevator.

They met on the third floor in an office that had a large wall map showing the Kennedy Space Center, Cape Canaveral Air Force Station, Merritt Island Wildlife Refuge, and Cape Canaveral National Seashore. Keith produced maps showing north Brevard County. Keith's readiness raised Bonnie's opinion of his participation. After some discussion, they determined that the team's area of consideration would include all of the government property and Merritt Island from the barge canal north.

"Let's go to the Vehicle Assembly Building," said Eduardo. "We'll find out how much space they gave us."

***

The Vehicle Assembly Building is one of the largest buildings in the world, 220 feet higher than the Statue of Liberty and equal to 3.75 Empire State Buildings in volume. Bonnie had seen it from the outside. From the inside, it was more impressive. When Bonnie looked up, the building went on forever, forming a gray sky of its own.

"I'll take you to the top floor when we're done," said Eduardo. "The view from the top is impressive."

"I bet," said Bonnie. "It's hard to believe the building's been here for more than forty years."

"Let's go meet Stan," said Eduardo. "He's the Vehicle Assembly Building facility manager. He'll tell us where our space is."

They followed Eduardo into the low bay of the Vehicle Assembly Building, walked to the second floor, and entered an office midway down the hall. The Vehicle Assembly Building manager was waiting for them.

"I'm going to put you in High Bay 4," Stan said. "There's nothing in there right now. I'll take you there. You'll have about 2500 square feet."

"Square?" asked Bonnie.

"Yes," said Stan. "Is that okay?"

"Perfect," answered Bonnie. "The flatbed is 37 feet long. Everything else will fit in easily. I want to see it anyway."

'Take a hard hat from the rack over there," said Stan. "We're going to be out on the floor."

"I can wait up here," said Keith. "I don't need to see it."

Eduardo nodded and slipped on a hard hat. "We'll come back for you. Do you want to go to the top floor with us when we come back?"

"Oh yeah," replied Keith. "I'd like that."

Bonnie and Eduardo followed Stan down the stairs and out onto the Vehicle Assembly Building floor. They walked to High Bay 4. Stan had their area marked off with yellow tape. Bonnie was impressed. Clearly, NASA took this exercise seriously. She wished she felt as comfortable about the county. However, she understood the rules that had their hands tied until the National Hurricane Center issued a watch. She walked around the designated space and came over to Stan and Eduardo, who were watching her.

"I'm satisfied," she said. "I'll tell my boss we can move our equipment out here."

"Give me a detailed operations plan in two days," said Eduardo, "and we'll set up the necessary support and badges for your personnel." He came closer to Bonnie and spoke to her in a confidential tone. "I'll call NOAA, of course, but where do you think the storm will be in two days?"

Bonnie scratched her head. She tried to picture a map. "About 750 miles east of Miami, I'd guess. Heading west by northwest."

"And, the winds?"

"A hundred and ten, maybe fifteen."

"Unbelievable. You seem pretty sure."

"A bird told me. A big bird."

"What do you think of Keith?"

"Other than that he's a chauvinist? The county has better. They'll get involved sooner or later."

Eduardo forced his tongue into his cheek and shook his head. "Let's go look from the top."

Bonnie thanked Stan for his assistance and followed Eduardo back to the low bay. Keith was waiting for them, hardhat in hand. They followed Eduardo out to the floor and over to a high bay elevator. They entered the elevator and Eduardo punched the button for the 34th floor.

"We'll have to walk up the stairs to go higher," Eduardo said. "I'm not sure if the crosswalks will be open or not."

Bonnie's ears popped on the way up. After they exited the elevator, Eduardo led them to a stairwell and they continued upward until Eduardo stopped and opened a door that seemingly went nowhere. In front of them were a screened-in cage and a steel door that Eduardo opened. Bonnie went through first.

"Don't look down just yet," said Eduardo. Bonnie had already looked straight down before he said it. The view was awe-inspiring. All of the trucks, cranes, and trailers they had walked by on the floor looked like diminutive toys for minuscule children. Across from them were two of the other high bays, one had a fully assembled space shuttle sitting on its pedestal. Keith and Eduardo stepped out to stand beside Bonnie.

"Wow," said Keith. "This is big."

Eduardo chuckled. "If I put a thousand dollars out on one of those beams," he asked, "Would you walk out there and pick it up?"

"No way," answered Keith.

"Could I keep it?" inquired Bonnie.

Eduardo nodded. "I suppose. It's a hypothetical

question."

"I would do it. Heights don't bother me much. I've rescued people from pretty high up."

"In Coreopsis?" Eduardo seemed surprised.

"No," Bonnie answered. "I worked around Atlanta before I came down here."

Bonnie was impressed with the size and history of the Vehicle Assembly Building, but she was eager to continue her preparations for the storm. "I need to get back to my car," she told Eduardo. "I want to look at north Merritt Island while it's still light."

After Eduardo dropped her off at the badging station, Bonnie drove south on State Road 3 and began exploring Merritt Island outside of the Kennedy Space Center. The area was a virtual maze of canals, dirt roads, and clusters of houses – some notable, most unpretentious. She found herself on Pine Island Road, a clay road with numerous potholes and uneven shoulders. Cabbage palms dotted the landscape.

Bonnie saw two boys coming toward her on bicycles. They each had a fishing pole and the taller boy had three fish on a stringer hung over the handlebar of his bike. Bonnie guessed that each was about nine or ten years of age. The shorter boy was husky and had reddish blond hair. The taller boy was thin with a burr cut. He had skin the color of milk chocolate syrup poured over vanilla ice cream, almost an island look. Bonnie thought of a young Harry Belafonte. She stopped to talk to them.

"How far to the river?" she asked.

"It's about another quarter mile to the shoreline,"

said the taller boy. "What're ya lookin' for?"

"I'm with Coreopsis Emergency Services. We're checking to see what we may have to do in a big storm."

The boy looked at the sky. "Don't look like no storm's comin' t' me."

"This is just in case. We want to be ready."

"What's your name?" the boy asked.

"Bonnie. Bonnie McConnell. I'm a paramedic."

The blonde-haired boy started to leave on his bike. "I gotta go," he said. "My mom wants me home before dark." He rode off.

The taller boy dismounted his bicycle quickly and pushed it out in front of him. He was looking at the road just in front of Bonnie's car. Bonnie turned her head to look. A large alligator, at least fourteen feet long had pulled itself unto the road in front of Bonnie's car.

"Where'd that come from?" Bonnie asked.

"From between those cattails over there," said the boy. "It may smell my fish." The boy pulled the string of fish from his handlebar and threw it in front of the alligator. The alligator ignored the bait.

Bonnie smelled the heaviness of a cloud descending on them and heard the wind shrieking through the cattails – a low steam whistle noise modulating up and down. She watched as the alligator transformed into a Native American man, dark, about five and a half feet tall, wearing a loincloth and carrying a short spear.

The boy stepped back and pulled his fishing knife from a sheath on his bicycle. "Stay there," he said to the Indian. "I'll kill you if you attack us."

"You see him too?" Bonnie asked.

"Yes ma'am. He's kind of scary."

"I think he's a friend," said Bonnie. "We're not in any danger."

The Native American stood in front of Bonnie's car and she heard in her mind, "Behold the wind."

"Did you hear that?" she asked the boy.

"Yes ma'am. 'Behold the wind.' I didn't hear it with my ears. I just heard it in my brain."

"That's correct," said Bonnie. "That's what I heard too."

"Who is he?"

"I think he's an Indian Chief, from the Ais tribes. From ancient times." The cloud continued to descend on them and Bonnie could smell the tropical seas and feel the depressed pressure. "He's warning us about a storm."

"Are you a witch?" the boy asked. "I've never met a witch."

"No. However, I know a witch and could introduce you sometime if you'd like. What's your name?"

"Simon," the boy said. "I'd like to meet a witch. That would be cool. How about pirates? Could you introduce me to a pirate?"

Bonnie shook her head. "I never met a pirate."

"How'd you know about the Indian?"

"A friend told me about the four ancient chiefs. A hurricane, a blue heron, an alligator, and a manatee."

"What do they want with you?"

"I'm not sure." Bonnie hadn't thought of it that way before, but she knew that sometimes children see things more clearly than adults do. "I'm not sure," she repeated.

The wind picked up and Bonnie saw the chief walk away into the cattails. The brown seed heads waved in unison as they marked the path of the departing man.

Simon laid his bicycle on its side and retrieved his string of fish. "I gotta go. Don't forget me. Simon Upton. I live over on Kangaroo. My mom's name is Aggie. My Dad's name is Ladamien He owns a company that builds airports. He knows some pirates too."

It was too dark to continue exploring Merritt Island. Bonnie turned her car around and headed back to Coreopsis.

***

It was Thursday, and Ladamien got out of bed at 4:30 in the morning

"Where ya goin'?" Aggie murmured.

"Gotta pack," answered Ladamien. "I fly today."

Aggie grunted and turned her back to Ladamien. He left the bedroom, went into the kitchen, and put on a pot of coffee. Next, he rummaged in the pantry until he found a half-full bottle of Bailey's Irish Cream that he placed on the table. He then sat down to wait for the coffee to finish.

Sitting there brought him back to a time when he sat at a table back in Belle Glade waiting to talk to his mother, Jezebel Upton. He was nineteen years old and had just graduated from high school. His mother had asked him to wait for her. She wanted to talk to him.

Ladamien knew what she wanted to discuss. Growing up in Belle Glade was not easy. Jobs in the cane fields were hard to come by and the future of a cane worker was not that good anyway. His grades had been good enough to graduate, but he was not going to college. He played football well, but not well enough to interest any college or professional scouts.

Before the graduation ceremonies, the leader of the Swamp Rattlers at that time, Cody Wilkins, had met with him. Cody had come to Florida from Wyoming and worked for a major crime syndicate boss in Atlanta – Alberon Randazzo.

"You've been a Swamp Rattler now for what – two years?" Cody had asked.

"Yes sir," Ladamien had answered, "since tenth grade."

"How'd you like to help us?" Cody asked. "How'd you like to make some real money?"

"Yes sir, I'd like that."

Cody had gone on to explain how the Swamp Rattlers helped people get out of countries where the government mistreated them, how they found jobs for them in countries where there were better opportunities. Ladamien had jumped at the chance. He thought he could make something of himself and marry Aggie.

Ladamien discussed it with Aggie later in the day. She said that whatever he had to do was okay with her. She knew he had to make a living. Ladamien explained that Cody thought he had a knack for management and wanted Ladamien to be the chief executive of a company owned by the Swamp Rattlers that built airports.

"You're no engineer," Aggie had said. "You don't know anything about building airports. You don't have any experience running a company."

"The Swamp Rattlers' gonna hire people to help me. Cody said I would have to go to school to learn about managing and polish my communication skills. He says my English is pretty ragged."

"Why does he want you to be the head of the company?"

"He said he needs somebody he can trust. Someone that will take orders and keep his mouth shut."

Aggie had agreed it was a good opportunity and consented to marrying Ladamien as soon as they could arrange it. She seemed satisfied that life with him would be just fine.

Ladamien's mother, Jezebel, had asked him that morning to meet with her right after the graduation ceremony. She came into the kitchen and sat down across from Ladamien with a worried look on her face.

"Ladamien, that gang o' yours gonna get you in heap o' trouble, an' runnin' aroun' with that white girl don' help none neither."

"Momma, they are my friends. We're not doing anything bad. Cody offered me a job to do good for people."

"Like what?" Jezebel asked. "Choppin'? Pimpin'?

Dealin'? Or, somethin' worse?"

"What I do doesn't hurt anybody what doesn't want it, or can't afford it. My new job is that I'm gonna build airports and help people get out of bad countries."

"An', that make what the gang do all right? Jes' because you have a job? You think them young girls wanna get laid. You think them rich folks wanna get robbed. You think that coke an' chop is legal?"

"It ain't all that bad, Momma," Ladamien said.

"What's that white girl's name?" asked Jezebel. "Aggie? What's she think of all that? Or, are you pimpin' her too?"

"I love her. She's no whore. She agrees with what I do." Ladamien fought to defend himself. "We're gonna get married."

"You ain't gonna live in no Belle Glade if'n you do. Ain't no white or black aroun' here's gonna let you live."

"We're gonna move, Momma. Go live some place where people will understand."

"Lawsy. Your sister is a good Christian. She got an honest job." Jezebel raised her hands to the sky, "Praise the Lord, your brother's got a scholarship to play football at Florida A&M." Jezebel reached across the table and took Ladamien's hands. "What happened to you, Ladamien?"

"I can't do what they do, Momma. Aggie and the Swamp Rattlers – they are my life. I can't give them up."

Jezebel had gotten up and walked away from her son, closing the door behind her.

Ladamien heard the coffee gurgling, indicating it was ready. He took a cup from the cupboard and filled it half full. He added enough Baileys to top it.

Aggie, he thought, *and the Swamp Rattlers – they had been the most important things in his life. Now, there was Simon. Ladamien loved his son. This last proposition from Leroy changed things, however.*

Cody Wilkins had eventually gone to jail. Afterwards, Alberon brought Leroy down from Chicago. Leroy was an old-time gang boss and kept his fingers in every pie. You could not put anything past Leroy.

Aggie had hinted at it. Transporting people out of a terrible situation into a merely bad circumstance was one thing. Laundering money for drugs, weapons, prostitution, and other criminal activities was something else. The memory of his mother's scolding bothered Ladamien.

Maybe if I talked to God, Ladamien thought. His mother was always big on prayer. Ladamien figured it could not hurt to try. He walked into the front yard and looked up at the sky. There was a half-full moon with a planet – *maybe Jupiter,* Ladamien thought – positioned above it.

"God, if you're there," Ladamien began. "I never much believed in you. My momma put a lot of stake in you, and she weren't a stupid woman."

"I done scads of things against man's law," Ladamien continued. "I ain't so sure about your law. I never studied it much, but I see you letting a lot of things go on. Maybe you'll understand."

Ladamien felt a mosquito buzzing around his ear and swiped at it. He walked out to Kangaroo Lane and ambled along the side of the road while he finished his communication.

"Lord, the Rattlers been good to me. I don't know how to say no to Leroy. I'm not scared for me, I'm afraid for Aggie and Simon. If I back out on the Rattlers, Leroy won't stop with me. He'll punish them too. If I go to the police – they're as bad as criminals are. I can't trust them."

Ladamien came back to the edge of his own yard. He put his hands together. "Show me what to do. Help me, and I'll do it. Thanks... I mean Amen."

There were no lightning flashes, but Ladamien felt better. He had made his case. In the meantime, he would go forward with the plan upon which he and Leroy had already agreed. He got to his feet and went back inside his house. Aggie was standing at the sink rinsing out his cup. The bottle of Bailey's was gone from the table.

"All packed?" Aggie asked.

"Just thinking."

"About Leroy and the business?"

"Yeah." Ladamien came up behind Aggie and put his arms around her waist. "You're not sorry you married me, are you?"

Aggie turned into his arms and kissed him on the tip of his nose. "I love you. You are my lover and my son's father. It's the best decision I ever made, to marry you."

Ladamien pulled her closer to feel the warmth and firmness of her body. She seemed warmer than usual. "I was praying to God, babe. I've never done that before."

"I don't know about God, but me and Simon; we're on your side. If we need to leave and hide out, we are with you. If you have to tell Leroy to go to hell, I'll pick up a gun and kill him before he hurts you."

Ladamien continued to hold her so she could not see the tears in his eyes. "Do you have a fever?" he asked.

"It was about 100, but I took an aspirin. It'll come down."

Ladamien shook his head. "I've probably been working you too hard."

"Don't be silly. It's just a little summer cold."

"You are wonderful," he said. "You are an angel." He knew his voice wavered.

***

Simon heard his parents in the kitchen from his bedroom. They didn't seem to be arguing, but their voices were serious. He thought they must be discussing the possibility of moving. He wanted to tell them about meeting the medical lady and seeing the Indian. He got out of bed and shuffled into the kitchen.

"Mom," said Simon, "can I have some milk?"

"Sure, honey," Aggie said. "Did we wake you?"

"Not really. I was done sleeping."

"Were you having a bad dream?"

"No. But, something weird happened to me yesterday."

"What was that, son?" asked Ladamien.

"Buster and I were comin' back from fishin', and

this lady stopped her car to ask us about Pine Island. Buster went on home, but I found out she's some kind 'a medical woman. She's a pear medic or something."

"Paramedic?" asked Ladamien.

"Yeah, that's it, and she said she was lookin' around to see what they would do if a storm was to come here. She said she was from Coreopsis."

"She was a good way from home," said Aggie. "You know what we've told you about talking to strangers."

Simon tilted his head. "I guess. She seemed okay. Anyway, while's we was talkin', this alligator came up on the road. I thought he wanted my fish." Simon paused a moment. He was sorry he had told his mother there were alligators where he and Buster fished. She might not let him go there anymore. "It was odd. We don't normally see any alligators."

"That's good," said Aggie. "They can be dangerous. Are you sure it's safe for you to go to Pine Island?"

"It's safe enough out there," said Simon. "We don't see gators that much. Anyway, this Indian man with a spear came up and chased the alligator away." He wasn't about to tell his mother that the alligator actually became the Indian. "I pulled my knife and told that Indian I'd kill him if he attacked us."

Ladamien chuckled. "That was brave of you. What did the Indian do?"

Aggie looked at Ladamien in disapproval. "That could have been dangerous," she said. Looking at Simon, she said, "You have to be more careful if we're going to let you go out on your own."

"Yes ma'am," said Simon. He looked over to see if his father was going to say something and then continued. "Anyway, the Indian said, 'Behold the wind,' and left. The paramedic lady said he was a friend — a chief."

"Behold the wind," said Ladamien. He ran his fingers over his chin. "That's a strange thing to say. I wonder if there's a storm coming." Ladamien walked into the living room and turned on the TV. "Let's see what Channel 13 says."

After five minutes of advertisements, Weather on the 1's came on and the weather woman was talking about tropical weather.

"The National Hurricane Center predicts that Dirk will continue its northwest movement for the next 72 hours and it is expected to pass north of the Bahamas late Sunday."

The TV picture changed to show people on the beach and surfers riding the waves. The weather woman continued. "Surfers can expect high waves over the weekend, and small craft are urged to stay alert for warnings. Swimmers should beware of rip currents. We will continue to watch Dirk closely and keep you informed of any threats to the US mainland."

"Sounds like it's going to miss us," said Ladamien. "I guess your paramedic was just checking things out."

"That's good news," said Aggie. "Especially, since you're leaving."

"Where are you going, Dad?" asked Simon.

"San Juan, Puerto Rico. I have to meet with my banker and a lawyer."

"Why don't they come here?"

"My business is worldwide. San Juan is closer to the bank I use."

"Are we going to move to San Juan?"

"No. If we move, we'll be moving to Boca Raton. Puerto Rico is too foreign."

"When are we going to move?"

"I'll know more after this meeting. We'll talk about it when I get back."

"That's enough questions, young man," said Aggie. "Your father's not going to do anything without telling you. Go get dressed. You still have school today. I'll fix you some breakfast."

Simon shuffled back to his room and picked through the clothes in his dresser until he found his favorite shirt. It showed a parrot in a pirate hat and read – Parrots of the Caribbean. He pulled on jeans, tied up his Adidas Superstars, and pulled on the parrot shirt.

He thought about the medical lady, the alligator, and the Indian. He wasn't going to tell anyone at school about it.

CHAPTER 5

"Every man's memory is his private literature."

Aldous Huxley

Bonnie decided to get in touch with Dr. Blaine. Dr. Blaine was the psychiatrist who had helped her when she had her first psychic encounter. He had called in forensic hypnotist, Deputy Marcie Reese. Marcie had revealed that the spirit of Julie Gustafson possessed Bonnie's soul. Marcie had helped Julie's spirit discover that Bonnie was the daughter she had birthed thirty years earlier. Bonnie and Marcie had discovered that the Swamp Rattlers had sold Bonnie, on the black market; to the parents she had known all of her life.

Now that preparations for Hurricane Dirk required her attention, Bonnie wouldn't have much time to deal with her latest visions. Perhaps, Dr. Blaine could help her interpret them. She watched the clock and called Dr. Blaine's office at exactly nine o'clock. Surprisingly, Dr. Blaine came on the line right after his receptionist told him who it was.

"Bonnie," said Dr. Blaine, "any more spiritual encounters?"

"Well yes, kind of," said Bonnie. "The possession

118

ended when my mother's spirit departed. I still have visions"

Bonnie recalled the scene in Atlanta when her mother's spirit released its possession of her and proceeded on its journey. She realized that she had never given Dr. Blaine a full accounting of that experience. "I guess you never got the full story of what happened in Atlanta?"

"No," Dr. Blaine agreed. "That deputy from Orange County, Marcie, she told me a little, but it didn't make a lot of sense." Dr. Blaine cleared his throat, and then continued, "What can I do for you?"

"You remember Justin? He was just a friend at that time."

"Yes, I remember. He's an architect, built that big sports complex out near I-95."

"That's him," Bonnie confirmed. "He's more than a friend now. We are getting married and having a baby."

"When is the wedding? I don't remember getting an invitation."

"We haven't completed the details yet." Bonnie figured she had better get to the point. "It will be real soon and I will make sure you're invited. I called you because I want to get this recent psychic thing cleared up."

Dr. Blaine started to say something but Bonnie cut him off. "There's something inside of me. I feel as if I'm still possessed and I'm not sure if it's harmless."

"Your previous case was so unusual," said Dr. Blaine. "I'd like to follow up. This could be related in some way."

"Do you think so?"

"Yours was the first instance I ever saw where I believe spiritual possession was at the root of your illness. There's no telling about the long-term effects."

"If you think that, I need to tell you something." Bonnie thought Dr. Blaine might be onto something. "Just before Julie's spirit left, it planted something in my heart or my brain – something different. It left me with some psychic abilities."

"That's interesting. I'll tell you what I'd like to do. I'd like to see both of you. I'd like to hear what Justin has observed. I gather you've been close over the past year."

"I didn't get pregnant over e-mail, if that's what you mean."

Blaine laughed quietly. "I remember your sense of humor." He resumed, "Justin might have noticed something that would help us. I'd like to have a session with the two of you. Then, I'll recommend a course of action. How does that sound?"

"It's what I hoped for," Bonnie answered. "I'll ask Justin and we'll call your office."

"That will be fine."

Bonnie hung up the phone. It was the best she could expect. She didn't know how much more time Justin had before he had to leave for Atlanta. She decided to call him immediately. He picked up on the third ring.

"Justin?" Bonnie couldn't tell if he was there. "Justin?"

"Sorry," Justin said. "I was just on the phone with Andre' D'aubigne. He wanted to know when I was going to come to Atlanta."

"What did you tell him?"

"I told him it would be sometime next week at the earliest. I told him we were getting married and having a baby. He said he understood."

"I'm glad you're not leaving right away. I need your consideration."

"Of course," Justin said. "You sound worried."

"I'm a little frightened. I talked to Dr. Blaine, about my incidents. Would you meet with him before you leave town."

"Just me? What are you afraid of?"

"No. He wants to see both of us. I need some answers about these visions. I'm concerned that there may be a possessing spirit that threatens out daughter."

"Before she's even born?"

"Yes. It's hard to explain, but this spirit may be more harmful than Julie's spirit was, maybe even evil."

"Of course I'll see Dr. Blaine with you. I'll look at my schedule and call him to set up an appointment. Is any time all right for you?"

"I'll make time. Look, I have to go. I have to take some equipment out to the Kennedy Space Center."

"Will I see you later?"

"Could we have dinner at Fran's? They have a new group with a hot piano player. Some jazz guy from Tampa named Perry Gallus."

"Okay. Can you be home before seven?

"I'll see you at home before seven."

***

Bonnie had seen Rusty checking on her twice while she was on the phone. As soon as she finished talking to Justin, she went to Rusty's office. "You were looking for me?"

Rusty looked up from some papers she was reviewing. She looked at Bonnie as if she were studying her.

"I was talking to Dr. Blaine," Bonnie said. She thought that perhaps Rusty expected an explanation. "I need some counseling."

"Will you want some time off?" Rusty asked.

"I'll work it in," said Bonnie. "I'll try not to disrupt my work schedule."

"I wanted to tell you that Vince has all the stuff you asked for loaded on the flat bed. He picked up his badge this morning, so you can go directly to the Vehicle Assembly Building. Eduardo called me. He wants to know when you'll be there."

"I'll alert him," said Bonnie. "Is Vince going to be permanently assigned to me?"

"Yes," said Rusty, "and, Mayor Moline borrowed four EMTs from Gainesville. Two of them will be on your team until the storm passes – one way or the other."

"Why Gainesville?" Bonnie couldn't figure the connection.

"Moline knows the mayor up there. They might be trainees from the university. It was the mayor's decision."

"When do they get here?"

"Tomorrow. They'll be bunking at the hospital."

"We'll have cots out at the Vehicle Assembly Building if they want to stay there."

"Don't start roughing it before you have to. If this storm comes through, you'll get your fill of that. I remember Katrina. You'll get sick of camping in a hurry."

Bonnie remembered the scenes from Katrina on the TV. It was hard to imagine what it must have been like to be there. "I'll call Eduardo. Do you want Vince and me to come back from the Vehicle Assembly Building?"

"No. Just keep me updated on what you're doing." Rusty picked up the papers she had been looking at and put them in a folder. "How are you coming with the operations plan?"

"I've got a first draft written. It needs editing."

"Give me a copy of the draft. I'd like to see it."

"Of course," said Bonnie.

Bonnie left Rusty's office. As confident as she was, the magnitude of what they might be facing was just starting to sink in. She put her hand on her stomach and thought – *you and me babe. You and me.*

She saw Vince waiting for her in the locker room.

***

After Bonnie left, Rusty reopened the folder she had put away while talking to Bonnie. The list of open issues still facing the newly opened station appalled her. None of the concerns was a showstopper, but Rusty felt uneasy about the impression she gave the mayor that her station was fully prepared for a major disaster. She picked up the phone and called Gus.

"What's up?" Gus asked.

"I've been going over the open items against my station," said Rusty. "I'm a little concerned about what I told the mayor. We may not be as ready for a major hurricane as I thought."

"Anything in particular?"

"Supplies. There are still many inventory items where we are short – waiting on deliveries."

"Critical items?"

"Not especially. However, I've been doing some reading. If this hurricane is as serious as Andrew or Katrina, we'll run out of ordinary items quickly."

"I imagine the whole east coast of Florida would have that problem. As soon as the National Hurricane Center issues a watch, supplies should start pouring in."

"I guess you're right. The other thing I noticed going through the open items was the number of process hazard analyses coming up next year. Almost every business in the area has its five year deadline coming up."

"You'll have to inspect for hazardous materials – make sure the tanks and storage containers are intact and safe."

"I know what it involves," said Rusty. "It's just that I haven't done much of that."

"Isn't Doug more or less an expert on risk management? Maybe you should put those inspections on him. As long as they're not overdue, I don't see an issue."

"Doug? Yes, that's a good idea." Rusty paused. "Gus, most of all, I think I'm nervous. Not just about this storm, but about the station. It's so new. I don't know how ready we are. I don't know if I'm prepared for this. I remember Katrina. We were even more unprepared than we thought."

"That's a natural feeling," said Gus. "When I first started, we worried about many things that we didn't know if we could handle – a nuclear attack or a major spill. Train wrecks where I was in Arkansas. You do your best. That's all anyone expects."

"I know you're right. Thanks for holding my hand."

"Maybe you can return the favor sometime."

Rusty laughed quietly. "I'll certainly do that." She hung up the phone, and went to her computer. Hurricane Dirk was still a category 3 storm, 850 miles from the United States' mainland. She shook her head. If not for Bonnie's vision, she wouldn't even be concerned about the storm this early.

"Relax," she told herself. "Just relax."

***

Bonnie and Vince arrived at the Vehicle Assembly Building shortly after noon on Thursday. She was pleased with the cooperation NASA provided. Vince drove the flatbed and its contents onto the center after a brief inspection at the badging station. He pulled the rig into High Bay 4 following a check of their paperwork at the guard gate. Two workers with the base operations contractor came over with a forklift to help them unload. Bonnie parked her car outside the Vehicle Assembly Building gate in a spot that Eduardo had reserved for her.

Bonnie approached one of the workers. "We'll need the low bay crane to unload the medical module when we come back."

"That's a different crew," said the worker. "Do you have it scheduled?"

"I told Eduardo," replied Bonnie. "I'll call him."

"I can check it for you," said the worker. "I have a copy of the schedule." He pulled a piece of paper from his coverall's pocket and traced it with his finger. "Yep. Here it is. Two o'clock this afternoon."

Bonnie turned to look at Vince. "We'd better go back to the station and get the unit. We don't have a lot of time." As she hoisted herself into the cab of the truck, she said, "I'll leave my car parked here."

It took almost five hours for Bonnie and Vince to drive back to the station, load the medical unit, deliver it to the Vehicle Assembly Building, and position it in High Bay 4. They picked up a hamburger along the way and ate in the cab while they drove. It was 4:30 p.m. when they finished.

Bonnie wanted to use the daylight time left to finish looking at north Merritt Island. She drove south on State Road 3 and turned on Tropical Trail just outside the entrance to the Merritt Island Wildlife Refuge. Tropical Trail wound south and, suitable to its name, displayed many varieties of tropical vegetation.

Merritt Island straddles the boundary between the southern temperate and northern subtropical zones. Mangoes and avocados that struggle to grow on the mainland flourish on the island. Citrus groves dot the landscape.

Bonnie finally exited Tropical Trail at Grant Road. She continued on SR-3 to an abandoned fish camp and trailer park on the barge canal. She drove down to a forsaken dock, left her car, walked out on the dock, and looked at the quiet waters of the canal.

She could see the drawbridge where State Road 3 crossed the canal off to her right. A manatee rolled in the water and approached the dock where Bonnie stood. It emerged partially from the water and took the form of a Native American man.

"Behold the daughter of the wind," echoed in Bonnie's mind.

"What did you say?" Bonnie asked the native.

Distinctly, she heard, "Behold the daughter of the wind." She watched as an apparition twirled across the water in front of her. It was the vision of a bronze nymph dancing across the water. A Renoiresque figure in golden hue. When Bonnie looked down, the man was gone.

Bonnie glanced at her watch and realized that if she was going to arrive home, clean up, and be ready to go out with Justin, she had better hurry. She took SR-528 to I-95 and reached their house at 6:20 p.m.. Justin wasn't there yet, so she showered and dressed in twenty minutes and waited for Justin.

"Did you call ahead for reservations?" Bonnie asked when Justin came in.

"Yes, but it's just Thursday. Fran said we didn't need them."

"Did she say anything about the pianist – Perry Gallus?"

"No."

"He has a trio – bass, drums, and piano," said Bonnie. "I've heard they're pretty good."

"We'll see," said Justin. As they walked to the car, he continued, "I called Dr. Blaine this afternoon. We have an appointment for tomorrow at 10:00 a.m."

"I'll tell Rusty I have to take the morning off."

As they drove to Fran's, Justin discussed his conversation with Dr. Blaine. "He asked me a lot of questions about you – what we did together, where you were living, how we made our work fit with our private lives. Nothing surprising really."

They arrived at Fran's and the waitress showed them to their table.

"Let's have calamari for an appetizer," said Justin. "They have non-alcoholic wine – Ariel. They say it tastes like Pineau de la Loire."

"That's perfect. I just want to relax for an hour. Listen to music, sip a little, and snack. Okay?" Bonnie closed her eyes and smiled. She decided to tell Justin about the alligator and the manatee. "I met an alligator that told me the same thing as the heron — 'Behold the wind.' Then, I saw a manatee that told me something different."

"What did the manatee say?" inquired Justin.

"Behold the daughter of the wind."

"That doesn't make any sense."

"Neither does 'Behold the wind.' And, there was a vision associated with each encounter."

"So, you think you might be possessed again."

"I don't know. It's not like the last time at all. This is real. I met a boy when the alligator approached me. He saw the same thing I did. A Native American with a spear."

"Didn't that happen last time? Didn't others see your visions?"

"Not the same way. This was different."

"I believe you. It seems like it's about more than the hurricane. Something here involves you personally. Don't you think? What did you see when the manatee was there?"

"A phantom girl, like a golden fairy, dancing across the water."

"The daughter of the wind?" asked Justin. "A wind you're supposed to behold? I don't understand what it means at all."

"Me neither," said Bonnie. "I'm tired of thinking about it. Order the wings and the beverage." Bonnie saw the trio setting up. She stood up and waved to get the musicians' attention. "Play something with a Latin beat," she said. "I want to dance."

The drummer picked up his claves and tapped out a bossa nova rhythm. Bonnie wiggled her hips. "Right on," she said. The pianist lit into a jazz rendition of The Girl from Ipanema and Bonnie moved into the space between tables to continue dancing. She beckoned Justin to join her. Justin approached her and tried to imitate her movements. He was no Fred Astaire, but Bonnie appreciated his efforts to please her.

***

It was Friday, and Bonnie woke up at 5:30 a.m. She had enjoyed herself the night before at Fran's, and had gone right to bed when they arrived home. She had talked Justin into coming to bed with her and had cuddled up to him before falling asleep. She would miss him while he was in Atlanta but figured she would be busy with the hurricane preparations.

Justin was sleeping soundly, so Bonnie threw on her robe, went into Justin's office, and checked the status of Dirk on the computer. The National Hurricane Center reported that Dirk was about 472 miles east northeast of the Turks and Caicos Islands and they expected the storm to strengthen to a category 4 during the next 48 hours.

Bonnie was not surprised. She wondered when the state would decide to act. Many previous Florida governors had moved out before the National Hurricane Center issued its first watch. It was becoming clear that this hurricane would come close to the Florida coast and possibly traverse the shoreline south of Jacksonville. She reckoned that she and Eduardo had two more days before the governor ordered an evacuation.

Bonnie went into the kitchen and started the coffee. From there, she progressed to the bathroom and undressed. She looked at herself in the full-length mirror. There was no sign of her pregnancy yet. Occasionally, she had felt a trace of movement, the fluttering of small butterflies inside her tummy. Up to now, she had very few symptoms from her pregnancy, but she knew that would start to change noticeably with the fourth month. She turned on the shower and adjusted the water temperature. When she stepped in, the water felt so good pelting her back that she just stood for a minute, letting it massage her until she rinsed her hair and bathed quickly.

When Bonnie finished drying off and dressing, the coffee was ready. She filled a cup and placed it on the table. She poured a bowl of bran flakes, sliced a banana over it, added sugar and milk, and sat down to eat. She felt a sense of urgency that was pointless. She went over the next steps in her mind. The detailed operations plan should be ready for her to print. The equipment and supplies were in place at the Vehicle Assembly Building. The two EMTs from Gainesville should arrive today. It all seemed so simple, yet she felt pressured. She was happy they were going to see Dr. Blaine. Maybe, her nervousness was a symptom of her pregnancy.

Bonnie brushed her teeth, rinsed and went out on the patio to wait for Justin. She smelled the air. It had the odor of a freshly mowed meadow and the feel of a sea breeze on an island shore. Warmth and moisture are typical for a Florida August. This, however, was the proverbial calm before the storm. It was indescribable, but Bonnie knew it was the source of her uneasy feelings. The sky was opaque, the wind was stationary, and the interlude seemed motionless. The world was in a state of foreboding.

Bonnie joined Justin while he had his breakfast. They drove separately to Dr. Blaine's office, so Bonnie could go directly to the Kennedy Space Center after the session. They waited twenty minutes before the receptionist ushered them into Dr. Blaine's conference room. Dr. Blaine came around his desk to help them take their seats.

Dr. Blaine opened the discussion. "Bonnie, you wanted this session. Why don't you tell me what's going on."

"When Julie's spirit left my soul, it was quite dramatic. I felt her spirit leave and as it disentangled itself, my own spirit returned. I was reborn in a sense. However, just before the spirit released completely, it snapped. It left something of itself with me. I thought it was out of love."

"What happened afterwards?"

"I was still connected to the spirit world. I came back to Coreopsis and visited the Ais Sanctuary. I thought I had found the truth, the big truth. I had visions. I could see into the past and the future, or so it seemed."

Dr. Blaine turned to Justin. "Did you know about this?"

"Yes, but I figured it was just Bonnie. It was strange, not threatening. She spent a lot of time out at the sanctuary. The Ais Sanctuary was within the boundaries of the sports complex I designed. I became interested in discovering if there was a connection between Bonnie's spiritual encounters and the Native Americans that once lived on the sanctuary."

"What did you find out?"

"There isn't much information available about the lost tribes of Florida – the Ais, Jobe, Tequesta, and many others. In 1597, the Spanish Governor of Florida was Mendez de Canco. He met with the leaders of the Ais, Mayaca, and Jororo tribes at the site of the Ais Sanctuary. They made an agreement. Afterwards, the tribes helped Spain fight the French.

The last mention of the Ais tribe is in 1704 A.D. when the British, allied with the Creek Indians invaded Florida and eventually took it away from the Spanish. From then on, historians assume that the Ais were absorbed into the general category of Calusa Indians. In 1763, the Calusa went to Cuba. Estimates are that there were about 80 surviving families."

"None of that seems to have anything to do with Bonnie's complaint," said Dr. Blaine.

"No," agreed Justin. "However, there is a story from that period that might explain this latest instance.

By the middle of the seventeenth century, disease, war, and societal collapse decimated the Ais tribes. The story goes that the original four chiefs returned to take their people to 'The Place of Ecstasy', their happy hunting ground. The principle chief was Ho-ta-lee – the Wind – rider of hurricanes. His daughter, Banna, was the spirit of the land that the Ais occupied. She refused to leave the land. As a result, the spirits of the tribe members stay bound to the earth until Banna changes her mind."

"The daughter of the wind," Bonnie said. "Where is she now?"

"It is said that her spirit possesses the souls of unborn children and lives vicariously through them."

"Our daughter?" Bonnie suggested.

Justin shrugged. "It seems far-fetched. What do you think?"

Both Bonnie and Justin sat looking at Dr. Blaine. Finally, he spoke. "After my last experience with Bonnie, I don't discount anything. Spiritual possession is out of the realm of science or medicine, but we have seen that it is apparently possible."

"I really feel helpless," said Justin. "I'm concerned for Bonnie and our baby, but this is bizarre."

"How did you get Julie's spirit to leave?" Dr. Blaine asked Bonnie.

"She found what she was looking for. When she found out I was her daughter and that the gang had her killed, she had completed her quest. She left willingly."

Dr. Blaine nodded. "Have you had any communication with this spirit, with this Banna?"

"No, but in another vision, an old man told me that something evil wanted my daughter's soul."

"Do you want to try hypnosis again?" asked Dr. Blaine.

Bonnie looked over to Justin. Justin scratched behind his ear. "I think we had better do whatever it takes," said Justin. "Don't you agree?" he asked Bonnie.

Bonnie nodded. "After the storm passes," she said. "After the hurricane."

***

After leaving Dr. Blaine's office, Bonnie drove north on US-1 and then took SR-3 south through the Merritt Island Wildlife Refuge to the KSC north gate. The landscape already showed the disheveled façade typical of central Florida in the late summer. Leggy wildflowers peeped between unruly vines. Shaggy cattails lined the ditches. Oak hammocks nested in savannahs interspersed with pines. Bonnie observed an osprey drifting toward an early fishing expedition. It soared unusually high, riding an unseen current.

As Bonnie passed through the Kennedy Space Center gate, she saw the Vehicle Assembly Building looming in the distance behind the orbiter processing facilities. It was early when Bonnie parked and walked to the staging area in High Bay 4. She turned on the computer and pulled up the operations plan. She printed a copy. Satisfied, she signed off on it and put the signed copy in Eduardo's in-box. Eduardo would have to approve it before it was official.

Next, Bonnie called Rusty. Rusty answered immediately.

"Did the EMTs from Gainesville get here?" Bonnie asked.

"They came in late last night. The last I knew Eduardo was checking them through security. Vince will escort them from the badging station and bring them out to the VAB."

The uneasiness that Bonnie had experienced earlier was still with her. She felt the baby stir gently in her abdomen. She called Vince and asked him when the student EMT's would arrive where she was. He said they were on their way.

Later, Bonnie sat down with the two students, Winona and Thad to lay out the plan for covering Hurricane Dirk from the Kennedy Space Center. Winona was a skinny brown-haired woman, maybe five feet six inches, around a hundred and ten pounds. Thad had light hair and a heavy build. Bonnie guessed he was six-feet-two-inches tall.

"Aren't we a little premature?" Winona asked after Bonnie explained what they were doing in the

Vehicle Assembly Building. "The hurricane is still a long distance from land."

"We have several indications that this storm will not veer north as they usually do," Bonnie answered. "My bosses believe that the risk of not being prepared outweighs the cost of early readiness."

"As long as they're not crying wolf," Thad said, "I guess that's okay. Apparently, your mayor convinced our faculty."

"When we start getting active," Bonnie said, "I want Winona stationed here all the time, taking care of any medical cases we have."

"What about me?" Thad inquired.

"You'll go out on search and rescue with me. I may need your muscles. Vince will handle transportation between here and Coreopsis."

"Is that it?" asked Winona. "Just the four of us?"

"NASA will assign a medical assistant to work with you in the Vehicle Assembly Building. They will also give us drivers and vehicles to help with search and rescue. You and the NASA medical people will have to share responsibilities depending on what kinds of patients we have. It's all defined in the plan."

"C'mon Thad," said Winona. "We'd better study that plan."

I know who is in charge of that team, Bonnie thought. She left them, to organize her own thoughts. She would sleep at home that night and return in the morning.

CHAPTER 6

"Man is born to live, not to prepare for life"

Boris Pasternak

Ladamien's plane landed in San Juan shortly after lunchtime. He took a taxi to the Caribe Hilton Hotel on Geronimo Street. Leroy was to meet him poolside at the Atlantico Pool Bar & Grill. Ladamien checked in and left his suitcase with the porter in the lobby.

"Please deliver it to my room," he instructed the bell captain, "I have to meet someone by the pool."

Ladamien strolled through the Oasis Bar and walked through the pool complex, turning right to enter the Atlantico. Leroy was sitting at an umbrella-covered table with two men in tropical business attire. Ladamien could see the ocean over the wall of the bar and grill.

Leroy rose and came toward Ladamien. He wore a decorative robe displaying orchids and hummingbirds over an orange bathing suit along with a pair of flip-flops. He pointed to the two men.

"That is Geraldo Jimenez, the banker, and Pasqual Avila, the lawyer," Leroy said. "They will fix you up."

Ladamien nodded and approached the two men. "Señor Jimenez," he said. "You are with the bank?"

"Si, Mr. Upton," said Jimenez. "The Regal Bank of the Caribbean. You may call me Geraldo."

Ladamien turned to the lawyer. "And, you are the lawyer. May I call you Pasqual?"

"Certainly," said the lawyer.

"Then you may call me Ladamien."

Leroy smiled. "I've been telling these gentlemen here about your business and what a good manager you are."

"I have good people working for me," said Ladamien.

"That is part of management," said Geraldo. "Putting together a good team."

"We have been discussing the new venture," said Pasqual. "Do you have a business plan?"

"I brought copies of our annual operating plan," said Ladamien. "I didn't want to put together a business plan before I understood the proposal."

Pasqual stroked his upper lip. "What do you need to know?"

"Where the money is coming from, what services my company is expected to provide, what are we building and where. I need details."

"True," mused Geraldo. "Very true. I can explain the money part. I think Leroy has the specifications for the project."

"We're talking a series of projects," answered Leroy. "I have clients lined up all over the world to contract with Ladamien for the design and construction of airports, seaports, and traffic terminals. Ladamien's company does the work, receives the money, and returns a percentage of the profit to me as a finder's fee."

"That's basic," said Pasqual. "It should be easy to put together the necessary documents. Don't you agree, Ladamien?"

Ladamien knew in his mind that it was not that simple. While Leroy's clients might be buying airports, seaports, and terminals, the money would be coming from the gangs. He would have to pad the books from Shasta to Shanghai and still make it look reasonable.

"I need details for each project," Ladamien said. "I have to make sure that the actual costs are in line with the contracted price. I understand that I'll be overcharging, but I need to distribute the additional costs so I can pass an audit. It has to look like I could win the contract on a competitive basis."

Pasqual looked over to Geraldo who nodded. "I agree we need a basis of estimate that can withstand scrutiny. That is why we need a written plan," said Pasqual. "If the authorities ever investigate your business, it will simplify things."

Ladamien understood that these men knew what Leroy was up to and he had hired them to help him. He spoke to Geraldo. "Does your bank have experience in dealing with these sorts of accounts?"

"Channeling money? That is what we do best." Geraldo pursed his lips and gave Ladamien a sly, just-between-us smile. "We have a great deal of experience with these sorts of accounts," he said quietly. "Your transactions will be above suspicion."

Ladamien felt relieved on one aspect but uneasy on another. He would still have to deliver on the contracts. How protected was he? He looked over to the lawyer. "What if we can't do the work under the terms of the contract?"

"I will prepare the contracts," said Pasqual, "in such a way that you can't fail. Leroy assures me that all of the clients will be satisfied."

"I have to approve all contracts," said Ladamien. "No weasel words, okay?"

Pasqual nodded.

Since the ultimate customers were the gangs that wanted to launder their ill-gotten funds, Ladamien knew Leroy could make sure they were satisfied. "What about the authorities?" he asked.

"It's not their contract. No complaints, no investigations."

Ladamien realized it all came down to money. Grease enough palms and you can get away with anything. No one would question the source of the gang's money as long as each got his piece along the way while the illegal funds were being made legitimate.

Ladamien turned to Leroy. "I'm satisfied. You give me the detailed specifications and I'll have a business plan in a month."

Leroy fluttered his left hand as if to wave away Ladamien's words. "Why don't you let Geraldo and Pasqual take care of the business plan? They know better what to say than you do."

"No," said Ladamien. "I doubt they know as

much about pricing an airport construction project as my staff does. I'll consult with them when I need them."

"Very well." Leroy dismissed the two specialists with his right hand, leaving Ladamien and him alone.

"Is something bothering you?" asked Leroy.

Ladamien bit his lower lip. *This is it*, he thought. *If I don't speak up now, it's gone too far to go back.* He put his hands, palms down, on the table. "Aggie doesn't like it. She thinks I'm supporting the wrong things."

Leroy smirked; there was no humor in his expression. "What does she think gangs do, Ladamien? Doesn't she know this is a business?"

"She does, and she's not gonna go all Miss Priss on us either. It's just the drugs, the prostitutes, the weapons. She sees all that stuff on TV."

"We're not like those people, Ladamien," said Leroy. "Drugs? Hell, drugs are natural. People have been using drugs since before civilization."

Leroy tapped his knuckles on the table. "Prostitution? They don't call it the world's oldest profession for nothing."

Ladamien could tell that Leroy had given this speech a thousand times. *Maybe he's trying to convince himself*, thought Ladamien.

Leroy continued. "Weapons? Half the time the same people as are against them want them. We're just in business. All those lawyers and politicians just make money off our business. That's all they want. I need for you to take what they consider to be dirty money and clean it so they will accept it."

Ladamien certainly had no use for lawyers or

politicians. He had no use for many supposedly upright people, including the police. *The love of money,* he thought to himself. *The root of evil. We're all bad. There isn't any good in any of us. So, what did he tell Aggie?*

"What should I tell Aggie?" he asked Leroy.

"Don't tell her anything. Let her keep the house, give her lots of money, and raise your son. You don't owe anybody an explanation. Doesn't she love you?"

"Yeah, she does."

"Then, be thankful. Be thankful you're one of the wealthy and not one of the needy. Be thankful you have a nice woman and a healthy son. Be thankful I'm your friend and that you're a Rattler."

Everything he says makes sense, thought Ladamien. "Thanks. I am glad you're my friend."

Leroy stood up, draped his robe across a chair, and headed for the pool. "You sure wouldn't want me for your enemy," he said, and laughed. "Now, why don't you go back to your room? I'll buy us dinner later."

***

It was Friday and Simon had just arrived home from school. "I'm going out to ride my bike," he told his mother.

"Be back home by seven," said Aggie. "I'll have dinner ready."

"Okay, Mom."

Ever since he had met the medical lady and seen the Indian chief, Simon had wanted to go back to Pine Island Road and investigate. He was sure something mysterious lurked there. Perhaps there was buried treasure or a secret village.

He knew all of the back ways and in about forty minutes was on the dirt road that led to Pine Island proper. He hid his bicycle in the bushes and walked up the path toward the water. A garter snake about two feet long slithered across the sand in front of him and disappeared into the damp grass. A large grasshopper flew by his ear and landed on a reed to his right.

Simon stopped and listened. It was eerily still and quiet. He heard the quiet rustling of dry grass heads in a light breeze. Occasionally, waves in the lagoon made a soft splashing sound. A dog in the distance yapped for a moment, and then yipped – possibly rebuked by its owner. The faraway hum of traffic on State Road 3 was barely discernible.

Simon saw a pickup truck with a boat trailer parked off the road about a hundred feet in front of him. He began to walk toward it slowly, looking to his right and left as he went forward. He heard a loud grunting sound come from a stand of reeds in front of him. A large alligator climbed onto the pathway. Simon stared at it.

The alligator transformed instantaneously into the chief, the one that Simon had seen earlier. The chief carried a bowl with the handle of a wooden ladle sticking above the rim.

"Are you a chief?" Simon asked.

The Indian stood looking at Simon for a moment, and then walked toward him.

I am chief, echoed in Simon's head.

Simon felt he should say something. He wasn't

scared. "You know the medical lady." Simon stated it as a fact. "Why are you here? Where did you come from?"

The chief came closer and placed his hand on Simon's shoulder. Simon flinched but he didn't back away. The chief's hand felt cold on his shoulder. The chief swept his other hand, holding the bowl, toward the sky and said, not aloud, but in Simon's brain – *Behold the daughter of the wind.*

Simon looked up in the sky and saw a shimmering fairy-like girl, draped in a gauzy negligee, twirling in midair and dancing across the sky. As quickly as she appeared, she spun away and disappeared. Simon felt the weight of the chief's hand recede and watched the large alligator vanish into a tangle of mangrove roots. He had no idea what he had witnessed, but he walked back to his bicycle and headed home.

What could he say to his mother? Simon parked his bicycle in the garage and went inside his house.

"How was your bike ride?" Aggie asked. "Did you see anything unusual?"

"It was good. I saw some frogs, and a garter snake." He asked himself should he mention the Indian and the girl. "Mom, have you ever seen a person come out of nowhere – like a ghost or something?"

"Your father sneaks up behind me occasionally."

"No. I mean like out of thin air."

Simon watched his mother look at him sort of weird-like.

"That's not possible, Simon," Aggie said. "People

don't just materialize from nothing."

"No, I guess not." *They do, I saw him*, he thought. "I just wondered," he said."

"Did you see something?"

"There were some people out fishing, but I didn't see them."

"Go get washed up, I'm ready to take up dinner."

"Okay. Have you talked to Dad?"

"He called. He is going to stay in San Juan overnight, and then Leroy wants him to go to Sao Paulo to meet a client."

"Where's Sao Paulo?"

"It's in Brazil, in South America."

"Do they have pirates there?"

"I know they do close by, in Guyana."

"I'll be glad when I can go with him."

"We don't want you doing what he does. Your Dad's job is too dangerous. If you get a good education you won't have to take the chances he does."

Simon washed his hands and returned to the table for dinner. *Some day*, he thought, *I'm going to hunt down pirates and put them in jail. I'm gonna be like my Dad.*

After dinner, Aggie asked Simon to clean up the dishes. She went into her bedroom and closed the door. Simon knew she wasn't feeling well.

* * *

Bonnie awoke Saturday morning at 6:00 a.m. In spite of Rusty's advice, she wanted to move out to the Vehicle Assembly Building and begin living there.

She had checked with Eduardo and he had said that if she felt that was the right thing to do, NASA would allow it. He would have someone acquaint her with the available facilities, including a restroom with a shower and a small kitchen.

Before she went to the VAB, Bonnie wanted to secure the townhouse. She had checked on Hurricane Dirk earlier and it was a category 4 storm 800 miles east southeast of Cape Canaveral. Justin wouldn't be back from Atlanta until Sunday night. Andre' D'aubigne had talked him into flying to Atlanta for a short meeting. Bonnie expected him back before the storm arrived, but she was taking no chances. Vince helped her install hurricane panels over the windows. She emptied the refrigerator, and turned off the water and electricity.

The neighbors came over to see what she was doing. She told them it was just caution; that Justin was out of town on business, and she had to leave for a while. She locked the door and walked out to her car at 9:30 a.m. She felt a twinge of foreboding, as if nothing from this point in time on would ever be the same. She had called her parents and told them about her pregnancy and Justin's proposal. Her mother wanted to come down and help, but Bonnie told her she should wait until Hurricane Dirk had passed.

The previous evening, she had spent two hours at the Ais Sanctuary. She had not seen anyone or anything remarkable – spiritual or otherwise. She sat by the lake and watched the sun set underneath a distant cover of violet-tinged clouds. As the sun went beneath the horizon, the entire sky lit up in a smoky orange blaze and then quieted to a subdued cobalt blue.

The morning advisory on Hurricane Dirk located it 485 miles north/northeast of the Dominican Republic. Bonnie calculated that it would be two days before the Florida coast began feeling tropical storm winds. Evidently, the National Hurricane Center agreed with her because it issued a tropical storm watch for the Florida coast along with the advisory. Bonnie also estimated that the eye of the hurricane would cross the Florida coast, just north of Cape Canaveral, in less than four days. Bonnie knew Dirk would not turn north. The wind was coming for her.

"Do you want to move out to the Vehicle Assembly Building with me?" Bonnie asked Vince.

"I'll wait," he replied. "Rusty may need me here for awhile, especially if they start an evacuation. I'll be there when it counts."

"I know you will. What about the two trainees?"

"Do you want them out there with you?"

"Yes. I want to get to know them." Bonnie put a finger to her cheek. "I'll call Rusty."

Vince drove with Bonnie out to the Vehicle Assembly Building. Bonnie insisted that he help her settle in. They had lunch at the Launch Control Center snack booth, and then Vince left to go back to Station #2.

Winona and Thad showed up at the Vehicle Assembly Building at about noon. Bonnie could tell immediately that Winona was a stickler for detail. She probed into every box and cabinet and created an inventory of supplies. Thad, on the other hand, found the most convenient source of coffee and doughnuts and relaxed in a chair reading the operations plan.

"Don't you think everyone will get off the island when the evacuation occurs?" he asked Bonnie.

"Most will," she answered. "Previous data indicates about ninety percent of the people will evacuate for a major storm. Some can't, some don't get the word, and some just don't want to."

"So, we have to help the remaining ten percent?"

"If they need us. Right now, we just need to prepare."

Winona came up and sat down with them. "We have everything we need for simple first aid," she said. "If there's anything serious, we'll have to get the patient to a hospital."

"That's Vince's job," Bonnie explained. "He'll have an emergency vehicle for evacuations."

Winona made a face. "Once the winds get too high, no one will be able to make it out that north road. It will be impossible to come across the causeways."

"That's true," said Bonnie, "but, we have a chance if we can get them here. Better here than if they're stranded out in the storm."

"If the storm comes here," Thad asked, "when will we begin to see the worst?"

"Tuesday," said Bonnie. "Late Tuesday night."

"That's only three days away," mused Winona. "When do you think the government will begin to act?"

"Soon," Bonnie speculated. "Probably tomorrow

night. The National Hurricane Center should issue a hurricane watch some time Sunday."

"Then what happens?" Thad inquired.

"They'll begin with a voluntary evacuation of the beaches. People will start boarding up their homes, the shelters will open, and the roads will get busier. Those on the mainland will rush to the store to stock up on water, canned food, batteries, etc."

"Haven't they already done that?"

"A few. Most will wait until the last minute."

"It's like having one's head under a guillotine, waiting for the blade to fall."

"Except," said Bonnie, "the blade is already half way down."

***

Rusty was already exhausted when Gus called her Saturday morning. Her third shift supervisor had called her at 4:00 in the morning from a house fire on Buzzard Roost Road. Two people had died in the fire and the TV media were already at the scene. Brad Pelham, the third shift supervisor could handle the fire and the medical emergency, but talking to the press was not his bag.

Rusty had been at the fire all morning getting investigation results and answering questions. She did not arrive at the office until after ten. When Gus called, he began the conversation immediately. "I saw you on TV this morning," Gus said. "That must have been tough."

"I felt so bad for the woman," said Rusty. "She got out with her son. The fire trapped her husband and daughter inside. It looked like they took a wrong turn. By the time we got there, it was all over."

"You handled it well on the tube."

"Thanks. Is that why you called?"

"No. Different subject. The National Weather Service called the governor's office. They said there was an 85 percent certainty that Hurricane Dirk would come ashore in Florida. They said it was still too early to issue an official advisory but they wanted to give the governor an early warning."

"How did Tallahassee react?"

"No panic, but the governor is going to come on TV at 3:00."

"What's he going to say, do you know?"

"Not exactly, but the county's been keeping us piped in. They suspect the governor will put the National Guard on alert status. He may ask for a voluntary evacuation from some areas. By Monday, the situation could be more serious. He'll probably recommend the schools be closed."

Rusty listened, but her mind wandered. It all sounded so familiar, much like the tone that prevailed before Hurricane Katrina. "So, it starts now," she said.

"What do you mean?" Gus asked. "What starts?"

"You know my history." – *How do I say this?* she thought. – "I was taking a post-grad course at Tulane when we started watching Katrina. We knew it was a gigantic storm, but we waited too long."

"I had always heard that Tulane's response was one of the bright spots in the disaster."

"That's true. The university evacuated all of the

students to Jackson State University on August 27, two days before landfall. Tulane University Hospital & Clinic received patients from other hospitals and the Louisiana Superdome. I was there. We were all taken out by helicopter."

"You think they waited too long?"

"Maybe not for Tulane," said Rusty, "but we acted too late for New Orleans and the Gulf Coast."

"You think we're responding too late on Hurricane Dirk?"

"With that evaluation by the National Weather Service, there should be a greater sense of urgency. How big a storm do they predict?"

"Category 5."

Rusty felt her eyes moisten. "Camille was the only category five I ever knew anything about. It was legendary in Slidell. There is no way we are ready for what is coming."

"I'm glad you're here," said Gus. "I think you'll make sure we're ready."

"I'll feel better if the governor understands what's coming."

"We'll just have to see what he says," said Gus. "I'll talk to you after his speech."

"Yes, please call me and we'll discuss it."

Rusty called Kathie Turbinov and Doug Forsythe into her office and rang Bonnie in on a conference call. She told them about her conversation with Gus and advised them to have the crews listen in on the governor's speech.

"This could be one of the more significant events in our lives," she told them. "We need to be ready."

At three o'clock, Kathie and Doug joined Rusty in her office to watch the governor's announcement. As expected, he put the National Guard on alert. Additionally, he asked for a voluntary evacuation for barrier dune and beach communities from Palm Coast to Fort Pierce. He specifically cautioned that individuals who might have difficulty getting out in a hurry or need assistance should get out early. He recommended that school boards in vulnerable areas make a decision on closing schools immediately.

After the governor's announcement, Rusty called Gus and Bonnie and put them on the speakerphone so Kathie and Doug could participate as well.

"It seems the governor is taking this storm seriously," she told Gus.

"You had better be ready to handle increased traffic on I-95," said Gus. "You'll start to see some results of the voluntary evacuation tomorrow."

"NASA is going to open State Road 3 through the center going north," said Bonnie. "That will help divert some traffic off of the causeways."

"Has the county decided where to open the initial shelters?" Rusty asked Gus.

"They're going to distribute a list later today," Gus responded. "I don't anticipate any surprises. They don't expect a lot of response this early."

"If I heard correctly, the governor said the National Weather Service predicted that Dirk could make landfall on Wednesday unless it turns north," said Gus. "Does Bonnie agree with that?"

"Yes," said Bonnie, "but if my intuition is correct, we'll start getting hurricane force winds before midnight Tuesday."

"If that's true," said Gus, "the National Hurricane Center should issue a watch Sunday night."

"What happens then?" asked Kathie.

"Probably," said Gus, "there will be a mandatory evacuation for Merritt Island, the beaches, and low-lying areas on the mainland. Increased traffic, people looking for shelters, runs on plywood, water, and batteries. In other words, general chaos."

"That's why we need to start early," said Doug. "It just keeps escalating once it starts. Until the storm actually hits, and then any emergencies become more difficult, what with the wind, rain, flooding, lightning…"

"It also explains why the governor recommended closing the schools," said Rusty. "We'll need the shelter space. Okay, we're going back to work. We should all try and get some rest before mayhem strikes."

"Good idea," said Gus. "I'll stay in touch."

After Kathie and Doug left her office, Rusty went over everything in her mind. "I wonder what I'm missing," she asked herself. "There's bound to be something."

***

Shortly after the governor made his announcement, Eduardo Martinez came to Bay 4 looking for Bonnie.

"The county called," said Eduardo. "They've taken Keith off our team and assigned someone else, a man named Ed Richardson. Do you know him?"

"Very well," Bonnie answered. "He's an emergency services manager. Very competent." Bonnie swept her hand out toward the Vehicle Assembly Building bays. "Do you mind if I ask a question?"

"Of course not."

"According to the news, the shuttle program is over. Is that true?"

"Yes. We still have one shuttle almost ready to roll out from here to the pad. It doesn't have a mission at this time."

"So that's why so much equipment is still here."

"That and we're making a transition to new launch vehicles."

"You're going to use the Vehicle Assembly Building for the new programs?"

"Temporarily. It's still a valuable asset. Eventually, we will phase it out completely, make it a tourist attraction."

"Because of that, it can't be used as a shelter?"

"It wouldn't be practical. We can stage stragglers through here but we can't handle a crowd."

Bonnie was satisfied with Eduardo's explanation. "What is NASA's reaction to the governor's announcement?"

"We expected it. It's reasonable to get a jump on the logistics of preparing to move and house what could be as many as a half-million people. It will take some time."

"A half-million? There's barely that many people in Brevard County."

"I know, but the governor has to be thinking that Dirk could threaten the coast from Flagler County all the way to Martin County and maybe Palm Beach County. That's a lot of beaches."

"That's over two hundred miles of shoreline. I doubt any storm would have hurricane force winds out that far."

"That's why we all have to wait for an official advisory before we can make major decisions. The center could still miss us."

"I see what you mean, but that eye is coming here."

Bonnie saw Eduardo's face take on the look of a hound that has treed a raccoon. She knew she had underestimated his interest in her relationship to the storm. "How big do you think it will be?" he asked.

Bonnie saw his point. He was getting her to see the wisdom of the governor's decision. "I don't know," she admitted. "Enormous. Huge enough to cover all of central Florida."

"That could be as much as three hundred miles across." Eduardo said as he walked to the edge of the area they had given Bonnie and sat down. "I actually came here to give you some good news."

"We could use some of that."

"Our big boss talked to the other administrators in Washington, and they went to the Federal Emergency Management Administration. FEMA agreed to start releasing non-perishable supplies early to the states possibly affected by Dirk. That included every state from North Carolina around to Texas."

"I'll bet Rusty was pleased. That's been one of

her concerns."

"FEMA doesn't want to be embarrassed again like they were with Katrina. Anything they can do up front will help."

"Mark that up to lessons learned," said Bonnie. "I say good for them."

Eduardo nodded, rose, and walked back toward the Vehicle Assembly Building low bay. Bonnie decided to call Justin and bring him up to date on her activities.

"Whatcha doin?" Bonnie asked after Justin answered his phone.

"André scheduled the meeting for later this evening," answered Justin, "I told him I would give him some notes but I have to get home. I'm almost done and then I'll be on the plane."

"I buttoned up our house and moved out to Kennedy Space Center this afternoon. Is your boat secure?"

"I heard that the governor asked for a voluntary evacuation of the beaches," said Justin. "My boat is secure. I always anchor it as if a storm were coming."

"That's good," said Bonnie. She continued, "Most people will ignore a voluntary evacuation. They'll wait until it becomes mandatory."

"What do you have to do right now?"

"Not much," answered Bonnie. "We won't start helping with the evacuations until they become mandatory."

"When do you think they'll issue a mandatory evacuation?"

"Probably not before Monday morning."

"I may be home by then. Do you think you'll be there?"

Bonnie would love to have said yes, but she knew that wasn't practical. "We're going to be short handed out here as it is. I'll have to stay put."

"Okay, I'll miss you. Stay in touch. This hurricane has your name all over it."

"I know. Isn't that weird?"

"I've thought so from the beginning. Be careful if you get out in the storm."

"I'd better let you get back to work. Love you."

"Love you too." Justin spoke hastily.

Bonnie saw Winona over at one of the storage lockers and walked over to her. "Do we have room for more supplies?" Bonnie asked. "Eduardo tells me that FEMA is going to send us more materials."

"We don't have much room," Winona replied, "but we're already well stocked." Winona stood up from her kneeling position. "Could you take me and Thad on a tour of north Merritt Island? We'd like to see the area."

"Sure," said Bonnie. "That's a good idea. Find Thad and we'll leave in half-an-hour."

"I'll find him," said Winona.

***

Bonnie headed south on State Road 3, known as the Kennedy Parkway on the center. She drove a government vehicle, a 2009 Chevrolet Tahoe that Eduardo had requisitioned for her use. Winona sat in the front with her and Thad sat in the back.

Bonnie pointed to her right. "Look up in that tree and you'll see an eagle's nest. It's a local landmark."

"Do the eagles still use it?" asked Thad.

"Oh yeah," said Bonnie. "There've been several generations of eagles born there."

As they approached the NASA Parkway, Winona asked, "Doesn't that go to mainland?"

"Yes," said Bonnie. "It comes out south of Titusville and north of Port St. John. The causeway will be closed when the winds go over forty-five miles per hour."

"That doesn't seem like much of a wind," said Thad.

"Maybe," said Bonnie, "but the officials have to draw a line somewhere. Remember, the water would probably cover the road and it will be raining heavily."

"Won't that also be true of State Road 3 going north?"

"It's not right on the water. Our driver may have to go around trees and debris, but he should be able to stay on the road. Undoubtedly, there's a point where that route may be impassable as well, at least temporarily."

After they passed under the NASA Parkway, they went through the south gate to Kennedy Space Center. Bonnie pointed to the west. "That's Space Commerce Way. It goes to the Visitor's Center. It's as close as you can get without a badge."

"What happens to the Visitor's Center if the hurricane comes through?" asked Thad.

"NASA will close it. I don't know what they do

about the rocket garden."

"What's that?" Winona's voice showed a hint of amusement.

"It's an outdoor display where all the historic rockets are displayed."

"I'd like to see that."

"We don't have time. Maybe we can go there after the storm is over."

Thad tapped Bonnie's shoulder. "All those orange groves we passed. Does NASA operate the groves?"

"They allow the owners to tend the groves and harvest the fruit. Many of the owners were here before NASA. One place we passed back there used to be a community, Orsino."

Bonnie pointed out a road to the east. "That's D'albora Road, our first road with housing. You can't see much from here."

"This far out in the country," remarked Thad. "Are there many people out here?"

"Quite a few. There are lots more as we head south."

"How far south," asked Winona, "and how many people?"

"About twenty-five miles from here and around thirty-six thousand people."

"We can't handle that."

"I figure all but a thousand or so will evacuate. The southernmost six miles probably won't be accessible. We're here to handle the real emergencies."

"Like what?"

"The injured, the sick, the very old, and the very young."

"What about the others?"

"They'll survive. Communication is going to be the real problem. Phones will be out eventually. We should continue to have radio contact within emergency services."

"Will water cover the island?" asked Thad.

"Not entirely," answered Bonnie. "The water will come up and there will be flooding but the Indian and Banana Rivers are lagoons, they're semi landlocked and shallow. They won't generate a surge wave."

Bonnie turned right on Tropical Trail. The first side roads were Kangaroo Lane to the left and McGruder Road to the right. She thought about the boy she had met near Pine Island. Simon Upton. *He lives right here.* "Tropical Trail is a main north-south thoroughfare parallel to State Road 3," she said. "There's another body of water to the east, Sykes Creek. It splits Merritt Island between the Indian and Banana Rivers."

"You could easily get lost out here," observed Winona. "I hope Thad is paying attention."

"It's not that bad," said Thad. "It's so narrow. What's it like to the east?"

"Most of it down to the barge canal is part of the Kennedy Space Center," replied Bonnie. "South of there, it's canal communities. Fairly vulnerable I'd say."

"What's on the other side of Sykes Creek?"

"Quite a bit of development. I hope that most of them will evacuate. I phoned Ed Richardson from the county. He's going to meet us at the Merritt Island mall."

Winona shifted around to face Bonnie. "Is he going to join us in the Vehicle Assembly Building?"

"I don't know. He said he had several things to discuss with us. I assume that's one of them. The county has a much bigger task than we do."

Bonnie parked the SUV outside the mall. Winona and Thad followed her to the Food Court. Bonnie spotted Ed Richardson seated in a booth and walked over to him.

"Let us get a cup of coffee and we'll join you," said Bonnie.

"Sure," said Ed. "These are Winona and Thad you have with you?"

"Yes. I'm sorry, I should have introduced you." Bonnie turned to Winona and Thad. "This is Ed Richardson from the county. You can learn much from him."

After they had their drinks, they all sat in the booth together. "What did you want to talk about?" asked Bonnie.

"A lot of people at county think you're a nut. You know that."

Bonnie smiled and shrugged her shoulders. "I've doubted my own sanity many times."

"I'm not one of them," Ed reassured her. "I checked you out a long time ago. Several people I know quite well told me they could not reveal the whole story, however, they assured me you were not making anything up. You have had paranormal experiences – contact with the dead, psychic precognition, otherworldly contacts – that sort of thing."

"Is that true?" asked Winona.

Bonnie shut her eyes and gave a blasé nod.

"No one told us this," said Thad. "Is that how you know so much about this hurricane?"

"I've had visions," Bonnie said.

"At any rate," Ed continued, "how bad is this storm going to be?"

"I don't know," said Bonnie. "In my vision, trees were uprooted and buildings were tumbling down – big buildings."

"And, it was coming here?"

"It was coming to me – to Coreopsis."

"Why to you? What has it to do with you personally?"

"I don't know. Something about the daughter of the wind and the original chiefs of the Ais Indian Nation."

"Do you think you are the daughter of the wind?

"No. It's something else." Bonnie took a sip of her coffee. "At any rate, you believe me. You, Gus and Mayor Moline. So, what did you want to tell us?"

"Assuming this is going to be a category 5 hurricane coming in north of Cape Canaveral, we will have to evacuate Cape Canaveral Hospital for one thing. Also we will have to evacuate all of the beaches, Merritt Island and flood-prone areas throughout the county."

"True."

"Patrick Air Force Base will want to keep a security force on the base. I figure they can handle that. NASA will want to keep some people at the center." Ed paused as if he were getting ready to make a point. "The county will continue to staff the Sheriff's office and the Fire and Emergency Medical stations on Merritt Island."

"I'm pleased to hear that," said Bonnie. "There's no way we can service all of Merritt Island other than with emergency evacuations."

"That's going to be your role then," said Ed. "We'll use your base in the Vehicle Assembly Building as a staging area to get people off the island to shelters or hospitals."

"Where will you be located?" Winona asked.

"I'll set up at the Sheriff's headquarters at Courtney and 528," said Ed. He looked at Bonnie. "When will the eye wall be here?"

"Early Wednesday, around three in the morning."

Ed looked at Bonnie in a peculiar way as if she were a two-headed cow or something. "I can't believe this is about you individually," he said, "but, if it is, I'll pray for you. God only knows what forces are at work."

"Thank you," said Bonnie, getting up to leave. "We'd better get back to work."

CHAPTER 7

"Human life is driven forward by its dim apprehension of notions too general for its existing language."

Alfred North Whitehead

Ladamien had been on the airplane for several hours. After a one-hour flight to Santo Domingo, and a two-hour flight to Miami, it was a nine-hour flight to Sao Paulo. The flight details indicated that he would arrive in Sao Paulo at 7:35 Sunday morning. He was accustomed to traveling long distances, so he had no trouble mixing sleep with alertness.

Ladamien called Aggie from Miami to tell her where he was going. He was worried about her. She had been sick to her stomach and felt listless. Her headaches had gotten worse.

"Don't you think it would be wise to leave the house and drive into Orlando?" he asked her.

"I'll feel better. It will be more restful to just button up the house and ride out the storm."

"Okay," Ladamien had said, "but don't hesitate to call 911 if you have to."

"I'll be all right," said Aggie. "Don't worry about me. Simon's here to help."

The airplane was out over the Atlantic when Ladamien began to go through some of the papers that Geraldo and Pasqual had given him in San Juan. Ladamien knew immediately that he was an executive. With the new investors, Airport Design Partners, LLC changed its name to Upton Planning & Design International. The company was truly international with sales offices on every continent, a simulation facility in France, and engineering branches in the United States, India, China, Germany, and Brazil.

The list of contracts and prospects filled ten pages with potential revenues of more than three billion US dollars. Nowhere was there a hint of a gang connection. Every deal appeared to be with a legitimate concern, many of which were easily recognizable. *Wow*, Ladamien thought. *I can hardly believe this. I wish Aggie could see this.*

The thought of his wife and son made Ladamien realize how much he was giving up to pursue his ambition. He couldn't deny his ambition drove him. He might blame the gang, or the system, but in truth, it was his ambition. He loved Aggie and Simon, but he wanted money and business success as much or more than he needed to be with them.

I can organize this enterprise, Ladamien thought, *and then I can spend more time at home. This will be enough, what I've always wanted.* He might have been fooling himself, but Ladamien was convinced he could say no to

Leroy when the time came. Ladamien flipped through the financial statements and returned to the executive summary.

I'm a lucky man. He closed his eyes and coasted into serene slumber.

* * *

Bonnie slept restlessly Saturday night into Sunday morning. NASA had set up monitors in the Launch Control Center where anyone could check on Hurricane Dirk at any time. Through the night, the storm had continued to strengthen to a category 5. It was becoming clear that Hurricane Dirk would not divert to the north and the National Hurricane Center predicted it would strengthen as it came into the warmer waters close to the coastline. Tallahassee put out advisory ordering schools in coastal communities to suspend classes for Monday.

Commercial television stations began running hourly updates shortly after the Tallahassee statement. They began to track the storm and issue lists of acceptable shelters. Traffic on highways going west picked up, and the state discontinued tolls on roads going east and west. Hardware and building supply stores began stacking plywood outside where people could easily pick it up. The TV reported that stores in the area had sold out of electric generators.

Winona and Thad came up behind Bonnie and sat next to her.

"Tell us about your paranormal experiences," said Winona. "How did Ed Richardson know about them?"

I guess I owe them some explanation, Bonnie thought.

If I dodge the issue, it will just peak their curiosity.

"It happened two years ago," said Bonnie. "It began with a seizure. I passed out on a picnic with friends. At first, the doctors couldn't figure out what was wrong."

"Did they ever find out?" asked Thad.

"A psychiatrist, Dr. Blaine, and a hypnotist, Marcie Reese, found out that I was possessed," said Bonnie, "by the spirit of a dead girl, a teenager."

"Wow, that's weird."

"That's what we all thought, but it happened. Her name was Julie Gustafson, she had returned from the dead to find her baby."

"How could she lose a baby?" asked Winona. "Didn't she know where it was?"

"She didn't lose it," answered Bonnie. "It was taken from her, shortly before she was killed."

"Who would steal a baby?" asked Thad. "What would they do with it?"

"A gang, the Swamp Rattlers, they stole it and sold it on the black market, to a couple in Georgia." Bonnie took advantage of the momentary silence. "They sold the baby, a girl, to my parents. I was Julie's daughter."

"Damn," said Thad. "That's unbelievable."

"Not as unbelievable as some of the other things that occurred during that time."

"Like what," said Winona, "how do you top that?"

"Julie's spirit had a protector, a spiritual being named Auriel," said Bonnie. "According to a witch in

Cassadaga, Lady Victoria, Auriel was Mother Earth's secular representative."

Thad chuckled. "There's an actual Mother Earth?"

Bonnie tilted her head and lifted her eyebrows to indicate to Thad that he could take it or leave it. "The Ais Indians thought so. According to Lady Victoria, Mother Earth wanted a certain property set aside as an Ais Sanctuary for their spirits. I spend a lot of time there. The spirits are definitely there."

"You can see them?"

"Yes. I think their ancient chiefs are showing me this hurricane. They have come to me in their original forms – an alligator, a blue heron, a manatee, and the storm. I have seen the first three in their human form. They have talked to me."

"You haven't seen the storm," asked Winona, "the storm chief?"

"I think he's coming."

"Why?"

"I don't know," said Bonnie. "There's an alien out at the Ais Sanctuary, Kameeshi – it might know."

"An alien!" said Thad. "What kind of alien?"

"Mother Earth brought it here, from some other world. It looks like a stick with a loop. It's a germanium-based life form. It communicates telepathically."

"What does it do?

"It protects the Ais Sanctuary."

"Why do you think you can see all of these things and others can't?"

"When my mother's spirit, Julie's spirit, departed, she left something of her spirit in my soul. It gives me psychic powers."

"Can you see the future? Are we going to be all right?"

"I don't know. I'm not sure I control the power. It just happens."

Winona put her hand on Bonnie's shoulder. "How many people know all of this?"

"I'm not even sure that I know the whole story, actually. I've only told you parts. Several people know bits and pieces. Ed Richardson, for example, knows enough to believe me and be concerned, but he doesn't know what I've told you."

"I can see why he's worried for you," said Thad. "You are involved in something really strange – and bigger than big."

"This hurricane is going to be enough for all of us. Don't worry about me."

Winona and Thad left to have lunch. Bonnie continued to watch the updates on Dirk. The NASA monitors had several views of the storm from space. Bonnie could see that Dirk was still in the cooler deep waters of the Atlantic moving toward the shallows closer to shore

It'll pick up a lot when it hits that warmer water, thought Bonnie. *It'll be a category 5 when it comes ashore.*

As she watched the spiral form of the storm, she pictured a face. She couldn't tell if it was real or imagined.

Don't lose it, she cautioned herself. *Don't go crazy on me.*

***

Simon was delighted when he found out the county had cancelled school for Monday. His mother gave him the news early in the afternoon.

"Does that mean we'll get a hurricane?" he asked his mother.

"Not necessarily," answered Aggie. "It's just a tropical storm warning right now."

"What does that mean?"

"It means we will get winds of forty miles per hour or more within 36 hours, by Monday night."

"Then, why are they closing the schools?"

Aggie sat down at the dining room table with a cup of coffee and motioned Simon to sit across from her.

"I grew up in south Florida," she said. "It's kind of a routine you get used to."

"What's a routine?

"Something you do over and over. When a tropical storm is coming, the first official notice is a tropical storm watch, that's a 48-hour alert. Then they issue a tropical storm warning, then a hurricane watch, and then a hurricane warning. The county is closing the schools early because they need them for shelters and parents want their kids at home so they can get ready to evacuate or button up their homes."

"Are we gonna 'vacuate?"

"Not unless they make us. We have a well-designed home, with storm shutters. We've kept the trees trimmed. Our yard may flood, but the water shouldn't get into the house. I don't want to leave.

Living in a shelter is the pits."

"If the storm doesn't come here, will I have to go to school on Tuesday?"

"Probably. We'll have to wait and see."

"Has Dad called?"

"No. He's on the plane from Miami to Sao Paulo. He'll call tomorrow."

"Can I go over to Buster's and play?"

"Yes, but be home for dinner."

When he stepped outside, Simon looked around. It didn't look as if a storm was coming. There were fluffy clouds in the direction of the ocean. The air felt relatively dry for August, and the oak trees across the street waved slowly in a gentle breeze. The constant drone of insects provided background noise.

Simon climbed into the fork of a small tree and watched a butterfly flutter from flower to flower on a wild vine. He saw Jennifer Purdy walking down the path toward him.

"Where ya goin'?" Simon asked.

Jennifer jumped. "I didn't see you up there," she said. "I was going over to Buster's house to see what he's doing."

"That's where I was going."

"Are your parents ready for the storm?" asked Jennifer.

Simon climbed down from the tree and started walking along the path ahead of Jennifer. "My Dad's out of the country. I don't think my mom's worried about it."

"I hope we can go back to school Tuesday."

"Not me. I don't care if we never have to go back."

"If we miss school now," said Jennifer, "we'll just have to go longer at the end of the year."

"I guess. I suppose school's okay, it's just that I'd rather go fishing."

"Did you go fishing today?"

"Nah. The water's kind 'a choppy. It messes up the river for fishing."

Simon didn't feel like talking anymore, so they walked in silence to Buster's house. Jennifer stood next to him while he knocked on the door. Mrs. Shockley opened the door.

"Is Buster here, Missus Shockley?" asked Jennifer. "Can he come out and play?"

"Hello Jennifer, Simon − you can come in. He's in his room."

Simon followed Jennifer back to Buster's room. His door was open, and he was watching *Zack and Cody* on his television.

Zack and Cody was a Disney show about two boys who went to school on a cruise ship. Simon thought it was silly and mostly for girls.

"I thought only girls watched that show," said Simon.

"You're a pimple head," said Jennifer, putting her hands on her hips.

"Nah, it's cool," said Buster. "Going to school on the high seas is neat. Can you imagine living on a cruise ship?"

Simon frowned at Jennifer. "I'm not a pimple

head."

"Yeah," Simon said to Buster, "Going to school at sea would be okay." Simon looked at Jennifer and then at Buster. "You wanna go outside and shoot some hoops or something?"

"Why don't we just stay inside and watch TV with Buster," suggested Jennifer.

"It's too nice outside," said Simon, "and Buster's got this neat basket and backboard."

Jennifer shrugged and sat down next to Buster.

"Can I use your ball?" Simon asked Buster.

"Go ahead. We'll come out later."

Simon took Buster's basketball off the shelf and headed outside. He ran into Mrs. Shockley on his way out.

"Aren't Buster and Jennifer going to play with you?" she asked.

"They'll come out later."

"I'd better check on them," said Mrs. Shockley. She headed toward Buster's room.

Simon went outside and started shooting baskets. It bothered him that Jennifer seemed to prefer Buster's company to his.

To heck with it, Simon thought. *I don't need them.* He dribbled the ball around the driveway and shot a few baskets. After fifteen minutes, he left the ball near the back stoop and started walking home.

When he came to the tree where Jennifer had found him, he climbed back up into the crotch of the tree and tried to think. He thought about being captain of a big ship, chasing pirates, and putting them in irons. He arrived home well before dark. His mother was in the kitchen cutting up vegetables.

"The National Hurricane Center issued a hurricane watch while you were gone," said Aggie. "We'd better start getting ready."

"What do we have to do?" Simon inquired. "Aren't we ready? Are we gonna have to 'vacuate?"

"I don't want to go to a shelter," said Aggie. I've already stocked some extra canned food, batteries, water, and gas for the car and the generator. You can help me hook up the generator and check it out. We'll lower the shutters and make sure they all work. You can pick up any loose stuff in the yard and make sure there's nothing that will blow around."

"What about school?"

"We can forget about school for a few days. Wash your hands, and set the table. Dinner's almost ready."

While Simon washed his hands, he pictured Jennifer and Buster together watching the TV. They're dumb friends anyway – especially Jennifer. She's a girl. He realized that was what bothered him most.

Simon was aware how quiet and lonely the house was with just him and his mother there. Thoughts of the storm troubled him and he wished his father would come home.

***

All day Sunday, Bonnie had felt the effects of sleeping on a field cot the previous night. She figured her pregnancy contributed to the backache she had tried to ignore. She found Winona and told her that she was going back to Coreopsis to sleep in her own bed.

Bonnie expected the National Hurricane Center to release a hurricane warning in the morning, but she figured she had time to drive back to Justin's townhouse, get a long rest, and come back to the Vehicle Assembly Building before the winds started to pick up. On her way to Coreopsis, she called Rusty.

"What's your day been like?" Bonnie asked.

"Pretty much normal," Rusty answered. "Almost no one is evacuating yet. Everyone is waiting for the National Hurricane Center to issue a hurricane warning."

"I'm going to stay at home tonight," said Bonnie. "Those field cots weren't made for pregnant women."

"I can imagine," said Rusty. "How are Winona and Thad working out?"

"Good. They listen and they are both hard workers."

"My two loaners are working out well," said Rusty. "Go home and get some sleep. The wind won't start picking up until tomorrow. I'll call you if anything changes."

"Thanks. I'll call you in the morning." Bonnie hung up and continued driving. She felt an urge to go to the Ais Sanctuary. She could call Justin later. As she came into Coreopsis, she lowered the car window. The sun was just above the horizon and was already creating a fiery panorama to the west. Dry, warm air blew across Bonnie's face and whipped her hair around her neck.

She parked the car at the Ais Sanctuary and walked up the path to Kameeshi's monument. The monument reminded Bonnie of a swooping silver bird. The bird banked over a spherical marble foundation and appeared to clutch a large football-shaped crystal egg. Within the egg was a fifteen-inch stick shaped like an Ankh cross. Only Bonnie and a few others knew that the stick was an alien life form — Kameeshi.

Bonnie realized that human and spiritual beings had deserted the Ais Sanctuary. A lone owl glided silently over her right shoulder and perched on a small black oak inside the Ais Sanctuary. Vermillion and lilac watercolors infused the sky starting at the peak and bleeding toward the horizon. It was a storm sky with ghost clouds creeping unseen beyond the shadows of the wind. Bonnie could feel the stillness pulsating – a steady heartbeat in her soul – stimulating the embryo in her uterus.

Bonnie closed her eyes and reached out to Kameeshi with her mind. *What's going on?*

The crystal containing Kameeshi began to flash – a lighthouse in the dusk. Bonnie heard Kameeshi's reply in her mind. *Ho-tah-lee, the chief of the Big Wind is coming. He rides the great bird Hurikon, and comes to see you.*

"Why would he want to see me?" Bonnie asked aloud.

You carry the spirit of his daughter. He wants her to return to her people so they can continue their journey into the great ecstasy.

Bonnie knew better than to question Kameeshi. The alien had insight into the spiritual world that she could not hope to match.

"How did that happen?" she inquired. "How did her spirit get into my body?"

When your mother's spirit departed, when she relinquished her possession of your mind, the wayward spirit she left in your soul was that of the daughter of the wind, Banna — Leaping Waters.

"What happened to my mother's spirit?"

Julie's spirit went on to the great ecstasy.

"What happens to my unborn baby if Banna's spirit joins the spirits of her people?"

Your daughter's spirit will be in limbo. Her soul might not develop.

"She could lose her identity? Her spirit might never be free?"

It would depend on the strength of her soul and the will of her spirit.

"I will fight the chief of the Big Wind. I will not sacrifice my daughter's spirit. How can I stop Ho-tah-lee?"

When you meet with the chiefs, you must convince them to release your daughter's spirit to you and persuade Banna's spirit to go on to the great ecstasy. Your love must overcome all other desires.

"Thank you Kameeshi."

Bonnie walked into the Ais Sanctuary. It was dissonantly quiet. The owl flew along with her, sometimes flying ahead and waiting and at others times letting her walk ahead and then catching up. Bonnie found a fallen log to sit on and pulled out her cell phone. She called up Justin's cell phone number and punched dial. Justin answered on the fourth ring.

"Justin," she said when he answered, "how much do you love me?"

"Totally," Justin answered. "What's wrong?"

"I'm upset, that's all. There may be something wrong – with our baby."

"Have you been to the doctor?"

"Worse. Kameeshi told me."

"What's happening?"

"Our daughter, she's possessed, before she's even born. There are powerful forces, supernatural powers that want her spirit."

"This sounds even stranger than when Julie's spirit possessed you."

"It is, Justin. I'm frightened."

"I'll fly back tonight. André will just have to do without me."

"Yes, please do. The hurricane will be here in two days. You can help. Just tell me you will always love me, no matter what happens."

"You know I will. I'll catch the earliest plane."

"Thank God. I can't wait to see you." Bonnie started to hang up, and then added, "I love you."

"Love you too," Justin said.

Bonnie hung up and walked back to her car. She drove to the town house, undressed and slid into the bed. The soft mattress, the warm covers, and the lingering odor of Justin comforted her.

I'm glad he's coming, she thought.

Bonnie fell asleep without setting the alarm.

***

The ringing of Bonnie's cell phone woke her up. She looked at the time. The clock said 5:43. Bonnie figured it must still be dark although there was no window in the bedroom.

"Hallo," she mumbled into the phone. She looked at the caller I.D. "Rusty, is that you?"

"Sorry to wake you up," said Rusty, "but the National Hurricane Center just issued an official hurricane warning for the east coast from Ft. Pierce to St. Augustine Shores. That puts us smack in the middle. The winds in the hurricane are up to 165 miles per hour and the barometric pressure is beginning to drop rapidly. You need to go back to the Vehicle Assembly Building and start preparing."

"You really think the advisory will change things that much?"

"Oh yeah. People will start evacuating now. They'll know it's just a matter of time. The county will start ordering them to leave."

Bonnie was still quite tired, but she understood she had to get moving. "I'll take a quick shower," she told Rusty, "and button up the house. Justin's coming back from Atlanta."

"I hope he can still get an airplane," said Rusty. "Call Eduardo when you're on your way. He's expecting you."

"What about Richardson, the county guy?"

"He's on his way to the sheriff's office on Merritt Island."

"How are you holding up?"

"I've got a forty-eight pack of doughnuts and two coffee pots. I'm good as long as the emergency power holds up, and it is a brand new system."

"Okay. See you when it's over." Bonnie knew that might be as much as a week. Before she took her shower, she poured a bowl of cereal and took it out on the back porch to eat.

Bonnie could feel the breeze fluttering in her hair and hear the whisper of the leaves stirring in the steady zephyr. She expected the intensity would increase throughout the day, eventually becoming gusts, and then gales. The hurricane was less than two days away. The air was still dry, but even in the pre-dusk, Bonnie could see rapidly moving clouds along the horizon. Soon, the rains would come. *What a way to start a Monday*, she thought.

After her shower, Bonnie pulled on her uniform over her clean skin and underwear. *Like a soldier preparing for battle*, she thought. After fastening the shoulder holster with a walkie-talkie, she picked up her EMS bag that contained foul weather gear and a trauma kit and headed out the door. Once outside, she secured the house and went to her car. She called Eduardo. "I'm on my way," she said.

"We're ready for you," Eduardo said. "If you haven't had breakfast, we've got a buffet set up in the cafeteria."

"Thanks," said Bonnie. "I'll be ready for it later."

The drive along State Road 3 was lonely and a little eerie. The animals sensed the coming storm. Bonnie opened the window on her vehicle. The frogs and insects were jamming in every octave with shrill buzzing and contrabass croaks. A brace of raccoons snuck along the side of the road seeking shelter. Wild pigs crossed the road headed toward higher ground.

Light from a three-quarter moon came on and went out as clouds scudded across its face.

As Bonnie approached the Vehicle Assembly Building, it stood out in monolithic relief against a graying sky. Kennedy Space Center security had opened the gates through State Road 3 and Bonnie passed four cars going north toward the safety of the mainland. The evacuation had begun.

Bonnie had to show her badge at the turnoff to the Vehicle Assembly Building. The parking lot was almost empty. NASA was already buttoned up for the storm. They had allowed non-critical employees to stay home and get ready to protect their families. Bonnie parked her car and entered the Vehicle Assembly Building. Eduardo met her at the entrance to High Bay 4.

"You just missed the action," said Eduardo.

"How's that?" asked Bonnie.

"One of our guys working the crane got his arm caught and broke his wrist?"

"Where is he now?"

"Thad is driving him to the hospital. Winona put a splint on his wrist. They really worked fast."

"Sounds like it was fortunate they were here." Bonnie spotted Winona sitting at a desk writing on a piece of paper. Bonnie walked over and sat across from her. "Eduardo here tells me you were a hero."

"I just put a temporary splint on the man's wrist," said Winona. "It needed to be x-rayed. I'm sure it was a multiple fracture. One of the NASA medical staff asked me to fill out this form."

"Where did Thad take him?"

"Cocoa, I think. That's probably closest."

"How did you sleep?"

Winona raised her head to look at Bonnie. Bonnie could see her eyes were a little bloodshot.

"So-so," said Winona. "There was a lot going on around us and those cots aren't too comfortable. I think Thad found a sofa on the third floor."

"You stayed down here?"

"I thought someone ought to look after our stuff. I heard the man scream when his arm got caught."

Eduardo had been listening in the corner. He motioned to Bonnie. "We've set up an area for transients," he said. "Let me show you where it is."

Bonnie followed Eduardo to the west low bay and up the stairs to the second floor. NASA had outfitted several rooms with cots and shelves.

"This one is for women," said Eduardo, walking into one of the rooms. "The one next door is for men. There are three rooms for families, bathrooms at each end of the hall, and a kitchenette in between."

"How many people can it accommodate?"

"Forty," answered Eduardo, "maybe fifty."

"That should be plenty," said Bonnie. "Most folks we'll just advise to stay put unless their dwelling is destroyed, or they're in imminent danger or injured."

"We've also stationed some of our heavy duty vehicles where you can use them. The crew rescue tanks can go anywhere and they are heavy enough to take a high wind. They are much like a SWAT carrier, or an armored car."

"How about fuel?"

"We've got plenty."

"Sounds like we're ready." Bonnie was still tired but her adrenaline was beginning to flow. She lay down on one of the cots and tried to relax.

CHAPTER 8

"Ever has it been that love knows not its own depth until the hour of separation."

Kahlil Gibran

Ladamien's plane landed at Aeroporto de Garulhos in Sao Paulo at 7:30 a.m. Monday EDT. He cleared customs and then called Aggie. She sounded over the phone as if she had a stuffy nose.

"Have you got a cold?" Ladamien asked.

"Yeth," said Aggie. "Just a little thummer thniffle."

"What're you doin' for it? Yu don' want it to turn into pneumonia."

"I'll be all right. How are you doing?"

"Fine. I'll be staying at the Monaco Convention Center and Hotel. I should be flying home tomorrow."

"I hope the storm doesn't hold you up."

"What storm?"

"Hurricane Dirk. It might be close to shore by the time you fly. They cancelled schools in the county

184

for today."

"I'll check with the airline. See what they say. Are you an' Simon gonna have to evacuate?"

"I'm not going to leave the house. We've got it all fixed up to withstand the storm and I need to rest and get rid of this cold."

"Alright, I guess you know best. You're on the scene." Ladamien glanced at his watch. "Look babe, love ya. Get some rest."

"Love you too. I will."

Ladamien hung up and hurried to catch a bus to the hotel. The hotel was only ten minutes from the airport, so Ladamien had time to check in and go down for breakfast. After he found a seat, a thin black man in a mudcloth Kofi hat came over to him.

"Mr. Upton?" the man asked.

Ladamien nodded firmly. He was curious and suspicious simultaneously. "Who are you?"

"Yusuf Zuberi at your service. May I join you?"

"Please. How did you recognize me?"

"Linebacker. American football. It wasn't difficult."

Ladamien looked around and chuckled. There was no one else in the restaurant that resembled him, in size or physique. "I guess not. And who are you Mr. Zuberi?"

"I am your buyer. We need a new airport in Tanzania."

"I didn't know Tanzania had any money."

"We have friends, friends with money."

Ladamien was getting an inkling of how the

money laundering worked. "What kind of airport and how much do you want to spend?"

Zuberi seemed to have the answers right in front of him. "A domestic airport," he said. "An international airport might attract the attention of the Financial Action Task Force."

"What is that?" asked Ladamien.

"It is a thirty-nation, policy-making group to combat money laundering and terrorist financing."

"I ain't worried about no policy-making group."

"Leroy said you might be naive. If they catch onto what we're doing, they'll destroy your business."

"What can they do?"

"Cut you off from the banks. Get Interpol on your case. Start making the connection to your gang's activities. You, Leroy, and I could end up in jail – or, dead."

It took a minute for this to sink in to Ladamien. Outwitting local officials or silencing petty crooks was one thing. Interpol, international banks – that was a different playing field.

"I can design and build a domestic airport for around $35 million US," said Ladamien. "How much you willing' to invest?"

"I think we can put in $200 million US for the airport and throw in another $15 million to pacify the African Development Bank Group," said Yusuf. "I don't think that will raise any eyebrows."

"The African Development Bank Group. I thought they were a big conservation and environmental group. How come they're interested?"

"It's a good citizen offer on our part. They'll help keep the heat off of us," said Yusuf.

"So," Ladamien summarized, "the Swamp Rattlers give you $215 million in gang money t' spend."

"That's right," said Mr. Zuberi, "and, I pay your company $200 million to build a $35 million airport in Tanzania. I further give the African Development Bank Group a charitable contribution of $15 million."

"That makes my gross profit for Upton Planning & Design about $165 million," said Ladamien. "Not bad. That'd be about $100 million after taxes, an' it's clean money."

"That's the idea," said Yusuf.

"Leroy comes away with $90 million in spendable cash and I keep around $10 million. Is that the way it works?"

"That's between you and Mr. Greene."

"That adds up quick if I can do it enough times. You sure it won't attract attention?"

"There's no guarantee. Just remember that you are running a legitimate business. If your customers are willing to accept a four hundred percent markup, that's just good business on your part."

"Ah guess. Just one question. Why'm I doin' a project in East Africa out of my South American branch?"

"The more we confuse the money track, the less chance we'll be detected." Yusuf scratched behind his left ear. "Just be sure none of your employees knows where the money comes from. Your financial officer is Leroy's man. The rest of your staff doesn't need to worry about money. Let them do the job they were hired to do."

Leroy glanced at his watch again. "Speaking of which, we're supposed to get together with them in fifteen minutes."

"I won't be there," said Yusuf. "Badro Erasto will represent my organization."

"What is your organization?"

"TZY Enterprises. It's a private company." Yusuf nodded and left.

Ladamien finished his breakfast and signed the room check. Ladamien was still dressed informally in his travel clothes, but he felt it was adequate for this meeting. He took the elevator to the third floor and entered the conference room. There were five others in the room. He only knew one of them.

Ladamien took a seat at the head of the table. "I'm Ladamien Upton, owner of Upton Planning & Design. Why don't we introduce ourselves?" He looked at the one woman at the table. "Why don't you go first ma'am?"

"I am Shu Lee, chief engineer, Upton Planning, & Design – Brazil."

Ladamien had known that his chief engineer in Brazil was a Chinese woman but he had never met her. "You sir?" Ladamien said, pointing to a dark skinned man sitting next to Shu.

The man wore a white Caribbean suit with an open dress shirt. "Tanase Duvalier, program director, airport design and construction."

The man next to Tanase spoke up without

prompting. "I am Badro Erasto, representing TZY Enterprises. I will be providing the specifications for building the airport. "

The man sitting next to Badro wore a dark blue suit and a dress shirt topped by a tie best described as presidential. He was strongly Hispânicos with dark wavy hair and dark brown eyes. "I am Antonio Medeiros, president of Upton Planning, & Design – Brazil." He nodded to Ladamien.

Ladamien knew Medeiros and trusted him. Ladamien glanced at the last man, a heavy-set man in a brown casual business suit.

"I'm Bruno," the man said with a recognizable mid-western accent. "Bruno Rococo, Chief Financial Officer."

"Of what?" Señor Medeiros inquired.

Bruno interlaced his fingers and looked haughtily at Medeiros. "Of everything," he said. "Of the whole shebang."

Ladamien immediately deduced the Chicago connection – Leroy's man. Probably an old acquaintance. He saw the bulge at the shoulder beneath the suit.

Bruno and Medeiros left the room. Ladamien and the others spent the next hour defining how to transmit and review specifications. When they finished, Ladamien called the airlines to see if he could get an earlier flight to the States. He was worried about Aggie and Simon.

***

At nine o'clock Monday morning, Bonnie received a call from Rusty.

"The governor has ordered a mandatory evacuation for the beaches," said Rusty. "That means we have to evacuate Cape Canaveral Hospital. I need your help."

"To take out the intensive care patients?"

"That's right. You and Kathie will accompany patients from Cape Canaveral and Dante and I will be on the receiving teams at Coreopsis Hospital. We're the only four experienced paramedics assigned to this station."

"What about Station #1, Gus and his crew?"

"We're handling two transfers and Gus' team is handling two transfers. Wuesthoff, Health First, and Parrish are handling all of the rest."

"Will I need to take a vehicle and a driver?"

"No, Health First will provide a special transporter and a driver. They just need an experienced EMT from our end."

"Okay. I'm on my way."

The rain started just as Bonnie turned off State Road 3 on to State Road 520. As she crossed Sykes Creek, the wind picked up and the shower pelted the driver's side of Bonnie's vehicle. The transfers would be difficult in this weather, but in ten hours or so, they would be next to impossible. Bonnie turned left into Cape Canaveral Medical Center and parked in the large structure next to the hospital.

Bonnie walked through the hospital to the quadrant where the emergency and trauma services were located. Dr. Hesbeth Kingsley, an anesthesiologist, met her in the trauma center.

"Who's the patient?" Bonnie asked.

"A special case," said Dr. Kingsley. "A baby with neonatal abstinence syndrome, methadone withdrawal. I was told you had some specialized training."

"A boy or a girl?" asked Bonnie.

"A boy, Thomas Samuel Gibson," said Dr. Kingsley, referring to a medical chart. "He's a week old and still experiences seizures. We'll have to monitor him closely. Fran Unkley will go with us."

Bonnie knew that Fran Unkley was a neonatal nurse specialist. Probably as expert as most doctors on the subject. "I'm honored," said Bonnie. "I've read some of her letters to the Journal of Neonatal Nursing. She's an authority."

"I agree," said Dr. Kingsley. "We're lucky to have her."

The trauma center bustled with medical personnel going in and out. Gurneys came down at the rate of about one every twenty minutes. Bonnie could hear the downpour turning into a driving rain. She pulled the foul weather gear from her EMT bag and put it on. Orderlies worked feverishly to clean and dry the floors. By the time they left for Coreopsis, the winds might reach tropical storm strength.

"They'd better start getting the regular patients out of here," said Bonnie.

Dr. Kingsley nodded. "I understand they have helicopters coming in already. It won't take long once they start." She motioned toward the door. "Here comes our little guy now."

Tommy, as Bonnie was already calling their

patient, was nestled in his Giraffe bed, used to protect and permit care for a premature newborn in the hospital's Neo-natal Intensive Care Unit. Bonnie almost cried thinking about the hardships this tiny person had already experienced in his first week of life. Get to work, she told herself. You're going to see a lot of suffering in the next few days.

Bonnie, Nurse Unkley, and Dr. Kingsley spent ten minutes going over a checklist and examining each connection and instrument of the Giraffe bed. A driver had backed the transportation vehicle into the loading area where it was relatively dry. The three of them loaded Tommy and his bed into the rear of the van. Unkley and Kingsley sat in the back and Bonnie slid into the jump seat.

The driver pulled out into the rain. Bonnie could see State Road 520 backed up into Cocoa Beach. The driver turned on the flashing lights and began weaving through traffic. They took the faster route back through Cocoa Beach and crossed State Road 528, coming out north of Cocoa. Interstate 95 going north still moved smoothly, so they arrived in Coreopsis shortly after lunchtime.

Dante and the Coreopsis neonatal team met them at the emergency entrance. Bonnie saw Rusty talking with Gus in the corner. She approached them.

"I left my car at Cape Canaveral," said Bonnie.

"Check out a city car," said Gus. "The administrators won't need them all for a while."

Bonnie drove the no-extras Ford Fusion across Kennedy Causeway and turned north to the Vehicle Assembly Building. The rain and wind were heavy but not blinding. In another three hours, Bonnie knew that the hurricane would set in and the winds would go up incrementally. From then on, none of them would get any sleep.

At the gate to the Vehicle Assembly Building, the guard spent more time than usual examining her badge. He came back with a special pass.

"Put that on your dashboard," the guard said. "Drive through the north entry door and park inside, next to your High Bay 4 area." He looked inside the passenger compartment. "Good luck, Ms. McConnell, it's going to be a long couple of days."

Bonnie nodded and drove in. She drove through the open door and watched it close behind her. She parked at High Bay 4 and Winona strolled out to meet her.

"Thad's out helping the Sheriff's office," said Winona, "in case they find some people that need assistance getting out."

Bonnie looked at Winona's young and serious features. She admired the dedication of youth – and the optimism.

"May I confess something to you?" Bonnie requested.

Winona nodded.

"I don't truly know what our role is in this crisis, but I think it's going to be quite clear to us as it happens."

"Sun Tzu wrote," said Winona, "In conflict, straightforward actions generally lead to engagement, surprising actions generally lead to victory."

"Meaning?"

"Perhaps we are the surprising action."

"Could be," said Bonnie. "Where is the conflict and what is victory?"

Winona just stared at Bonnie. "Look inside yourself," she said. "Anyone can see there is something you carry with you that isn't resolved."

Bonnie didn't argue with her.

***

Simon quickly found out that not going to school did not mean vacation. His mother did not feel well, but she wanted to be ready for the hurricane. Simon was putting the hurricane panels over the screens on the back porch when Aggie came out to help him.

"Did you find all of the fasteners?" Aggie asked.

"I'm missing one," said Simon, "but I left it off on the inside middle. I don't think the panel will come loose."

"Let me look." Aggie got down on her knees and examined the panel. "That'll hold," she said. "Help me up." Simon saw his mother lose her balance as he helped her up. She had been coughing since early afternoon and appeared pale.

"You'd better lie down, Mom. I know what to do."

"We'd better check the generator, and then I'll let you finish."

"How do we do that?"

"It's called back feeding. Come with me and I'll show you where the main breaker is located."

Simon followed his mother outside to the power meter.

"Okay," Aggie said. "Here goes." Aggie pulled

the main breaker handle down. "Now," she explained to Simon, "we don't have to worry about electrocuting anyone. If you ever have to do this, it's the first thing you do, always. Now we'll go to the inside breaker box."

Simon followed his mother into the utility room and watched her turn off all of the breakers.

"Do you know where the generator is, and the big cable that fits the plug into the house?"

"Yes ma'am. It's the 220 receptacle. Dad showed me."

"That's right. I'll go start the generator. When I tell you it's okay, you can plug in the cable. You can come watch me start the generator."

Aggie explained every step of bringing up the generator to Simon as she did it. "You might have to do this when I'm not here to help."

After the generator was running and hooked up, Simon and Aggie turned on breakers and made sure that the lights, refrigerator, stove, and pump all worked. They then reversed the process and disconnected the generator.

Aggie talked aloud to herself as she went over the preparations. Simon could tell she was struggling to stay alert and not get sick. "Shutters, water, yard, flashlights, first-aid kit…" Her voice tapered off and she arose and went back to her bedroom.

"I love you son," she said as she stood the entrance to her bedroom. "I just need some rest. " Aggie closed the door.

Simon went into the living room and turned on the television. Every station was broadcasting news about Hurricane Dirk. Evidently, Dirk was a little over a hundred and twenty miles off the Florida coast and gaining strength.

Mandatory evacuations were in effect for the beaches from Daytona to Jupiter. Various reporters talked from the beaches with their clothing blowing in the wind. The TV showed surfers taking advantage of the big breakers and riding the waves.

Simon quickly lost interest in the weather reports and looked for something more entertaining. He found a program on the SyFy channel call Scariest Places on Earth that looked interesting. He had just settled down with a cookie and some milk when the phone rang. He answered quickly so it wouldn't wake his mother.

"Hello, Upton residence."

"Simon, this is your father. Is your mother there?"

"She's sleeping. She has a cold."

"Wake her. I understand there's a storm coming that way and I want to make sure she's still okay."

"Okay. We spent the whole day getting ready. The shutters are up, the generator's ready. We got lots of water and canned goods."

"Get your mother. I want to talk to her."

Simon woke his mother. "Dad's on the phone. He wants to talk to you."

"Hello," said Aggie.

Simon watched his mother. She said, "I'm not feeling that bad. I would prefer to ride out the storm here. When will we see you?"

After a few moments, Aggie said goodbye and hung up. "Your father is coming home," she told Simon. "He got the last flight they think will be allowed to land in Orlando. He's going to drive home the north way. It's supposed to stay open."

"When will he get here?" Simon asked. I'll be happy to see him."

"I will too honey. He said real early tomorrow morning. Maybe five or six."

Simon went back to watching TV but quickly found out that the scariest places weren't truly that scary. He turned off the television and went to the front door. He could hear the wind and rain but couldn't tell how severe it was. After all, Florida often had heavy thunderstorms. He peeked out. The trees were blowing vigorously, and some brown palm fronds skittered along the street. He saw nothing remarkable in that.

Simon decided it was a good time to get out the model ship his father had given him for his birthday and see if he could assemble it. He cleared the dining room table and covered it with newspaper. He went to his room and got the box with the model in it. He opened it and read the instructions. All he needed was some model glue, which he had.

Before he started on the model, he cracked open his mother's bedroom door to check on her. She was lying on her stomach in a slip with the covers pulled up to the tops of her legs. He heard her wheezing and thought she might be having trouble breathing normally. He was careful not to wake her and pulled the door closed.

For the next several hours, the model completely

absorbed his attention.

**

Since the National Hurricane Center had issued the hurricane warning, most people in the area knew Hurricane Dirk was coming their way and they were making preparations. The news media were comparing Dirk to other devastating hurricanes – Hugo, Camille, Andrew, Ike, and Katrina. Of course, Dirk was its own animal, so comparisons were insignificant.

Hurricane Dirk was a model category-5 hurricane, with wind speeds of 175 miles per hour, a barometric pressure of 911 millibars, and an inner wall radius of 20 miles. Hurricane force winds extended out seventy-five miles to the north and forty miles to the south. There were tropical storm force winds as far as one hundred and thirty miles from the center.

The National Hurricane Center predicted that Hurricane Dirk would come ashore somewhere between New Smyrna Beach and Patrick Air Force Base as a category-5 hurricane but would lose strength rapidly as it came ashore. The center also forecast that Dirk would remain a hurricane as it crossed central Florida and eventually entered the Gulf, probably around Steinhatchee.

Rusty took only a few minutes to go over the technical details provided by the National Hurricane Center. Meteorology was not her concern. Her job was to make sure there were no casualties resulting from the storm. Even in that, her role was limited to Coreopsis, which was not going to be a major focus of the storm. The greater threat was to the coastal communities – Cape Canaveral, Cocoa Beach, Patrick Shores, Satellite Beach, and Eau Gallie. Even Bonnie's post at the Kennedy Space Center was somewhat removed from the main storm.

Rusty's crews had helped move some elderly people into shelters. Older people not experienced with hurricanes, mostly living in highly vulnerable mobile homes. Many of those would be gone after the storm. There had been several traffic incidents, minor injuries associated with poor driving conditions and overcrowded highways. Considering, it had been relatively quiet so far.

Rusty was having another doughnut and reviewing the shelter status when a man knocked on her office door.

"May I come in?" the man asked.

Rusty recognized Justin but was surprised to see him at the station, especially since the weather was foul. She wasn't busy enough to send him away. She figured he wanted to know about Bonnie.

"Come on in," she said. "Help yourself to some coffee and a fat pill."

Justin poured a half cup of coffee into a Styrofoam cup and picked out a doughnut with a napkin.

"You checkin' on your gal?" asked Rusty. "She's out at the Cape helpin' people get out of the storm, which is what you ought'a be doin' – gettin' out of the storm, that is."

"The last time I talked to her, she was back at our place. She said something about losing our baby."

Rusty was dumbfounded. "She never talked to

me about that."

"She said it had something to do with the baby being possessed."

"I wouldn't know about that."

"I didn't know what to do, so I did some research on the Native American chiefs. I found something that may help. I need to talk to Bonnie."

Rusty was determined to deal with one thing at a time. Right now, Dirk was her first priority. "Look, this whole thing will be over in a couple of days. Bonnie will be all right until then, and you can spend some time talkin' about it."

"You think I should just go home and wait."

"Yes," said Rusty.

"Well," said Justin, "I can't do that. I'm in love with Bonnie and she may be in considerable trouble out in that storm."

"You think this storm has something to do with her personally?"

"I know it does. It has to do with what I found out about Chief Ho-tah-lee, the chief of the wind, and his supposed daughter, Banna."

"Is it urgent?" Rusty asked. "Can't it wait until this hurricane passes?"

Justin shook his head. "That's the whole point. This storm is all about Bonnie, our daughter, Chief Ho-tah-lee and Banna. Bonnie could be in a lot of danger."

Rusty sighed. "Let's call her." She went to the radio communicator and set it for the correct channel. "Bonnie. Rusty. Go to seventeen."

"Bonnie here," Bonnie's voice came over the radio. "What's up?"

"Justin's here in my office. Where are you now?"

"I'm just heading out with the sheriff's department. Is there a problem?"

Justin moved closer to the radio. "I'm worried about you. I found out something about the chief of the wind and his daughter. It might help us."

"I don't have time to think about that right now," said Bonnie. "Can you come out to the VAB? We may get a chance to talk."

"Will the storm allow me to get out there?" Justin asked.

"It's still navigable," said Bonnie. "There's still time."

"I'll make arrangements for Justin to go out there," said Rusty.

"I've gotta go," said Bonnie. "See ya in the VAB."

"How long do I have?" Justin asked Rusty.

"The sooner you leave the better," said Rusty, "but you have at least eight hours before it becomes impossible to get out there."

"Thanks," said Justin. "I'm on my way."

Rusty watched Justin leave. She wondered what the spirits of an Indian chief and his daughter had to do with this storm.

***

The sheriff's office was in charge of coordinating a mandatory evacuation of the beaches and Merritt Island. Bonnie had decided that her crew could do the most good by going out in the field, being available to attend to, and transport residents who needed medical assistance.

Bonnie instructed Winona to stay in the Vehicle Assembly Building and deal with transients. She left Vince and the Coreopsis ambulance with Winona to move any disaster victims. The KSC Visitors Center provided two buses and drivers to take evacuees to shelters in North Brevard and South Volusia counties. Bonnie and Thad rode in two vehicles with drivers provided by Kennedy Space Center to support the evacuation of north Merritt Island.

Bonnie realized that most of their calls would be for medical evaluation and assistance with defining special needs for evacuation. Thad patrolled the east side of Merritt Island and Bonnie scouted the west side. They soon had a variety of evacuees with multiple health problems requiring special transport or assistance. Through the day, they dealt with patients on dialysis, others needing oxygen or respirators, and some with mobility difficulties. It soon became apparent they would work well into the night with the storm worsening.

Hurricane Dirk was just over 100 miles offshore, so the rain was constant and wind gusts of forty miles per hour hammered their vehicles. As Eduardo had promised, the heavy-duty transporters provided by the National Aeronautics and Space Administration were stable in the high winds and maneuvered well through the flooded streets. It was late Monday evening and Bonnie guessed the roads on Merritt Island would be impassable, even to these sturdy vehicles, by Tuesday evening.

Frequent lightning bolts brightened the sky with amusement park fireworks. A distant transformer erupted in blue flame; streetlights extinguished briefly and then came back on. Thad called Bonnie on the walkie-talkie.

"How much longer do you think we can stay out in this?" he asked.

"It's not that bad yet," answered Bonnie. "We need to stick with it until we're done. It'll be worse if we don't."

"Where's the hurricane? Do you know?"

"Yeah, I've been talking to Rusty. The National Hurricane Center expects the eye wall to come into Cape Canaveral in about twenty-eight hours, around one a.m. Wednesday morning."

"But we'll experience hurricane-force winds before that, right?"

"Probably by tomorrow afternoon. It'll be a category five when it comes on shore."

"Look," said Thad, "I'm loaded. Gonna head back to the Vehicle Assembly Building and drop everybody off."

"Okay. Call me when you get back." Bonnie hung up and motioned to the driver. "Go up in there, on Wind-chime Road. One of the deputies said there was an older couple at the end of this road. We'll check on them."

Bonnie opened the window between the front and the back and spoke to the other two passengers in the rear. "We have to pick up an elderly couple and then we'll take all of you to catch a bus to a shelter." She did not wait for a reply.

The driver maneuvered skillfully around mud holes and ruts on the side road. The end of the street was unpaved. Up a narrow lane, Bonnie saw the small bungalow that the deputy had described. She pulled her foul weather gear around her and walked up the path to the front door. She opened the screen and knocked on the wooden door. A thin old man with obvious osteoporosis answered her knock.

"Mister Iverson," Bonnie said, "are you all right"

The hunch-backed man lifted his face to Bonnie. "Can I help you?" he asked.

"Mister Iverson, there's a hurricane coming. You need to evacuate. Do you need help – a ride?"

Bonnie saw that the man seemed confused.

"My wife," he said, "she's in the back. She's sleeping."

"We need to get you both out of here," said Bonnie. "This house won't be safe once the storm gets here."

The man appeared to think about this. Finally, he spoke. "We'll go with you. You'll have to help my wife. Her name is Pat."

"We'll get the van up here. Does she need a stretcher?"

"No, she can walk. Can you keep her dry? It looks mighty wet out there."

Bonnie stepped off the stoop and signaled the driver to bring the motor vehicle up closer. She watched as he turned the van around and backed up to the front door. Bonnie went to the vehicle and opened the back. She retrieved two ponchos from under the seat. She took the ponchos and stepped into the small house.

"Show me your wife and we'll figure out what we have to do to get her into the van," she told Mr. Iverson.

The old man led Bonnie to a small bedroom in the back. She saw an elderly woman dozing on a double bed. "I'm going to wake her," she said to Mr. Iverson. "Is that okay?"

Iverson nodded. "Let me do it." He leaned over his wife and whispered into her ear.

Pat Iverson opened her eyes and looked at Bonnie. She sat up slowly. "I need to pack," she said. "We'll need a few things."

"I'll help you," said Bonnie.

Bonnie assisted Mrs. Iverson in packing a small suitcase with clothes, medicine, and sundries. When they were done, she had the two elderly people put on their ponchos and led them to the van.

"This is four," she said to the driver. "We'll take them to the Vehicle Assembly Building and catch dinner while we're there."

On the way, Bonnie called Rusty.

"Is Justin on his way to the VAB?" she asked.

"He left here a couple of hours ago," said Rusty. "He should already be there."

"Okay," said Bonnie. "That's fine. I think we're doing the right thing."

"I estimate you have until about 14:00 tomorrow to continue assisting with the evacuation," said Rusty. "Then, we'll have to pull the plug on staying out in this. You'll start getting sixty-mile gusts about then."

"I think we'll be done by then."

"Good."

Bonnie looked out the windshield as they drove onto the center. She could barely see the road. Every few seconds, a frog would leap across the road in front of them. Each amphibian gleamed like a bouncing white streak in the headlights.

***

Ladamien took a charter from Miami to Orlando and his plane landed at five o'clock in the morning. He was traveling light and the line at customs was unusually short, so he cleared through and rented a car in short order. On the drive east on State Road 528 – the Beach-Line – to Merritt Island, Ladamien noted the crowded highway headed west and the empty lanes going east. The state had discontinued tolls on the road, so Ladamien managed a quick pace going home.

Where Ladamien crossed the St. Johns River, the wind began to gust and the rain increased. Driving into the sunrise, he saw the hurricane sky over the ocean. Clabbered gray clouds moved menacingly from north to south interspersed with glimpses into a mauve-colored sky morphing to lilac overhead. Ladamien kept his eyes on the road and his hands gripped the steering wheel tightly as he kept the car on the road against the steady crosswind and the frequent gales.

As Ladamien came to the intersection of State Road 528 with US-1, he saw a blockade ahead with a sheriff's car flashing its red lights. He stopped and a deputy, wearing a flapping raincoat and a full-brimmed hat came toward him. Reluctantly,

Ladamien rolled down his window, even though the rain came from that side.

"What is it officer?" he asked.

"Can't go any farther," the officer said. "Mandatory evacuation."

"Can I go north?"

"Yep. Just can't go across the bridge."

Ladamien closed his window and turned onto US-1. He thought that perhaps he could cross over the Indian River at the NASA Causeway. He was driving into the rainstorm now and it limited his vision more than before. The traffic going north was heavy, so he had to stop and wait periodically.

As Ladamien went through Port St. John, sheriff's deputies were out directing traffic. He approached the NASA causeway and saw that the police had it blocked it off as well. After driving through Titusville, he decided to try the north road to Playalinda Beach and see if he could turn south on State Road 3. He was pleased to see that the SR-3 was open and he drove south until he came to the entrance gate to the Kennedy Space Center. The guard stopped him at the gate.

"Where are you going?" asked the guard.

"My family's on Merritt Island. I've got to get them out."

"Can't your wife drive out?"

"I talked to my son. I think my wife may be a lot sicker than she believed at first."

"There's a medical contingent in the VAB. I'll let you through and call ahead to the guard at the VAB gate. See him and he'll let you talk to the medics."

Ladamien wanted to drive through and go directly to his house. He realized, however, that crossing the authorities would just delay getting help. He drove to the VAB gate and parked outside. He walked to the gate. The wind was blowing strongly. It pushed him around as he walked.

"The guard down there said you could help me," Ladamien said to the guard at the VAB gate.

"Yeah, he said that your wife and son are on the island and you want to go get them."

"Yes, my wife is sick and my son is just nine years old."

"I'll get the medic out here. She can take you into the VAB and you can talk to her."

"All right."

Ladamien waited while the guard talked on the phone. After ten minutes, he saw a thin young brunette woman in foul weather gear leaning into the wind and laboring to the gate.

"Hi," the young woman said, "I'm Winona. Let's go inside."

"Ladamien. I'll follow you."

The wind was pushing them, so Ladamien and Winona half-ran to the VAB door. When they were inside, Ladamien followed her to the southwest corner of the building. Winona threw him a towel.

"Here," she said, "dry off."

Ladamien was thankful for the chance to get the water off his face and wipe off his arms and hands. "Thanks," he said.

"We've had units out all night," said Winona. "I

haven't heard any report on a sick woman and a boy."

"We're kind of isolated, out at the end of Kangaroo Lane. Your teams might not find it."

"That's possible. Kangaroo is about at the end of the cautionary zone. Let me call Bonnie."

Ladamien watched Winona fetch a walkie-talkie.

"What's your address?" asked Winona.

"1145. 1145 Kangaroo Lane."

"Okay, Bonnie's already on her way in. She will take you with her to check it out. She'll be here in twenty minutes."

"What am I supposed to do in the meantime?"

"There's a transient room on the second floor. You can have a cup of coffee or a soft drink. Maybe, some chips or a cookie. Bonnie asked me to put together a medical kit, in case you are stuck out there. The wind is up to 65 miles per hour."

"Can I drive and follow her?"

"No. We have a special vehicle, the Avenger. We will have someone drive you out on the carrier and then you and Bonnie will go in on the Avenger. She says the water is already two feet deep on Kangaroo."

"God. It may already be in the house."

"That's right. Let me find someone to walk you up to the coffee pot."

Ladamien followed a young man Winona directed him to, and helped himself to a cup of coffee and a muffin after they arrived at the transient room. He would have preferred to handle this situation alone, but he knew the county and NASA –

NASA for Heaven's sake – would have better equipment and trained personnel. The storm was strengthening even as they waited.

It was only twenty-five minutes, but to Ladamien it seemed like hours before Winona came to the door of the transient room and motioned for Ladamien to follow her. They returned to the medical staging area. An athletic-looking woman in a paramedic uniform met Ladamien as he walked into the area. She approached him and held out her hand.

"I'm Bonnie McConnell. I'm in charge here. I'm taking you with me because it may help put your wife at ease if you are with me. I trained to drive the amphibious vehicle we're taking to your house. What's your name?"

"Ladamien Upton. I own an engineering company."

As Ladamien watched, Bonnie smiled and lifted her eyebrows. "I met your son," she said.

Ladamien was astonished. "How did you meet my son?"

"He was out fishing, with a friend. We saw an alligator."

Ladamien chuckled. "You were the medical lady. I'll be damned."

Winona brought Ladamien a pair of waterproof pants and a zip up rain parka. "Put these on," she said. "They were the largest I could find."

Ladamien put on the rain gear. It fit pretty well considering his size. "This is fine." He watched Bonnie stow the waterproof case with the medical supplies in the Avenger.

"We'll leave in a moment," said Bonnie. "I need to talk to my fiancé."

***

Bonnie walked back to the room where Justin was waiting. "I have to go back out," she said. "There's a man out there who believes his wife and son are in danger. What's this about the chief's daughter?"

"Banna," said Justin. "She's not really the chief's daughter. He found her and adopted her, but long before the later tribes occupied Florida. She was a queen. Queen of the ancient tribes, the old ones."

"So how is she holding the spirits of the tribes here? Why can't they leave?"

"She doesn't want them to leave. Apparently she has the power to keep them here."

"And," Bonnie was pondering the consequences, "the chief is coming here to convince her spirit to release the others and go on to the great ecstasy. What happens to our daughter's soul?"

"If Banna's spirit stays, she will possess our daughter all of her life. If she leaves, our daughter's soul will be free and her spirit will be her own."

"I want to meet the chief," said Bonnie. "I want to talk to Banna's spirit. They're coming and I'm ready to fight for our daughter's soul."

"I want to help," said Justin.

"You have. Just be here when I get back."

"Couldn't I go with you?"

Bonnie kissed Justin, "You stay here and help Winona. Our vehicle can only carry four people.

We'll need the room to transport the patient."

Bonnie turned and went to the carrier truck where Vince was waiting. "Let's go," she said to Vince as she seated herself in the front passenger seat.

***

Ladamien sat in the back seat of the carrier truck. Before he stepped into the truck, he had seen the small amphibious vehicle on the trailer. He didn't recognize the truck driver or the other medic. Thad climbed into the rear of the carrier vehicle cab. Bonnie sat up front with Vince.

"This is Vince," Bonnie said, pointing to the driver, "and Thad. Vince, Thad, this is Mr. Upton – Ladamien."

Vince grunted and started the truck.

"There is a gas station with a garage right behind Ladamien's house," Bonnie was telling Vince. "We'll park the carrier there and take the Avenger to the house."

"Can we park inside the garage?" asked Vince. "Is it sturdy enough to survive the hurricane?"

"We can park inside," answered Bonnie. "I called the owner. I think the carrier will be safe."

"I know the station," said Ladamien. "The front roof will probably blow away but the main building will hold."

"Have you ever been in a category five hurricane, Mr. Upton?" asked Bonnie.

"Felix, on the Mosquito Coast, in 2007."

"Then, you know what we're up against."

"Better than most folks," said Ladamien. "That's why I'm so worried about my Aggie, and my boy, Simon."

"I'm sure you are, Mr. Upton. We'll get them out safely."

Ladamien looked out the side of the cab just in time to see lightning split a large oak in two. A second later, a loud thunderclap shook the truck.

CHAPTER 9

"Life is either a great adventure or nothing."

Helen Keller

"Where have you been?" Bonnie asked Ladamien. "It seems like you've been out of touch."

"I was down in Sao Paulo on business."

"Brazil? Tell me about your business"

"I own a company that builds airports and terminals. It's an international business."

"That must be exciting. Your son seemed mature for his age."

"Simon is a smart boy. Aggie and I are real proud of him."

"Did you get any idea from Simon what's wrong with your wife?"

"I talked with her earlier and she had something like a cold. Simon said she had headaches, was sick to her stomach, and finally went to bed. I had him wake her up because I thought she might need to call 911. She said she felt better and didn't want to evacuate."

"That wasn't a good decision," said Bonnie. "We

would have helped her get off the island."

Bonnie continued, "Maybe what she has is not serious. I brought everything I could think of to treat almost anything. Usually, oxygen, a saline IV, nutrients, and antibiotics will assure survival even with a serious illness. Dehydration or pulmonary failure can kill anyone."

Bonnie saw the worried look on Ladamien's face. "I didn't mean to scare you," she said. "I was trying to let you know we're prepared for anything."

"I understand," said Ladamien. "It's just that I do business in many underdeveloped nations, and I've watched people die of disease. I hate to think of Aggie being seriously sick."

"I doubt it's anything like you've seen in those countries, but we won't take any chances. Okay?"

"Yeah, okay."

Bonnie could tell Vince was fighting the wind, the road, and the water. Fortunately, there was no traffic on the road anymore. Those that were getting out had gotten out. All others had barricaded against the storm and holed in for the duration. The sky was a gray soup that extended upward from the ground into a heavenly abyss. It was dark enough that the street lights had turned on automatically, fooled into thinking night had come. Soon, power outages would extinguish even these mindless sentinels.

Vince pulled the flatbed into the service station on Courtenay Parkway. The owner was waiting for them.

"I thought you might not get here," said the owner. He went to the garage door and opened it.

"You can back right in there."

"We.ve got to take the Avenger off first," said Vince.

It took them twenty minutes to unload the Avenger and back the flatbed into the garage. Vince walked around the station. "I'm going to stay with the truck," he said. "This building will stay up."

"Fine," said Bonnie. "We'll stay in touch. She climbed into the Avenger and started the engine. Thad and Ladamien climbed aboard with her. "What's the best way to your place?" she asked Ladamien.

"Will this thing float?" asked Ladamien. The wind muffled his voice.

Bonnie yelled into the wind. "Yes. It's totally amphibious."

"Go behind the station," said Ladamien. "Head through those pine trees. There should be enough room to work our way through to the house. I have a key if Simon doesn't hear us."

Bonnie drove the Avenger around the station and off the concrete into the long grass. The wind was coming from her right side and had definitely gained strength. It had broken several large branches from the pines, and Bonnie had to detour around two of the larger ones. When she turned into the wind, the Avenger strained to move forward.

She shouted to Thad. "There're a couple of poles in those side clips. You and Ladamien push us off the trees if it looks like we're going to hit them. We don't want to get wedged in here."

The Avenger had a compass on the dash, so

Bonnie kept going west as well as she could. Visibility was poor and the stands of pines all looked alike. The Avenger alternated between floating and grabbing traction. Whenever she felt the tires take hold, she gunned west and made as much distance as she could. Finally, she saw the silhouette of a house appear out of the mist. A lake of roiling water separated them from the residence.

Bonnie looked back at Ladamien. "Is that your house?"

Ladamien waved his arm forward. "We're across the street, and farther south. We must have been going northwest."

Bonnie went around the house on the left side and looked for the road. The Avenger was more boat than truck all the way to the street – which was likewise more stream than road; however, the tires grabbed and Bonnie turned left onto Kangaroo Lane. The wind was pushing the Avenger now, so they picked up speed.

"You'll see my house in a minute," said Ladamien, "on the right. We can get to the front door."

Blue flashes lit up the horizon and the few streetlights on Kangaroo Lane went out. "There goes the electricity," said Thad.

"We have a generator," said Ladamien. "I don't know if Simon knows how to work it or not."

"Is that your house?" asked Bonnie, pointing to a shape in the distance.

"That's it," said Ladamien

As she maneuvered the Avenger toward the front

door, Bonnie saw a light appear in one of the windows. She pointed it out to Ladamien. "That answers that," she said. "Simon's on the ball."

Ladamien didn't answer. Bonnie watched him jump out of the Avenger and wade to the front door. Even over the wind, she could hear him knocking on the door. She saw it open and recognized Simon. Simon jumped into his father's arms. He must have been scared to death, Bonnie thought. *I'm glad I brought his father with us.*

"Carry the medical supplies inside," she said to Thad. "I'll park the Avenger in a safe place."

Thad hopped out of the Avenger and pulled out the bag containing the medical supplies. Bonnie knew the bag was heavy, but Thad carried it easily and slogged to the front door. Ladamien opened it for him. Bonnie parked the Avenger in a protected nook on the east side of the house. The water wasn't so high on that side. She retrieved the remainder of the medical supplies and plodded around the corner to the front door. When she came inside, Thad handed her a towel.

"If you want to change," said Thad, "Ladamien says he has some clean exercise outfits that would probably fit us."

Bonnie had removed her foul weather gear and was wiping off with the towel. "You go ahead," she said, "I want to check the patient."

"Where is your mother?" Bonnie asked Simon.

Simon looked at her. "You're the medical lady," he said. "The pear medic." He motioned her to follow him and led her down a hall to an open bedroom door. Ladamien was kneeling next to a half-naked white woman who was lying face down on the bed.

Bonnie could see that the woman had trouble breathing. She heard Aggie cough, softly but wetly. "Is she talking?" Bonnie asked Ladamien.

Ladamien turned his face to Bonnie. There were tears in his eyes. "I think she's delirious," he said. "She asked me if I'd seen Diesel."

"Who is Diesel?"

""Diesel was a cat Aggie had when she was young."

"Would you mind leaving the room while I examine her?" Bonnie saw disappointment cross Ladamien's face. "I know you want to be here, but I'll be able to work better alone. Please, ask Thad to bring me the medical kit."

Bonnie didn't know exactly what Aggie had, but she had some ideas. She stopped Ladamien before he left the room. "Did your wife travel out of the country recently?"

"We went to Jamaica. I had to leave, but she stayed behind to take photographs."

"What kinds of photographs?"

"Birds, jungle birds."

"I won't be long. Ask Thad to bring the kit. Tell him we'll need the oxygen and he'll have to help me set up an IV."

Ladamien left the room and closed the door behind him.

***

Bonnie cleaned Aggie and positioned her in the

bed so she would be comfortable with the peripheral intravenous cannula and oxygen nasal cannula connected. She and Thad got a simple saline IV drip and an oxygen flow going and then Bonnie fetched Ladamien and Simon.

"I laid out some clothes for you," said Ladamien. "In the back bedroom."

"I know," said Bonnie. "Thad told me. You can sit here with Aggie. Don't expect anything, but if she gets hydrated and oxygenated, she may wake up a little."

"Thank you," said Ladamien

"In the meantime," said Bonnie, "I'm going to talk with a doctor. Do you have a phone?"

"I'll show you," Simon said.

Bonnie preferred to talk directly with an internist, so she dialed the Coreopsis Medical Center. Beverly, a receptionist that Bonnie knew, answered.

"Beverly," said Bonnie, "This is Bonnie. I have a patient out here in the storm with symptoms of a viral disease, perhaps a Hantavirus or something similar. I need to talk to an internist."

"Dr. Nieves is here. I will see if I can locate him. Are you on a house phone? I don't recognize the number."

"Yes. We're out on Merritt Island. I didn't want to tie up the official communication links. I figure they're busy."

"Can Dr. Nieves call you back on this line?"

"Sure, that's fine."

Bonnie called Vince on the walkie-talkie. "How

ya doin' out there?"

"I'm comfortable," said Vince. "How's the patient?"

"She has a viral infection with pulmonary involvement. We're going to have to get her to the hospital as soon as we can."

"That's not going to happen for a while. There are probably hurricane force winds out there right now and it's just beginning. I've been listening to the radio in the truck and the eye wall is still several hours away."

"How's the outside world holding up?"

"They don't know. At least the evacuation seems to have gone well."

"That's good. Hopefully, we won't have any fatalities."

"You never know. Good luck with your patient."

Bonnie took advantage of the short break to strip, dry her body, slip on the dry clothes that Ladamien had laid out, and call Justin. She used her cell phone, hoping to get through and keep the conversation short. Justin answered after four rings.

"Where are you?" Justin asked.

"I'm in a house on North Merritt Island. The woman here is quite sick. I think she picked up a virus in the tropics."

"Are you in danger? Is it catching?"

"I'm fine. It's probably not contagious, but we're being cautious. How are things there?"

"We've stayed busy, especially with the kids. A lot of families didn't get out until late. They're actually a lot of fun."

"Enjoy yourself. I think we're pretty much socked in for the duration now."

"Well, you be careful. I can't help worrying about you."

"Oh. How do you like the name Crystal for our daughter?"

"I like it."

"Good. I'll call again later. Love ya."

"Love you, too."

Bonnie clicked off. It felt good to get rid of the wet apparel. She had barely finished talking to Justin when the house phone rang. Bonnie answered it. It was Dr. Nieves. She explained Aggie's symptoms and the steps she had taken so far to care for her.

"You have only a cannula inserted for the oxygen?" asked Dr. Nieves.

"Yes," answered Bonnie. "Should we intubate?"

"Yes, if you have the equipment. That way, we will know the airways stay open. We want to prevent pulmonary edema."

"We can do an intubation. Do you think the virus is contagious?"

"Probably not, but until we can get a lab analysis and find out exactly what the patient has, we had better treat it as if it were. Pneumonic plague has similar symptoms, but it's not likely. I'll notify the Centers for Disease Control that we have something but can't pinpoint it yet."

"Good. I was concerned about that. We don't have any provisions for quarantine here."

Dr. Nieves sniggered. "I guess the hurricane takes care of that. Just limit contact with the patient as much as possible. Wear facemasks. I would guess your choices are limited."

"Definitely. Her family is here with us."

"Bring her directly to the hospital when you can," said Dr. Nieves. "I'll make sure we are ready for her in intensive care."

"Thank you, doctor," Bonnie said. "You've been very helpful."

Bonnie went back into the bedroom with Ladamien and Simon. Ladamien was holding Aggie's hand.

"Has she awakened at all?" Bonnie inquired.

Ladamien shook his head.

"I talked to the doctor," said Bonnie. "He wants me to do a procedure called intubation that will help her breath better. It would be best if you and Simon left the room while we perform it."

Ladamien nodded and released Aggie's hand. He went over to Simon. "Let's go finish that model of yours," he said to Simon. "It'll take our minds off the storm."

"Before you leave," said Bonnie, "there's some possibility that what Aggie has is contagious. You and Simon should avoid unnecessary contact with her."

Ladamien glowered at Bonnie. Bonnie could only imagine what words were going through his mind.

"I'll consider myself warned," said Ladamien.

What can I say? Bonnie thought. *I would have gladly died to save Walter or Timmy. I know how this man feels.*

Ladamien and Simon left the room. Bonnie went to find Thad.

"Do you know how to do an intubation?" she asked Thad after she located him.

"We practiced," he said, "on dummies."

Thad brought in the medical bag and retrieved a laryngoscope while Bonnie positioned Aggie's head, took off the cannula, and started suction. She lubricated the tubing and inserted the laryngoscope. She then inserted the tubing and checked the airflow to Aggie's lungs. She and Thad secured Aggie to the bed.

"Much better," Bonnie said to Thad. "Maybe she'll be responsive in a few minutes. I don't think she suffered any brain damage."

Aggie's color seemed to improve and Bonnie could see she was coming around. Aggie's eyes fluttered and half-opened. She tried to move against the restraints and made a burbling sound. Bonnie could see Aggie's eyes taking in the scene.

"Wha' happen'?" Aggie said softly.

"You are very sick," said Bonnie. "I'm a paramedic, here to help you."

"'s Simon okay? Does know 'm sick?" Aggie struggled to speak around the tubing.

"He's been taking care of you. He's fine. He's in the other room. He'll be glad to know you're better. Your husband is with him."

"'s all right." Aggie closed her eyes and appeared to relax. Bonnie left her to sleep and motioned to Thad that he should stay to keep an eye on her. Bonnie crept from the room and closed the door behind her. She found Ladamien and Simon in the kitchen working on the model.

"Your wife," she said to Ladamien, and then looking at Simon, "Your mother, she's a very sick woman. She needs to be in intensive care and we need an ambulance to take her there. With this storm, that may not happen for several hours, even days."

Ladamien interrupted as if Bonnie was telling him something he did not want to hear. "You've got that super vehicle out there. Why don't we just take her to the hospital?"

"It's already a hurricane out there and it's going to get worse. We'd never make it."

Even inside the house, Bonnie could hear the storm tearing at the trees and hurling objects around. She knew the others could hear it too. She watched Ladamien bite his lower lip and nod.

"Have you been listening to the radio? What do they say?"

"The eye-wall will come over the coast through Cape Canaveral at 10:30 p.m., and the winds are up to 185 miles per hour. The eye should cross over Merritt Island at 2:00 a.m."

"Do me a big favor," said Bonnie. "Go get Thad and bring the rest of the supplies in from the Avenger before the storm becomes so bad we can't get out there."

"What kinds of supplies," asked Ladamien?

"There's a portable aspirator, some different IV packages, more oxygen bottles, and so forth. Thad will know what we might need."

"Wanna help me son?" Ladamien asked Simon.

Bonnie thought about stopping Ladamien from taking Simon with him but realized this kind of reassurance was exactly what Simon probably needed.

"Stay safe," she said, "and, don't stay out too long."

***

Simon sensed that he would be able to stay up as long as he wanted. He had never stayed awake the whole night through, so the prospect of watching the clock creep past midnight and seeing the sun come up out of the night thrilled him. He was worried about his mother, but the medical lady seemed to know what she was doing, so he figured it would be okay. He liked helping his father and being responsible. They had almost finished the model but Simon had another one stashed away in his room, so he and his Dad would have something to occupy them during the hurricane.

"We'd better refill the generator tank while we're out here," said Ladamien.

They had gone out through the side door to get to the Avenger because the house partially blocked the wind. Simon could see that the wind had toppled a sand pine in the woods next door and it had fallen across a bunch of wires. They probably would not have electricity for several days. It was remarkable that the telephone still worked.

Simon asked his father, "Can I help?"

"The diesel can is too heavy and the wind is too strong," said Ladamien. "You'd better let Thad help me."

"Okay," said Thad, "but then we have to get the

stuff from the Avenger. We may have to make two trips."

They walked in single file with Ladamien in front and Simon sandwiched between his father and the medic. Simon was more than knee high in the water, and he had to use his hands under his legs occasionally to keep his balance in the wind. It would be difficult to carry much and not slip or fall.

It took a long time to fill the generator tank and return everything to where it belonged. The three of them struggled to the Avenger and opened the stowage lockers. Thad handed Simon a canvas duffle bag. "Try and keep it out of the water as much as possible," Thad told Simon.

The bag was heavy and the wind caught it and pulled Simon along with it. Simon guessed it was like rigging the sails on an old-fashioned sailing ship in a storm at sea. He pretended he was carrying the sail up the mast and preparing to unfurl it into the wind. "Pirates on the horizon," he shouted. "Prepare to come about." Somehow, make-believe made the task easier. He lost track of his father and Thad in the storm and plodded to the side door. The wind was shifting and the rain stung the back of his neck. When he opened the side door, the wind slammed it open. Simon stepped through and dropped the bag on the garage floor. Thad followed him through and pointed at the duffel.

"Don't let that bag sit in the water," Thad said.

Simon had not even noticed that the water had flowed onto the garage floor, and was now about two inches deep.

"If it keeps this up," Simon said as he lifted the

duffel off the floor, "it'll be in the house by morning."

"That's likely," said Thad. "This is a low area."

Ladamien came in last and pulled the door closed. "It's getting windier out there," he said. "Is this all of it?"

"We'll have to ask Bonnie," said Thad. "She's in charge. How much do you think it will flood here?"

"It may go up another foot," said Ladamien, "and then it should start draining to the west. The garage will flood, but I don't think it will come into the house."

Simon carried the duffel into the house. The medical lady saw him and pointed toward the living room. "I've covered the carpet with plastic," she said. "Lay the stuff down there so I can go through it."

Simon hefted the bag, carried it through the kitchen and dining room, and deposited it on the plastic in the living room. He undid the tie at the top and peeked into the duffel. Inside were things he recognized, like syringes and bandages, and others with which he was not familiar. He decided it was best not to take anything out of the container until the medical lady was there to direct him.

He walked back to the kitchen. "Is your name Bonnie?

"Yes. Bonnie McConnell.

"May I call you Miss McConnell?"

"You may call me Bonnie. I don't believe in being formal."

"I saw one of those chiefs when you weren't there. He was an alligator, and then he was an Indian, and told me to, 'Behold the daughter of the wind' I saw her – briefly."

Bonnie left the stove and sat down at the small table. "What did she look like?"

"She was in the sky, all silver, and gold, dancing and twirling. I think she was a ghost or something."

"Anything else?"

"She wasn't wearing any clothes, just a gown you could see through. Oh, and the Indian said he was a chief."

"Did you tell your mother?"

"Nah, she wouldn't believe me."

"Thank you for telling me." Bonnie went back to the stove and stirred something in a small pot. Thad and Simon's father carried the other items retrieved from the Avenger through the kitchen and into the living room. Simon heard a loud thunderclap. It rattled the dishes in the cupboard above Simon's head.

Simon was relieved that Bonnie had not questioned him more about the chief and had not seemed surprised by what he told her. Whatever secrets she had, these strange occurrences failed to upset her. She had promised to introduce him to a witch. He was eager to have her fulfill that promise. He wanted to look out at the storm, but they had closed the shutters on all of the windows. He felt tired, so he went back to his room, took off his wet clothes, put on his pajamas, lay down on his bed, and went to sleep.

***

The first hurricane force waves from Hurricane

Dirk began crossing the Florida coastline at 6:00 p.m. on Tuesday. Rusty felt that her station was ready for the storm – prepared for the worst it could deliver. Her confidence was not bravado. She had been there when Katrina struck New Orleans and knew it would not be easy.

This time, however, the state and federal governments recognized their roles and started early preparations. The citizens recognized the danger and responded by evacuating or boarding up. Everyone was as ready as could be expected.

The west side of Coreopsis was not as threatened as other areas of the county. It was not directly on the coast, nor was it as populated as Melbourne or Palm Bay. While the St. Johns River flood plain presented problems, very few people lived on the lowest areas. Many large trees in Coreopsis had never experienced hurricanes or been trimmed to withstand high winds. That concerned Rusty. They would probably cause a great deal of damage and perhaps some medical emergencies. She did not want to send one of her crews out in the tempest, but the occasion would almost certainly happen.

It did not take long. The call came in at 6:15. Rusty listened in as Kathie and Dante responded to the alarm. Doug Forsythe, her fire chief came into her office.

"I saw Kathie go out on a call. What's the emergency?"

"There was a tornado out near Whiskey Lane," said Rusty. "It went through a trailer park and apparently two people hadn't evacuated."

"Worst place to be," said Doug. "Who's driving

the ambulance? Not Dante."

"No," answered Rusty. "One of the temps from Gainesville. Gus thought that would be the best way to use him. Young fellow named Burgess."

"Last name or first?"

"No, that's his given name. People name their kids all kinds of things nowadays." Rusty looked over her journal. "I see you've been out a few times already today."

"Mostly traffic. One lightning fire. It'll get worse as the hurricane gets here."

"I don't like to think that's true, but I know it will get worse. Hundred and eighty-five. That's one hell of a wind."

"Could be worst ever."

"Not quite, but close. It'll go down in the books." Rusty heard Kathie's voice on their side channel.

"Hey boss," said Kathie. "You there?"

"Yeah," said Rusty. "What's the scoop?"

"We got two, a man, and a woman. He's okay, but she has a head injury. We're transporting to emergency."

"Okay. Let me know when you're on your way back."

"The storm has only begun," said Doug. "It could be a long night."

Rusty nodded and watched Doug leave the room.

**

Bonnie checked on Aggie every half hour. She sensed that the congestion in her patient's lungs had reached critical levels. Aggie's blood oxygen level was under ninety percent, indicating hypoxemia – Bonnie could not determine exactly how severe. She considered calling Dr. Nieves, but decided there was nothing he could suggest she did not know. She understood they had to get Aggie to intensive care as soon as possible.

The wind, rain, and lightning continued to increase by the minute. It came in waves, separated by about fifteen minutes. Bonnie comprehended that these were the bands of the hurricane coming across. Occasionally, she heard a loud thump as the wind tore something loose and propelled it against the side or roof of the house. Bonnie imagined it was a war zone outside the shutters.

Thad came into the room. "How's she doing?" he asked.

Bonnie shook her head and buried her face in her hands. "We might be losing her, her blood oxygen levels keep dropping."

"Any ideas?

"Yes, but we don't have the equipment for extracorporeal membrane oxygenation, or lowering her metabolism. She should be in intensive care."

"How about nutrients?"

"She's getting enough as long as she's inactive. It's her lungs, whatever she has, it's causing severe bronchitis."

"What about antibiotics?"

"I asked Dr. Nieves about that. He said it would just be a guessing game without knowing what she has."

"I guess keeping her on oxygen is the best we can

do."

"I'll call Dr. Nieves and ask. It can't do any harm."

Bonnie tried to use the house phone and found it was not working anymore. She called the hospital on her cell phone. The central desk answered her call.

"This is Bonnie McConnell. I'm a paramedic at station 2. I need to talk with Dr. Nieves."

"I think he left the hospital. It's been pretty hectic here, so I'm not sure."

"I need his phone number. I'm in the storm and I have a patient. He helped me earlier."

"I have your number. I'll find him and have him call you."

"That's fine. Tell him I'm afraid we might be losing his patient." Bonnie hung up, and went to the door. "Keep an eye on her," she told Thad, and left the room.

Bonnie found Ladamien in the kitchen. He had an open can of Vienna sausages sitting on the table in front of him.

"Have you eaten anything?" Ladamien asked her.

Bonnie looked at the half-full can of sausages and decided she wasn't hungry. "I haven't even thought about it," she said. "I'll just have some water."

"How is Aggie?"

"The same. I called the doctor. Maybe he'll suggest something."

"Can I see her?"

"Yeah, go ahead. Thad's in there with her."

Shortly after Ladamien left the kitchen, Bonnie's

cell phone rang. It was Dr. Nieves.

"I understand our patient isn't doing well."

"Her blood oxygen is around point eight seven. The congestion is worse.

"What about her temperature, pulse, BP…"

"The last time I took her temperature it was 99.4, slightly elevated. Her pulse was sixty-two, blood pressure 117 over 76."

"Actually, that sounds pretty good, except for the blood oxygen."

"That's what I thought, but with the hypoxemia, how long will it stay that way?"

"Probably not long. In addition, I am concerned about oxygen to the brain. I take it the intubation went all right."

"Yes."

"Do you have any anti-viral medications with you," asked Dr. Nieves, "like oseltamivir?"

"I think so," said Bonnie. "That's the drug they thought would help prevent H1N1, called Tamiflu, isn't it?"

"That's it. The results weren't spectacular, but it might help and it won't hurt."

"It's out in the Avenger," said Bonnie. "I'll have to go out in the storm to get it."

"Is that a problem?" asked D. Nieves. "I haven't looked outside, but I've heard the noise."

"Only if you're not crazy," Bonnie answered. "Fortunately, EMT's are certifiably insane. It's a job requirement." Bonnie thought about the prospect of going out in the hurricane. It was almost out of the question. She decided to ask Ladamien to go out with her. They could save one another. If something happened to them, Thad would still be there to look after Aggie and Simon.

"Thank you doctor," she said.

"Call me if things change – for better or for worse."

Bonnie finished her bottle of water and went to fetch Ladamien. She approached the bedroom, opened the door, and motioned to Ladamien to come out. "Strip down to your skivvies," she said, "we're goin' swimmin'."

Ladamien looked surprised but came out into the hallway. "What's the deal?"

"I've got some medicine out there that might help Aggie. I need a buddy to help me get across the stream."

Ladamien removed his shoes and socks, dropped his pants, and took off his shirt. Bonnie noticed the ripple of the muscles beneath his undershirt, and the bulge of his biceps. She admired people who kept themselves in shape. "We might as well go out the front," she said. "God only knows what direction the wind is coming from."

Ladamien held the door against the wind while Bonnie slipped outside. The wind caught her immediately and caused her to go to her knees. The rain stung her skin everywhere it came in contact. It was as if she was being pressure cleaned and her underclothes plastered against her body. She felt Ladamien holding onto her and helping her work her way around the side of the house toward the Avenger. The depth of the pond surrounding the house helped break the force of the blustery weather. When they rounded the corner, the house blocked the wind and they crawled as if in the shallows of a lake to the flank of the Avenger.

Bonnie could barely hear Ladamien's voice over the squall, even though she was sure he was screaming. "Can you get to the medicine?" he called.

Bonnie pulled herself to her feet, climbed into the Avenger, and retrieved the medicine bag from a coffer. She closed the cover and didn't try to speak. She pointed to the side door to the garage. She thought it would be easier to get there than to go back around the house. She waded through about two and a half feet of water and Ladamien followed her. He caught up and went ahead of her to open the door. After they entered the garage, they found themselves standing in a pool, out of the wind and in almost total darkness.

"What is that medicine?" asked Ladamien.

"To be honest," said Bonnie, "it's a shot in the dark. The medicine is Tamiflu, and we're supposed to administer it in the first two days that flu symptoms start. Without knowing what Aggie has and how long she has had it," Bonnie shrugged, "it's…well, it's the best we have. It's going to be hard to administer as it is."

"You don't sound very optimistic."

"If I could do more, I would. Let's go inside. Can you find the door?"

Bonnie heard Ladamien moving through the water and then saw a square of twilight when he opened the door to the house. She followed him inside. "Can you please bring me those dry clothes I left at the front door?" she asked. Then, she went to the bathroom to find a towel. Ladamien brought her the exercise suit.

"I could bring you some of Aggie's underwear if you wanted," he offered.

Bonnie shook her head. "It wouldn't fit," she said. "I'll be fine without it."

Ladamien took a towel from the bathroom closet and headed toward the east wing of the house.

Bonnie closed the bathroom door, undressed, dried, and put on the exercise clothes. Well, we'll see how this goes, she told herself as she took the Tamiflu out of the medicine bag. Fortunately, we have the suspension as well as the pills.

As she walked toward the bedroom, Bonnie heard a thunderous noise come from the direction of the garage.

CHAPTER 10

"God moves in a mysterious way, His wonders to perform. He plants his footsteps in the sea, and rides upon the storm."

William Cowper

Ladamien had just turned on the radio when he felt the house shake and heard an enormous noise from the east side of the house. He took a flashlight from where he kept it at the door and stepped into the garage. The low pressure of the hurricane jerked the door handle from his hand and he was looking into the blackness of night. He shined the flashlight around and realized that there was a giant oak trunk in front of him. The storm had ripped away most of the garage roof and was already eroding the sidewalls. Soon, it might begin to work on the house roof. The flapping of the roof boards sounded like an elephant on a rampage in a lumberyard.

Ladamien stepped farther into the garage. The walls still protected him from the fury of the wind. The oak trunk must have weighed more than ten tons. It had come through the roof and crushed Aggie's car. As Ladamien stepped closer to examine the car, he saw a peculiar movement in the clouds overhead. Something darker than the clouds moved through the sky. It was a gigantic bird whose wings spanned the visible horizon. Ladamien discerned the yellow beak and the eyes that flashed with the lightning. He retreated to the house and used all of his strength to pull the door shut.

The shock of seeing the garage destroyed had diminished with the astonishment of seeing the enormous ghost bird. Ladamien was accustomed to physical devastation but was unprepared for the monstrous apparition within the storm. He scuffled hastily into the main part of the house and back to the bedroom where Bonnie was watching over Aggie.

"How is she?" he asked, pointing at Aggie.

"Her pulse is erratic and her blood pressure has dropped some. It's not good."

"A tree shattered the garage, ruined Aggie's car." Ladamien put his hand on his forehead. "You'll never guess what I saw, in the sky."

"Swirling black clouds?"

"Yeah, those too, but I saw the damndest gigantic bird you can imagine."

Bonnie didn't look as surprised as Ladamien expected.

"A big black bird, with wings that covered the sky?" she asked.

"How did you know?"

"A friend told me that the Big Wind will ride in on the great bird Hurikon to see me."

"You gotta be shittin' me," said Ladamien. "That or you're crazier'n a turnip pie."

"You saw the bird, not me."

"What in the hell is goin' on? Who are you?"

Bonnie was frustrated by the distress of the situation. "We're in the middle of a record-shattering tropical storm, your wife is critically ill, and this house is disintegrating around us. What more do you want?"

"An' the biggest fuckin' bird that ever flew is comin' ta see you. It's a pissin' nightmare."

Bonnie laced her fingers across her breasts and spoke so softly that Ladamien could barely hear her. "That it is," she said. "It certainly is."

When she looked up at him, Ladamien could see that her eyes were bloodshot. "How long since you had any sleep?" he asked.

"I don't remember," said Bonnie. "I've tried, but my mind keeps running on. I feel like this whole mess is my fault."

"That's absurd," said Ladamien. "You can't create hurricanes, and you didn't make Aggie sick."

"True. What about the house, will it stand up to the hurricane?"

"We'll be all right. The eye wall is going through and we'll be in the eye soon. We're probably experiencing the worst right now. How about Aggie?"

"I can't do any more without equipment we don't have. We've got to get her to a hospital."

"When do you think we'll be able to get out of here?"

"Eight, nine hours." Bonnie got up and stretched. "They should be able to get a helicopter in by then."

Ladamien knew that Bonnie was not expressing her true thoughts. "Why don't you get some sleep?" he said. "I'll sit with Aggie."

Bonnie came over and took his hand. "Wake me if anything happens."

After Bonnie left, Ladamien saw the bedroom door crack open and Simon's face peeked through the gap. "I heard a loud bang," Simon said. "Did something blow up?"

"A tree fell on the garage," Ladamien answered. "We're lucky it missed the house. Come on in."

"How's Mom? Simon asked, looking at Aggie with a worried expression.

"We're gonna fly her out of here as soon as the storm lightens up."

"She sounds terrible," said Simon. "Like she can't breathe."

"I know, but Miss Bonnie's got her fixed up so she's getting oxygen. She'll be okay." Ladamien wasn't sure of this, but he wanted to reassure his son. Inside, he was already thinking what he would do if Aggie didn't make it. His and Simon's lives would change drastically. "She's not going to die," he said – almost too dramatically.

Simon began to cry.

"It's okay, son," said Ladamien. "It's okay to worry."

Thad came into the room. "Bonnie said you two should get some rest also. I'll watch Missus Upton and let you know if anything changes."

Ladamien took Simon's hand and led him into the kitchen. "Why don't you go back to bed? I'll go sleep in the study. Miss Bonnie's in the spare bedroom."

Simon went back to his room. Ladamien stretched out on the recliner in the study and closed his eyes. He couldn't sleep, but lay back fitfully. Visions of the destruction going on outside flitted through his mind. He could hear the wind screaming, a banshee out of its cage.

Overriding all else, however, was the image of that great bird. Its eyes had the fatal glare of a raptor diving onto its prey. Its beak was the scythe of death, hungry for carnage, honed to razor sharpness. Its wings captured the sky, beating in a devastating rhythm that swept everything from its path. Ladamien shuttered, not at what he had seen, but comprehending there were forces at work he couldn't see. That woman – Bonnie – he couldn't figure her out.

***

Rusty had just gotten off the phone with the county emergency center when Bonnie called.

"Rusty," said Bonnie, "when do you think we could get a helicopter out here. I'm losing this patient. She needs to be in intensive care."

Rusty looked at the anemometer on her office wall. "The wind is blowing in excess of one hundred and forty-five miles per hour here. What's it like there?"

"We're still getting heavy duty winds, but the eye should be coming over soon."

"They won't try and fit a helicopter flight between the walls of the eye," said Rusty. "It's just too risky. Bad enough that Doug and I have to go out in an engine."

"You're going out in this? Why?"

"The county confirmed an explosion out near Rogers Road, where that plastics plant is located. The plant uses potassium cyanide, so I have to investigate."

"Potassium cyanide. That's bad stuff. Isn't that what they use for executions?"

"Sometimes," Rusty agreed. "It releases hydrogen cyanide if it gets wet."

"That could require an evacuation. What a mess in this weather. How is the rest of the county faring?"

"It's hard to get information. The winds were one hundred and eighty-five miles per hour when Dirk came ashore. The surge at Canaveral National Seashore was eighteen feet."

"There go the turtle's nests," said Bonnie, "and, there go the condos."

"Maybe," said Rusty. "We'll have to wait and see. Let me check on that helicopter for you."

First, Rusty called the ready room at the station and asked her fire supervisor, Doug Forsythe, and lead paramedic, Kathie Turbinov to come to her office. Then, she called the county emergency center.

"When could I get a medical evacuation helicopter to fly into north Merritt Island?" she asked the dispatcher. The dispatcher went off line to find out and came back shortly.

"The Coast Guard says they can get a chopper in when the winds go below twenty knots," said the dispatcher, "but you have to guarantee a landing area at least one hundred and fifty feet on a side. They figure the wind will be down early tomorrow morning."

"Can they talk to my paramedic direct?" asked Rusty. "I'll give you her number."

"What about radio contact," asked the dispatcher? "The phones are intermittent."

"She has a radio. You can talk to her. I'll make sure she knows."

Rusty hung up the phone just as Kathie and Doug came into her office. She checked the closed circuit TV. It looked out on the parking lot, which was an incomprehensible blur of gray and white. She heard the wind from outside. It whined and moaned, alternately.

"We have a mission," Rusty told them. "There was a tornado, somewhere near Rogers Road. Several people saw an explosion. There's a plant out there that might be on fire, but more importantly, there may be a hazardous gas release."

"What gas," asked Doug?

"Hydrogen cyanide."

"That's terrible stuff," said Doug. "How's it stored?"

"Actually, its potassium cyanide," said Rusty, "but, in this rain, it'll make the gas."

"We need to find out quickly," said Doug. "You ready to go?"

"You can't drive in this wind. The eye will be passing over shortly. I figured we could get on the road then."

"Good plan. We'll take the big Hummer. It has a high wheelbase. Bound to be a lot of water out there."

"What about protective gear?"

"It's already packed in the Hummer. Let me know when the winds get down to seventy miles per hour. I can handle that."

Rusty looked at the anemometer. It read one twenty-five. "It won't be long," she said. "Go ahead and get ready."

While she waited, Rusty decided to call Bonnie and let her know about the helicopter. Bonnie picked up on the fourth ring.

"Hey Rusty," said Bonnie.

"The Coast Guard will be calling you about landing an evacuation helicopter. You need to monitor the radio as well as your phone. How're you doing?"

"Not good. A tree fell on the house. My patient, Aggie, is still going downhill – pulmonary difficulty – and there's something strange going on."

"Strange? Like what?"

"There's some kind of spiritual presence. Aggie's husband saw it, but I've known it was coming."

Rusty shook her head. *What now?* she thought.

"What did he see?" Rusty asked.

"It's almost too weird. He saw an enormous bird, in the hurricane. I had a premonition about this."

"Are you in danger?"

"I don't know. I don't think so. We'll have to wait and see. I'll be glad to see the helicopter. When will it be here?"

"The dispatcher said not until tomorrow morning."

"The patient may not make it."

"Tell the Coast Guard it's urgent. I have to go out on another vital call. Good luck."

"Yeah," said Bonnie. "You too."

***

Bonnie was curious to see what Ladamien had seen. She started to go back to the garage when she became aware of the storm outside subsiding. The eye was coming. However, it was more than the eye of the storm. Bonnie saw the foot-and-a-half long stick shaped like an Ankh cross.

Kameeshi!

The alien spiraled slowly just below the ceiling of the living room.

As the extraterrestrial spun, it worked its magic and the scene began to change. The ceiling opened up into a soft amber sky and the carpet spread out into a grassy turf. The walls disappeared, replaced by a corral of tropical shrubbery. A friendly bonfire appeared in the center of the scene with a ring of pine stump stools arranged around it. On Bonnie's left, a lazy river meandered through the glen. To her right, she saw Aggie in her bed and Thad sitting next to her, apparently oblivious to the changes that Bonnie observed.

Inside her head, Kameeshi spoke to her. *"The chiefs are here."*

Bonnie parked herself on a grassy knoll and

awaited their appearance.

***

A clamor of calm awakened Simon. The sound of the wind was gone. It was two o'clock in the morning, but inside of Simon's room, there was a hushed brilliance, reminiscent of the setting in a movie theater before the show starts. Simon slipped out of bed and went into the hallway, except the hallway was gone.

The sky was a soft yellow with the texture of a baby's blanket. Thin shrubs blocked the path, but Simon was able to push them aside and work his way toward an open glade that he could see through the leaves. When he emerged into the clearing, he could see Bonnie sitting on a mound on the other side of the open space. His mother was visible in the background lying on her bed with Thad monitoring her vitals.

In the center of the dell was a small bonfire around which were eight pine logs positioned like chairs around the fire. Above it all, rotating slowly at the dome of the sky was a strangely shaped stick. Farther away, to the right, a river quietly rippled by. Simon saw an osprey perched on a small tree at the water's edge. In the heavens, a large black bird remained suspended, flapping its wings slowly.

"They're coming," said Bonnie.

"The chiefs," asked Simon, "and the daughter of the wind?"

Bonnie nodded. "I think so."

"I saw her," said Simon.

"So did I," said Bonnie. "She didn't look real,

more like a whisper."

"I know. Kinda fairy like."

Ladamien walked into the clearing looking confused. "What's up?"

"The chiefs are coming," said Simon.

Ladamien started to say something but stopped when an alligator came out of the bushes and transformed into a brown-skinned man before their eyes. The man ignored them and walked over to where Aggie lay. He touched her forehead, knelt down to hear her breathing, and then came back to face Simon.

He spoke to Simon, not in sounds but directly to Simon's brain, with deep compassion. *"She is your mother."* The chief phrased this not as a question, but as an affirmation. *"She will not live."*

At this, Simon arose and went to his mother's bedside. Her face was tranquil. She was so beautiful to him. He came back and faced the chief. "Maybe she will live," he said. "Perhaps the big chief will cure her."

The alligator-chief only nodded, cocked his left eye, and smiled. *"You may ask him. Tell him Chief Pak-taw, the merciful one, told you to ask."*

Simon saw a manatee rolling in the water. Before his eyes, the water mammal slowly changed into a heavyset man who climbed from the river and sat on the bank.

"That is Chief Ga-pa," said Chief Pak-taw. *"He is the keeper of secrets. The silent one."*

Simon saw a blue heron coming out of the water. "Here's another chief," Simon said, as the heron began to take on the form of a man.

The heron chief sat next to where Simon's father had been sitting.

Simon's father had been pacing around the fire. Finally, he asked, "Who are these men?"

"They're the chiefs, Dad," answered Simon.

"The chiefs of what?"

Bonnie answered. "They are the four ancient chiefs, the original leaders of the Native Americans who lived here before the Spanish came – the Ais, Hororo, Surruque, Mayajuaca – and their great chief, Ho-tah-lee, Chief of the Wind."

"What do they want?"

"They want the spirit of Banna, queen of the old ones. Her spirit has possessed my daughter, the child I carry within me now."

"How do you know all of this?"

"Do you see that stick in the sky? It is alive and it told me."

"Unbelievable," said Ladamien. "Can they save Aggie?"

"I don't know," Bonnie replied.

Ladamien walked around the fire, obviously disturbed. "Where is the hurricane? It can't just go away. Where is my house?"

"They're all still here," said Bonnie. "Somewhere."

The fire continued to burn, and Simon felt a peace settle over him. He went back to his mother and put his small hand over hers. She appeared to be breathing more easily and her face was serene. Thad was apparently unaware of their presence. "Please," he said to the sky, "please make her better."

As Simon peered upward, he saw an apparition begin to descend from the great black bird. It looked like a swirling mass of dust, or water. It started small and grew slowly larger as it came closer to earth. After some time, Simon could make out the shape of a tall man, lean and well muscled, but older in appearance than Simon had expected. Simon knew it was Ho-tah-lee. The man held a staff and when he finally landed, the osprey flew from its perch in the tree and settled on his shoulder.

Ho-tah-lee looked around and then went to Bonnie. Apparently, he was communicating with her because Simon could see the concentration in her eyes. As Ho-tah-lee stood in front of Bonnie, Simon saw the spirit of the daughter of the wind twirling in the sky. The chief looked up to see her also, and then looked back at Bonnie.

Bonnie tented her hands and looked intently at the Chief of the Wind. Simon listened to hear what she would say.

"No," she said. "I can't do that."

***

Bonnie had watched the entry of the chiefs and the descent of Ho-tah-lee with a measure of detachment, as she might view a parade. When Chief Ho-tah-lee approached her, she expected him to speak inside her mind. Instead, he welcomed her into his mind without saying a word. It was similar to walking onto the stage set of a play in mid-progress. She stood on the beach while the chiefs and their tribes set up camp along the shore. She knew it was their first day in Florida, the beginning of an era.

She saw Chief Ho-tah-lee standing at the top of the dunes and she approached him.

"Where did you and your people come from?" she asked.

"From the place of spirits," answered the chief. "From the great ecstasy."

The scene rolled quickly before Bonnie's eyes. She watched the tribes separate and war against one another. Later, other native tribes came from the north and invaded the territory of the aboriginal people. More wars transpired but most of the time, the tribes lived in peace. The chiefs had sons and daughters that inherited leadership of the tribes, but one stood out – Banna, the daughter of Chief Ho-tah-lee– the daughter of the wind. The chief found her in the forest, abandoned in a basket, and adopted her as his own.

Bonnie saw Banna briefly, standing next to the chief holding a bow with a quiver of arrows slung over her shoulder. She was a warrior and a hunter who chose not to marry and spent her time in the bush, living separate from the tribes and the camps.

When their souls departed the Earth, the spirits of the four chiefs resided in the land between the living and the great ecstasy. The spirits of some tribal members went on to the great ecstasy, others stayed with the chiefs. Banna's spirit endured, inhabiting one soul after another, like a supernatural parasite. Her spirit had found a conduit to immortality. The Europeans – the Spaniards, the French, and the British – exterminated the tribes; the few Native Americans remaining alive went south to the islands with the Spanish. It was time for the chiefs to continue to the great ecstasy.

Chief Ho-tah-lee did not want to go to the great ecstasy without his daughter's spirit accompanying his spirit. However, she had hidden herself, secreted in an innocent soul. The Great Mother gave the chiefs the Ais Sanctuary near Coreopsis to await the submission of Banna's spirit. The spirits of many tribe members stayed with the chiefs to await Banna's return. The Great Mother brought Kameeshi from another world to assist the chiefs and to guard the Ais Sanctuary.

Then, Bonnie saw Julie's spirit possessing her as Kameeshi had observed it. Kameeshi had seen Julie's spirit depart Bonnie's soul and leave a spiritual presence behind; the alien knew it was the spirit of Banna. He made the chiefs aware of the status of Banna's spirit. Chief Ho-tah-lee rushed to Bonnie so he could appeal to her for Banna's deliverance.

"If you abort your baby," said Chief Ho-tah-lee, "Banna's spirit will be released and we can all proceed to the great ecstasy."

Bonnie found herself outside of the chief's mind. Several hundred Native Americans encircled them – the spirits of men, women, and children – long dead. Bonnie looked up at the chief who was bent over her.

"No," said Bonnie, "I can't do that."

"Do you understand that your daughter's spirit will never be free," said Chief Ho-tah-lee, "that she will be possessed from birth?"

"I don't know what that means," said Bonnie. "Won't she still be herself? What about the unborn spirit, the spirit of my daughter?"

While the chief appeared to mull over an answer, Bonnie added, "It wouldn't matter. She is my daughter. I have carried her for three months. I'm not about to give her up. I'm not going to kill my baby."

"I don't need your permission," said Chief Ho-tah-lee. "I could abort your baby. I could kill you."

Bonnie contemplated the chief's remark. She knew he was making a threat, but something told her he couldn't carry it out, that he needed Bonnie to convince Banna's spirit to go with him. Bonnie pointed to Aggie. "Can you cure her? Chief Pak-taw said we should ask you."

"Perhaps. If I wished. Right now, she will die soon."

"I know," said Bonnie. "I'm not even sure what disease she has."

"She has what you would call Hantavirus pulmonary syndrome. Her lungs cannot get enough oxygen into her blood."

Bonnie knew this was probably an accurate diagnosis. It didn't change her assessment of Aggie's chances, but it did show that the chief was being honest with her. In addition, it told her the condition was not contagious, something that had concerned her.

"If you had compassion for this boy," Bonnie indicated Simon, "her son, you would at least help her to stay alive until we get her to the hospital."

"If you felt anything for my tribe and my daughter," said Chief Ho-tah-lee, "you would release Banna's spirit to join us."

"I don't know how to do that without denying my own daughter's spirit her right to life." Bonnie tried to communicate with Kameeshi. "Is that possible? Can Banna's spirit leave my daughter's soul without harming her natural spirit?"

"It is possible," she heard Kameeshi reply in her head.

Evidently, Chief Ho-tah-lee could overhear their conversation. "I don't have time for that," he said. "The great bird is moving on."

Bonnie had not thought that there might be a time limit on the chief's appearance. It changed her approach. "If you will help Aggie stay alive until we get her to an intensive care unit," she said, "I will attempt to have Banna's spirit leave my daughter's soul and rejoin your tribes."

"I don't have to wait."

"Yes, you do. You cannot force Banna's spirit to join you. She has to make the decision for herself."

"As you wish," said Chief Ho-tah-lee. He dismissed the other chiefs and rose into the sky toward the great black bird. The spirits of the deceased began to whirl around the glade, becoming a cyclonic hodgepodge.

Kameeshi spun more quickly. The sky closed in and the walls of the house reappeared. Bonnie, Simon, and Ladamien sat in the living room. Bonnie could hear the wind picking up outside. Dirk's eye had passed and the fury of the hurricane returned intensified two-fold.

Thad came in from the master bedroom. "It's miraculous," he said. "The oxygen level in Aggie's blood is almost back to normal."

Bonnie got up from the sofa to go check her patient. As she walked to the bedroom, she heard a loud ripping sound and felt the air rushing around her toward the kitchen. The lights flickered, and then went out. She ran up the hallway to the counter where she had placed a flashlight earlier. When she beamed the light toward the rear of the kitchen, she saw a gaping hole in the roof.

Ladamien came up beside her, also holding a flashlight. "I'll go see what knocked the electricity off," he said, and continued through the kitchen toward the garage.

CHAPTER 11

"Seeing death as the end of life is like seeing the horizon as the end of the ocean."

David Searls

As the eye approached Coreopsis and the wind speed dropped to ninety miles per hour, Rusty and Doug moved the protective gear into an off-road Hummer. As the eye approached, the wind speed dropped, not quickly but steadily. After they were about a mile from the station, there was an uncanny calm. It was dark, but the sky had a slight color to it, as if there were a violet night light above the clouds. There was no sound and a moist blanket swathed the surroundings like the insides of a just-used sauna.

In the headlights of the vehicle, Rusty could see the incredible devastation from the storm. Debris of every description littered the streets, the yards, and every open space. Tree limbs, entwined with power wires and electric poles had rearranged themselves everywhere, intermingled with displaced trailers and whole parts of roofs. A bedraggled cat took advantage of the tranquility to seek a better shelter. Coreopsis was a town in shambles. Rusty could only imagine what the more vulnerable coastal communities must be like.

Rusty noticed that Doug was picking his way through the jumble, driving off the road onto sidewalks and lawns when necessary. "Are we gonna make it?" she asked.

"I think once we get out on US-1 and the main streets," Doug said, "it'll go easier. I figure we've got twenty minutes to make it to the plant on Rogers Road."

"Are you familiar with that plant?" Rusty asked.

"Not really. I know they manufacture high impact plastics."

"It's a virtual storehouse for toxic and flammable materials."

"That figures. They should have it all locked down. When did we last inspect them?"

"Nine months ago." Rusty was still bothered thinking about it. "Something could have been released, what with the explosions and all."

"The fumes from the fire could be toxic. I don't know how much we can do about it in the storm."

They had gone about five miles when the Emergency Operations Center came up on the radio. "Hey Rusty," it was Ed Richardson's voice. "We got in touch with the general manager and the chief chemist at that plant. They say they moved all of the toxic materials to a vault two days ago."

"What about the fire," asked Rusty?

"Yeah, we asked them about that. They say their plastics won't release anything more harmful than a forest fire would. Not to worry about it."

"Should we check it out? I don't want to get

caught in the eye wall when it comes back through."

"Just check out the extent of the fire. They think the flammables in the plant will burn off quickly, but you might make sure no residential dwellings are threatened."

"Okay, but it'll be a quick look."

"All right. Call me back."

"For once," said Doug, "I'm glad it's a false alarm."

"We'd better check it out before we assume that." Rusty checked her watch. She knew they only had about a half-hour window inside the eye. "We need to think about where we're going to find shelter. We'll never make it back to the station."

"There's a farm out on Buckram Road. They have a specially designed storm shelter. I know the owner. He'll let us park there."

"How do you know him?"

"We're in the rifle and pistol club together."

"How far from the plant is it?"

"Only about three miles." Doug turned right onto Rogers Road.

Rusty could see the plant, dimly lit by the remaining fire inside. Smoke still poured from a hole in the roof and several broken windows. "Looks like we still have an active fire," she said.

"It could still be an explosion hazard," said Doug. "They have all of the ingredients in there."

"I'll call Ed," said Rusty. She picked up the microphone to the radio. "Central this is Coreopsis 2."

"Go ahead Coreopsis 2."

"Ed, we're at the plant on Rogers. It appears there is still a healthy fire inside. It could explode again. We don't have the equipment to put it out."

"What's your assessment?"

"There isn't any danger to residential areas. We think we should just let it burn itself out until you can get some heavy equipment in here. Right now, we're only about fifteen minutes away from the wind returning. There's a shelter close by. We're headed there."

"Okay Rusty. I'm sure their insurance is paid up."

As Doug backed the Hummer to turn around, Rusty saw a bright flash of light and felt a low frequency shock wave go through her. The roof of the plant lifted fifty feet into the air and flames escaped from the building as it disintegrated before her eyes. Several booming noises shook the air around her, similar to an aircraft breaking the sound barrier. The fire flared to twenty feet high in several places. Almost as if on cue, the wind began to pick up and a heavy rain blew across the road.

"We'd better get a move on if we want to make that shelter," said Rusty.

"Doug gunned the Hummer and they hurried away from the scene.

***

Ladamien had watched the episode between Bonnie and the chiefs without understanding what was happening. In his worldly travels, he had seen many astounding things, but he had never seen anything to match the disappearance of the house and the storm and the sudden visitations from the heavens. If someone had described to him what he had seen, Ladamien would have assumed that person made it up. When Thad came in and announced that Aggie was better, it made up for whatever had gone on. He started to follow Bonnie into the bedroom to see if Aggie was better.

Ladamien knew the sound coming from the kitchen. It was the roof tearing up from the garage and breaching a portion of the roof covering the house. As soon as he felt the wind rush past him, he knew the storm had penetrated into the house. He grabbed a flashlight from inside the bathroom and headed toward the door to the garage. The lights went off at just about the time he brushed past Bonnie. He panned the flashlight at the ceiling and saw where the roofing had busted the wiring. He had heard the snap of the electricity shorting when the wires broke.

Ladamien waded back to the circuit breaker box. The short had popped the 30-amp breaker feeding the lights but the main breaker was still closed. Ladamien searched around the garage until he found a drop light and an extension cord. He plugged both of these into outside receptacles just below the circuit breaker box and unrolled them into the house. Once inside, he turned on the drop light.

"Ah," he heard Bonnie say. "The miracle of light. Is that power you bring?" she asked pointing at the extension cord.

"Should be," Ladamien answered. "I thought you might need it."

"It will save the life of the battery on the

ventilator. Give it to me and I'll plug it in."

"How is she?" Ladamien asked after he had watched Bonnie examine Aggie.

"Much improved," said Bonnie. "It's a double miracle, that the chief knew what was wrong with her and that he was able to arrest its progress. What's the deal with the roof?"

"There's nothing we can do about it. I think it will hold. That was probably the worst of the wind. Can I talk to Aggie?"

"Let her know you're here. Don't expect her to answer. The intubation will make it difficult for her to speak. She's very weak."

"Aggie. It's Ladamien. I love you, honey." Ladamien saw Aggie's eyelids flicker, but she didn't open her eyes. He took her hand and she squeezed his fingers. He pressed back lightly, and then released her hand.

Ladamien looked at Bonnie. "I know what I saw, and what I heard. Who were those men?"

"They were spirits, or spiritual beings. The first chiefs of the Native American tribes that lived in this area originally, before Columbus and before the Seminoles."

"I've never believed in spirits. What did they want from you?"

"A few years ago, I was possessed by the spirit of a girl, a teenager who turned out to be my mother. When she abandoned my soul, she left something behind – another spirit – the spirit of the chief's daughter."

"An errant spirit," asked Ladamien, "so to

speak?"

"Precisely," said Bonnie. "At least, according to the chief."

"So you are possessed by this errant spirit?"

"Worse. The spirit of his daughter, Banna, has possessed my unborn child. If she departs, my baby might not develop normally."

"What happens if she stays?"

"She will be a parasite on my daughter's soul, depriving her spirit of the life it was meant to fulfill."

"I guess we don't think about our spiritual lives a whole lot," said Ladamien. "Do you think our spirits are judged for what we do with our lives? Like in the spirit world."

"I don't have any idea," said Bonnie. "Most religions have some version of Heaven and hell, some accountability between being good or evil."

"My momma always said that what I do is evil, that Jesus will judge me and my spirit will go to hell."

"Simon told me you owned a business. Something to do with airports."

"I do," said Ladamien. He thought about telling Bonnie more, and then decided that wasn't a good idea. "My momma wanted me to be a lawyer."

"I think it's more how you live your life," said Bonnie, "as well as what you do."

Ladamien thought about Bonnie's remark. The whole question was not so academic when he realized that spirits existed, that his spirit might go on after he died. *How have I lived my life?* Ladamien realized he didn't know for sure. The sound of the hurricane broke off his ponderings.

Ladamien asked, "Will Aggie make it until the helicopter gets here?"

"I think so," said Bonnie, "as long as whatever the chief did continues. Will the house hold up?"

"I think so," Ladamien told her. He knew enough about construction to feel confident.

Ladamien returned to the living room and sat in the easy chair. Almost losing Aggie was just beginning to sink in. *What am I doing?* He thought. *Running around the world, breaking the law, avoiding the police. It has to change.*

Simon had gone back to his room and Thad returned to take up the vigil with Aggie. Bonnie came into the living room and sat on the sofa.

"There's something you're not telling me," she said. "Something that's bothering you."

"Are you familiar with gangs?" Ladamien asked.

"I had a bad experience with a gang called the Swamp Rattlers," said Bonnie. "They kidnapped me."

Damn, thought Ladamien. *Who is this woman?*

"Cody Wilkins was my father," Bonnie continued. "He was the gang's leader."

"Would you believe I'm a member of the Swamp Rattlers?" said Ladamien. "I work for them."

Ladamien saw Bonnie's jaw drop and her eyes widen. She tented her hands and looked at him, evidently waiting for him to say more. "My business," he said, "is a money-laundering operation for their activities."

"How did you get tied up with them?"

"I couldn't go to college. I couldn't get a good job. Cody gave me an opportunity. Without money and stability, I could never have married Aggie."

"And now you think it was wrong."

"I'm not sure. I never did the bad stuff. I helped other people get out of terrible countries and go to places where they had more opportunity."

"Human trafficking? You engaged in human trafficking?"

"Yes, but that's not so bad, is it?"

"It's terrible. Did you ever see where those people ended up?"

"I saw where they came from. It was worse."

"You did it for money. You didn't care what happened to them. The money laundering is even worse. You're financing drugs, prostitution, extortion, and even murder." Bonnie paused and took a breath. "Judge yourself. Don't wait for Jesus to do it for you. Save yourself if you can."

Ladamien felt as if Bonnie had spoken for him. In essence, they were the same words he knew his mother would have used on him. "It's not going to be easy."

"Not doing it will be disastrous," said Bonnie. "I'm not sure how, but I'm pretty sure there are consequences in the hereafter."

I wish I knew for sure, Ladamien thought, knowing he didn't want to find out from experience.

***

Rusty watched Doug turn the Hummer around and start south on Rogers Road. The headlights barely pierced the deepening dark as the storm picked up intensity.

"Here's my phone," said Doug as he handed a cell phone across to Rusty. "Find 'Plug' on the list of contacts. That's my friend."

"Plug?" said Rusty. "Is that his real name or a nickname?"

"We all use nicknames at the gun club. Tell him 'Deadeye' needs his help."

Rusty felt relieved that the cell phone call went through. She half-expected a busy signal. A woman answered the phone. "Is Plug there?" asked Rusty.

"Who is this?" said the woman.

"My name is Rusty. I'm the chief of Fire and Emergency Station Number Two in Coreopsis. We need to use your shelter. Tell Plug that Deadeye is calling."

Rusty heard the woman calling Plug to the phone, except she called him Paul.

"Deadeye?" the man asked. "Is that you?"

"He's busy driving," said Rusty, "trying to keep this vehicle on the road."

"You're driving in this?"

"We had to check out a fire on Rogers Road. We need to get to shelter before the eye passes and the winds pick up."

"Okay. The shelter is unlocked, but you will have to open it. I think Doug knows how to do that."

"Plug says the shelter is unlocked," Rusty said to Doug. "Do you know how to open it?

"Yes," said Doug. "Tell him we'll be all right."

"Doug says he knows how to get in," said Rusty. "Thanks, and we'll see you in a little bit." Rusty closed the phone.

"Keep it," said Doug. "The wind is picking up rapidly."

In a matter of seconds, the outside turned so black that Rusty could not even see the reflection from the headlights against the gloom. The inside of the Hummer was a world onto itself moving through a void. The low wailing of the hurricane drowned out the noise of the engine. Rusty could feel the vehicle yawing from side to side.

Rusty spoke loudly in order for Doug to hear her. "Are we still on the road?"

"I don't know for sure," said Doug. "The wind is pushing us."

Rusty felt the Hummer start to bounce up and down.

"I've lost the road," said Doug. "We're airborne."

Rusty felt the bottom of the car seat come up hard against her butt, and the impact threw her forward as the back of the Hummer came up behind her and the vehicle rolled counter-clockwise.

"We're flipping," Doug yelled. "Hold on."

It was more terrifying than any roller coaster ride. Rusty felt an eternal sense of weightlessness, a seeming hour to figure out how the Hummer would land – to brace for the inevitable impact. Then it came. In the interior light, Rusty saw the roof of the van collapse toward her and felt her shoulder strap bite into her chest, knocking the air from her lungs. The airbag deployed and slammed her backwards.

Her head snapped forward, violently elongating her neck. Her seat belt compressed her stomach, almost forcing its contents into her throat. The lights stayed on for a few seconds, and then extinguished, leaving her in total darkness.

"Doug," said Rusty. "Are you okay?"

Doug did not answer. Rusty heard water running into the vehicle from outside. She could not tell where it was coming in or where it was going. *Oh shit,* Rusty thought, *we must be upside down in the retention pond.* She remembered passing the pond on the way into Rogers Road. It had flooded almost to the road, so the fence around it was under water. *It must be eight to ten feet deep by now,* she thought.

Rusty did not know if she were floating or sinking. She tried the handle just in case the door was above the water. The resistance told her that the door was already under water. She felt around for something with which to break a window. The Hummer had safety glass on all of the windows, but if she could equalize the pressure, she might be able to open a door. She thought of the compressed air tanks that went with their protective gear. One of them would be heavy enough to break through a window.

That is fortunate, Rusty thought, *having an air supply so we won't suffocate.* She heard Doug moan. "Are you coming to?" she asked.

"Damn," said Doug. "My head feels like I lost a fight to Mike Tyson. What happened?"

"I'm pretty sure we went off the road and flipped. I think we're upside down in a retention pond."

"Reach under your seat," said Doug. "There should be a flashlight there. Maybe we can figure out exactly what we're faced with."

It was difficult for Rusty to search under the seat when she was hanging upside down. She released her seat belt and knelt on the roof. Soon, she located the flashlight, retrieved it, and turned it on. A murky brown coating that looked more like mud than water covered her window. They were totally submerged. When she examined the window on Doug's side, she saw that the fence from around the retention pond had embedded itself against the outside of the driver's side of the Hummer.

"I don't know if we'll be able to open the doors," she said, "even if I can break a window and equalize the pressure."

"We might have to break out the window in back," said Doug. "We can't open the hatch from the inside, but I might be able to reach outside. I can unlock it from inside."

"The water will come in like a hammer," said Rusty. "I'll have to brace myself."

"What about the air in the tanks," asked Rusty, "can we use it underwater?"

"The regulators aren't designed for that, but open one of them so we will have air if the van floods."

"Maybe we should just sit tight," said Rusty. "We'll have plenty of air. Someone will come looking for us after the storm clears."

"What are we going to do when the water floods the van?" asked Doug.

"You're right. We've got to get out of here. I'm

thirsty. Want some water?"

"Yeah. I'm going to unfasten my seatbelt and join you. It isn't comfortable being suspended."

Rusty fetched the water while Doug released his seatbelt and settled on the roof. She gave Doug a bottle of water, opened one for herself, and turned off the flashlight. "We'd better think this through before we do anything," she said.

Rusty heard nothing except the sound of their breathing. *Thank God, we have air*, she thought as she opened the valve on one of the tanks. The water was making her seat wet.

***

Rusty sat in the dark and thought about their predicament. She had trained people to escape from a submerged vehicle. It was ridiculous that she felt helpless under the circumstances. Her training, however, did not include a category five hurricane, extra-strength car windows, or blocked doors.

"You're probably stronger than I am," she said to Doug. "You can most likely make a hole in the rear window with one of the air cylinders in one swipe."

"I can get to the linkage from inside," said Doug, "and unlatch the door before we equalize the pressure."

"What's the advantage to that?"

"With the water rushing in, I might not be able to grasp the outside handle through the hole. This way, we know the door is unlatched before we let the water come in."

"Okay. That sounds reasonable," said Rusty.

"How deep do you think we're submerged?"

Doug asked.

"Maybe eight, ten feet. Deep enough to get a lot of pressure."

"Do we have enough air just to let one tank run continually?"

"Yes," said Rusty." I already have one going. Let's get another flashlight out as well."

"Okay," said Doug. "We'd better strip down to the essentials. We'll have to swim our way out of here."

Rusty took off everything except her bra and panties. Doug took off all of his clothes except his shorts.

"You ready?" asked Doug.

"Let's go." Rusty turned on the flashlight and aimed it toward Doug's seat.

Doug searched above the seat bottom and found another flashlight. He snatched an air tank from the rack and positioned himself in the rear of the Hummer.

"Shine your flashlight at the top of the hatch," he said to Rusty. "Remember, the vehicle is upside down, so I'm working from bottom to top."

Rusty watched as Doug removed the panel from the hatch. After Doug had removed the panel, Rusty could see the linkage to the door latch. She watched Doug pull on the chain and heard the door latch release. Doug pushed the door forward and inserted a plastic tongue depressor to secure the unlatched position. Water seeped around the hatch seal.

"Can't you just push it open?" Rusty asked.

"It took all of my strength just to shove it out an eighth of an inch for an instant. I don't have the leverage to push it open."

"Can you get in position to break the window?"

"I'm going to get over on the left and brace against the cold chest," said Doug. "You ought to get over to the right, because the water will come straight through the hole."

Doug moved to the back of the Hummer and Rusty propped against the rear of the passenger seat. She grabbed a support stay on the floor of the Hummer that was now over her head. Doug lined up with the center of the Hummer's rear window and swung the air tank hard against the window.

"It didn't break," said Rusty. She saw the window crack into a spider web of cracks. Water trickled through in small drops and Rusty released her hold on the floor strut.

Doug drew back to take another swing at the window when the dam burst. The window bowed in momentarily, as the water pressure stretched the bonding impregnated in the glass. Then, it split, opening up like an overstretched grocery bag. The air bubble evacuated the back of the van with explosive force and the deluge hit Rusty squarely in the chest, throwing her over the front seat into the front windshield. The impact stripped the flashlight from her hand and she found herself in total darkness.

Rusty felt around the dashboard to get her bearings. She turned in the water and found the headrest for one of the seats. She pushed back with her legs against the console toward the back of the vehicle. She came up short. Something had wrapped itself around her ankle. She bent over to remove it, but it seemed to have many layers of wrap, something like a fish net. She could not extract her ankle, so she decided to see if she could pull it loose.

She now recognized that holding her back was the webbing that separated the front of the Hummer from the back. Rusty put her foot against the back of the seat and pulled on the webbing. It should pull away from the fasteners. Sure enough, the webbing came away from the roof of the vehicle one rivet at a time. Rusty kept working at it until the webbing came loose. She was running out of air and could not remove it from her ankle. As Rusty began swimming toward the rear of the Hummer, the webbing snagged, holding her back.

Rusty's lungs were on fire. She had to resist the urge to take a breath. The water was working its way up her nostrils, flooding her sinuses. She sneezed pulling water into her mouth and starting a flood down her trachea into her lungs. She knew she was losing consciousness. One final desperate attempt failed. Rusty felt her flailing body going limp.

Rusty's spirit lingered for an indeterminate time, perceiving not so much the scene below it as taking in the totality of the life it had shared for thirty-five years. The little girl growing up in the Mississippi bayous. The determined Tulane student – honor student and gymnast. The paramedic, willing to serve and work hard. Finally, the successful medical professional that earned the title "Chief" in a small Florida town. Rusty's life sealed in that unfathomable manifold we call existence. Timeless in its eternity, without space in its infinity.

CHAPTER 12

"The wise man in the storm prays to God, not for safety from danger, but deliverance from fear"

Ralph Waldo Emerson

In spite of her denial, Simon had decided that Miss Bonnie was a witch. Ordinary people did not bring spiritual chiefs out of the sky. Only a witch would stand up to an ancient chief, a powerful figure in himself, and make him cure Simon's mother. Simon knew from the Wizard of Oz that there are good witches and bad witches. He figured that Bonnie was one of the good witches. Maybe, that is why she denied it. She did not want Simon to think she was a bad witch. He decided to ask her again.

"You are a witch, aren't you?" he asked.

"No, Simon," Bonnie answered, "I'm not. It might be easier if I were."

"Then, how come the chiefs are coming to see you? How come they act like they know you?"

"It started with my mother."

"Was she a witch?"

Bonnie chuckled softly. "Hardly. She wasn't much older than you are. She died young."

"Were you an orphan?" Simon thought that unusual things often happened to orphans.

"Not that I ever knew then. I was adopted, but I didn't know it until my real mother came back from the dead to find me."

"I didn't know people could come back after they died," said Simon. Simon did not doubt that they could, but he had never seen anyone that was supposed to be dead.

"I didn't either." Bonnie tilted her head. "Mostly, they don't or can't. I think my mother had some spiritual help."

"Wow. Like an angel?" Simon couldn't think of any other spiritual beings.

"From friends of the witch I told you about. She lives in Florida, about fifty miles away from here."

"What kind of friends? Were they angels?"

"I don't think they were angels. They were spiritual friends. You can't see them unless they want you to."

"Where is your mother now? Could I meet her?"

"She went on the great ecstasy, as the chief referred to it."

"So she's really dead now?"

"Yes, but she left something behind. The spirit of the chief's daughter. That's why he came to see me."

"Is she the girl I saw, the 'daughter of the wind'?"

"I think so. I'm not sure if that was her."

"Do you know where she is?"

"Her spirit is inside me. I'm carrying a baby. The chief's daughter 's spirit has possessed my baby."

"So you're married?"

Bonnie shrugged her shoulders. "Not yet," she said.

"What're ya gonna do," asked Simon, "about the chief's daughter?"

Bonnie shook her head. "I don't know."

"I think you should ask my mom. She knows everything."

Simon saw a tear form in one of Bonnie's eyes. "Is my mom okay?" he asked.

"She's going to be all right," Bonnie said. "She's just not up to answering questions right now."

Simon wanted something to drink. "The refrigerator is still cold," he said. "It's not running any more, but the drinks will still be okay."

"Sure," said Bonnie. "What've you got?"

"Coke, tea, ginger ale, water..."

"Just water would be fine."

Simon and Bonnie walked into the kitchen. In the light of the droplight, Simon could see that the wind and rain had soaked the walls and floor next to the garage. Simon fetched a Coke for himself and some bottled water for Bonnie. They carried their drinks into the living room. "Ya know me and my mom; we spend a lot of time together 'cause my dad works all the time."

"I could tell you love her very much."

"I love my dad too, but my mom, she puts up with stuff, and she's real smart."

"What do you think she would tell me to do?" asked Bonnie. "About the spirit of the chief's daughter."

"The girl I saw was kinda pretty. I think my mom would say that she's your daughter too, and you just ought'a love her as she is." Simon was sure that was what his mother would do.

"That might work. I would love her, but I keep thinking about the unrealized spirit of my real daughter. I have to love her too."

"Maybe they would be like sisters," said Simon, "just sharing the same body."

Simon felt Bonnie's intense stare. "How would you like to share your mind and body with an unborn brother?" she asked.

Simon tried to imagine what that would be like. "I don't think I'd like it," he said.

"I shared my soul with my mother's spirit for a couple of months," said Bonnie. "I already had a well-developed psyche, and it was still quite uncomfortable. I couldn't put my daughter through that."

"So, what're you gonna do?"

"Maybe I'll talk to the witch that helped me before," said Bonnie.

"Can I go with you?" asked Simon.

"Only if your mother and father approve."

"Neat." Simon could hardly wait to meet a real witch

***

Bonnie knew that Chief Ho-tah-lee would return later. She knew they had not settled the fate of her daughter or the issue of Banna. She also knew that

Aggie's sickness was temporarily allayed, but not cured. The storm went on incessantly, wave after wave of wind and rain. The clock ran on past seven o'clock, and Bonnie knew it should be daylight. Shuttered in as they were, she had no idea if it was brighter outside or not.

She wanted to know how the storm was progressing, so she walked back to the kitchen where she found Ladamien glued to the radio.

"Where is the storm now?" she asked him.

"The highest winds are in the Sanford area," Ladamien answered. "They've reported gusts as much as one hundred and thirty miles per hour near Lake Monroe."

"There won't be anything left standing. How about Orlando?"

"The hurricane has stayed a little north. Winter Park is taking a beating. They expect Dirk to go west of Deland and then curve north."

Bonnie went into the bedroom and came back with her emergency two-way radio. "I'll see if my station knows what's going on," she said. Bonnie powered the transmitter. "Coreopsis station 2," she said, "This is Bonnie McConnell checking in."

Kathie Turbinov's voice came up on the receiver. "Hey Bonnie, you still in Merritt Island?"

"Yes," said Bonnie. "My patient is improved, but we still need that Coast Guard helicopter when they can get it here. Is Rusty there?"

"She and Doug went out on a call. We're somewhat worried about them. They were supposed to check in hours ago."

"It's probably chaotic out there."

"Definitely. We're still getting one hundred plus winds here."

"Have you heard from Winona? How're they doing at the Vehicle Assembly Building?"

"They ended up taking in about sixty people all told," said Kathie. "They're all going to be stuck there for a couple of days."

Bonnie thought to herself, *I had better check on Justin.* "How about the beaches," asked Bonnie? "How did they fare?"

"The National Guard just sent two surveillance teams out from Patrick Air Force Base about an hour ago. We oughta get a report around ten or so."

"When do you think they might send me my helicopter?"

"It won't be today," said Kathie. "Maybe later, early tomorrow."

"I don't think we can manage a transfer in the dark," said Bonnie. "There'll be too much water and too many fallen trees."

"You want me to set the helicopter up for daybreak tomorrow?"

"Yes, let's say eight o'clock."

"I'll let you know," said Kathie, and hung up.

Next, Bonnie tried to call Vince on the radio. After several attempts, he came on the air.

"Are you still in that gas station?" she asked.

"Yeah," said Vince. "It hung together pretty well. The overhang is long gone, the pumps are stripped, the store windows are broken, but me and the truck, we're pretty much in one piece."

"You're not flooded out?"

"Nah," said Vince. "There's a lake out there, but we could drive through it if the wind would die down some."

"We're gonna be stuck here all night," said Bonnie. "They're gonna send a helicopter first thing in the morning, and then we can pack the Avenger and head home."

"I'll be okay," said Vince. "I have water and food. I can sleep in the cab. The wind should let up during the night."

"Good," said Bonnie. "That's what we're all hoping for. See you tomorrow." She turned off the radio.

"Will Aggie be all right until tomorrow," asked Ladamien?

"Near as I can tell," said Bonnie. "It's kinda out of my hands."

"You think the chief might let her die?"

Bonnie didn't have any idea about the chief's intentions, but she didn't think Aggie was one of his concerns. "I don't think he's angry with Aggie. He's probably forgotten about her."

"Is he gone for good?"

"I'm sure he'll be back. I just don't know when or how." Bonnie wanted to change the subject. "Have you checked on the garage? Is the house holding up?"

"Yes. It's okay. Did you know it's daylight out there?"

"It should be. Can you see anything?"

"The rain seems lighter, but the wind is still quite strong. You couldn't drive in it."

"Could we go out in it?"

"I can't tell from the garage. I suppose we could go out in an emergency. Isn't your husband worried about you," Ladamien asked, "being out here pregnant and all?"

"I'm not married," Bonnie said. "The pregnancy was kind of unexpected,"

"You don't seem the type."

"What type is that?"

"Oh, I don't know," answered Ladamien. "The thoughtless type, I guess."

Bonnie had never made that association. She did not know what to say. "We were careful, but Justin and I have been together for a long time." Bonnie realized that sounded foolish as well. "We are getting married."

"How do you feel about giving up your independence?" Ladamien asked.

"I was married before and lost my son and husband in an auto accident. I was kind of afraid of getting hurt again."

"You don't have to explain it to me," said Ladamien. "When is the wedding?"

"Right after this hurricane blows over."

"I bet he's worried sick with you out here. I would be."

"Yeah," Bonnie admitted. "I would too. I'll text him and see if he's paying attention."

"Why texting?" asked Ladamien.

"It takes up less network space," said Bonnie. "Voice communication ties up the system."

"I'll leave you alone," said Ladamien. "I'll go check on Aggie." He left the room, so Bonnie was alone.

Bonnie turned on her cell phone and sent a text message to Justin. *How r u? I'm ok on Merritt Island.*

Bonnie didn't expect Justin to respond immediately, so she was surprised when her phone chirped less than a minute after she sent the text message.

I'm ok too, Justin responded. *Busy in VAB – winds 90 kt. Helping Winona – about seventy evacuees here.*

Gr8, Bonnie answered. *C u soon. All my love.*

Bonnie was relieved to find out that Justin was weathering the storm. Ninety knots was hurricane strength, but survivable. The worst was probably over.

***

Bonnie went to the kitchen and obtained a candle. She lit it and went to the bedroom, which she had confiscated as her control center. She preferred the candlelight to the electric lamp. The soft flickering glow seemed to her to be more appropriate to the recurring waves of wind and rain that echoed through the walls of the house. It reminded her of a scene from a thirties' Peter Lorre movie, except the terror of the wind seemed less sinister than the murderer in "M", perhaps because it was physically in the present, instead of unseen.

Bonnie relaxed on the bed and closed her eyes.

Then she heard the internal voice and felt the sensation that had haunted her once before. "Who is there?" she asked.

No one answered, but she still discerned the other presence, the unseen manifestation of a possessing spirit. "I know you are there," Bonnie said. "Who is it?"

Slowly, an apparition formed before her eyes. The young woman she saw was not at all ghostly. She was genuine and strikingly beautiful. She wore the clothes of a princess – a gossamer blue overgarment, gauzy with shimmering gold undergarments. Her onyx black hair sparkled in the candle light and her skin had the burnished appearance of a smoothly tanned model. She spoke with quiet assurance in surprisingly clear English. "I am Banna, the spirit of your daughter."

Bonnie considered Banna's words. "I've been led to understand that you are an intruder, that you have taken over my daughter's soul and replaced her true spirit."

"Whoever told you that is lying."

"I believe Kameeshi. The alien has never lied to me before."

"Perhaps not lying," said Banna. "Maybe, just misleading."

"What are you saying?" asked Bonnie.

"At this point in its development, your embryo has no chosen spirit. I can be that spirit just as readily as any other."

"Aren't you depriving another spirit the opportunity to live?"

"It's not a privilege. A fresh spirit does not know about the denial of life. Other opportunities abound."

"My mother, Julie, had her own spirit. You were a parasite, assuming her identity. I may not want you as a daughter."

"You can't deny me without rejecting the spirit of your natural daughter." Banna tented her hands in a begging posture. "Let us share our existence. Love us both. You will barely know I exist."

Bonnie believed that Banna's view was probably true. It agreed with what Kameeshi had told her. "I'm not going to have an abortion, if that's what concerns you. I don't seem to have a choice."

"When you accepted Justin's proposal, I knew you were not thinking about an abortion."

"Of course I wasn't. I want our baby." Bonnie sat up on the bed so she could look directly at Banna, who appeared to be standing next to the dresser. "You say I won't know you exist. How do you explain Julie's wildness?"

"That wasn't me. Julie's spirit was like that without my help."

"How many times have you pulled this trick; sharing a soul?"

"Dozens. Since I was conceived."

"I know your father was the wind. Who was your mother?"

"My mother was the fire beneath the Earth. I am fire and air."

"So, you achieve your human existence by occupying unborn souls?"

"Yes. I cannot be human on my own, and nothing can destroy me. I must live vicariously."

Bonnie had ceased to question the impossible. Her experiences with Julie had conditioned her to accept the existence of the spirit world and its inscrutabilities. "And the spirit of my true daughter, it is still intact and in possession of its soul?"

"Sure. I would not harm it. I waited for your pregnancy so I would have a soul to enjoy."

This explained to Bonnie why she had become pregnant in spite of precautions. "You're a sneak," she said.

Banna's image adapted a smug look. "I do what I have to do, but Justin is still the father."

"That's nice," said Bonnie. "I'd hate to think something happened I don't remember."

"I need to show you something," said Banna's spirit.

The image before Bonnie changed dramatically. She was outside in the storm, looking at a large pool of water. Beneath the water was a large dark object, a small truck, or a large van. She went beneath the water where she could look inside the vehicle.

"Oh my God!" Bonnie said. "Is that Rusty? She looks dead."

"It is your friend. She is not dead, not yet."

Unwelcome tears came to Bonnie's eyes and she sobbed. "That's terrible," she said. "What do you mean, 'not yet'?"

"There is air in the van," said the spirit. "She became tangled in that webbing and almost drowned. She will revive"

Bonnie shook her head. "Are you some kind of monster? What kind of evil thing created you?"

"Nothing evil, and nothing good," said Banna's spirit. "Only fate and the capriciousness of the universe."

Bonnie found the two-way radio and took it back to the bedroom with her. She turned it on and selected a channel.

"Hurricane central, this is Bonnie McConnell. Is Gus there?"

"I'll get him," said the person at the other end.

"Bonnie," said Gus, "how're you doing?"

"We're okay. Look, I had another vision. I saw Rusty dead in a lake or a pond. Is she okay?"

"Damn," said Gus. "They just pulled her out not forty minutes ago. Doug made it to a friend's house and called for help. They rolled their Hummer into a retention pond. Doug thought she had followed him to the surface, but he couldn't find her. Kathie sent out a search party and they found her inside the vehicle."

"But, she's still alive?"

"It was a kind of miracle. They opened an air canister before they tried to get out and when she passed out; she floated up into the air cavity."

"Is she going to be all right?

"I'll let you know after the doctors get a chance to look at her."

"At least she's not a casualty."

"No, but we have some, seven so far. This is one of the worst hurricanes ever. It is really devastating inland."

"What and where is it now?" Bonnie wanted to get an idea of what they could expect in the morning.

"The eye is just passing over Lake Mary. It's a marginal category two and the National Hurricane Center expects that it will still be a hurricane when it enters the Gulf."

"What about the beaches?"

"The search teams have been out for a couple of hours. They sent back photos. The devastation is remarkable. The water cut the foundations out from under the older houses, especially around Pelican Point. They collapsed. The pier is gone. Port Canaveral held up astonishingly well. There was severe beach erosion."

"Nothing unexpected really," said Bonnie. "You say the inland is taking a beating?"

"Yeah. They didn't take it as seriously as they should have. The coastal counties did all right, considering. Orange, Osceola, and Seminole underestimated Dirk. We don't know about Lake or Marion. The storm hasn't finished with them yet."

"How did Coreopsis fare? Do Justin and I still have a house?"

"Probably, unless a tree fell on it. You may not have a roof."

"Has anyone contacted Rusty's family?"

"Not yet. Someone will call them soon."

"I feel better knowing she's alive."

"Yeah. Take care" said Gus. "I'll see you later."

Bonnie put the radio away and lay on her back,

trying to regain her composure.

***

Until her conversation with Banna, Bonnie had not considered the possibility that the spirit possessing her was malevolent. After all, Julie's spirit had been that of a sixteen-year-old waif, innocent and buoyant. Until now, Banna's spirit had been a porthole to an unseen world, apparently blissful and serene. Now, suddenly, Bonnie recognized the scenario for the Lewis Carroll parody that it was. She was Alice, bandied about by the Mad Hatters and Cheshire Cats of a capricious nightmare – the unknowing pawn in a sinister game.

What could she do about it? Whom could she ask?

Bonnie thought that formal religion, in order to gain converts and mislead the innocent, had oversimplified the conflict between good and evil on the cosmic scale. She had no doubt that there was a world beyond this one, perhaps more than one, even an infinite number. Julie had shown her that there is a path between the domains of the living and the dead. Bonnie had seen that some detached spirits could be well intentioned and good, while others were definitely self-serving and evil. *How could she learn more? Whom could she trust that would be expert in such matters?*

Bonnie did not have faith in the emissaries of organized religions. All manner of friends and relatives had quoted the Christian scriptures to her to the point of brainwashing indoctrination. As far as she was concerned, they did not know, they did not believe – they only preached. She had no evidence that the Buddhists, Pagans, Muslims, or Hindus were any different.

She certainly could not rely on any of the actors in this lampoon – not even Kameeshi. Some of them, such as the witch, Lady Victoria, undoubtedly knew a great deal, but their motivations were suspect. Bonnie finally decided that the two people she could have confidence in, who might have some insight were the psychiatrist, Dr. Blaine, and the hypnotist, Marcie Reese. She would talk to them after the storm had passed. She thought that Banna could read her mind, but she was determined to find the underlying cause of the situation and solve it to her satisfaction. Part of that solution had to include freeing herself and her daughter from any possession.

Having thought out a plan of action, Bonnie felt better. She blew out the candle and went into the bedroom to check on Aggie. Thad and Ladamien were standing watch.

"Where's Simon?" Bonnie asked.

"He went back to his room to play Tetris," said Ladamien. "He's getting bored."

"I can't say I blame him," said Thad. "I'm feeling kind of house bound myself."

"How's Aggie?" asked Bonnie. "Have you checked lately?"

"Little change," Thad answered. "Blood oxygen dropped some, but it's still acceptable. I just hope she stays stable until the helicopter can get in."

"Have you thought about how we're going to get her out to the road?"

"You can bring the Avenger around to the

front," Thad answered. "Ladamien and I should be able to bring Aggie out. We can throw a waterproof sheet over her to keep her dry. We should follow the road this time. Taking the Avenger through the woods would be too risky."

Bonnie left Aggie's room and went into the living room. Ladamien followed her.

"You look upset," said Ladamien, "like you've been crying."

"It's just the strain," said Bonnie. "The storm, the chief..." Bonnie paused, "...and some other things."

"Yeah," said Ladamien. "I got some of those other things too. I have been thinkin' about what you said, about the human traffickin' and all."

"You have a legitimate business," said Bonnie. "Why don't you just quit the other stuff?"

"You don't just walk out on the gang," said Ladamien. "Leroy, the boss, he'd have me killed."

"Bad dude, huh."

"Tough. Besides, it's the law of the gang. Nobody just quits."

"I understand," said Bonnie. "Look, I ran into a federal agent in Atlanta – Chris Zirkle. He specializes in investigating criminal activities by gangs. Maybe, he could help you. I'd trust him."

"How'd you meet him?"

"He captured my father, Cody Wilkins, and put him in jail. Cody was the one that convinced you to join the gang. Isn't that what you told me?"

"Yeah, Cody was the boss, just like Leroy is now. Leroy runs a tighter ship than Cody did."

Ladamien ran his left thumb over the fingers of his left hand, almost as if he were going to snap them. Bonnie had noticed he had the habit of doing this when he was thinking.

"You think this Zirkle fella could help me without my going to jail?" asked Ladamien.

"I don't know," said Bonnie. "After the hurricane passes, I'll get in touch with him and see what he says."

"He's gonna want details. What are you gonna tell him?"

"That it's confidential. I won't tell him about you specifically."

"You run the risk of being charged with a crime."

"I'm past being afraid of the law anymore."

"You must be in serious trouble if that doesn't scare you. What's up with you?"

"The spirit of the chief's daughter – it has possessed my unborn child. I don't know how to get rid of it, and I don't know who to ask."

"You need an exorcist," Ladamien said emphatically.

"I'm not sure I believe in all that stuff," said Bonnie, "what with the priests and the spitting up and all those incantations."

"Maybe it isn't like that," Ladamien said. "My momma would know. She's very religious."

"Why would I trust your mother?"

"You kiddin'?" Ladamien smiled. "God and the devil himself would trust my momma. If she don't know, she'll tell you so."

"Tell you what," said Bonnie. "After the storm, I'll talk to Chris and you talk to your mother. No commitment, just to see what they say. Okay?"

"You got a deal," said Ladamien. "We'll probably have to go to Belle Glade if my momma agrees to talk to you. Will we have to go to Atlanta to see the agent?"

"I don't know," said Bonnie. "I'll let you know after I talk to Chris."

Bonnie and Ladamien looked at each other with a sense of accomplishment.

***

Ladamien went into the bedroom to check on Aggie. Bonnie was in the room changing out Aggie's I.V. He saw that tubes from two machines ran into Aggie's body. He assumed they regulated the delivery of air and nutrients. They were plugged into the extension cord that he had hooked up in the garage.

"It looks like you need the electricity to run those machines?" Ladamien remarked. "The generator probably needs refueling."

"They can run on batteries," said Bonnie, "but it would be better if we had external power. Batteries run down quickly."

"I'll get Thad and we'll go outside and fill up the tank."

Ladamien found Thad in the kitchen. "You up to going outside?" he asked.

"It'll break the monotony," said Thad. "What're we going to do?"

"Fuel up the generator. We got to keep Aggie's life support working." Ladamien beckoned Thad to follow him. "The fuel cans are in the garage."

Ladamien went through the kitchen, which was now water-soaked, stepped into the garage, and surveyed the destruction. Rain still came down heavily and obscured the scene, and he could see that the continued onslaught had totaled Aggie's car. The garage roof was completely gone and there was more than a foot of water covering the floor. Water-soaked boxes and their contents floated in the pool and plastic containers half-filled with discolored water sat on shelves and on the floor. Ladamien spotted the fuel cans sitting on a floor rack in the back of the garage.

"It may take two," Ladamien told Thad. "You take one and I'll take one."

They waded to the holder and retrieved the fuel cans. Ladamien led the way out of the side door and to the protective barrier behind which Simon and Aggie had positioned the generator. He and Thad filled up the tank and fought their way back into the garage.

"That should last until we can get Aggie out of here," said Ladamien. "I heard Bonnie schedule the helicopter for eight o'clock tomorrow morning."

Ladamien went into the bathroom and dried off. From the bathroom, he slipped into his room and put on a pair of shorts and a knit shirt. He walked down the hall and entered the bedroom where Aggie lay on a bed. There was no one else in the room. He moved to Aggie's side and lightly clasped her hand. She opened her eyes briefly and smiled at him – a smile that brought back memories – the smile she had given him fourteen years ago when he picked her up for her senior prom.

The Swamp Rattlers' leader, Cody Wilkins, had arranged for the tuxedo and the limousine. It had taken a week to get the tuxedo ready for Ladamien and an equal length of time to get Ladamien ready for the tuxedo. By four thirty in the afternoon, Ladamien had put on the tuxedo, hair neatly trimmed and bow tie appropriately straight. It had been difficult for him to stay spick and span while waiting for the limousine. He had never met Aggie's parents before, so he was as nervous as a pig in the slaughter enclosure. When he had asked her about them, she had only said, "It's alright. They'll adore you." He wasn't so sure.

The florist delivered an orchid corsage just before Ladamien left his house in the limousine. He thought Aggie would have preferred a gardenia, but Cody had insisted an orchid was more fashionable. Ladamien sat in the back of the luxurious automobile as if he were a prisoner going to the gallows – stiff and unmoving. When the limousine stopped in front of Aggie's house in suburban Bradenton, he departed the vehicle gingerly after the chauffeur opened the door for him. Aggie's home was ample but not ostentatious, and Ladamien approached the front stoop slowly and walked up to the front door. He pressed the doorbell and Aggie's mother opened the door almost instantly.

"Come in," said Aggie's mother. "Aggie will be down shortly."

Ladamien stood at the base of the stairway and noticed Aggie's mother inspecting him.

"So you're a football player," Aggie's mother

said. "Are you going to be a professional player?"

"No ma'am. I'm not that good."

"What are your plans?"

"I'm going to run a company, a company that designs airports."

"Oh. That sounds exciting. Are you going to college to learn about management?"

"No ma'am. I couldn't get into no – uh, any university. I'm going to be the owner."

"Oh, your family has money."

"No, ma'am. I have a sponsor."

"Oh, that's nice."

Aggie came down the stairs with her hands folded in front of her. She came down slowly, like a queen coming to her coronation, and stopped halfway down. She looked at her mother and smiled pleasantly. Then, she looked at Ladamien and gave the kind of smile that launches ships, that starts and stops wars. Ladamien noticed that Aggie's mother saw it as well.

"You look like a prince," Aggie said to Ladamien. She looked at her mother. "Why don't you ask Daddy if he would like to meet Ladamien? Maybe, they can talk football sometime."

Aggie's mother went to get Aggie's father. He came, clearly unwillingly, into the living room. He shook Ladamien's hand. "Hey," he said. "When you gonna bring her home?"

"We should be back by midnight," Ladamien answered.

"Yeah, okay." Aggie's father turned to leave.

"Good to meet you."

Ladamien turned to look at Aggie. She still had that wonderful smile, the same one she had shown him a moment ago. She came the rest of the way down the stairs and took his arm. "Lead me to our chariot, sir," she had said.

Now, her face was relaxed. The machines continued to make their metronomic puttering and it seemed that Aggie's vital signs continued within acceptable limits. Ladamien bent over and kissed her lightly on the forehead. He left her side and settled in a chair.

***

Rusty's lungs automatically sucked in air. She regained consciousness slowly, moving through a tunnel of kaleidoscope lights. Every nerve in her body tingled as each recovered from oxygen deprivation and regained sensation. She comprehended that the air tank she opened earlier had filled the cavity where her head now emerged. She floated motionless and let the oxygen-rich atmosphere penetrate her being.

She had no idea how long she drifted, suspended inside the Hummer, before she heard thumping outside the vehicle, and then was aware of hands working along her almost naked body. She couldn't see anything but she felt the mask slide over her face and the rush of water as the divers removed her from the Hummer. As they placed her on a gurney, she looked around to see her rescuers. She was relieved to see Doug's face, so she knew he had gotten out safely as well.

***

Bonnie checked her watch. It was almost midnight and the storm continued. The rhythmic waves of wind and rain played their percussive symphony against the outside trees and shrubbery. She could tell that the ferocity of the hurricane had subsided, so she ventured outdoors and stood on the front portico. The wind was coming in gusts that Bonnie estimated to be forty-five or fifty miles per hour. The rain whipped around, sometimes nearly horizontal and at other times merely swirling. It was too severe to attempt leaving in the Avenger.

Thad had evidently heard her open and close the front door. He came outside and joined her.

"Kind of stimulating, isn't it?" said Thad. "It's like being in on the beginning of creation."

"I hadn't thought of it that way," said Bonnie, "but the air is super fresh. The universe is somewhat exposed. I can't describe it, but I'm impressed. Beautiful, but deadly, like so many things in nature."

"We're both going to need to get some sleep," Thad said. "I'll keep watch on Aggie and wake you up at four."

"Good. I need some rest."

Thad opened the door and ushered Bonnie inside. The wind slammed the door shut just after he stepped inside.

Bonnie went back to the bedroom and collapsed on the bed. Her mind kept returning to Banna. It was uncomfortable knowing that a spirit possessed her daughter that did not intend to go away. She was dozing and images kept running through her mind.

Images of natural Florida. Impressions of life in the Ais village. Visions of the Spanish conquerors and their annihilation of the Native Americans. The aura of an apparition that had lived hundreds of times. A nightmare in immortality. She was fast asleep when she heard Thad's voice.

"Bonnie. Bonnie." Thad was shaking her. "Bonnie, it's four o'clock."

Bonnie struggled to open her eyes. "You ready to get some rest?" she asked Thad.

"Yes. Wake me when you're ready to leave."

"It'll take us about two hours to prepare Aggie and get to State Road 3. I'll check on the helicopter at five forty-five and wake you at six if they're coming."

"I'll be glad to get out of here," said Thad.

"Don't be so sure," said Bonnie. "We haven't seen the worst until they start search and rescue."

"Good night," said Thad. "Close the door behind you."

Bonnie left the room and closed the door. She found a flashlight and checked on Simon. He was sleeping soundly. When she went to the bedroom, Ladamien's snoring told her that he was in with Aggie. She gave Aggie a thorough examination and found that she was stable. Her blood oxygen was just below normal and her breathing was steady.

We're going to make it through this, she told herself.

CHAPTER 13

"We feel free when we escape - even if it be but from the frying pan to the fire."

Eric Hoffer

Simon woke up at 6:30 a.m. on Thursday morning. His mouth was dry and his body felt scummy, like moldy bread. Normally, he wouldn't mind missing a bath, but between the portable potty and the humidity, he was ready to jump in a fresh clean lake and wash off the residue of the last three days. He went back to the bedroom where his mother lay and found Bonnie rearranging the tubes that supplied Aggie with air, water, food, and medicine.

"Are you getting ready to take my mom to the hospital?"

"A helicopter is supposed to pick her up in an hour and a half," said Bonnie. "I have to get her ready to go out to the highway."

"Can I go up in the helicopter?" asked Simon. "I've never flown in a helicopter."

"I don't know if there will be room," said Bonnie. "I'll have to go with your mom. We'll see when the 'copter gets here."

Simon could hear that the wind outside had died down. "Can I go outside?"

"You'll have to ask your father. It could be dangerous out there. There are probably fallen power lines and God only knows about snakes and alligators and such."

"I ain't afraid of no snakes."

"Go ask your dad."

Simon found his father in the living room laying on the sofa and listening to the radio. "Dad, can I go outside? There's no wind and I want to see how many trees got knocked down."

"I'll go with you," said Ladamien. "I'm curious to see what the house looks like from the outside. Why don't we put on our trunks and flip-flops? The water's pretty deep out there."

Simon ran back to his room and put on his bathing suit. He found an old pair of sneakers and put them on. He thought they would stay on his feet better than sandals. He waited for his father in the hallway. Ladamien joined him in a few minutes. They exited through the front door and waded out to the road. Simon looked around and saw that the wind had torn the roof from the neighbors' house. It was laying in pieces around the adjacent lawns and woods. One utility pole had broken at the base and leaned across the road supported on the other side by an oak tree.

"Bonnie's gonna have a hard time drivin' that

amphib around that power pole," said Ladamien. "She's gonna have ta go behind that shed over there. Let's go take a look-see."

Simon followed his father down the street and to the right of the power pole. He remembered what Bonnie said about fallen electrical lines but noticed the wires were all to the left of where they were wading. From farther down the road, Simon looked back at his own house. The enormous oak that Simon had climbed numerous times had split in two and one part had fallen onto the garage roof. The wind had blown away most of the garage roof. The hurricane had uprooted the two pine trees in the side yard.

Ladamien stopped and looked back toward their house. "It appears we can get Aggie out by bringing that amphib between those two trees and going around the shed. Looks like the house came through pretty good except for the garage and the roof right near the garage."

"Are you gonna get it fixed up?" asked Simon.

"Yeah, but it might be a good time to move to Boca Raton. We can afford to sell. Won't get much for it anyway, what with the economy and the storm."

Simon and his father continued wading up the road. A couple of times, they stumbled in ruts under the water that they could not see.

"We'd better go back and tell Bonnie what we've seen," said Ladamien. "She ought to be about ready to leave. We'll just stay in our suits. Make it easier to get around."

Simon and his father returned to the house and

dried off before going to the bedroom to check on Bonnie and Aggie. Thad was there as well.

"There's stuff scattered everywhere," said Simon.

"The eye just passed north of Eustis," said Thad. "Dirk is a category two headed for the Gulf."

"Does it threaten any major cities?" asked Bonnie.

"Maybe Apalachicola," answered Thad, "Ocala will get some of it. West of there is a lot of scrub and swamp – Cedar Key, Suwannee, small towns."

Simon listened as his father gave Bonnie and Thad a quick rundown on the conditions outside.

"Aggie's ready to go," said Bonnie. "I'll bring the Avenger around and you and Thad can bring her out." Bonnie looked at Simon. "You want to come with me?"

"Can I help?"

"Of course you can help. You can help me push us off after I get the engine started."

"Cool. Can I drive?"

"No. I had special training to learn how to drive the Avenger."

"Are you gonna wear a bathing suit?"

"I don't have one. I brought a wet suit because I thought we might have to do a water rescue. I'll go put it on now."

When Bonnie emerged from the bedroom, Simon thought she looked a little like a seal.

"Can you go under water with that suit?"

"If I had my scuba gear I could, but I didn't bring that. You ready to go fire up the Avenger?"

Simon nodded.

"We'll go out through the garage," said Bonnie. "It's closer." She led the way and Simon followed her, into the garage and out the side door. The wind still gusted and a light rain persisted. Bonnie removed the cover from the Avenger. Simon helped by unfastening the side nearest the house. Bonnie boosted Simon over the side and then clambered in herself. She started the vehicle and moved toward the west, finding a path between the two fallen pines.

She positioned the Avenger in front of the entryway to the house and climbed out of the vehicle, then went to the front door and knocked. Thad opened the door. Bonnie climbed back into the Avenger and took one end of Aggie's stretcher from Ladamien. Ladamien then scrambled into the Avenger and took the other end of the carrier from Thad, who boarded the Avenger and strapped Aggie's bed in place. When everyone had taken a seat, Bonnie started the Avenger engine.

Maneuvering through the neighborhood in the boat-like motor vehicle gave Simon a first-class view of the hurricane's destruction. Most houses were still standing. Two trailers had blown in from somewhere. They were totally ruined. Parts of roofs and sheds hung in trees and fences. Trees were down everywhere. Simon saw a dead dog floating alongside the road. He recognized it. It was a stray the kids called Pooch. Finally, they came around the corner and saw the filling station where Vince had parked the flatbed.

Simon looked to the north and saw a large helicopter painted red and white. "Look," he said, "there's the chopper."

Simon watched as the HH-65 Dauphin helicopter came overhead and hovered in front of the service station. He saw Vince come out of the station and wave them in. The helicopter sat down and the main rotor stirred up the standing water in State Road 3. The medic from the helicopter jumped into the water and came over to help Bonnie with Aggie's carrier. They carried Aggie to the helicopter and lifted her onboard. The medic jumped into the helicopter and Bonnie stood in the water. She waved at Simon.

"You want to come," she yelled. "Hurry up or we'll leave you behind."

Simon couldn't believe he was going to fly in the copter, but he looked at his father and saw him smile reassuringly. Simon waded to the helicopter as quickly as he could and Bonnie gave him a lift inside. As Bonnie climbed aboard, the helicopter started its assent. Simon saw that his mother was resting peacefully.

***

After making sure Aggie's hookup was in place and checking her vital signs, Bonnie glanced out of the helicopter window to survey the damage from Hurricane Dirk. At first, she saw little, other than the high water, which covered the roads and overflowed into fields and yards. After they crossed the Indian River to the mainland, however, she saw many signs of destruction. Piers that once connected to boathouses now ended abruptly. In some cases, the storm had detached and demolished the boathouses and swept them to various parts of the river.

The Dauphin followed the shoreline north

passing over Titusville and Mims. Bonnie looked down on the marinas and saw that several boats had broken loose from their moorings and been tossed onto the docks. There was almost no traffic on the roads. Clearly, the storm had closed businesses and schools. People were apparently waiting for an all clear from local government before they resumed their normal activities. As Bonnie's eyes adjusted to interpreting the aerial view, she realized that trees and utility poles were scattered like toothpicks and trailer parks looked more like salvage yards than residential complexes.

As Bonnie watched, the scene spun around before her. The houses and boats were gone. Troops of Spanish soldiers marched along swaths between the trees, dressed in body armor and carrying medieval weapons. Before them, they herded small gaggles of dark-skinned people – men, women, and children – bound and chained together with rope. Bonnie watched as the Spaniards slaughtered them and pushed their bodies into shallow graves.

"Miss!"

Bonnie felt someone shaking her by the shoulder. She came out of her trance and looked at the Coast Guard medic. He was trying to get her attention.

"Your patient is in trouble," he said. "She's gagging. I tried to open her passages but we're losing her."

Bonnie crawled to Aggie's side. She was checking the intubation when Chief Ho-Tah-Lee appeared before her.

I could let her die, he intoned in Bonnie's mind.

Bonnie projected her thoughts, something she

had learned from the previous possession by her mother. *What do you want? Let her live.*

I want my daughter's spirit to return to me.

So do I, I want her out of my daughter's soul.

Make it happen.

Chief Ho-tah-lee's image disappeared and Bonnie saw Aggie's vital signs recover.

"What did you do?" asked the medic. "That was quick."

"Bonnie," said Bonnie. "My name is Bonnie."

"Oh, Mike," the medic said. "Lieutenant Michael Bakker, Public Health Services. Now, what did you do?"

Bonnie knew that Lieutenant Bakker had watched her adjust Aggie's tubing. He would see through any implausible explanations.

"Nothing special," she answered. "I just adjusted the tube. It had slipped a little."

Mike looked at her with his eyes aslant. "You must have the magic touch."

"Sometimes," Bonnie agreed, "but not always. Have you been out to the beaches?"

"We spent the last three hours out there. It's an unusual sight. I've never seen anything like it."

"In what way?"

"The sand, most of it is gone. The ocean just ate it. There are big buildings standing on their pilings and you could drive underneath them. The sand is gone."

"That must be weird. How about people? Are there many dead?"

"We only picked up one. Almost everyone evacuated the part of the beach where we went. A few individuals rode it out. Some of them were injured, lucky to be alive."

"That's good news. I bet they were glad to see you."

"We flew over to Orlando Regional Medical Center with one victim. The St. Johns River looks like a lake. It will flood all the way to Jacksonville."

"That's happened before. Remember Fay?"

"This was more. It came faster and harder. Fay was just a tropical storm."

"Where is Dirk now?" Bonnie asked.

"It's just north of Wildwood. The National Hurricane Center downgraded it to a category one."

Bonnie felt the copter spin slowly. "Are we there?" she asked.

Mike nodded, and took his seat. Bonnie took her seat and fastened her harness. She checked Simon to make sure he had buckled his seatbelt. "Did you enjoy the ride?" she asked

"It was cool, real cool," said Simon.

The pilot set the helicopter squarely in the middle of the helipad at Coreopsis Hospital. Two orderlies and a nurse came out to meet them. Bonnie and Lieutenant Bakker lifted Aggie's carrier down to the orderlies. As they left with her, Bonnie jumped out of the helicopter and helped Simon disembark. She saw Dr. Nieves standing at the entrance to the hospital. Taking Simon's hand, she walked over to Dr. Nieves.

Dr. Nieves looked at Simon. "Is that your mother?" he asked. Pointing toward the entrance.

"Yes sir," said Simon. "Will she be alright?"

"We'll do our best," said Dr. Nieves. "She's made it this far. I'd say her chances are good."

Dr. Nieves turned back toward Bonnie. "We're going to put her in isolation until we know for sure what we're dealing with. The Centers for Disease Control requires that we take no chances with possible pandemics."

"Is there anything we should be doing?" Bonnie asked, indicating Simon.

"You're probably tired and yucky," said the doctor. "Why don't you take some time to clean up? I'll have one of the nurses dig up some scrubs for you and the boy. Then, you can get some decent food and rest for a while. I'll know where you are and let you know what we find."

Bonnie was relieved to have the responsibility lifted from her shoulders for a time. One of the nurses came and led them to a small room on the sixth floor. Bonnie followed her willingly. She needed to call Justin.

***

Ladamien had watched the helicopter lift off and head north. He was relieved to know that Aggie would now receive proper medical care. Bonnie would look after Simon.

"What're you guys gonna do now," he asked Vince and Thad. "Are you gonna head back to the barn?"

"The Emergency Center wants us to stay right here," said Vince, "at least for the time being. We'll join the search and rescue effort shortly."

"Can you get me a ride to wherever they've taken my wife and boy?"

"I'll check with the Sheriff," said Vince. "They may be able to pick you up. Do you need to go back to your house?"

"Yeah," Ladamien answered. "I need to secure the generator and pick up a few things."

"I can run you back in the Avenger. Thad can wait here for us."

As they rode back in the Avenger, Ladamien realized that he and Aggie would probably not live in this house again. He appreciated how fortunate he was to have the money to write off a home and not worry about how to pay for another. The Swamp Rattlers made that possible. How could he turn against them? They had earned his loyalty.

"Have you ever been out of the country?" Ladamien asked Vince.

"I was in Kuwait," said Vince. "Stationed at Camp Doha in Ad-Dawhah. Third Army. No recreational travel if that's what you mean."

"No. I was wonderin' more if you'd ever seen what conditions are like in other countries."

"Couldn't judge. A country at war isn't much for comparison. I think they had it pretty good there until the Iraqis came in."

"Yeah. Kuwait, Dubai, they're pretty well off, especially if you're among the rich."

"We have poor people everywhere, even in the U.S."

"I know. However, we treat our poor people pretty well. Many places in the world, they don't.

Countries like Myanmar, Iran, North Korea, Sudan, and Uzbekistan."

"Have you been to all those places?" Vince asked.

"Yes," Ladamien replied, "and, lots of others where people are treated badly."

"What were you doing there? Sounds like a lot of travel."

"I own a company that builds airports." Ladamien realized what an excellent cover his business made for him to travel and account for large amounts of money. Leroy must know how valuable he was to the gang.

"Doesn't seem to me that poor people fly much," said Vince, "but I guess it would give you a chance to see many countries. Show me where you live."

"Over there, to your right."

Vince maneuvered the Avenger until he found a firm purchase. Then, he parked. "Can I help you with anything?" Vince asked.

"No," said Ladamien "It'll only take me about fifteen minutes."

Ladamien went through the house to the generator. He turned it off and went back to the house to disconnect the cable and cover it. He turned off the circuit breakers. He grabbed a knapsack from the hall closet and stuffed it with a change of clothes and personal toiletries. He lifted the mattress and saw his 9mm. He left it there. There was too much possibility that the authorities might search him. On the way out, he locked all of the doors and waded to the Avenger.

"Let's go," said Ladamien. "That's as secure as I

can make it."

Vince started the Avenger and circled around to follow the road. "I've been thinking about what we were talking about," he said. "Don't you think the United States and United Nations are doing something to help people in those places?"

"It's gotten better in some spots," Ladamien admitted, "but there are many places they don't really know what's going on. Local officials get paid off and lie."

"I imagine that goes on everywhere. Money talks all over the world."

"You're right about that," said Ladamien.

Why would I give that up? Ladamien thought to himself. *The Rattlers give me the best of all worlds. Money and status. I'd be dumb to give myself up.*

Ladamien no longer kidded himself that what he had done was good for the people he had transported. They were the lost anyhow, but it wasn't his burden to save them. He had done what he did because it paid well. Besides, what else could he do? Join the lost. Screw it; he was just making it, like everybody else.

"What'd you do in the military?" Ladamien asked Vince.

"Motor pool. Trucks and engines have been my life. I took the medical training because Uncle Sam paid for it."

"You're not a bleeding heart?"

"Wasn't. Seven years in this job rather changed that. You see so much misfortune, people needing help. It touches you in a peculiar way." Vince turned the Avenger toward State Road 3. "Like this hurricane. Think how many people will lose everything? Their homes, their money, their jobs, even members of their families or their lives. They need us."

Ladamien thought about what it would be like to feel needed, but he knew. Aggie and Simon needed him. So did Leroy.

"It's a good feeling to be needed," said Ladamien. "Is there a way we can check on Aggie? Make sure she's all right."

"I'll call the hospital when we get back to the truck," Vince answered.

"I gotta call my momma, too," said Ladamien. He wanted her advice. He wasn't sure if he felt inclined to keep his promise to Bonnie about the federal agent, but some time with Jezebel Upton would be good for both of them.

"Your cell phone probably works," said Vince. "You can most likely call her on it."

Ladamien called up his contacts on his cell phone and dialed his mother. She answered after four rings.

"Son," she said, "How y'all doin' up there? Is everyone okay?"

"Aggie's real sick, Momma. They flew her to the hospital. I'm okay and Simon's fine, but the house is ruined. That was some kinda hurricane."

"Ah been watchin' the news. Ah's worried mos' pow'ful 'bout y'all. What's wrong wi' Aggie?"

"She caught some tropical disease down in Jamaica."

"All them foreign places. Wonder you ain't died

of the typhoid or the tetanus."

"Momma, I need to come see you, and bringin' a friend. We need your counsel."

"You didn' get some girl pregnant did you?"

"No Momma. She's carryin' a baby, but it isn't mine. We need spiritual advice."

"You need to pray. Jesus is the only one can help you."

"I tried that, Momma. It don't work."

"When you comin'?"

"Prob'ly Saturday."

"Well y'all come on. You are my son, and any friend of yours is welcome in my home." After a short pause, Jezebel continued, "Cept'n that skunk Leroy. He ain't welcome here."

"Thanks Momma." Ladamien clicked off and gave a sigh, not of relief but of foreboding.

CHAPTER 14

"Promise me you'll always remember: You're braver than you believe, and stronger than you seem, and smarter than you think." Christopher Robin to Pooh

A. A. Milne

Bonnie settled Simon and then crept out of the room, wearing her scrubs, and approached the nurses' station.

"Do you have a phone I can use?" she asked.

"The phone service has been a little iffy," said the nurse, "but there is a guest phone in the office next to the waiting room over there. Just go through that door to the right."

Bonnie went through the waiting room and entered the small office. She dialed Justin's cell phone figuring that he might not be close to the phone in the VAB. The phone rang five times and then asked her to leave a message.

"Justin. It's Bonnie. I'm at the hospital, fifth floor. Call the nurses' station. I want to know you're okay."

She went back through the waiting room and found the floor nurse.

"I'm Bonnie McConnell," she told the nurse. "I'm a paramedic with station two. I'm expecting a call. Would you please come get me from the waiting room if a call for me comes in?"

The nurse nodded indicating she would take care of it. "Did you get enough rest?" she asked. "You were out in the storm a long time."

"I feel better rested just getting cleaned up, thank you."

"That was a close call about Rusty," said the nurse.

"I found out that she survived the accident," said Bonnie.

"She did, but it was a miracle. She got to the air in the nick of time."

"We need miracles in times like these." Bonnie walked back to the waiting room. In addition to worrying about Justin and the house, she was concerned about Aggie. She had done her best and the chief had helped, but Aggie's condition was still tenuous. After she talked to Justin, she would locate Dr. Nieves and find out more about Aggie's prognosis.

The waiting room had a television. Several people sat around watching the news. The station kept switching from one site to another showing the damage from Hurricane Dirk. The storm was entering the Gulf headed for Carrabelle. It had cut a fifty-mile wide swath from Cape Canaveral to Suwannee. The storm had decimated Cocoa Beach. Scenes from Titusville, Orlando, and Ocala looked like landscapes from a war. Estimates of casualties and property damage escalated every fifteen minutes.

The National Hurricane Center was predicting that the hurricane would reform and strengthen before it hit the panhandle. Cities from Perry to Panama City braced for the storm. No one was ignoring the fact that Hurricane Dirk still had a punch. It would go down in the annals of hurricane history along with Hugo, Camille, Andrew, and Katrina.

Bonnie saw a nurse's aide beckoning her from the hallway. She left her seat and went to the aide.

"You have a call in the office," said the aide. "Nurse Brantley asked me to come and tell you."

"Thanks," said Bonnie. "Can I take it in the side office next to the waiting room?"

"Yes. Look for the flashing light."

Bonnie went into the small office and picked up the phone. It was Justin.

"How did you do?" she asked. "Have you had a chance to check our house?"

"I guess an advantage of being an architect is that you design your own place. Everything came through okay, even the boat."

"Good," said Bonnie. "How did things go at the VAB?"

"It was kind of exciting. NASA saved some lives by providing a shelter convenient to the island."

"I think the government can be proud of how it responded to this storm."

"How about yourself. What's been going on?"

Bonnie caught Justin up to date on how she spent the hurricane stranded on Merritt Island with a sick woman and on Rusty's accident.

"We got the patient to the hospital," said Bonnie "Her son is here with me. I still need to catch up on my sleep."

"How's the baby doing?"

Bonnie didn't know how to answer that. "Physically? First-rate as near as I can tell. Spiritually? There's still an impasse. It's too complicated to discuss over the phone."

"Come home for dinner," Justin suggested. "I know you still have a job to do, but take a break."

"You don't mind if I bring a nine-year-old boy with me?"

"Of course not. I'd love to meet him."

"Okay. We'll be there around seven."

A nurse had opened the door and was motioning to Bonnie to hang up and come with her.

"Look," Bonnie said, "I have to go. See you at seven."

Bonnie hung up and followed the nurse to the nurses' station. Nurse Brantley came up to meet her.

"Dr. Nieves is looking for you," said the nurse. "He's in the Intensive Care Unit and wants you to meet him there."

"Alright," said Bonnie. "There's a boy in my room. I don't want him to wake up and find himself deserted. Would you please check on him occasionally?"

"We'll watch out for him," said Nurse Brantley.

Bonnie took the elevator to intensive care and checked in at the outer desk. "I'm Bonnie McConnell. Dr. Nieves is looking for me."

"He's in there," said the desk monitor. "Go on in."

Bonnie went in and saw Dr. Nieves talking to another doctor.

"I'm glad you came down," said Dr. Nieves. "There's something different about the patient you brought in. Did something unusual happen during the hurricane?"

"Like what," said Bonnie.

"I'm not sure," said Dr. Nieves. "According to all the rules, that woman should have died hours ago, yet she comes in here in apparently stable condition. Your intubation was good for a field job. We still treated her for hypoxemia and administered oxygen therapy. Her condition is still the same, stable but unresponsive."

"What does that mean, exactly?" Bonnie asked.

"She should be talking or even dancing. Instead, she appears to be in stasis."

"Just listen to me," said Bonnie. "Don't prejudge what I'm going to tell you."

"Is this a long story?"

"Somewhat."

"Let's go to the coffee nook outside ICU. I need a cup of coffee and I need to sit down."

Bonnie and Dr. Nieves left ICU and sat at a small table in the coffee nook.

"Go ahead," said Dr. Nieves.

Bonnie told him the whole story, about Chief Ho-tah-lee, Banna, the visit by the chiefs during the hurricane, and Ho-Tah-Lee's remarkable intervention. After she finished, Dr. Nieves sat looking at her with a blank stare.

"That's quite a tale," he said after a few seconds. "How does it help me cure her condition?"

"Chief Ho-Tah-Lee will be back to visit me. He still wants his daughter's spirit to leave me and go with him."

"If I believe your story, and it is hard to swallow, I should think you would want that as well."

"Not if it means that I lose my own daughter's soul in the process."

"So you think Aggie will stay in this suspended state?"

"More or less'"

"Okay. I have to take into account what you have told me, although I'm not buying it completely. We'll continue to watch her. Maybe the virus will exhaust itself. That might help. Until then," said Dr. Nieves, "I will keep her in isolation."

***

Bonnie left the intensive care ward and started upstairs to check on Simon and call Ladamien. As she entered the elevator, she heard a page for her to report to the Emergency Department drop-off area. She had been out of the main stream of emergency response for almost a week. *OK girl*, she to herself. *Are you ready to get back in the pool? She knew the page meant her unit was looking for her.*

She had no idea what they might have been facing the past two days – what with Rusty's mishap and all. She sighed, headed toward the ambulance entrance, and then she changed her mind. She turned on the walkie-talkie on her shoulder harness.

"This is Bonnie McConnell calling central."

"Hey Bonnie, this is Denise. Whaddaya need?"

"I'm at the Coreopsis Hospital. Someone paged me from the Emergency Department. Would you please find out who it was and connect me?"

"Stand by," said Denise.

Bonnie waited and watched the hospital corridor. The hospital was busier than usual. Many people looked as if they were lost, looking for a place to light until someone told them what to do next. One old woman, evidently noticing Bonnie's walkie-talkie came up to her.

"Would you please tell me where my son is?" she asked.

"Take the elevator to the lobby," said Bonnie. "The information desk is there."

The woman nodded and went to the elevator.

"Bonnie?" It was Denise. "I've got Kathie on the line. She wants to talk to you."

"Hey, Kathie. It's Bonnie. You paged me?"

"Yeah. Are you ready to go back to work? Dante, Doug, and I haven't had any sleep for the last twelve hours."

"I don't have my uniform. We cleared out of Merritt Island real quick. It was a lake."

"I don't care if you are in a bathing suit. I need a coordinator, someone who knows the local territory."

"I would think you were shorthanded for workers."

"You wouldn't believe what's happening," said

Kathie. "We've got first responders down here from Georgia, South Carolina, Tennessee – but they need direction. One unit from Baton Rouge heard about Rusty and drove through the storm to get here. They're wonderful."

"That's amazing," said Bonnie. "Is there that much to do?"

"Have you been outside?"

"I flew in, in a helicopter. I saw it from the air."

"You haven't seen anything until you are out in it," said Kathie. "Homes broken up like matchsticks and Lego blocks. People wandering around with nothing but the clothes on their backs – and sometimes, not even that."

"What about food, water, medicine?"

"FEMA, the Red Cross, everyone was down here faster than you can say Withlacoochee, but people are hurting. Everything is gone for some of them."

"Where do they go?"

"Neighbors, churches. I've never seen people being so good to one another."

Bonnie could hear the fatigue in Kathie's voice. I've got to go out there, a voice in her head said. They need me. "Can you give me an hour?" Bonnie requested. "It's important or I wouldn't ask. I have a nine-year-old boy and his father to consider."

"I've got the ambulance down in receiving," said Kathie. "If you can make it fifteen minutes, we'll wait."

Bonnie thought about it. She wanted to take Simon with her and she wanted to talk to Justin and Ladamien. "Okay," she said, "I'll see you in twenty.

Okay."

Bonnie phoned Justin. He answered immediately. "I don't have time to explain," she said, "but my unit called. They need me to go out on search and rescue."

"Call me when you're coming home," said Justin.

Bonnie went up to the room where she had left Simon. He was still sleeping. Bonnie shook him lightly. "Wake up, sweetie," she said. "We're gonna go where I can get in touch with your father."

Simon sat up and rubbed his eyes. "Gotta use the toilet," he said. "Can we get something to eat?"

"Go ahead. I'll see what I can do." While Simon went to the bathroom, Bonnie went to the nurses' station. "Do you have something for a hungry boy to eat?" she asked the nurse.

The nurse went to a small refrigerator. "There's half a bologna sandwich and a vanilla shake of some kind. Is that all right?"

"Sounds yummy," said Bonnie.

The nurse handed Bonnie the sandwich and the plastic container. "Are you leaving?" she asked.

"Yes. I have to get back to my unit. I'm taking the boy with me. If anyone is looking for us, we'll be at station two."

"Gotcha," said the nurse.

Bonnie saw Simon come into the hallway. "Ready?" she asked him. "I'm going to call your dad from here. Do you want to talk with him?"

Simon nodded and followed Bonnie to the telephone. "Will my dad be able to find us?"

"We'll tell him where we're going. He'll get to us eventually."

"What about my mom?"

"She's better off here. We'll check on her later."

Bonnie got Vince on the phone. "Is Ladamien still there with you? I want to talk to him. Simon wants to talk to him also."

"He's here. We're trying to get the Sheriff's office to take him to the hospital."

Ladamien came on the line.

"I don't have much time to talk," said Bonnie. "Aggie is in the hospital. She's stable but they need to keep her here. Simon is with me. I'm taking him with me to station 2. I have to go back on duty for awhile."

"Okay," said Ladamien. "I'm going to go to the hospital first – to try and see Aggie. I'll catch up with you and Simon."

"That's fine," said Bonnie. "When you're done at the hospital you can come to our house. It's 2637 Indian River Drive."

"Let me write that down," said Ladamien.

"Can you say hello to Simon?" Bonnie asked.

Bonnie waited while Simon talked to his father and then they walked to Emergency Intake where Kathie was waiting. Bonnie motioned to Simon to get into the ambulance beside her.

"We're gonna ride in the ambulance?" Simon asked.

"Yes," said Bonnie. "We're going to where I work."

"Cool," said Simon. "Is the driver gonna blast the siren and flash the lights?"

"I don't think so," said Bonnie. "Not unless there's an emergency."

Kathie and a driver that Bonnie didn't know got in the front. "This is Sid," said Kathie. "He's with the county."

Sid backed the ambulance out of the hangar and pulled out on US 1. Bonnie could see the damage caused by Hurricane Dirk. Kathie was correct. From the air, one could survey the scene with detachment. On the ground, it was personal. The storm had scattered sheet metal, plastic and wood all over the landscape. Trees, power poles, signs, automobiles, furniture, glass, pieces of houses, clothing, everything imaginable littered the streets, yards and ditches.

Crews worked everywhere. Tree cutters, power electricians, cleanup squads, trash collectors, and teams handing out water, food and clothing. The scene reminded Bonnie of pictures she had seen of Turkish bazaars and oriental markets. It had a businesslike efficiency in the midst of chaos. Change was in the air, in the water, and on the land. Nature at its worst and best, shaping the human soul.

Bonnie looked over at Simon. He was silent and still, but his eyes were wide – and moist.

***

Ladamien slid into the front seat of the deputy's car. "Thanks for agreeing to take me to the hospital," he said. "I'm worried about my wife and son."

"I called ahead," said the deputy. "Your wife is still at the hospital, but your son is with a paramedic.

A Miss Bonnie McConnell. I guess you know her?"

"She saved my wife's life. Rode out the storm with us."

"Got stranded out there, did ya?"

"Aggie got sick before she knew to get out of there. She and my son were trapped in the house."

"Yup," said the deputy. "Happens."

Ladamien could tell that the deputy had already talked more than he was used to doing. They rode in silence the rest of the way to Coreopsis Hospital.

"Thanks," said Ladamien as he got out of the patrol car.

The deputy saluted and drove off. Ladamien marched into the hospital and approached the reception desk. "I'm here to see my wife," he said. "Upton. Aggie Upton."

The receptionist fingered her keyboard and stared at the monitor. "She's in intensive care. You will need Doctor Nieves' permission."

"How do I find Doctor Nieves?"

"We have a locator. Let me check." The receptionist worked at the computer. "Doctor Nieves is in pathology – third floor. You can go up there and check with the floor nurse."

"Thank you." Ladamien went to the elevator and rode to the third floor. Two doors blocked the entrance to the ward. Ladamien tried them both. Locked.

"Can I help you?" Ladamien heard a voice to his left. He turned to the voice and saw a nurse inside of a cubicle on the other side of the doors.

"I'm looking for Doctor Nieves."

"Who are you?"

"Ladamien Upton. My wife is a patient of his."

"Have a seat over there. I'll tell him. It may be a while."

Ladamien sat where the nurse had indicated. There was nothing in the room, no TV, no magazines, not even any music. He figured it was a good time to call Leroy. A woman answered.

"Leroy's phone. Sapphire here. How ya doin' Ladamien?"

"Not good. Aggie is real sick. I lost my home to the hurricane."

"You wear that white chick down?"

"No. She picked up some disease in Jamaica," said Ladamien. "Nice talkin' to you. Is Leroy there?"

"He's here."

"Ladamien," said Leroy, "that hurricane battered you peeps up there."

"It did. Lots o' folks lost it all, including me."

"You need money?"

"I got money. I'm worried about Aggie."

"What can I do for you? Why'd you call?"

"Me an' Aggie, we wanna move to Boca Raton. I thought that perhaps one of your sterling contacts could find us a nice place. Near to a good school, on the water, secure, out of the way."

"I'll give you a name and a phone number. How's that?"

"I'll take it," said Ladamien. He knew that Leroy

would not do the work himself.

"Harold goes by Slick, Lindenwold. Came down from Chicago with me. He's elite."

Ladamien knew that meant Slick was a high-ranking gang member. "What's his phone number?"

"Sapphire will text it to you, I don't remember right now."

Leroy did not hang up, so Ladamien stayed on the phone, Finally, Leroy spoke. "When you gonna be ready to talk to some clients, fly out to Delhi?"

"India?"

"Of course India. You think I care about Delhi, Minnesota?"

"I didn't know there was a Delhi in Minnesota."

"Don't play dumb ass on me, Ladamien," said Leroy. "When can you go?"

"When I know Aggie is okay. Maybe, Monday."

"I'll set it up. Call Slick." Leroy terminated the connection.

A nurse was motioning at Ladamien, trying to get his attention. "You can come in, Mr. Upton," she said. "Doctor Nieves will see you shortly."

Ladamien tried the door and it opened.

"In the office." The nurse pointed to a door to Ladamien's left. Ladamien opened the door and went inside. Several plaques hung on the wall. Ladamien sat in one of two chairs in front of a large desk. The desktop was bare – no papers, no pad, nothing. The two cabinets in the room had solid wood fronts – closed. Very tidy, very organized.

Doctor Nieves entered the office and shook

Ladamien's hand. He took a seat behind the desk. "Well," he said, "at least we now know what your wife has. It's called Hantavirus Pulmonary Syndrome. Rodents spread it, through their feces. Aggie probably contracted it in the jungle of Jamaica."

"How bad is it?" asked Ladamien.

"In its advanced stages it is often fatal. Fortunately, it is not contagious. We get about forty cases a year in the United States."

"Can you treat it?"

"That paramedic, Bonnie, she did all of the right things. Keeping the blood oxygen level high is essential. Hydration and nutrition are also important." Doctor Nieves leaned forward and looked intently at Ladamien's face. "Bonnie told me a story that was difficult to believe."

"She told you about the Indian chief?"

"So, is it true?"

"I was there, and I'm not sure I believe it," said Ladamien. "An enormous bird hovered over us, and this chief came down from the sky. He put some kind of spell on Aggie, and she got better. It happened."

"Mr. Upton," said Doctor Nieves. "I'm a medical doctor, so I can only treat her disease. I'll do what I can to save your wife's life regardless of what some spiritual apparition does."

"Thank you, Doctor," he said. "Just don't let Aggie die."

The doctor nodded. "I'll do my best, Mr. Upton. Go take care of your son. I understand the ambulance crew will take you to where he is."

CHAPTER 15

"I hate having my life disrupted by routine."

Caskie Stinnett

When Bonnie had called Justin and told him that she had to be on duty, she had no idea how long it would be before she would be relieved. The time went quickly and the emergency squads fell into a routine. Search and rescue teams from the National Guard and local law enforcement went from neighborhood to neighborhood in a carefully planned fashion. As they found persons needing medical assistance, they identified the condition and it was Bonnie's job to determine the type of response needed and dispatch the appropriate crew.

Of course, there were surprises and true emergencies, but for the most part the cases were predictable. Medics treated minor injuries resulting from the high winds or storm-related accidents. They brought in people suffering from fatigue, dehydration, and exposure. The outside help from other states was invaluable because it meant the first responder crews could follow along with the search and rescue teams providing real time treatment.

Slowly the displaced and the homeless settled in and waited for the search and rescue efforts to finish so they could go in, and assess the damage to their property. Almost everyone agreed that it would be years before life returned to normal, especially in the hardest hit areas of the beaches. Insurance representatives and federal agents had an enormous job ahead of them making settlements.

Hurricane Dirk left the coast of Florida at Cedar Key and entered the Gulf of Mexico. It was a weak category one storm. It would gain strength before barging into Crawfordville in the Florida panhandle. The storm would bring seventy-five mile per hour winds to Apalachicola and Tallahassee before crossing into Alabama. Mississippi and Louisiana could breathe a sigh of relief this time after suffering so much before.

At two o'clock Friday morning, Gus walked into the command center where Bonnie was working.

"How much sleep did you get?" he asked Bonnie.

"Four hours," she answered, "more than a day ago."

"Go home, get out of here. The boy's father called. He said he still has business at the hospital. He asked me to have you take Simon home with you."

"Alright, I'll do that. When should I come back to work?"

"Don't call us, we'll call you. Take a day off."

Bonnie took off the headset and started to walk away when Gus took her arm and turned her to face him. "You know," he said, "because of your premonition, we were probably ahead of this thing. At least, that's what Mayor Moline thinks."

Bonnie nodded. "I hope so," she said. "How much worse could it have been?"

Gus shrugged. "We'll never know, but thanks."

Bonnie saw Simon standing outside the command center. She went to him.

"Gus said I should take you home with me," she said. "I have to call Justin, have him pick us up."

"I can wait," said Simon.

Bonnie didn't know if she would be rousing Justin or not. He answered on the second ring. "Did I wake you," she asked.

"I was sitting here in the chair dozing."

"Would you mind coming to get us? I'm bringing Simon with me. His father might show up anytime."

"All right. We still don't have any power here."

"That's okay. I think we're going to sleep mostly."

"I'll be there in half-an-hour."

***

Ladamien started to leave Dr Nieves' office, and then hesitated. Every sort of thought was spinning in his mind. He had to call Aggie's family. He had to call his mother. He had to make a decision about Leroy. There was Simon, and the house, and the business, and Bonnie.

"Does the hospital have a counselor?" Ladamien asked Dr. Nieves. "Someone who could help me sort things out."

"Yes," said Dr. Nieves. "I know they do. I have

to go back to the main building. I'll have my nurse set you up with a counselor. I have other patients I must take care of. The storm. We're in a state of emergency."

"I understand," said Ladamien.

After they arrived at Dr. Nieves' office in the main building, the physician summoned his nurse. "Please escort Mr. Upton to counseling. See if they can match him up with someone."

Ladamien thanked the doctor and prepared to follow the nurse. Dr. Nieves stepped out of his office.

"Mr. Upton," Dr. Nieves said, "We'll get your wife through this."

Ladamien did not say anything. He was confused. Be a man, he told himself. Make Aggie proud.

Ladamien walked quietly behind the nurse until they arrived at the counseling department.

"Would you please make sure that Bonnie gets the word I need to stay at the hospital for a while," Ladamien said to the nurse. "She's expecting me to come to her house."

"I'll do that," said the nurse.

Ladamien sat down between a black woman with a small child and an old man with a long white beard. After a twenty minute wait, he heard his name called. He walked to the main desk and was met by a small athletic woman whom he immediately nicknamed "Chipper." With her round face and compact body, she looked like a chipmunk, a cheerleader for a girl's soccer team.

"Mr. Upton?" she asked. "You wanted to talk to

somebody? I'm Kitty, Kitty Bradshaw. I'm a psychologist."

Kitty. That worked. It was almost like Chipper. God, she was young.

"Hey Kitty. Where'd you go to school?"

"I'm a Gator, Mr. Upton. Just graduated last year."

Ladamien smiled. "Good school" he said. *She must be twenty-three going on sixteen*, he thought.

"My office is right over there," she said. "Let's go inside and talk."

CHAPTER 16

"For everything you have missed, you have gained something else, and for everything you gain, you lose something else."

Ralph Waldo Emerson

Justin was waiting in the break room. Bonnie was pleased to see him. Lately, it seemed that very little in her life had been stable. She had been able to bathe and get fresh scrubs at the hospital, but her personal belongings were scattered all over the county. She had hung onto her purse and shoulder harness. Justin was the steadiness that she needed to reestablish control. Bonnie rushed into his arms and held him close.

"Miss me?" Justin asked.

"It seems like a lifetime," Bonnie answered. "It's hard to believe the storm is over. I thought it would never end."

"It'll be two weeks before they get power restored everywhere," said Justin. "We're lucky my house was built to code. It's dry inside. Dark, but dry."

"I'll just be happy to put on real clothes and brush my teeth with my own toothbrush. Little things seem so big." Bonnie saw Simon standing alongside her. "Oh," she said, "This is Simon. His mother was my patient."

"Is she getting better?"

"Her condition is unchanged. She should recover."

Justin bent down to Simon's level. "You want to come home with us?" he asked Simon.

"Sure," Simon answered. "My dad told me to go with Miss Bonnie."

"Look," said Bonnie. "Could you wait here for me for a few minutes? There's something I want to tell Gus." Bonnie left Justin and Simon in the lobby and returned to the command center. She found Gus inside. "Can I talk to you for a moment?"

"Why not?" Gus walked out into the hallway with her. "What's up?"

"When Kathie talked to me and I realized I had to come into work…" Bonnie stopped.

"Yes," Gus prompted.

"I realized I didn't have the enthusiasm I once had. It was an effort to say I'd come in."

"So?"

"I have decided to quit, what with the baby and all."

"Think about it. Take a leave of absence. I've seen it happen. You've been under a strain."

"I can do that?"

"Would I say you could if you couldn't?"

Bonnie shrugged. "I guess not. Thanks." *At least I can think about it,* Bonnie reflected. *Gus didn't seem upset.*

"That didn't take long," said Justin. "What did you talk about?"

"I just asked for some time off. Gus said it was okay."

"Good. Maybe you'd like to go up to Atlanta with me."

"I'll think about it. Simon has to go to school and his father and I have to attend to some business in Belle Glade. There's a lot to get done."

"How are you going to get Simon to school?"

"I guess I'll drive him. I have to get my car back. I've forgotten where it is."

"Winona drove it back to my house yesterday. I think she said you left it at Cape Canaveral Hospital and someone brought it back to the VAB."

"Oh, good. That's one more thing I can take off my worry list."

They drove to their town house in the F-150 pickup truck. Justin had evidently abandoned his Prius in favor of the truck with its higher wheelbase. It was still dark, but Bonnie noted that the cleanup crews had made remarkable progress over the last twelve hours. They had cleaned off the streets, many of which were still under water, and piled tree parts into neat piles. Small color-coded flags marked the houses where evaluation teams had made a determination whether to demolish or repair a dwelling. One in three houses appeared to have survived relatively unscathed, at least from the outside. The wind had scoured the trees, removing Spanish moss and dead branches.

Justin parked the pickup in the area between the house and his office. The three of them went to the door and Justin unlocked it. He went inside and returned with a lighted candle.

"Take this," he said to Bonnie. "I'll light a few more candles and we'll be in business."

After milling around for a while, they assembled in the dining room. Simon broke the silence. "Do you know what my dad had to do?" he asked Bonnie.

"Not really," she said, "but I can guess. He probably wants to talk with your mother's parents and to his mother. He has a business that needs his attention."

"Do you think he'll come here?"

"I understand that he will. He'll probably call before he comes. The hospital has our phone numbers."

"May I talk to him when he calls?"

"Of course. I'm sure he'll want to find out how you're doing." Bonnie turned her attention to Justin. "Did Winona say anything?"

"She told me that they were escorting people from the Vehicle Assembly Building back to their homes to see if their places were still standing. NASA wants them to clear out as quickly as possible."

"Are she and Thad going back to Gainesville?"

Justin shrugged. "Beats me. She didn't stay for long."

Justin sat still for a long time. Bonnie could tell

he was thinking about what to say next. Finally, he spoke. "You said something about our daughter being possessed. What's that about?"

"When Julie's spirit left my soul, in Atlanta that time, she left something behind. The errant spirit, Banna, which you uncovered, it had possessed Julie in life. Julie's spirit left it with me. Now, that errant spirit has occupied our baby's soul. Evidently, I was the carrier, like Typhoid Mary"

"How does that happen? Are you cursed?"

"Maybe. I don't know."

"We have to get to the bottom of it and I don't know how to help."

"I bet the chief knows," said Simon. "He's going to cure my mom."

"Who is the chief?" asked Justin.

"The chief is a spirit of some kind," answered Bonnie. "Claims to be the father of the errant spirit Banna, daughter of the wind. I don't think the chief is the only answer to Aggie's recovery."

"It's beyond me," said Justin. "Why don't we go to bed?"

"Simon can sleep in the game room," said Bonnie.

"Fine." Justin said to Simon. "There's a potty in the back, in the game room, in case the water isn't running yet. Even if the water comes on, don't drink it. I'll put some bottled water in the room."

***

Justin gave Simon two sheets and helped him make up the sofa in the game room for his bed. After

Justin left, Simon slipped between the sheets and tried to sleep. Visions of his mother inundated his mind. Simon recalled simple things. Aggie standing at the sink rinsing dishes. His mother sitting at the coffee table folding clothes. The two of them shopping for cereal in the grocery store. His mom using pliers to remove a fish hook from a bluefish. Tears flooded his eyes.

Simon got out of bed and walked through the half-light to the door to Bonnie's bedroom. He knocked softly and heard a rustling on the other side of the door. He heard a match strike and saw the soft light of a candle under the door.

"Come in." Bonnie's voice was soft, almost a whisper.

Simon opened the door and stepped into Bonnie's room.

"What is it, sweetie?" asked Bonnie. "Can't you sleep?"

"I keep thinkin' about my mom."

"I know. I think about my mom sometimes, too. She died before I knew her."

"How'd you find out about her?"

"She came back from the dead to find me, except she didn't know it was me until later. She was only sixteen when she was killed."

"My mom is thirty-four. I think she's about your age." Simon tried to recall what else he knew about Bonnie.

"Let me tell Justin I'm going to sit up with you for a while."

Bonnie went back to her bed. Simon heard her

whisper something to Justin. She motioned Simon to go back to the game room and followed him there.

Simon waited for Bonnie to come in and sit down on a divan. He sat next to her. She smelled different from his mother, older somehow. "You had a son and you were married?"

"Several years ago. An automobile accident killed them. Timmy was only two."

"An' you're gonna have another baby, a girl? Are you gonna marry Mister Justin?"

"Yes. We've already applied for the license."

"Your daughter," Simon paused. "She's in some kind of danger, from the chief and his daughter."

"That's part of it."

"Your daughter will be like my cousin. I'll protect her from the chief."

Bonnie chuckled. "You have quite an imagination. We're not related, but my daughter can be your friend. Friends are important, too."

Simon felt embarrassed. "I'm sorry," he said. "I didn't mean it."

"No. It's okay. You love your father and you miss your mother. It's quite all right."

Simon leaned back and lay down on his back. He felt much more comfortable in the room with Bonnie than he did in the living room. "Can you sleep in here, with me?"

"I guess it's okay," said Bonnie, "for a while. I told Justin I'd come back to bed, so just for a few minutes."

Simon wrapped a sheet around his body. Bonnie

leaned over and kissed him on the forehead.

"Sleep tight, sweetie," she said. "You want to be rested when your father gets here."

Simon still had images of his mother running through his brain, but now they were comforting instead of disturbing. *Good night, Mom*, he thought. He imagined that he heard her answer, "Good night, Simon."

***

Ladamien followed Kitty Bradshaw into her office.

"Have a seat, Mister Upton," Kitty said. "Help yourself to water if you wish."

Ladamien saw the pitcher of water and a clean glass on a small table next to the wall. "Thank you," he said and poured himself a glass. He settled back in his chair and waited for Kitty to speak.

"You asked for a counselor? What do you need?"

"My wife is in a coma. She's going to be in intensive care for a long time. It was unexpected. I have a lot to deal with."

"I'm sure that's hard to deal with. What's wrong with her?"

"Doctor Nieves said it was a Hantavirus, oxygen starvation put her in a coma."

"I've never heard of it," said Kitty.

"It's a tropical disease. She brought it back from Jamaica."

"Is she suffering?"

"Not that I can tell. Like I said, she's in some kind of coma."

"How can I help you?"

"Several things," said Ladamien. "Is our session confidential?"

"Within limits. Have you broken the law?"

Ladamien thought about how to answer. He could not see how that made any difference as far as what he wanted to talk about, so he lied and said. "No, nothing like that."

"That's good. I'm obligated to report any criminal activities."

"I'm more concerned with the publicity aspects. I own a business that is very sensitive to bad publicity."

"I don't talk to the media. Anything we say stays in this room."

"That's what I wanted to hear. The first thing I'm concerned about is breaking the news to Aggie's family. Aggie is white and they feel that I took their little girl away from the good life. They don't like me. This could be the final straw."

"Is race the main issue?"

"It's one problem. The other is that I come from a poor neighborhood in Belle Glade."

"Sort of a class bias, eh?"

"That kinda sums it up."

Kitty leaned forward and put her elbows on her desk. "They're not likely to change their opinion. Do you and Aggie have any children?"

"Our son, Simon."

"How do Aggie's parents feel about him?"

"They think he's too black to be fashionable – an

embarrassment."

"That's too bad. Maybe they'll soften a little. You can't avoid it. You have to tell them how sick she is. You should probably do it in person. Where do they live?"

"Bradenton. On the Gulf Coast."

"That's not far. You should probably phone them first."

"Would you call them for me?"

"You have to talk to them."

"I will, but it will help if you talk to them first."

"Okay. What are their names?"

"Buchholtz, Edward, and Cynthia Buchholtz."

"Dial the number," said Kitty, "and, I'll talk to them."

Ladamien dialed the number for Aggie's parents and handed the phone to Kitty.

"Hello, Missus Buchholtz? My name is Kitty Bradshaw. I am a counselor at Coreopsis Hospital in Coreopsis, Florida."

Ladamien watched as Kitty apparently listened to Cynthia Buchholtz.

"Yes, Missus Buchholtz, it is about your daughter. I have her husband here in my office. He needs to talk to you." Kitty handed Ladamien the phone.

"Cynthia?" said Ladamien. "It's Ladamien. I have bad news. Aggie has a disease. She's in a coma, in intensive care."

The phone was silent from the other end, and then Ladamien heard Cynthia screaming away from the phone. After a short wait, Edward's voice came over the phone. "Cynthia is hysterical. She says that you told her Aggie is dying. Ladamien, are you there? Ladamien?"

"Aggie is very sick. I didn't say she was dying. The doctors are optimistic."

"We need to come see her."

"I think that's a good idea. The hurricane destroyed our house. Simon and I are going down to Belle Glade until we can find a new place. We'll probably move to Boca Raton after Aggie gets better."

"Who is the doctor? Why didn't they take her to Orlando?"

Ladamien was getting impatient with Edward's questions. "I have a counselor here at Coreopsis Hospital, Kitty Bradshaw. You can talk to her when you get here."

Ladamien handed the phone back to Kitty.

Kitty gave Edward her name and phone number. "I'll be glad to help you in any way I can."

Ladamien watched Kitty nod while Buchholtz talked, and then she gave him the high sign.

"Mister Buchholtz," Kitty said, "You and your wife have my most heartfelt sympathy but from what Ladamien tells me I believe your daughter will recover eventually."

Kitty puckered her lips and hung up the phone. She smiled cautiously. "That wasn't so bad, was it?"

"No. You helped a lot."

"Is anything else bothering you?"

Ladamien thought about all of the tasks he had to complete. He had to call his momma. He and Simon had to relocate and settle in somewhere. He could handle all of these without help. The real dilemma involved his business and Leroy. Bonnie had offered a solution – the FBI agent, Chris Zirkle. Should he step over that line?

"There is something else, but I'm not sure you can help."

"I can try," said Kitty.

"How rigid is that rule about breaking the law? Can you overlook some things?"

"Not really. It's cut and dried. I have to report any criminal activity, even a suspicion."

"How about business questions?"

"I'm not a business expert." Kitty leaned back as if taking a momentary break. Finally, she spoke. "It's a matter of conscience, isn't it?"

"Something like that," Ladamien admitted.

"One piece of advice. Do the right thing. You probably know what that is. Do it." Kitty hesitated again and then continued, "Is there anyone you trust absolutely, beyond any doubt?"

"My momma, Jezebel. I'd trust her with my life."

"Have you called her yet?"

"Once, but I'm going to go see her."

"Call and go see her first, before you meet with Aggie's parents. I gather money's not a problem for you."

Ladamien shook his head. "No. Money's not an issue."

"Take the time. Leave the arrangements for Aggie's care in the hands of her parents and one of our facilitators. It'll cost a little, but you don't need to be bothered with all those details. Take your son with you and go see your momma. It sounds like she is your best counselor."

Ladamien liked that advice. "The paramedic, Bonnie McConnell, she has become sort of a friend. Would it be okay if I took her with me to see my momma?"

"If she is comfortable with it, and you are comfortable with it, I can't see any harm. Is there any particular reason?"

"Something happened within the wind, during the hurricane. We had a spiritual visitation."

Kitty cocked her eye. "Oh."

"It involves Bonnie. I told her my mother could help. I still believe that."

"Maybe you need to see a preacher."

"My momma's an ordained minister. She'll do just fine."

"Well, spiritual visitations are certainly out of my field of expertise, so good luck with it."

Ladamien rose to leave. "You've been helpful," said Ladamien. "If you could stay in touch with Aggie's parents and keep an eye on Aggie, I'd appreciate it greatly."

"I'll do that. Does the hospital have your information?"

"Yes. I filled in all of the forms when we admitted Aggie."

Kitty shook Ladamien's hand. "Best wishes, Mr.

Upton. I hope it all works out."

Ladamien found an empty waiting room and used his cell phone to call his mother. She picked up on the fourth ring. He noted that his battery was down to sixty percent.

"Momma, it's Ladamien."

"How're y'all doin'," asked Jezebel. "Is everyone okay?"

"Aggie's in a coma. Her life is still in danger, Momma."

"Ah is right sorry t' hear that. What happened?"

"She caught a virus, down in Jamaica. She's never come out of the coma."

"How's Simon takin' it?"

"I don't know. I had to leave him with a medic."

"Is he sick too?"

"No, he's fine, but I had to stay at the hospital. The hurricane's passed but it's still hectic around here. I need to talk with you, about Leroy. I'm thinkin' about givin' him up."

"Oh. That would be a big step. C'mon, down. Ah'll cook us up a pork shoulder."

"I'll be bringing a friend, a white woman."

"What kind 'a friend? You ain't been foolin' around?"

"No, Momma. A real friend. She's the paramedic that tried to save Aggie an' she's takin' care of Simon right now."

"You be sure and bring Simon with you," said Jezebel. "The schools will be closed for a few days anyhow. I haven't seen my grandson for a while"

"I'll do that, Momma."

"All right, Ah'll fix up Corrine's room. Your sister's doin' good up in South Carolina. The medical woman can sleep in her room. What's her name?"

"Bonnie, Momma. Bonnie McConnell. We'll see you tomorrow afternoon, and thanks."

"Son, about Leroy – I'll be prayin' for ya. God bless."

"God bless, Momma." Ladamien clicked off the phone and gave a sigh. *God bless, indeed*, he thought.

CHAPTER 17

"To live is so startling it leaves little time for anything else."

Emily Dickinson

The hum of the air conditioner and flashing lights of the bedside clock awakened Bonnie. Florida Power and Light had restored electricity. Bonnie watched Justin get out of bed and head toward the kitchen. Bonnie rose, unplugged the clock, and left the bedroom to check on Simon. Simon was still sleeping in the game room, so Bonnie went into the kitchen. Justin was measuring coffee into the coffeemaker.

"I guess things are coming back to normal," said Justin. "Cable's still out, though."

"Would you please pop a bagel into the toaster for me?" Bonnie requested. "I'll need something to smooth out that coffee."

Justin took a bagel out of the package and cut it in half. He put both halves in the toaster and pushed down the slide. He opened the refrigerator and retrieved a container of cream cheese. He took off the top and smelled it. "Smells okay. A little soft maybe."

"It'll be fine," said Bonnie. She separated a paper plate from a stack and took a knife from the silverware drawer. Somewhere in the distance, she heard her cell phone ring. Simon came straggling down the hall holding it out in front of him. He brought it to Bonnie and handed it to her just before it stopped ringing. Bonnie checked the call history. She didn't recognize the number.

"Thank you," Bonnie said to Simon. "I'll call them right back." She was about to return the call when her phone rang again. It was Ladamien.

"Can you pick me up here at the hospital," asked Ladamien. "Can you be my chauffeur for a few days?"

"I'll have to ask Justin, but I am on leave of absence. Where do you need to go?"

"Belle Glade."

"At least we're going in the right direction. The roads should be good down there."

"I-95 South may be messed up a bit, but it'll be clear once we pass Vero."

Bonnie knew that hurricane force winds had extended beyond Fort Pierce, but she believed Ladamien's opinion was well founded. "Are you still at the hospital?" she asked.

"Yeah. I just finished with a counselor. I can wait outside the main entrance."

"All right. I'm going to finish breakfast and then I'll call you. It'll be about an hour."

"I'll see if I can get breakfast here," said

Ladamien. "Call me when you get close."

"I will," said Bonnie and clicked off.

"I could pick up Ladamien if you wanted to stay here," said Justin.

"I'll do it," said Bonnie. "I want to hear what he has to say." She looked at Simon. "You don't mind staying here with Justin, do you?"

"No ma'am," answered Simon. "Maybe Mister Justin can fix me somethin' to eat."

"Stove's working," said Justin. "You got your choice, scrambled eggs, or eggs scrambled. What's your order?"

Simon just giggled and said, "Scrambled, I guess."

"See ya," said Bonnie after she finished her bagel. "Do you have the keys to my car?" she asked Justin.

"In the dish next to the front door."

Bonnie gave Justin a quick kiss. "I won't be long," she said.

Bonnie found her keys and went to her car. She started it and backed out onto Indian River Drive. She decided to drive along the river and see what the hurricane had done. She noticed that while their house and boat had survived, the boathouse and dock had not done so well. Part of the deck was gone and the boathouse was leaning into the river.

Bonnie knew that the Indian River was not a true river. The Indian River was a part of the Indian River Lagoon, a huge brackish basin that extended from Jupiter to Halifax – connected to the ocean by several inlets in between. Hurricane Dirk had raised the level of the lagoon and even though it was going down, the water still came over the road in many places.

Bonnie drove north from Justin's house, often diverting to the left lane to avoid washouts where the road had fallen into the lagoon. She had driven this way many times before and noted how many docks the hurricane had swept away completely. Old trees – twenty, forty, and sixty years old – lay split and broken, mostly on the left side of the road. She drove around them when necessary.

Eventually, Indian River Drive merged with US-1 and Bonnie ran into more traffic – people on errands and looky-lous curious to see the storm's aftermath. Just beyond the town limits, she turned into Coreopsis Hospital. She called Ladamien on her cell phone. He answered immediately.

"I'm here," Bonnie said. "I'm driving up to the front door."

"I see you," said Ladamien.

Bonnie saw Ladamien waving from the curb. She pulled up and unlocked the car doors. Ladamien slid into the right seat.

"Thank you," said Ladamien. He fastened his seat belt. "Have you had time to think about driving me and Simon to Belle Glade?"

"Normally I'd say no, it isn't a good idea to become involved with my patients' families."

Ladamien started to say something, but Bonnie held up her hand to stop him. She continued. "I feel some responsibility for Aggie's condition," said Bonnie. "You and Simon are friends – we went through something special together – a category five hurricane. Besides, I'm on leave of absence. In a sense, I'm not really working now. Justin has to meet with his employer, so, yes. I'll do it."

Ladamien let out his breath. Bonnie could tell he was relieved. "When do we have to leave?" she asked.

"We can drive to Belle Glade in half-a-day," said Ladamien. "How about tomorrow morning?"

"Fine. Where will we be staying?"

"My momma is fixin' up my sister's room for you."

"Where is your sister?"

"Corrine lives up in Florence, South Carolina. She teaches medical records management at Florence-Darlington Technical College."

"I almost went there for my EMT training," said Bonnie. "I'm from Calhoun, Georgia."

"It's a small world," said Ladamien, "although my job takes me to almost every part of it."

"What are you going to do about your job?" asked Bonnie.

"That's why I need to see my momma. The counselor says Jezebel is probably my best advisor."

"I can't wait to meet her," said Bonnie. As she turned into the driveway at Justin's house, she thought, *I wonder how much she knows about spiritual possession. What will she say about Banna?*

***

Friday evening had passed quickly. Bonnie, Simon, and Ladamien packed enough clothes for two days. Ladamien promised that they could get more clothing and other sundries in Belle Glade if they ran out. Justin's employer, Andre' D'aubigne, was coming down to meet with Justin and survey the damage to the sports complex he owned. Bonnie wanted to return quickly from Belle Glade and arrange for their marriage. However, she also thought that if Jezebel could solve the Banna situation it would be best to do that before she and Justin married.

Simon seemed eager to go. He told Bonnie about his Granny Jezebel and all of the marvelous things she could do. She told stories about the Indians, and pirates, and the poachers that stalked in the Everglades. She could make pineapple upside down cake that you could eat forever and barbeque ribs that were the best anywhere. She grew greens and herbs in her back yard, things you never saw in a store. Bonnie helped him make up his bed and got him to promise her that he would sleep through the night without disturbing her.

The city restored water service around five o'clock and they had hot water by eight. Bonnie took a long soaking bath, including lavender bath salts, and felt relaxed and ready for bed by nine. Through her closed door, she could barely hear Justin and Ladamien talking in the kitchen. Their voices did not keep her awake.

Bonnie awoke to the sound of the alarm at six in the morning. Ladamien had wanted to get an early start to Belle Glade, so they all dressed quickly, ate a light breakfast, and packed the car. They were on the road before nine. Bonnie allowed Ladamien to drive her car since he knew exactly where they were going. Bonnie sat in the back seat with Simon and played word games with him. After they passed Viera going south on I-95, the scenery was monotonous − wind-blown, but repetitive.

"We'll be in Belle Glade before one," said Bonnie, "at the rate we're going."

"There's a place on Kanner Highway," said Ladamien, "serves the best Cuban sandwich outside of Tampa. I thought we'd stop there for lunch. Momma's not expecting us until three."

Just south of Stuart, Ladamien took the exit onto State Road 76 – southwest Kanner Highway – west toward Indiantown. The road straightened and flattened out, a precursor to crossing the Everglades. They soon left the busyness of the West Palm Beach outskirts and entered the serenity of inner Florida. Bonnie's mind turned briefly to Chief Ho-tah-lee and the ancient lives of the Native Americans. Not only were they forgotten tribes, but the land they left behind was rapidly becoming ancient history as well. She thought of the Ais Sanctuary. What would it become without Banna and the enduring spirits of the Native Americans?

They stopped outside of Indiantown and had lunch. It was as good as Ladamien had said and Bonnie hoped it wouldn't make him sleepy. "Are you all right to drive?" she asked.

Ladamien gave her his 'don't annoy me mother' look and sat in the driver's seat of her vehicle. He drove along the eastern shore of Lake Okeechobee until US-441 bent slightly east going into Belle Glade. Ladamien maneuvered the car skillfully through the back streets until they pulled up in front of a clapboard house at the edge of a large muck field on the outskirts of town. The house was moderately large and painted with whitewash instead of conventional paint. Bonnie saw a small chicken yard off to her right.

It's right out of a 1920's Saturday Evening Post, Bonnie thought to herself. *I wonder if there's an outhouse.*

"Here we are," said Ladamien.

Simon jumped out of the rear door and ran toward the house.

A stocky black woman wearing a bright colored skirt and a red blouse came out to greet him. She had her hair covered by a green and yellow bandana and wore a necklace of oversized fake pearls around her neck. She picked Simon up bodily and hugged him so enthusiastically that Bonnie thought she might break his back.

Bonnie opened the car door, exited and walked toward the woman. The woman placed Simon on the ground and looked at Bonnie. Bonnie had seen those eyes once before in her life. At the zoo – the elephant matriarch. They were wise eyes that looked through the body and the physical world into the soul and the essence of a being. Eyes that had known motherhood and family since a primordial era. Eyes that accepted pain without complaint and gave love without conditions. Aged eyes like polished onyx, gleaming from years of seeing with wonder and appreciation.

"You must be Miss Bonnie," said Jezebel. "Ah is Jezebel, Ladamien's mother..." Jezebel looked down at Simon, "and Simon's grandma"

"Missus Upton," said Bonnie, "Ladamien asked me to come with him." Bonnie hesitated. She was thinking about where the conversation might lead. "But, I'm here for my own reasons as well."

Jezebel came forward and put her hand on Bonnie's tummy. "Let me talk to your chil' fo' a moment," she said. Jezebel closed her eyes.

Bonnie felt strange standing in the middle of the path to the front door with Jezebel bending down with her hand placed firmly on Bonnie's stomach. She did feel something, however, going on inside her, a slight stirring.

Jezebel removed her hand and stood straight. "Ah knows that spirit," she said. "Don' you worry none. Your baby's goin' t' be all right."

Bonnie bleated out her next words. They surprised her. "You know this spirit?" She emphasized the word, "know."

Jezebel nodded. "An old friend and a known troublemaker." Then, she chuckled under her breath. She looked over at Ladamien. "Why don' y'all come inside. It is your home ain't it?" She turned and moseyed toward the front door. "Simon," she said, "There's some cookies in the jar and sweet tea in the fridge. Why don' you show Miss Bonnie what a genteel young man you are, and serve us in the back garden?"

The back garden turned out to be an arbor covered with a passionflower vine. The floor was made of concrete steppingstones and under the arbor was a concrete table with two concrete benches. Jezebel ushered Bonnie and Ladamien to the table. "Have a seat," she said. "I'll go see if Simon needs any help."

After Jezebel was out of sight, Bonnie leaned over to Ladamien. "Your momma is something else," Bonnie said. "I've never met anyone else like her."

Ladamien rolled his eyes. "You ain't seen nuthin' yet. Wait 'til she deals with that spirit of yours."

"You've seen her do that kind of thing before?"

"Oh yeah," said Ladamien. "My momma is famous around these parts. She can send the devil into hiding."

"Why didn't she ever help you?"

"She said I'd have to deal with my own demons when the time came."

"What do you think she'll tell you to do about Leroy?"

Ladamien shook his head. "I don't know. I never did know what momma might do next."

Jezebel came from the house and stood by the concrete table looking out over the field behind her house. "You want t' know about Leroy?" she asked. "Look out in that grassy place over there. See that rabbit?"

Bonnie saw the rabbit. It was standing in the middle of a small pasture looking from side to side. Suddenly, Bonnie saw a large hawk coming out of the sky diving toward the rabbit. "That hawk's gonna get him," said Bonnie.

"That hawk is Leroy," said Jezebel. "The rabbit is Ladamien."

Just before the hawk grabbed the rabbit, the rabbit transformed before Bonnie's eyes. The rabbit became a large dragon-like lizard that grabbed the hawk and swallowed it in a single bite.

"The lizard is Ladamien with guts," said Jezebel. She put her knuckles on the table and glared at her son. "Get rid of that demon," she said. "Use what you know to purge the Earth of Leroy and his immorality."

Simon came out with a tray carrying four glasses of iced sweet tea and a platter of chocolate chip cookies.

"You have a good son," said Jezebel. "Make him proud."

Bonnie bit into a cookie and wondered what Jezebel had in store for her

***

Simon loved his Granny Jezebel. She had been the first person to read to him when he was very young. He knew there was something about his father of which Granny Jezebel disapproved. He waited until they were alone and asked her, "Does my dad do something you don't like?"

"What gave you that idea?" she asked.

"Just the way you act, like he stole somethin'."

"Your dad's a good man, but he has some bad friends. They have him doing some things that are wrong."

"Why doesn't he just tell them he won't do bad things?"

"Did you see that hawk this afternoon, chasin' that rabbit?"

"I saw it. The rabbit changed to a lizard and ate the hawk."

"What do you suppose would have happened if the hawk had got hold of that rabbit, before it could change?"

"I guess the hawk would have eaten the rabbit."

"So if you were the rabbit, would you have been afraid?"

"Yes ma'am. I wouldn't be sure if I could become a giant lizard or not. I'd be scared to death."

"Well your father is like the rabbit and his friends are the hawks that already got their talons under his skin. An' he's scared. He's got to become that giant lizard, or they'll eat him alive."

"That's terrible. He never told me."

"Worse," said Jezebel, "he's never told his self, 'til now, maybe."

"Is Leroy one of those bad friends? I know my mom never liked him."

"He's the worst. He's not only bad, he's evil."

Simon was not sure what to make of the comparison. "I know my dad will do the right thing. He'll do it for my mom."

"He's got to do it for his self, and for you."

Simon decided to change the subject. "Miss Bonnie says she knows a real witch and she's gonna introduce me to her."

"Why do you want to meet a witch?"

"So's I could write about her, I guess. I wanna meet pirates, and witches, and Indians, and cowboys before they all disappear. So's I can write about them."

"Ain't none a' those gonna go nowhere. They's cowboys, and Indians, and pirates, and witches right here, in the Everglades." Jezebel went to the refrigerator, opened a soft drink, and sat back down. "Tell me about what you saw during the hurricane."

"You mean with the chief and the big bird?"

"Yes. I wants t' know about it."

Simon told his grandmother how the hurricane had stopped while the chiefs appeared. "I watched the big chief, Chief Ho-tah-lee, come down from this giant black bird, a bird that covered the whole sky."

"The great bird Hurikon that brings the hurricane and the chief of the wind. I've heard about them."

"Well, the chief and Miss Bonnie, they have this kinda quiet argument. Something about the baby she's carrying."

"What'd she say?"

"She said, 'No. I can't do that,' and then she asked him to look at my mom."

"What did he say about your mom?"

Simon tried to remember. "The chief and Miss Bonnie argued some more, and then he did something to make my mom better." Simon decided to change the subject. "What happens if my dad turns in Leroy?"

"Leroy likely have him killed. You and me too maybe. He's a bad person."

"Wouldn't the police protect him and us?"

"The poh-lease!" Jezebel laughed. "They's more scared of him than we are. Ain't nobody gonna stop Leroy lessen he's dead."

"You want my dad to kill Leroy?"

"No chil', no. Ah don' want your dad to kill no one, but somebody has to put Leroy out of business. Maybe Interpol or the FBI."

"There was something else," said Simon,

"something weirder than the chiefs."

"What was that?"

"There was this big stick flying in the air, Miss Bonnie said it was an alien."

"Kameeshi," said Jezebel. "I don't know much about it, but I've heard about it. What did it do?"

"I'm not sure. I think it closed the roof and let the hurricane start up again. It was creepy."

"Your Miss Bonnie has got herself tied up with some strange things. She may not have many choices."

"Won't God help her?"

"That's not up to me to decide. We can pray, but if God wants to help her, that's up to Him."

"I don't understand how that works," said Simon.

"Neither do I chil', but I have faith in the Lord to do the right thing."

"He didn't do the right thing lettin' my momma get sick. I don't trust him to do right by my dad or Miss Bonnie."

"You don' mean that."

"I do mean that," said Simon. "I think my dad oughta do to Leroy exactly what that rabbit did to the hawk, change into a dragon, and kill him."

"What about Miss Bonnie?"

"She oughta just have her baby and keep her mouth shut. She oughta marry Mister Justin."

"Nine years old an' you got it all figured out."

Simon felt confused and angry. He left the table and started toward the back door. "I'm gonna take a walk," he said as he marched out.

Simon meandered through the garden. Almost everything had gone to seed. Late summer was not a good time for gardens in south Florida. He scared a black snake out of the underbrush and it slithered over the mud flats.

Life should be simpler, he thought, as he sat down in the grass and cried. He missed his mom.

CHAPTER 18

"Courage is the ladder on which all the other virtues mount."

Brendan Francis Behan

Bonnie saw the Sunday newspaper, the Palm Beach Post, folded on the breakfast table. The headline read, "Dirk Leaves 21 Dead in Florida – deluges southern Alabama." She sat down while Jezebel dished up grits, eggs, and bacon.

"You look all dressed up," said Bonnie.

"Ah's takin' Simon to church," said Jezebel. "Someone gots t' pray for y'all."

"Ladamien said something about you being an ordained minister. What's with that?"

"Through the White Lily Ministries, but Ah don't preach. Ah can perform weddings, and such."

"I see," said Bonnie. "So, you've studied the Bible a bunch?"

"Every day. It's a big part of my life."

"Thanks for breakfast," said Bonnie. "I can clean up. Where's Ladamien?"

"He went over to see a friend. Someone he knows from high school."

A large black Lincoln pulled up in front of Jezebel's house. Jezebel yelled toward the back of the house. "Simon, our ride is here. Let's go." Simon came running and followed Jezebel to the car.

Bonnie watched them depart. She washed and dried the dishes and placed them into the rack to dry. There was coffee in the pot, so she poured herself a cup and wandered to the back garden. She sat on one of the benches and looked out over the scene beyond Jezebel's yard.

There was something magical about the place. She saw several yellow legs, a bird she knew, foraging in the swampy fields. A feral cat stalked them from the underbrush to Bonnie's left. The air had a sulfurous smell Bonnie associated with swamps, not polluted, but redolent from decaying vegetation. The sharp chirp of an unseen osprey or hawk punctuated the air. Bonnie heard the voice in her head.

"Beautiful, isn't it?" said the voice.

She looked around to see if anyone was there, but she knew the voice was inside her. The spirit of Banna was talking to her.

"In its own way," Bonnie answered. "Why are you talking to me?"

"This woman, Jezebel, she's not what she appears to be."

"What is she? I know she's different."

"She is a Holhkunna, a spiritual sorceress. She practices magic."

"I gathered that," said Bonnie, "from the rabbit

incident." *Maybe Banna is suggesting something*, thought Bonnie. "Do you think she can help us?" Bonnie emphasized the "us".

"We do not need help," answered Banna, stressing the "we". "We especially do not need her."

Bonnie got the message. Banna was afraid that Jezebel could make her do something that she would not be willing to do otherwise. Bonnie decided to push the issue. "Jezebel seems knowledgeable. Maybe she's exactly the person who could help us."

"You don't know what you would be getting into," said Banna. "You would not like it."

"It would have to be better than aborting my daughter."

"I never suggested that you should have an abortion," said Banna. "I want to share your daughter's soul."

"You mean possess her soul – dispossess her spirit."

"You will not be able to tell the difference. She will still be your baby and your little girl."

"I'll know you are there," said Bonnie. "I can't accept that. I don't want you in my daughter's mind. There has to be a better solution."

"Not for me," said Banna. "Do you know where I would go, as a disembodied spirit?"

"Not really. Do you?"

"I would cease to exist," said Banna, "or…" The spirit stopped.

"Or what?" asked Bonnie.

"Or, I go back to where I was."

"Where was that?"

"I am not going to tell you. It is not important."

"Your father said something about going to the great ecstasy. That doesn't sound so bad."

"And give up my identity. Millions of spirits choose not to go to the great ecstasy."

"Where do they go?"

"They are lost. They get reassigned – to grasshoppers, rocks, trees – or they just wander around."

"Is that what happened to you?"

"Something like that. Only, I found a way out."

"By possessing unborn babies."

"Yes. It is my talent."

Bonnie sensed that Banna had retreated and shut off communications. She had many questions and no answers. She searched for her own spirit and couldn't find it. Apparently, she could not address it separate from her body and soul.

I wonder how that works, thought Bonnie. *What power assigns spirits? What force integrates my spirit with my body and soul, and makes it unique?*

Bonnie heard the back door close and watched Ladamien sit across from her. "Did my momma take Simon with her?" Ladamien asked.

"Yes," said Bonnie. "They left about forty-five minutes ago. Can I ask you a question?"

"Sure."

"How much do you know about your momma and her powers?"

Ladamien's eyes went glassy, as if he did not hear

the question. He just sat rubbing his chin. Bonnie waited, wondering if she should rephrase her question. Finally, Ladamien answered.

"Nuthin'," he answered. "Nuthin' at all."

"You do know she has a special gift."

"My brother, and sister, and me – we always took it for granted?"

"What about your father?"

"I never knew my father. He died before I was born."

"Oh, I didn't know."

"Many people believe that Jezebel has a serious mojo, that she can work miracles. People come to see her about sickness and love and to have their fortunes told. She usually helps them."

"That's why you thought she could help me."

"I know she can."

"I guess we'll find out," Bonnie said. "That's why I came."

At least I don't think she'll do any harm, thought Bonnie. *It couldn't get any worse.*

***

Bonnie felt that Jezebel had avoided her all day. Jezebel had brought Simon home from church and immediately gone out with her friends. Ladamien had also left early in the morning but returned around two in the afternoon driving a luxurious convertible.

"Wow, nice car," said Bonnie when she saw Ladamien drive into the driveway. "Where'd you get that and what is it?"

"A friend drove me into Palm Beach. It's a BMW

650i convertible. No sense you havin' t' drive me around."

"No, I guess not. Are Aggie's parents still in Bradenton, or did they go to Coreopsis?"

"They said they would drive over to Coreopsis. I'll call the counselor at the hospital and see if they arrived." Ladamien started toward the house. "Is my momma home?"

"She's been gone all day. She brought Simon back after church and left immediately."

"Where's Simon?"

"He and I were working a jigsaw puzzle in the back. Wait until he sees that new convertible. He'll flip."

Ladamien smiled. "He will, won't he?"

"Does your mother always stay out all day on Sunday?" asked Bonnie.

"Not that I remember," Ladamien answered, "but keep in mind, she's on her own now. I haven't lived at home for a long time."

Bonnie was about to go back and get Simon when he came into the living room.

"Go see your Dad's new car," said Bonnie. "It's real snazzy."

Ladamien and Simon went out the front door and Bonnie collapsed on the sofa. She was upset that she had wasted a whole day waiting to see Jezebel who seemed to be ignoring her. She was about to doze off when Jezebel came storming in from the front.

"That boy has no sense 'a the value of money,"

said Jezebel. "An eighty thousand dollar toy, that's what it is. An' honest people 'round here workin' to make a dollar."

"Where have you been?" Bonnie asked.

"Ah've been gettin' ready to he'p you, that's where Ah've been. My friends an' me, we got somethin' planned. Are you ready?"

"I guess. I've been waiting for you."

"Well," said Jezebel, "Sadie's gonna pick us up in a half hour. She has some rice with beans and some collards. We're gonna eat at her house."

"Then what?" asked Bonnie.

"We's goin' t' a place out in the 'Glades. Kind of a refuge in the marshes. You'll need some mosquito spray."

Bonnie knew that mosquitoes in the Everglades were more than a nuisance. If Jezebel, who lived there, thought they would be bad, they would probably be intolerable.

"Do you have something?" Bonnie asked.

Jezebel nodded in the affirmative. "Ah'm goin' t' freshen up, an' have some sweet tea."

Sadie came by on schedule. There were two other women in the car with her, Gladys and Ruth. Jezebel introduced all around and Sadie drove everyone to her home where the full meal included buttermilk to drink. Bonnie had never developed a taste for buttermilk but she drank it since it seemed to be the tradition with the greens and beans. After dinner, Jezebel rubbed a nasty mosquito repellant all over Bonnie's arms and ankles and let Bonnie apply it to her own face. Bonnie thought the concoction would ward off not only mosquitoes, but alligators, panthers and big foot.

Sadie drove with amazing skill through high fields of sugar cane and saw grass. The headlights barely showed enough between the vegetation to stay on the rutted road into the 'Glades. After forty minutes or so, Bonnie saw a ramshackle building barely visible against the backdrop of the star-filled heavens. It was a scene from a nineteenth century ghost story. Bonnie expected to see bats flying around the steeple and a werewolf stalking the grounds. Sadie parked in front of the building.

"We's here," said Ruth. "Ah'll go get the inside ready."

Bonnie stood outside the building with Jezebel and watched as first Ruth and then Gladys went inside the building. She saw candle light appear in the window nearest them. Sadie went inside and Ruth came out. She beckoned to Jezebel, and Jezebel said to Bonnie, "We can go inside now."

Bonnie followed Jezebel into the building. Inside, they had arranged the chairs in a circle. Bonnie could tell that someone used the building frequently. There were no spider webs anywhere and the carpet was clean.

"We're gonna have to tie you down," said Jezebel. "We don' want that spirit o' yours to hurt anyone, 'specially you."

The thought of restraints repulsed Bonnie, but she had come here to cooperate with Jezebel, so she consented. Gladys approached her with a jigger of yellowish liquid.

"Drink this," said Gladys. "It'll force the spirit

out of your body."

Bonnie drank the liquid. It had a sweetish flavor with a taste like strong tea and an aftertaste like alfalfa or some other grazing plant. Bonnie could not identify it. After a few minutes, she began to feel light headed. Jezebel started undressing her.

"Do you have to do this?" Bonnie asked.

"We's got to get the egg all over your body," said Jezebel. "If we leave any part uncovered, the spirit will take refuge there."

When Bonnie was naked, the women tied her to a center post and checked her bindings to assure their security. Jezebel and Sadie brought a bowl of raw eggs over to her and started rubbing it all over her body. Bonnie figured that if the mosquitoes didn't like the other stuff, they would really dislike this. As the egg dried, it made Bonnie's skin feel tight and sticky. Ruth was sitting to Bonnie's right, chanting. Her chanting grew louder and louder but it was in a foreign language. Bonnie thought the chants could be prayers, but she could not be sure.

These women are idiots, Banna said in Bonnie's mind. *I'll give them something to bring them to their senses.*

"The spirit's talkin' t' ya," said Jezebel, "ain't it?"

"Yes," said Bonnie. "It says y'all are fools."

"We'll see," said Jezebel. "Spirit. Talk to me," she continued.

Bonnie felt her body tingling and burning. She felt as if she had contracted a serious rash, as if she had rolled around in poison ivy. Then, the room began to fade away. Ruth's chanting diminished to a whisper and then stopped. Bonnie's heart began to pound.

***

Bonnie walked over a field of death. Disease had overtaken the entire tribe of Native Americans and the spirits of the dead hung around awaiting the call to pass on. From within the throng of corpses, Bonnie heard a baby cry and picked her way to where the infant, a girl, lay upon a straw mat. Squatting next to the mat was the spiritual image of a young Chief Ho-tah-lee. He was beseeching the heavens, "Save my daughter. Let our spirits go in peace, but save my daughter."

Bonnie did not know what to do. She examined the bodies of the dead and surmised that the killing disease was most likely small pox. Bonnie could not account for the baby's survival when all of the others were dead except that it had a natural immunity or perhaps, judging by its appearance, some European blood in its heritage. As Bonnie walked around the compound, she felt the wind increase and looked up to see the great black bird, Hurikon, coming over the horizon. It finally hovered over the site.

Bonnie saw a fairy-like spirit prance from the earth and flit around the little girl. *The wind and the daughter of the wind*, thought Bonnie.

"That was me."

Bonnie turned to see a young woman with nutmeg hair and eyes standing just behind her and to her right. The woman had fawn skin that showed through her gossamer nightdress.

"Banna?" asked Bonnie.

The woman nodded.

"Which one," Bonnie inquired, "the baby or the spirit?"

"Both," said Banna. "We were inseparable. The child and the spirit of the land."

"When the baby grew up, what happened to her?"

"I was found by the Spaniards and given to the Calusa tribe. I went south to Cuba with a Spanish sailor. Banna's body died down there, but her spirit stayed with her daughter."

"And, you have hitchhiked from mother to daughter ever since."

"More or less, until Julie. You got away from me."

"So it was through you that Julie came back from the dead to find me?"

"Yes. I did not want to stop living. I did not want to go to the great ecstasy."

"And, now?"

"You do not want me," said Banna. "The spirit of your unborn child does not accept me. I loved Julie, and the spirits of the tribes want me to go with them. It is time to go, to leave the land, and follow the wind."

Bonnie felt the wind begin to swirl around her, gaining force. She saw Hurikon flapping its wings and Chief Ho-tah-lee ascending into the darkening sky. The ground trembled beneath her feet and the dead bodies disappeared beneath the earth. Banna's spirit flitted across the heavens, flashing and glistening in the light of an unseen sun.

After the wind subsided and the firmament

cleared, Bonnie stood naked on the shore of a lake. Waves shimmered in the moonlight and a multitude of stars shone above her. She saw a grass mat spread on the beach and reclined to take in the fresh air and the ambience of the night. She ran her hand along her abdomen to check on the tiny life she knew it held. She felt a response; a current of love that she knew came from her baby's spirit.

***

Bonnie came to in a bathtub full of warm water. Jezebel was washing her body with industrial grade hand soap.

"What happened?" asked Bonnie.

"We raised the spirit," said Jezebel.

"Hmm, hmm. We did," said Sadie loudly, in a singsong fashion. "The spirit came to us."

"So you saw the spirit, Banna?" Bonnie asked.

"We did," answered Jezebel. "It talked to us."

"What did it say?"

"It told us a story," said Ruth, "about the Ais people and the Spanish invaders. Banna is the spirit of their land."

"That's true," said Bonnie. "I had thought spirits only dwelt in people's souls."

"Oh, no," said Gladys. "Everything has a spirit. Rocks, trees, animals, the water, the land and even the sky."

"Like Chief Ho-tah-lee is the spirit of the wind," said Bonnie.

"At least a part of the wind," Jezebel agreed.

"Why do you think a spirit of the land would

want to possess my daughter, the soul of a human being?"

"To remain in the present," said Jezebel, "hoping to restore the past."

Bonnie looked into Jezebel's wise eyes, feeling like a child trying to understand its parent. "That would be hopeless. The past is past. Isn't that what past means?"

"In the material world, perhaps," said Ruth, "but in the spiritual world, not necessarily."

"Do you understand what you are saying?" asked Bonnie.

"Let me dry you off," said Jezebel. "We've got some clean clothes here for ya."

Bonnie stepped out of the bathtub and let Jezebel dry off her body. It felt good to be clean and internally, she felt scrubbed clean as well. The old women may or may not have pulled off an exorcism, but Bonnie felt spiritually cleansed. "Banna left," Bonnie said.

"Are you sure?" asked Gladys, who was bringing a white smock and a pair of sandals to Jezebel. "Or did the spirit only agree to leave."

Jezebel handed the smock to Bonnie. She said, "Here, pull this down over your body."

Bonnie fluffed out the smock and held it in front of her. "No. It is gone. I watched it leave."

Jezebel pushed the sandals over to where Bonnie could slip her feet into them. "I expected a thunderclap, a fiery demon."

Bonnie smiled. "What did you think of Banna?"

"The four older ladies looked at one another."

"Selfish," said Ruth.

"Headstrong," said Gladys.

"Irreverent," said Sadie.

"Needful," said Jezebel.

"Actually," said Bonnie, "she was none of those and all of those. Jezebel, would you please say a prayer for her."

Bonnie was comfortable bowing her head and listening to Jezebel intone a long prayer asking God to forgive Banna and guide her on the right spiritual path. The four women looked at Bonnie with sympathetic eyes and said in unison, "Amen."

Bonnie said, "Thank you," out of appreciation.

"The potion I gave you will keep the mosquitoes at bay," said Gladys. "We can leave anytime."

Bonnie walked out of the building into a starlit night. Frogs and insects filled the dark with sound and the 'Glades smelled fresh, as if every plant in the world had released its oxygen there. She sat in the back seat of the car next to Jezebel. "Did y'all see anything while Banna talked to you?"

"Images," said Gladys. "Images in our heads of the old days for them natives. Eatin', gatherin' oysters, jus' livin', even fightin'. It made us feel fer them."

"What did the spirit say about them?"

Ruth answered. "That the Great Mother, Mother Earth, gave their spirits permission to stay until they were ready to proceed to the great ecstasy."

"And they all waited for Banna?"

"Exactly," said Jezebel, "they wouldn't leave

without the spirit of their land."

"What are you going to do about Ladamien and Simon?" Bonnie asked Jezebel.

"We'll talk to them," said Jezebel. "Convince Ladamien to do the right thing."

Bonnie was not sure if that would be easy to do. "Did Ladamien tell you that I have a contact in the FBI, someone who specializes in gang activities?"

"No," said Jezebel, "Ah don' believe he mentioned it.

"I'll call Agent Zirkle when we get back to the house," said Bonnie. "I'll tell him about Ladamien and Leroy. He'll want to see Ladamien."

Jezebel cocked an eye toward Bonnie. "Won't that be dangerous?" asked Jezebel. "Aren't you forcing Ladamien's hand?"

"I'll talk to Ladamien first," said Bonnie. "Get his permission."

"We'll tell him it's the right thing," said Jezebel. "I'll talk with Corrine too. She may end up takin' care of Simon."

"Corrine's your daughter?" asked Bonnie. "Simon's aunt."

"That's right," replied Jezebel. "Simon's aunt. She and her husband live in South Carolina. They have a daughter, Lancia."

"Are you scared for Ladamien's life?"

"Always have been. Gang life's always been dangerous."

"Maybe agent Zirkle, Chris, can find a way out for him," said Bonnie. "A way to pursue a normal existence."

"That'd be nice," said Jezebel. "It'd be an answer to my prayer."

The old car pulled up in front of Jezebel's house and Bonnie stepped out into a warm breeze. The mosquitoes did not bother her.

***

Dirk was now a rainstorm dumping water on Tennessee. The damaging winds had reduced to gales and the system had dispersed. Crews throughout northern Florida and southern Alabama were busy restoring power and assessing the property damage. They had completed the search for missing persons and bodies of the dead. The final death toll was twenty-seven.

Ladamien listened, first to Bonnie, and then to Jezebel. They were sitting in the dining room after breakfast. It was advice he did not want to hear.

Justin had driven down from Coreopsis. He came in while they were talking, and told them that Aggie had come out of her coma and was recovering rapidly. Ladamien knew that Simon had to go back to school on Wednesday. Ladamien just wanted to return to the way things were before the storm. Jezebel and Bonnie wanted him to throw away the money and the position that he had struggled for since he graduated from high school.

"It ain't easy," Ladamien explained to Bonnie, "walkin' away from a hundred million dollars."

"I can imagine the temptation," said Bonnie, "but the gang's money is poison. It'll corrupt your soul and taint Simon's future."

"I don' know if the feds can protect us, me and Simon. The Swamp Rattlers got a long reach."

"Will you let me talk to Chris? Find out what he can do."

Ladamien knew that once the authorities knew anything about him and his connection to Leroy, the game was up. He might just as well surrender. Ladamien hated indecision and he knew that eventually he would have to confront Leroy – directly or indirectly.

"You've already made up your mind," said Jezebel, "haven't you son? You gonna do the right thing."

"Get your FBI friend on the phone," said Ladamien. "Tell him I'll talk to him."

Ladamien watched Bonnie leave to use the telephone in the front room.

"Chris helped Bonnie a lot," said Justin. "The gang might have killed her too."

"Once I turn myself in," Ladamien said, "it isn't likely I'll see any of y'all again for a long time. Momma, do you think Simon and Aggie will be safe with my sister; with Corrine and her family?"

"Safe as anywhere, I'd guess, until Aggie can get settled." said Jezebel. "If the feds put Leroy away, not likely the gang will go all the way to South Carolina for your wife and boy. They'll want you."

"I could just bump off Leroy myself."

"You'd get you' self killed tryin'. It ain't worth it. Let the FBI do its job."

"They're gonna put me in the pen too. I'll never make it there. The gangs run the prisons."

"You make it right with God, and God will make it right with you. No coward ever made it to Heaven."

Ladamien had heard a phrase similar to this from his mother for most of his life. He knew that she believed it. Having no faith in divine intervention, Ladamien figured he was bound for hell either way. "I'm not a coward," he said. "At least I got that workin' for me."

Ladamien and Justin chitchatted until Bonnie came back into the room.

"I finally got Chris on the line," said Bonnie. "It took some doing. He wants to talk with you."

"Now?" asked Ladamien. "He's on the phone now?"

"That's right. It took a lot of talking to get through to him. He's an inspector up at Langley now."

Ladamien went to the phone. He was nervous. "Hello," he said. "Ladamien Upton here."

"Hello Ladamien," said Inspector Zirkle. "Bonnie says you know a lot about the Swamp Rattlers, that you are willing to turn yourself in and help us bring in Leroy Greene. Is that true?"

"Yes sir. Leroy has pushed me too far. I'm not afraid of him anymore."

"I understand from Bonnie that your wife is sick and you have your son with you."

"That's correct, but my wife is recovering. Right now, I plan for them to go up to South Carolina and stay with my sister."

"We'll see," said Chris. "I'm going to have

someone meet you in Belle Glade. They will take a preliminary statement and then stay with you until you can come into the Atlanta office. Okay?"

"What do I do about Aggie and Simon? I want to see my wife before I go to Atlanta."

"Our agent will make sure you are safe. We'll work with Bonnie and Justin to make arrangements for your wife and son. I'm sure you will be able to see her before you go to Atlanta."

"All right," Ladamien interjected quickly. "You and Miss Bonnie must be good friends for you to believe her so quick."

"We go back a long way," said the inspector. "We've had our run-ins with the Swamp Rattlers. You do know that Cody Wilkins, the former leader of the gang, was Bonnie's father?"

"Yes. She told me."

"You can expect our agent later today or early tomorrow. I'll see you when you get to Atlanta." Inspector Zirkle hung up the phone.

Ladamien returned to the dining room. "He's sendin' an agent over," he told Bonnie and Jezebel. "Bonnie, you and Justin can take Simon back to Coreopsis, and then Inspector Zirkle wants me in Atlanta. I guess you better call Corrine, Momma."

"Simon's going to have to return to school," said Bonnie. "Today is Labor Day but I imagine the schools will be back in session sometime this week."

"He goes to Lewis Carroll," said Ladamien. "We can work something with the school to get him transferred. Can you help me with that?"

"I would be happy to talk to them," said Bonnie.

"You need to let Aggie know your plans as well. I'll go see her as soon as we get back home."

"Inspector Zirkle said I'd be able to see her before I go to Atlanta."

"All that red tape," said Jezebel. "Don't you worry, son, Simon will get his education, and he always has a home with his family. We'll take care o' Aggie too."

"Thanks," said Ladamien. It was reassuring to know that his family and friends would take care of Simon and Aggie in his absence.

Ladamien walked out of the kitchen into his mother's back garden. Even in September, he could feel the hot, lazy days of summer receding. He could smell freshness in the breeze that was not there in July or August. Northerners felt there was no change of seasons in Florida, but natives knew there were three hundred and sixty five seasons, each day a shift from the last and a foretelling of the next. Hurricane Dirk had passed hundreds of miles away, but the spoor of its departure spread far beyond its path.

What went on within the wind still lingered in the present.

CHAPTER 19

"Life has taught us that love does not consist in gazing at each other, but in looking outward together in the same direction"

Antoine de Saint-Exupery

"I brought the license with me," said Justin, "and the ring. I thought maybe we should just find a justice of the peace and get married."

"You two don't need no justice o' the peace t' marry," said Jezebel, "Y'all are family. Ah can do it right here in this house."

"She could," said Bonnie. "Ladamien told me his momma is ordained, licensed and a notary. I'll just call my parents and tell them we'll visit soon."

"This is exciting," said Jezebel. "We haven't had a wedding in my house since Corrine married Terrell."

"Fine with me," said Justin. "Long as it's legal."

"You let me an' the sisters take care of all the arrangements," said Jezebel. "We'll have music and flowers and everything."

"Sounds better than grits," said Justin.

Bonnie hoped he wasn't being sarcastic.

"Ah'm glad we could get rid of your errant spirit," said Jezebel. "Ah have faith that everything's goin' ta be all right with you and your baby. Now, you and Justin run off and enjoy one another."

"Maybe we should check into a motel," Bonnie said to Justin. "Practice being married."

Justin took her up on her suggestion, very quickly. They rented a room near Lake Okeechobee. After a long nap, Bonnie and Justin walked near the locks that regulated the height of the lake.

"Everyone seems to know what happened out in the Everglades except me," Justin said.

Bonnie gave him a long rundown on her vision and what she thought the story was behind Banna, Chief Ho-tah-lee and their daughter's spirit.

"So you think Jezebel saved our daughter?"

"I don't know, Justin," Bonnie said. "I'm just thankful it is almost over."

"Almost?"

"It won't be completely over in my mind until we are married, safely home, and I am holding Crystal in my arms."